Fort St. Jesus Bait & Tackle

Louis Tridico

Steven:
Hope you enjoyed this
little "trip" down the bayou.
A lot safer than the real thing;
You'll never know what you'll find,
or what will find you!

[signature]

This is a work of fiction. All characters, events, organizations
and some of the locations portrayed in this novel
are products of the author's imagination.

FORT ST. JESUS BAIT AND TACKLE
Copyright © 2012 by Louis Tridico
Duke Street Press

Copyright © 2012 Louis Tridico

ISBN-10: 0-6156-9886-7
EAN-13: 9780615698861

Dedication

In memory of my father
Louis P. Tridico
1914—1986

Thanks for those great times fishing on the bayou. Especially the ones where I heard all those weird, scary noises in the swamp.

And in memory of my mother
Juanita Tridico
1918—2012

For taking everything we caught and making some of the best-tasting meals a seafood fan could want.

Table of Contents

Chapter 1:
"Hot, Horny and Hungry"

September in the swamps of south Louisiana is like the last few minutes of a simmering, slow-cooking gumbo. Summer is almost over, and the liquid heat of the region has cooked out, with nothing left but a rich mix of the weird, the surprising and the flavorful. There's a thickness to the air, too, broken only by the occasional hurricane that stirs the pot.

Deep in the Atchafalaya Basin, Floyd Guidry wasn't thinking about gumbo, or hurricanes, or much of anything else, because he was having a very good day. On the bottom of his large aluminum boat lay four dead alligators, ranging in length from seven feet to 11 feet. Yes, indeed, a very good morning of gator hunting. But that's not what had him smiling. Because at the bow of the boat lay the nude, voluptuous form of one M'Lou Marchand, a drop-dead redhead with luscious lips, green eyes and more-than-ample breasts. The 23-year-old waitress stretched out and tried to catch what little sun filtered through the cypress trees. She had her face up to the sky, eyes closed, elbows resting on the gunwale. Her long ginger hair was spread out like a goddess, and she had one knee up, slowly waving her leg from right to left. The sign to steal home was on. To Floyd, she was a living, breathing, *Playboy* centerfold, and she was right here in his boat.

Floyd was old enough to be her father, but was still a handsome man, with a full head of brown, wavy hair. He had a strong jaw, straight nose and a smile that would get a woman out of her clothes in an instant. Which it had. His sun-bronzed skin was smooth and wrinkle-free. He had his shirt off, revealing an admirable six-pack for a guy his age, with the lean, sinewy form of a man who worked with his hands.

Which was what he was about to do with M'Lou.

M'Lou was not part of his approved sexual playlist, though. That role belonged solely, in theory, to his wife of 26 years, Felice. Not present at the moment. Floyd, in his own words, had a penchant for "neighborhood sport fuckin'," a term he had heard in a movie once and liked very much. And M'Lou was about as sporty as it got.

She gave him a dreamy smile. "Floyd, you're pretty good at baggin' those gators, but can you handle this?"

Floyd felt a gator moving in his pants, or some other kind of large reptile. He smiled and scratched his head. In his classic Cajun accent, he said, "Baby, dat I don't know, but I sure as hell gonna die tryin'."

He had driven the boat off the bayou and deep into the forested swamp. Or deep enough that he wouldn't be seen, anyway. He had gone to some trouble to sneak M'Lou onto the craft at the dock early this morning, before anyone else got there. While he was packing up, other fishermen and gator hunters had arrived, but he had already covered his biggest catch of the day with a canvas tarp, like a captive mermaid. She had giggled a lot, and he warned her to keep it down, or word of her presence might get back to Felice.

They had successfully departed the dock and within an hour were in prime gator-hunting territory. She had watched him throughout the morning check his lines, and then shoot the four gators and winch them into his boat. But by noon, she was getting a little needy. And as her clothes had begun to come off, so had Floyd.

He took one last look around before he devoted himself to the pleasures of M'Lou. The air was still, and the girl's sweet perfume freshened the wild, earthy smell of the quiet swamp. He heard the *tap tap tap* of a woodpecker in the distance, banging away into the bark of a tree, looking for a morning meal. Not a thing in sight.

Including the thing underwater next to the boat.

Floyd didn't know anything about that thing. He had his mind on other things. M'Lou had eased her delicate hand down her thigh, like a catcher giving the sign to a pitcher to bring the heat. A fastball high and inside. Floyd had played a little ball in high school. He was definitely going to bring the heat.

But all that changed in an instant.

Floyd's brain never really had time to process what happened next. About the only data it could download was that of something big, fast, grayish-white and wet coming up on his left out of the water. There was a deep inhalation of air, a foul smell, semi-darkness, and then total darkness. The permanent kind.

M'Lou's brain, however, had a fantastic front-row seat for the excitement. Her brain got to process the whole event in all its glory. First there was Floyd, reaching down to unzip his pants, and then there was the giant thing that came up over the top of Floyd and swallowed him whole. There was a distinct snapping sound before the thing went back into the water. Where Floyd had been was now just an empty space. The boat rocked violently back and forth. Because M'Lou's brain couldn't figure out exactly what it had seen, it locked up the rest of her body while it tried to handle the particulars. It was while this was going on that the thing came back up and went to work on the dead alligators. It took its time with those, since they weren't going anywhere in their present condition.

M'Lou now heard a startling sound that seemed to come from all around her. It was a shrill, high-pitched scream. Her own.

Later, below the algae-covered surface of the swamp, the creature lay still again. He loved the flavors he'd just enjoyed. In fact, they were some of his favorite flavors from the swamp. And there was *lots* to eat. Normally, a meal of that size would have been satisfying. Not today. Something had changed. It wasn't caused by the quick meal. Nor the water itself. It was the same refreshing liquid he had known for well over 100 years, as time was measured in this place. Not in the temperature of the nitrogen-rich air he breathed into his lungs, or what passed for lungs. That air was essentially the same, although over the last 50 years or so, it contained some rather odd chemicals. And the light from the single star still burned down as it always had.

No, the change wasn't in the environment. It was in *him*. His metabolism had been dramatically dialed up. His senses were somehow heightened. His *awareness* was more acute. He understood things he hadn't before. It was like some chemically induced high.

He had never felt this way before. Certainly not since he had been dropped in this place when he was very young. In many ways it was like home, but in others, it was not. Sure, there was plenty to eat, and places to hide, and things to think about. After all, he was a near-sentient being. He was aware of himself and his place in the universe. Well, sort of. Not like the things that had left him here. They were very smart. A lot smarter than him. They could manipulate their environment. They built things. Traveled places. Across the land and across the stars. It was they who took him from his home and put him here. He held no resentment about it, though. He was a very adaptable creature and for the most part enjoyed his youth in this place.

His kind wasn't a social species, though. Not like the ones who brought him here, who did so much with each other. He stayed alone for most of the time, eating, drinking, sleeping. Seeing what he could see, learning new things.

There were all kinds of creatures in this swamp, and just about all of them made for excellent food. Some were smart, some were stupid, some lived in the water, some on land. But it didn't matter to him much. He could pretty much catch and eat anything. Now, there was one creature that was both very smart and very stupid at the same time. He wasn't sure what they called themselves, but they reminded him of the beings who dropped him in this place. They could change their environment, too. They made things. But somehow they fell well short of the others on the thinking scale. Maybe somewhere between him and the things who left him. He'd even eaten some of these local things over the years. And in the last few minutes. A savory flavor he enjoyed immensely. But they were kind of dangerous, just the same. But easy to catch. So there was that.

But something was definitely changing. He was now aware of that female who had been dropped here with him. He hadn't seen her in decades, and up until now didn't really care one way or the other. But now he sensed her out there. Not a smell. Or a sound she made. It was more like a vibration through the air and water. Calling him to find her and mate. Well, to be honest, she was already pregnant and carrying her young. They had done the first part of their mating ritual over 50 years ago. Now it was time for the second part, when he would release the chemical into her that would initiate the final birthing process. That would lead to the delivery of the young ones. More than 50 were the norm. He was guessing there'd be more. After all, this was a very good place for food, and he suspected the female had eaten well over the years, as had he. The young would flourish, too.

He rose to the surface, took another deep breath and looked up at the sky. A group of flying creatures soared overhead and squawked loudly. Oh, yes, something had changed in him. He was restless now, focused and full of an energy he hadn't felt for a long while. Time to get moving. He had things to do.

He wasn't bad. Nor was he good. He was just *horny*.

And he was still very, very hungry.

Chapter 2:
"Must Be Something In The Water"

Cam DeSelle's stomach growled. Not the quick gurgle of most people. No, this was a seismic event of the gut. It came with sheet music. He took a deep breath of the cayenne-pepper-infused aroma of boiling shrimp and smiled. He grabbed a thermal glove without bothering to slip it on and pulled the top off the steaming pot. The roiling water revealed big pink shrimp, new potatoes and corn on the cob dancing together in a spicy mix that made his eyes water. He reached down and turned the fire off the old gas stove and placed the top back on the deep pot.

"Don't let those things soak too long, Cam!" yelled a husky-voiced woman from the next room. "You know I don't like 'em too spicy."

The next room was the combination bait and tackle shop and grocery store Cam ran, inside a neat but aging old wooden building that served the active fishing needs of folks in Alcide, Louisiana, population 273. It was located southeast of Butte La Rose, in St. Martin Parish. If you were in the Google Earth mood, which might help you find it better, you'd see a slight smudge of high ground on the satellite photo, surrounded by bayous, swamps and diversion canals.

The pier-and-beam structure had solid wood floors and a high-pitched roof in the Acadian style of architecture that dominated this part of the world. The corrugated tin roof was almost completely rusted over, but it still kept the rain out.

The inside was jam-packed with just about everything a fisherman might need, from rods and reels to artificial bait, line, hooks, traps and even some high-tech depth-finding hoo-hah the idiots from New Orleans and Baton Rouge liked to throw in the boat. Out back he kept live bait like night crawlers, crickets and minnows, and some nasty stink bait for the catfish lovers.

Although technically not a restaurant, he had put four stools along the wooden counter and served whatever he happened to cook in the small kitchen in the back. There was no menu. If Cam cooked something, he'd sell you some. If he was too busy, you grabbed a bag of chips and a soda and went on your way.

Today, Carla Fontanelli was lucky. She had a stool and Cam had a pot of boiled shrimp.

Cam stepped out from the little kitchen to the counter area and gave Carla his million-dollar smile. She eyed him from head to toe. At 34, he was a year older than her, about six-two, lean. Dark, wavy hair and almond eyes. Good cheekbones and a chiseled nose and jaw. He wore an old blue chambray shirt, with a couple of buttons undone that revealed a nice tanned chest. Khaki board shorts and Topsiders completed the ensemble. She figured if someone didn't come in the store in the next 60 seconds, she'd do him right now behind the counter.

"What's shakin', Carla?" he said. For Carla, that was a legitimate and reasonable question. She was petite, with a little *budonkadonk* out back, nice chest out front, and the dark olive complexion and black, lustrous hair of her Sicilian ancestry. A lot of Sicilians had settled South Louisiana at the end of the 19th century. Somebody had to cut the cane after the slaves high-tailed it to the north during Reconstruction.

"Had a pretty good run this morning," she said. "Mary Kay's got a new line out, and I've been selling that shit like hot cakes." She took off her denim jacket to reveal a tight white cotton tank top. Cam's eyes dutifully drifted south for a moment to enjoy the view.

Carla was the official queen of the deal. At any given time, she sold Mary Kay Cosmetics, Avon or AmWay all up and down the bayou. She also sold sex toys and various other bedroom sporting equipment out the back of her trunk, too. She always said people really liked the junk in her trunk. She was just the consummate saleswoman. Won herself a pink Caddie from Mary Kay, too, which she promptly donated to Father Mike over at the Catholic Church. She preferred Audis, anyway. Father Mike would have preferred another color.

She eyed him again. "I got some stuff for guys, too. In case you need to exfoliate that gorgeous face of yours."

"Forget it," Cam said. "Real guys don't do that shit."

"Hey, it's perfect for today's metrosexual. Or bayou-sexual, if such a thing exists."

"It doesn't."

"You gonna fix me a plate, or what?"

"Hang on." Cam went in the back and loaded up a tray full of shrimp, potatoes and corn. He brought it out and put it in front of her.

"Beer or soda?" he said.

"An Abita Amber, if you got one."

Cam pulled out a bottle from the cooler, popped it open and set it by her tray. She grabbed it and put the longneck up to her mouth and gave it a long, slow pull. He thought she was giving it something else, so he thought about his grandma in a bikini for a moment to get things settled down a bit.

Carla was also pretty shrewd. She knew which shifts the men worked in the oil fields, when they were home and when momma wasn't at home, and vice versa, and timed it perfectly to sell her wares to whoever needed it most. Cam thought maybe that was a poor choice of words. Or maybe not.

"What's the word down the road?" Cam said.

Carla started peeling and talking at the same time. "Same old shit. Lyin', cheatin' eatin'. Fishin's good. But you'd know that. Some drunk coonass sliced up a redneck during a cockfight outside of Catahoula." She popped a shrimp into her mouth. "Oh, yeah. Floyd Guidry didn't come back from a gator hunt the other day. Wife thinks he's got a woman back up in there, so we'll see how that turns out." Carla smiled at that thought.

The screen door squealed open. "See how what turns out?" Lexie Smith walked in and surveyed the place. She was a St. Martin Parish sheriff's deputy, the closest thing to being Alcide's official top cop, and at age 28, the youngest ever. And at five-eleven, with blonde hair and blue eyes, the hottest ever, if you asked Cam. Cam stood straight and sent a charming smile her way.

"Hey, Lexie. Hungry?"

"Hey, Cam. Carla." She nodded her head and walked to the counter and sat next to Carla. Her leather belt, holster and boots squeaked as she sat down. "Mmmm. Shrimp."

Carla scooted her stool over. "Floyd Guidry went missing the other day."

"Huh," Lexie said. "Was that reported? I haven't heard anything."

Carla bit into a potato and mumbled. "Beats me. You know how those guys are."

"Probably got too late and bedded down in some old camp," Cam said. "My dad and I did that a few times when I was a kid. I hated it. The swamp makes weird sounds at night."

"I'll take a plate," Lexie said. She pulled out a small notebook and jotted something down. "I'll call the sheriff and see what's up."

"Oh, I got that...foundation...you ordered, out in the car," Carla said. "Let me know if you need anything else." Carla looked down at her food, a smirk on her face. Cam was pretty sure the "foundation" or "anything else" wasn't going on Lexie's face.

Lexie blushed a bit, and Cam gave her a dreamy look, turned, and walked back into the kitchen.

She was a widow and still recovering from the death of her husband 18 months earlier. He had died in front of her at home. Right after he had come at her with a machete and she blew most of his head off with her Colt Anaconda.44 Magnum revolver. Everyone knew he got drunk and beat her up from time to time. The machete took it to a whole new level, though. Well, for him anyway.

"I see you finally got the photo up," Lexie yelled a bit so Cam could hear her. She was looking up at the wall behind the counter at a framed 8 x 10. It showed eight soldiers standing on a dusty street, dressed in desert camo, holding automatic rifles, looking badass. Also in the picture were five German Shepherds held on tight leashes. They looked badass, too.

Cam returned from the kitchen with Lexie's order and glanced back at the photo. "Yeah, baby, the 'hounds from hell.' Those were some good old dogs," Cam said. "Scared the shit out of the Iraqis."

Cam had been with the Louisiana National Guard and got called up a few years back. Before being deployed, he ran Alcide's only vet clinic, a small building next door to the bait and tackle. When he went over, he was assigned to care for the war dogs that fought alongside the troops. His dad had run the store until he retired last year, and now Cam was doing double duty running the vet clinic and the bait and tackle shop.

When Cam said "dogs," there was a slight chuffing sound from behind the counter. A big yellow Lab stood up, ears alert and tail wagging.

"Not talking about you, Huey," Cam said and scratched the dog's head. The big dog licked his hand.

The screen door slammed open again and he, Carla and Lexie turned as one. An emaciated young man with long greasy blond hair walked toward the cooler. He wore faded jeans, no shirt and some beat-up Nike's. His rib cage pressed tightly against his bronze skin.

"Oh boy," Carla said under her breath and turned back to her food. Cam gave Lexie a look. Huey growled.

"You got any cold Keystone in here, Dee-Sale?" the man said.

"Yeah, Roland. To the right. And grab some fried pies while you're at it. You look like you haven't eaten in a year." He smiled and winked at the girls.

"Fuck you, Dee-Sale," Roland said.

"Right back at ya, douche bag," Cam said.

Roland dropped a six-pack on the counter. "Camels," he ordered.

Cam tossed a pack next to the beer. "Sure you don't want some deodorant to go with that? You smell a little ripe there, buddy."

Roland squinted at Cam and grinned. A jack-o-lantern had better dental hygiene. "You know, I could take my business down the road, dude. You shouldn't be so rude to your customers."

"Just friendly advice, asshole," Cam said. He rang up the order and Roland walked out, leaving behind a fragrance that made even Huey's eyes water.

"I'm gonna bust that bastard," Lexie said as she ate. "He's been cookin' up meth back in that swamp long enough."

"Looks like he's been sampling the goods, too," said Carla.

"Did seem a little twitchy," Cam replied. "But you gotta catch him with the goods."

"He moves that lab around somehow," Lexie said. "I can never find it. Need more manpower."

"You should call the State Police. Or DEA or something," Carla said.

"Nah, he'd spot 'em and go to ground," Lexie said. "I'll just play dumb ol' deputy girl and wait for him to make a mistake."

"Me and Troy could go in there and do some recon for you," Cam said. "You could deputize us or something."

Lexie stopped eating for a moment and gave that some thought. "Maybe. You got time for that? I mean, with everything else you're doing." She waved her hand in front of her.

"Yeah, I could sneak out a bit. Get Zach or somebody to watch the store for a while. Just let me know."

"Would it be okay for them to just shoot him?" Carla said with a snort. "Save everybody some trouble."

Lexie smiled. "Interesting thought. Angola is so overcrowded now anyway."

Cam heard big tires over gravel and the squeak of brakes outside. A moment later, a tall black man in chinos and a lavender golf shirt walked in. He gave Cam a wave.

"Yo, Cameron. What's happenin' at Fort Saint J?"

"All good, Lee. Whatcha need?"

"Hooks, bobbers, lead weights. Some small cane poles if you got 'em."

Cam smiled. "Goin' after some big trophy bass, are you?"

"Funny," Lee said. "Macy's birthday party is Saturday. We'll let all the kids do some fishing off the bank out back. Biggest fish wins something or other. More fun than pin-the-tail-on-the-donkey, anyway."

"Maybe not," Cam replied. "You're gonna spend most of the day untangling line."

"Tell me about it."

Lee walked around the store to finish his shopping. Carla and Lexie finished their meals, paid up and said their goodbyes.

"I'm serious about that recon," Cam yelled as Lexie walked out. She gave him a smile and a thumbs up. That would hold him for the rest of the afternoon.

Lee brought his supplies to the counter. "Damn, those two are some kind of talent," Lee said. He craned his neck to watch Lexie put her long frame into the police cruiser. "I mean, what is it about this town? Everybody around here is hot. Hell, I picked Deanna up at some garden club thing—you know, a bunch of old ladies. In their seventies—and *they* were hot. For old broads, at least."

Cam stared at Lee. "Dude, you been in the sun too long. Shit, Lee. Don't be greedy. Deanna is smokin' hot. That caramel skin. Those green eyes. Hell, I can't wait for you to die, man."

"Yeah, get in line. And all four of my girls look like her, too. Gonna have to get a shotgun before long and just sit on the porch to keep the boys away. My oldest is already thirteen."

"Damn near jailbait," Cam said. "Send her to that convent in New Orleans. The one Sister Joanie went to."

"There's a thought." Lee handed Cam his debit card." But seriously. It is kind of weird, isn't it? Did you know that four of the last ten Miss Louisiana's came from this parish?"

"I might have read that somewhere," Cam said. "I've lived around here all my life. Guess I'm just used to the beautiful people."

Lee took his bag of supplies. "I can get used to it," he said.

Cam nodded. "It's like my *grandmère* always said. 'Must be something in the water.'"

Chapter 3:
"Dinner at Floyd's"

Father Mike Fallon pulled out of the rectory driveway of Sacred Heart of Jesus Catholic Church and on to the
parish road. His Cadillac CTS Sports Sedan's engine roared
as it grabbed the sizzling hot blacktop and gathered speed.
He liked the smooth, quiet ride and all the techno bells and
whistles, but he hated the pink makeup. He thought about
getting Troy over at the garage to give him a new paintjob.
Black would be good, to go with the uniform.

He slowed through Alcide's single, blinking yellow
light and let his momentum carry him a few more blocks
until he passed Fort St. Jesus Bait and Tackle. He shook his
head and smiled when he passed the place. "Fort St. Jesus"
was Alcide's nickname of sorts and Cam had taken the name
for his store to further the joke. It had all started a few years
back when Father Mike's parish, Sacred Heart of Jesus, absorbed the nearby struggling parish of St. Alphonse after the
death of its ancient pastor, Father Alvin Arceneaux. Word was
the old priest, who was rumored to have gone to high school
with St. Peter, was finally catching up on old times with his
classmate. Like most mergers, it was an equitable arrange-
ment for one of the parties, and the new parish was called
Sacred Heart of Jesus. It was a pretty good deal for Mike. He
picked up 300 more parishioners, their money, a pretty good

electric organ, some new hymnals, a few relic bones of St. Alphonse himself, a cute young nun and an undisclosed free agent and three second-round draft picks. Of course, the local Cajun jokemeisters had some fun with the news. They got to thinking and slammed some thoughts together, which was always a dangerous endeavor. First, they thought about calling the new parish "St. Jesus," with a nod to both parish names. That got them laughing. But they thought something was missing. So one local genius remembered the old Civil War cavalry "fort" down the road that had an historical marker next to it. Wasn't anything but an open field where some Confederate horse troopers had camped for a month or so on their way to Texas. Or on the way back from Texas. No one could remember. Anyway, that gave them a fantastic idea, and the name "Fort St. Jesus" was hatched and it stuck like a big fat leech on somebody's ass.

Mike was a native, and understood the people around here. He was popular with his parishioners, especially the ladies, who had pegged him as marrying material since he was five. He was a shade under six feet, with auburn hair and pale blue eyes. His model good looks usually packed the church on Sundays.

Today, he had gotten the call from down the bayou about a distraught Felice Guidry whose husband had gone missing during a gator hunt. Some of the church ladies thought it'd be good if he swung down there and made a quick visit and said a few prayers. Her husband, Floyd, was a bit of a hound, and was known to disappear for a few days during a hunt. Usually this involved hunting women of all shapes, colors and ages, so

Mike wasn't worried about Floyd's health, but maybe a little about his soul.

The drive down the two-lane took him out of Alcide and along the western edge of the Atchafalaya Swamp—600,000 acres of rivers, bayous and wetlands that cut a 20-mile-wide by 150-mile-long swath through south-central Louisiana all the way to the Gulf. Mike was a sportsman since birth, and had spent many a great time inside the swamp. His work demands as pastor had cut into his recreational time, but every now and then some of the men would invite him along for a hunting or fishing trip. Of course, he was expected to say a prayer for success. The outcome of that prayer either increased or decreased his chances for another invite.

The road snaked its way through the swamp, the lush wetlands still and hot. The sky was clear, but the blue had a milky, washed out hue. Mike cranked up the satellite radio and tapped the steering wheel to some old song from the nineties. He slowed the car as he came around a curve and noticed something across the road ahead, like a black and brown stain. It looked like mud and dirt had been tracked across the highway by a tractor or a big four-wheeler. Odd, though, because there were no trails or roads coming out of the swamp on either side of the highway. The Caddie thumped across the mud and dirt, and as soon as it did, Mike was overcome by an odor that gagged him. It was a hot, pungent chemical smell that made him catch his breath. For a moment, he thought it was a combination of skunk and road kill, but it was too toxic for even that. He hit the automatic window button and got all four windows down to let the nasty odor out of the car.

"Yeeecchhhhh!" he shouted. He spit out the window to get the smell-taste out of his mouth. "What the hell was that?"

It wasn't a natural smell, he thought. More like a chemical. Were they doing some drilling out here? The oil-and-gas people pumped some weird shit into those holes to extract crude and natural gas, but he didn't see any wells nearby. Which probably meant somebody had dumped some chemicals out here, or had illegally cleaned out a tanker or something. Bastards. The last thing they needed was a toxic spill to mess up the eco-system. He'd report it to the sheriff.

The creature watched through the willow and cypress as the car zipped down the highway. He counted its occupants. Only one. He had never run down one of those things, but the thought excited him. He was fast on level ground, and could probably catch one if it wasn't moving too quickly. Maybe he would risk it if there were more people inside to eat. Damn, he was hungry again. It was the mating thing. He had to eat a lot to produce the chemical he needed to spray in the female and cause the birth of the young ones. The acids in his stomach were now very potent, and they digested his meals at a rapid pace in order to produce and store the mating chemical. He was hungry almost constantly now, and was eating his way through the swamp at a blistering pace as he tracked the female. She was still far away, but he was making good progress as long as he could find something to eat. And the bigger, the better. Wouldn't hurt if it tasted good, either.

Thirty minutes later, Father Mike slowed the Caddie down and made a right onto a gravel road that ran a quarter mile through a small pasture. A lone cow stood comatose under a live oak, stunned by the heat and staring at nothing in particular. At the end of the road sat a white doublewide, trimmed in blue, tricked up to look like a real house. A curtain of aluminum siding covered the gap between the ground and the house, and it gave it the illusion of a house on a solid foundation. The yard was well kept, with a flower garden around the steps leading up to the door. A gray barn sat behind the house, its pitched roof leaning a bit to the left. A small John Deere tractor was parked under a pecan tree.

Two sheriff's cruisers were parked out front. Three other cars were pulled in at odd angles. Three men stood in a tight circle near the front, smoking and talking.

"This doesn't look good," Mike muttered. He got out, adjusted his Roman collar, and walked over.

The men stood straight and looked toward the approaching priest.

"Father," one said, nodding his head and tossing a cigarette butt to the ground. He blew a stream of smoke out of the corner of his mouth.

"Boys," Mike said. "What's the what?"

"Dudn't look good, Father," the smoker said. "Not good at all."

Mike looked toward the house, and then leaned in. "Sure Floyd's not out chasing some tail?"

The men all looked at their feet, not quite sure how to respond to that one, especially from a priest. Smoker said,

"Naw, it's the real deal. He went out for gators. Cops found out something, too. Wouldn't tell us. They inside."

"Thanks." Mike walked up the steps and knocked. Lexie opened it for him.

"Hey, Mike," she said in a low, serious tone. Instead of letting him in, she eased out the door and herded him into the yard, away from the cluster of men.

"He's dead," she said. "Found his boat an hour ago."

"Crap," Mike said. He shook his head. "What happened?"

Lexie frowned and looked up at the sky. She scratched her forehead. "Uh, hard to say. I wasn't there, but this is what the sheriff told me. Floyd's boat is tied up to this cypress knee. Inside the boat is what's left of four gators. Big ones, too. Must have had a good day."

"What do you mean, 'what's left?'"

"Just that. A piece of a head, a leg or two, the tips of a couple of tails, with Guidry's tags still on 'em. Chewed up. Blood everywhere."

"Something ate them?" Mike said.

"Yeah, ate 'em *in the boat.*"

"Shit."

Lexie looked at the ground. "So, you gonna ask me about Floyd?"

"I'm almost afraid to."

"They found his boots still in the boat."

"Okay," Mike said.

"Feet still in 'em."

Mike rubbed his hand through his thick hair. "Dear Lord."

"Yeah," Lexie said. "Pretty much a bad day for Floyd. And the gators."

Both Lexie and Mike looked off toward the highway. Neither said anything as various horror movie scenarios played through their heads. Mike broke the silence.

"So, Guidry's in the boat. Four dead gators in there with him. Then something *else* gets in the boat and pretty much eats them."

"That about covers it," Lexie said. She looked at the three men in the distance. They were lighting up another round of smokes.

Mike shook his head.

Lexie said in an almost whisper, "The sheriff's theory is that Floyd caught and shot a fifth gator, a *really* big one, and winched it into the boat, thinking it was dead. Maybe the bullet stunned him or something instead of killed him. Anyway, the big gator wakes up and kills Floyd in the boat. Then eats him. Then has his gator cousins for dessert before slipping back into the water."

Mike frowned. "This thing is big enough to eat a full-grown man *and* four alligators?' C'mon."

"I'm not buying it either," she said. "The big gator might have gotten Floyd. Maybe some other gators got in the boat later and ate the four dead ones over time. Something like that. But, I always thought gators ate their kill in the water."

Mike sighed. "Okay, they told Felice?"

"Yeah."

"Then I guess I'm on," Mike said, and looked toward the front door. "How's the food situation inside?"

"Etouffee,"

"Awesome."

Chapter 4:
"Idiot Savant Avant"

Roland Avant sat back on the deck of his floating meth lab and inhaled the Camel cigarette smoke deep into his lungs. He looked up at the sun that floated in and out of the cypress branches and closed his eyes. The nicotine gave him a little jolt. It would have to do. He'd run out of weed yesterday and his man was still over in Breaux Bridge making deliveries. Might be tomorrow before he got some more. Of course, he could always hit the meth, but that shit seriously fucked him up, and he had *bidness* to attend to.

He let his head tip forward and took in his floating domain. It had started out as a beat-up pontoon party barge he bought from some old Cajun down in Morgan City who needed cash to cover his gambling needs. He had hauled it back to Alcide, tinkered on it some behind his trailer, and then floated it out into the swamp to become his personal love nest with the ladies. That was a bit optimistic, given his dubious hygiene and lack of a sustainable income. So Roland, a stack of skin magazines and his left hand got very acquainted with each other over the years together out on his love boat.

But everything changed a year ago. Roland's cousin from Monroe had visited and given him a quickie degree in the fine art of cooking meth, and the rest, as they say, was mind-blowing, teeth-losing, appetite-suppressing history.

It might have ended all there—passed out, totally wasted inside his boat, one hand on the meth pipe, the other on his pecker—had not a curious possum walked up his stomach at 3 a.m. and raised Roland's consciousness. That's when his ninth-grade dropout brain had the epiphany that he could sell this shit. Not just to the dumb fucks who lived around here, but to the *real* dumb fucks in New Orleans.

So it began. He painted his party boat in an abstract brown, green and blue camo pattern, gathered the necessary supplies, and started his own business. And because he could move his stealth kitchen, as he called it, anywhere in the swamp, that Lexie Hot Ass Smith would never find it. But he did have fantasies she would, and he'd jump her, and use her as a recreational device during his breaks. That movie was a popular one in his brain, and he filed it away in his personal spank bank.

Over time, Roland had developed quite an inventory, and he had to move it. A few phone calls here and there, a couple of trips to the Big Sleazy, and he'd found himself a *distributor.* They looked like gangbangers, but he suspected they were muscle for what was left of the old Mob in New Orleans. Didn't matter one way or the other to him. He was about to score some serious cash, and the boys from the city were days away from showing up and taking delivery.

Roland planned on spending his windfall in New Orleans, with a suite at Harrah's and a couple of hookers to help him pass the time. It would be epic. All he had to do was sit tight and wait for his customers.

He tossed the cigarette butt into the algae-covered water and smiled. Okay, maybe just one little hit wouldn't hurt.

The back of Fort St. Jesus Bait and Tackle faced the bayou, and Cam's dad had built a long porch years earlier that ran the length of that side of the store. A short set of wooden stairs led down from there to a small pier where fishermen could pull up, grab some beer and bait, and be on their way. The porch had some old gray rocking chairs, an assortment of cheap folding lawn furniture, a few picnic tables, and various bar stools Cam had collected. It was a perfect place to hang out. His dad knew that fishermen would come in for the day, tie up, and have a few beers and snacks out back and talk about the day. Money in the bank.

Cam sat in one of the rocking chairs, beer in hand, and stared out as the sun set over the willow and cypress across the bayou. A lone fisherman in a beat-up aluminum bass boat puttered past in the fading light, its old Evinrude motor whining like a giant bumblebee. Seated next to Cam was Troy Pitre, also with beer in hand, eyeing Cam's dog, Huey, who sat between them. Troy was broader and taller than Cam, with brown buzz-cut hair, big, brown eyes and a long, aquiline nose with a slight angle to it, as if it had been broken and reset more than once. A slight scar ran above his left eye.

"What the fuck's wrong with that dog?" he said.

Cam let out a long burp and leaned forward. "What?" He looked down at the dog and rubbed Huey's back. The dog stared off in the distance, ears back. He wasn't even tracking the fisherman.

"Look at his lips," Troy said.

Cam stared closer at the dog's mouth. Huey curled his lips up in a snarl, revealing his large teeth. But he wasn't growling the way a dog would if making that face. He was quiet.

"Hell if I know. What ya see, boy?"

Huey didn't even acknowledge his master. He was in the zone.

Cam looked in the direction that had caught Huey's attention. He squinted his eyes, but could see nothing. Satisfied that all was well, he sat back and rocked a bit.

"You busy tomorrow afternoon?" he said.

Troy sighed. "Pulling an engine in the morning. Couple of brake jobs, but that's about it. Why?"

"I dunno. Wanna go snoopin' around Roland's world? Lexie's trying to bust his operation and might need some undercover help."

Troy snorted. "Undercover help? Yeah, I bet you'd like to help her with that. When are you gonna close that deal, man?"

Cam shook his head. "Ahhh. She's still screwed up about her ex. Like the moment she blew his head off, she closed shop or something."

"That'll do it to a woman. Hell, you just need to find the right key to open that door." Troy grabbed his crotch and gave it a squeeze.

"Off limits, shithead," Cam said.

"Whatever. We've been chasing the same chicks since 11th grade. What's one more?" He gave Cam a punch in the arm. "Remember how dorkie she was then? All legs. No boobs. Skinny ass. She wasn't getting anywhere near our illustrious all-district quarterback Cameron DeSelle."

Cam pointed a finger at him. "I was never mean to her. There were just...other girls."

"Yeah. Carla was rockin' a great rack even then. I swear, coach yelled at me that whole season for watching more of her ass than the game. I wanted to quit and become a cheerleader, just so I could grab that nice little bottom all night."

"Quarterbacks outrank receivers, even in that department," Cam said, a thin smile on his lips. "If I could have figured out how to make a football look like her ass, you would have never dropped a pass all season."

Troy threw his head back and burst out laughing. "Shit, I'd be all-pro by now," he said.

Cam looked back down at Huey. The dog was still frozen, teeth bared in a classic display of aggression. Now the big Lab's hackles were up, and Cam could finally hear a deep, resonant growl from the big dog.

"What's the matter, Huey? I thought that was pretty funny."

The parish office of Sacred Heart of Jesus Catholic Church had officially closed 30 minutes earlier. The building was connected to the church itself, an old white clapboard thing made of ancient but sturdy red cypress with a high steeple. The office ran perpendicular to the church and consisted of meeting rooms, a small parish hall, offices for Father Mike and Sister Joanie, a business office for the clerical and administrative staff, and a tiny chapel for small services.

Father Mike sat on a green vinyl love seat in the small lobby, his feet propped up on a beat-up faux-wood coffee table. He'd taken off the Roman collar, so his unbuttoned black shirt now looked like a Nehru jacket from the sixties. He stared at a six-month-old issue of Outdoor Life magazine, some article about elk hunting somewhere up north. He tossed it on the table.

"Look in the back, behind the potato salad," he yelled.

"Shut up, I see them," a woman's voice cried from the kitchen off the lobby.

Mike put his head back and rubbed his eyes. The consolation of Felice Guidry earlier in the day had not gone well. She'd been married to Floyd for 26 years, and after the kids moved out, they had begun to do more things together. Whenever Floyd wasn't boinking some wayward waitress, that is. She'd put two and two together and got the gist of his demise—that he'd been *eaten*—which kind of freaked her out. She'd asked the obligatory questions of her priest, about why God let this happen. Was it punishment for his philandering, etcetera, etcetera. Mike wasn't very good at the death thing yet. To be honest, death still kind of freaked him out, too, seeing as he was still pretty young. So he muddled through it, did some praying with Felice, and then pigged out on some fantastic crawfish etouffee before hightailing it back to the church.

The clink of beer bottles shook him out of his reflection. He opened his eyes and watched as Sister Joan Allemand walked into the room. She carried two Bud longnecks in one hand, a bag of Doritos in the other.

"You look like crap," she said, and handed him one of the beers. She dropped the bag of chips on the coffee table and plopped down in a matching vinyl chair next to the love seat.

Joanie was 28-years-old, with hazel eyes and long chest-nut-colored hair in a simple ponytail. She wore cut-off jeans, sandals and a black-and-gold New Orleans Saints T-shirt. A blue bandana was tied up on her head. Her legs and arms were tan from the long summer outdoors. There were dried green paint splotches here and there. The T-shirt did little to hide her curvy figure. Certainly not hard to look at. Like every-body else in these parts. Except she was a nun. Which added some chatter to things.

"Thanks," he said. "I also *feel* like crap, so there, I don't have to explain any inconsistencies." He took a pull from the beer and reached for the Doritos. "Finish painting the office?"

Joanie nodded. "All done. We'll put the furniture back in tomorrow." The church ladies were getting tired of the brown décor in the bookkeeping offices and decided on a little makeover. "When's the funeral?" she asked.

Mike mumbled something between crunches of the chips, took another swallow of beer. "Wake's Friday night. Service is Saturday morning."

"He never came to church," Joanie said. "But he gets the send-off anyway."

Mike smiled. "I used to tell him it would take six strong men to get him back into church. Am I a prophet, or what?"

"So what exactly are we burying? Heard it's gonna be a pair of boots."

"Not my problem," Mike said. "Maybe he won't need six strong men after all to carry the casket." He winked at her.

They drank in silence for a few minutes and thought about that. Mike said, "She kept asking me why God let something like that happen to Floyd. Like God was some redneck who got everybody up there together and said, 'Hey, watch this! This is gonna be cool' and chomp, chomp, Floyd is lunch."

"Maybe He did," Joanie said.

"I continue to see why you almost got thrown out of the convent twice," he said.

"Four times," she answered, and held up four fingers. "The third was the night I snuck out and went partying with those Tulane students. The fourth was the bottle of Jack they found in my room."

Mike gave her a level gaze. "I'm sure your parents were very proud."

Joanie shrugged her shoulders. "Yet here I am."

"Here you are," he replied.

Joan, or "Joanie" as everyone called her, was another local girl with the beauty and brains to do whatever she wanted. Her smart mouth, impulsiveness and free spirit had most taking equal bets it would be Hollywood, politics or the women's prison at St. Gabriel. But God had zapped her during the summer between her junior and senior year at the University of Louisiana at Lafayette, or "U La La" and off she went to the Sisters of the Cypress convent in New Orleans. The bets remained on the table, however.

After a tumultuous stretch at the convent, she'd taken her vows and was immediately posted to a small school in Northern Alaska, teaching Inuit children. The Mother Superior had wanted Mongolia, but had to settle. Lucky for Joanie, her parents had some pull with the Bishop in Lafayette and gotten Joanie back home in a hurry. To the Mother Superior, swampy, isolated Alcide, Louisiana wasn't a bad third option.

Mike had picked her up in the massive trade for St. Alphonse Parish. She helped him with the large, far-flung combined parish, and spent part of her week teaching at the local public elementary school, which needed the help.

Mike looked her over, and she caught his gaze.

"Are you checking me out?" she said.

Mike rolled his eyes. "You don't look like any nun that taught me."

"Pity for you," she said.

"What would happen if Sister Lavelle walked in right now and saw you dressed like that?"

"She'd die of a heart attack?" Joanie said. "I'd pay good money to see the Mother Superior have a little episode."

Mike laughed and held out his bottle for a toast. Joanie leaned over and tapped his bottle with hers. "To Attila the Nun."

"Attila the Nun."

Somewhere in her closet, Joanie possessed her "full-on nun battle dress" as she called it, but rarely wore it. She hated the "nun tan" it gave her, she would say. A bronzed, sun-kissed oval face, and a pasty white body everywhere else. The locals, rather than being shocked by her casual dress, embraced it. She was "their Joanie" after all. Screw those old nuns in New Orleans.

Joanie filled Mike in about her day, the start of school, something about an upcoming fundraiser and other assorted parish business. He nodded, but he wasn't listening. He thought about how glad he was that she was here. She was perfect for the parish and a great asset for the people. And she was a good friend. That's what he kept telling himself. Over and over and over again.

Might need to pay a visit to Father Marion over in the next parish to hear his confession, Mike thought. He watched as Joanie crossed her long, lean legs. *Yep. Might want to take care of that ASAP.*

Chapter 5:
"Game On"

Cam kept his Ford F-250 pickup at a comfortable 45mph down the two-lane road that wound its way through the parish. The sun had gone down and he was headed home, a mild beer buzz had put him in a mellow mood and Led Zeppelin was playing from the CD deck. *Whole Lotta Love'."* He didn't particularly care for Led Zeppelin. Maybe because he was pretty sure when their music was coming out, his Mom and Dad were listening in, doin' the dirty to Mr. Plant and his buddies' wailing guitars and suggestive lyrics. The thing was, it was Huey's favorite band. He looked back into the crew cab and checked on the big Lab, who had his head out the passenger side of the truck, nodding, strangely keeping time to the licks those Led Zeppelin boys were laying down.

"Roll with it, Huey!" he yelled. "Duh duh, duh duh duh, wanna whole lotta love!" The dog barked and Cam laughed. Suddenly the music cut out and Cam looked at the readout on the sound system. The Bluetooth was cutting in with an incoming call. He hit the answer button.

"This is Cam," he said loudly over the road noise and wind.

"Cam? It's Lexie. Got a minute?"

Cam sat up. "Yeah, hang on. Huey, in the car," he ordered. The dog pulled his head back in and Cam rolled the window up. The road noise dropped. "Hey, what's up?"

"Need to tap into your vet brain a minute," she said.

"'Vet' as in animals, or as in *Iraq*?"

"Animals," she said.

"Okay, you finally get a pet?"

"No, got no time for a pet. You on the way home?"

"Yeah."

"Close to my place?" she asked.

"Close enough. You want me to drop by?"

"Can you? Better than you talking and driving. I need your undivided attention."

Cam looked at Huey and raised his eyebrows a couple of times. The dog cocked his head, ears up. "On my way."

Lexie's house was not too far from Cam's. He drove another half mile and turned off the parish road down a narrow two lane. The willows seem to close on the road in the harsh light of his headlights. Bugs shone in the high beams and splattered against his windshield. The road opened onto a small pecan orchard and Lexie's modest ranch home was on the right. Cam pulled into the oyster-shell driveway and parked next to her cruiser.

Lexie came out the front door. "That was quick," she said.

Cam stepped out of the truck. "No problem, I make house calls." He turned to Huey, who looked expectantly out the window. "You stay, Huey."

Lexie walked up and gave the Lab's head a rub. "It's okay, he can come in."

Cam opened the door and Huey jumped out, tail wagging. They all walked back to the front door, but Huey stopped and turned toward the dark, swampy woods behind Lexie's house. His ears were up and his nose went into the air. He whimpered a bit, and then the whimper turned into a growl as his ears went back and his tail dropped.

Cam stared at the dog a moment. "Huey, what is it, boy?"

"Probably that big fat coon that's been digging in my garbage can every night," Lexie said.

Huey backed up toward Cam and Lexie.

"Okay, let's go boy," Cam said. Huey was eager to oblige and ran ahead to the front door.

"Sorry, he's been acting weird all day," Cam said.

"It's been a weird day for everyone," Lexie said. She showed Cam in. The door opened into a spacious den, with a tasteful, contemporary décor. Sofa, love seat, a big easy chair—all in muted earth tones. A big flat screen hung from one wall near the fireplace. The other had floor-to-ceiling shelves full of books and various bric a brac. The walls were full of family pictures. None contained a picture of her late, great, headless husband, Kevin.

"You eat yet?" she said as she walked into the adjacent kitchen. "Got half of an oyster po'boy I'm not gonna touch."

Cam had caught the faint smell of fried seafood when he came in. He was starved. "Sure, wouldn't pass that up."

He sat at the bar while Lexie warmed the sandwich. Huey lay down on the floor nearby, a faint growl somewhere in his throat. Cam had a nice perspective of her at work. She wore tight blue jeans with a thin, clingy white top. Her blonde hair was down and cascaded over her thin shoulders. He thought he caught a faint whiff of perfume.

A few minutes later, Lexie put the po'boy and a cold beer in front of him. "Dig in and I'll fill you in."

"Great. Thanks."

"First question," she said. "What's the biggest alligator ever caught in Louisiana?"

Cam chewed on the sandwich a moment and thought about it. "I think the record is something like 19 or 20 feet," he said. "I can't imagine them getting any bigger."

"And how much food would a gator that big eat in a day?"

Cam didn't know where this was going. "That big? I don't know. They're apex predators. Top of the food chain, which means they eat whatever the hell they want. Truth be told, though, gators don't need that much protein to survive. Maybe 10 pounds a day? Huey needs more meat in a year than a 600-pound gator."

"Do they eat other gators?"

"Sure, all the time."

"What about people?"

"Rare, but they will indulge if the opportunity presents itself. They're wary of people, though. Especially us Cajuns. We eat them right back."

"Uh huh," Lexie said.

"What's this all about?"

She explained how Floyd Guidry's day had gone. And her working theory of what might have happened.

"Shit," Cam said. "That's the guy Carla was talking about at lunch?"

"Yeah, lunch," she said. "Finish your sandwich. There's something I want to show you when you're done."

"It's okay," he said. "I can look now."

"Trust me. You should wait."

Cam knocked back the po'boy and the beer while Lexie cleaned the kitchen. When he was done, she led him into the den. He sat in the recliner, she on the love seat. A brown manila envelope lay on the square coffee table. Lexie opened it and pulled out a stack of eight-by-ten color photos.

"Take a look," she said. "Floyd's...boots."

Cam stared at the photo of a pair of work boots. One sat upright on the bottom of Floyd's boat. The other had tipped over, revealing the ragged edge of a tibia bone and calf muscle sticking out the top of the boot.

With a straight face Cam said, "This was no boat accident."

"What?"

Cam looked up, a mischievous twinkle in his eye and a slight smirk. *Jaws.* The movie? When Hooper examined the girl's remains in that tub?"

Lexie shook her head slowly. "Cameron DeSelle. Could you be serious for a moment?"

"Sorry."

Cam looked through the rest of the photos.

"What do you think?" Lexie said.

Cam peered closer at one photo, frowned and looked up. "I can get the bit about the stunned gator waking back up, biting Floyd's feet off, maybe he falls overboard, gator slides back in the water and drags the guy off," Cam said. "Crazy, but weirder shit has happened. It's the other four gators. Was the boat pulled up on the bank?"

"No. Had it tied off in about 10 feet of water. Far from dry land," she replied.

"Right. No way that gator could climb back into that boat. And if he could, he couldn't possibly eat four other gators in one sitting. And not in a boat. Gators usually eat in the water, after they drown their victim."

"So what happened?" she asked.

Cam furrowed his brow and looked through the photos one more time. "I suppose the medical examiner is working on this?"

"Sure. In Lafayette. Sheriff said we might get a prelim report tomorrow."

Cam took a deep breath. "There's only one other creature back in those swamps that could do this."

Lexie leaned forward.

"Humans," Cam said. "I'd say somebody or bodies murdered Floyd and staged this weird scene to cover their tracks."

"You mean, like, poachers?" Lexie said. "Moving in on Floyd's action?"

"Maybe," he replied. "Or somebody else. Maybe Floyd saw something he wasn't supposed to."

They both stared at each other a moment. Lexie said, "Roland?"

Cam nodded. "Maybe Floyd found Roland's meth operation. Roland shot him, then staged the scene to look like a gator attack. Might've gone a little over the top on the staging, though."

Lexie sat back in the love seat and folded her arms. "Roland. That asshole. Game on, you little shit."

Southeast of Alcide, near Bayou Chene, the female creature lay bloated in a shallow pool of muddy water and tried to get comfortable. She looked up at the night sky to see low clouds sailing across the stars. She made a grunting sound, low and undulant until it faded. That was not quite correct. The sounds became so low a native animal couldn't hear them. But they sent out a tone that her mate would be able to hear from great distances. At the sound, the young squirmed inside of her, active but unable to exit her body. They were anticipating the final stage of the birthing process.

The creature's normally gray-black hide was now a mottled pink, and the spots grew larger and smaller with each large breath she took. Her eyes had grown twice their normal size, and she had doubled her weight. Earlier in the day, she had been at the bank where the water on the bayou was abnormally clear. She took a long gaze at her reflection in the water and cried out. It was undeniable. She looked like shit.

Before this she had been sleek and nearly black. When she walked upright, which she preferred, she stood nearly 15 feet tall. Not as tall as the male, but impressive nonetheless. Her huge mouth was loaded with orange teeth, and her sleek gray oral arm was long and powerful, able to snatch prey from 20 feet away. Now, she could barely get the thing out of her mouth. And standing on two legs hurt her back.

She was ready to get this show on the road. Where the hell was that male? She knew he would be going out of his mind with lust and hunger by now. Prone to stupid decisions as he made his way to her. If he didn't get here soon, she would do what her kind always did under those circumstances. Delicately tear open her own belly and release the young, who would die in minutes without being "set" by the male's chemical spray. She would recover, but her long pregnancy would be for naught. Then the bastard would come around and impregnate her again.

The female had constructed a solid birthing area around her little pool. She had cut small trees with her teeth and lashed the trunks together to create a wall around her, protecting the young from predation and camouflaging herself from intruders. Her specialized hands were highly adapted, enabling her to run very fast on all fours, rip prey with lethal claws, or use her opposable thumbs to do delicate work. At the moment, they came in handy to scratch her hide, which itched terribly, another by-product of her pregnancy.

She sighed, closed her huge eyes and tried to sleep. If the male didn't show up tomorrow, she would have to go looking for him. Not an ideal plan, but she was getting more irritable by the day. She looked like shit. And felt like it, too.

Bastard.

Chapter 6:
"Tammy Stirs the Pot"

Titus Worthy knelt on the soggy ground of the swampy southwest edge of Lake Pontchartrain. Mosquitoes feasted on every exposed part of his body, which at that moment was rather extensive since he was completely naked. His ebony skin glistened with sweat by the light of the car's headlights.

"C'mon, Tree!" he pleaded. "You can have the money. I just needed a…needed kinda an advance. Thass it. Some upfront to take care of a couple of tings."

"Shut the fuck up," Trey "Tree" Taylor barked. "I can't have the money, punk, cuz you ain't got it." Taylor's six-foot-seven frame towered over the kneeling man. He loosely held a Glock pistol in his right hand, letting it dangle from one huge index finger. Four other young black men surrounded Titus, each one similarly armed.

Titus nodded in the affirmative. "I know. I know. But I can get it. Dat's what I meant. Just need to talk to my man over in Algiers. Aw, man, you don't want to do dis." Titus's sobs sounded like he was choking.

"The fuck I don't," Tree replied. "You had a job to do. You deliver. You bring my cash back. Done. Pretty fuckin' simple." Tree pulled the slide back on the Glock and a round entered the chamber.

Titus whimpered, then his bowels let loose.

The four other men jumped back. One said, "Aw, man. Dude shittin' on hisself. Shoot that fucker, Tree."

Tree tightened his grip on the pistol, put it to Titus's head and said, "Fuck you," and pulled the trigger. The *pop* of the Glock dissipated into the vast dark swamp.

"Whatch you wanna do with the body, man?" another said.

Tree looked around the swamp, then down at Titus. "Nuthin'. Gators'll drag his body away in the morning. Fuck this punk."

"Gator gonna fuck him up fo' sure," another said, and laughed.

Tree looked at his watch. "I pronounce the time of death as... 2:11 a.m," he said. That's what the doctors always said on those emergency room TV shows. He liked to "pronounce," as they said. He'd done a lot of pronouncing over his young, violent life.

They walked back up to the big black Lincoln Town Car, its engine idling smoothly in the still night. They had parked it sideways on the overgrown gravel road that ran down to the low shoreline, so the headlights could give them some light to work by. The overgrown road was used by fishermen to get down to the lake.

"Crank that AC up," Tree ordered as he slipped his enormous frame into the passenger side of the car. His driver, Raymond, a wiry 20-year-old with jet-black skin and cornrows, was one step ahead and flicked the blower on high. He backed the car out and headed back up the road to the levee.

Tree still held the Glock between his knees, stroking the thing like a lover. No one spoke.

"Fucker ruint my night," Tree said to no one. "Had some cooch lined up and then this shit happens."

"Punk," someone affirmed cautiously from the backseat. Everybody felt more at ease when Tree was getting regular cooch. He tended to get a little unpredictable otherwise.

"Wayne, you talk to that cracker about pickin' up our shit?" Tree said, and turned to the back seat.

"Yeah, Tree," Wayne, the man in the middle, said. "Saturday morning."

"And where the fuck is this place?" Tree said, his big dumb face now looking especially dumber as he squinted his eyes.

"Alcid, Alseed, some fuckin' coonass name," Wayne replied. "Other side of the Basin, 'fore you git to Lafayette somewhere."

"Shoulda made that punk bring it to us," Tree said. "Don't like haulin' on I-10. State police all over that road."

"We be cool," Raymond said. "I keep it right under 65 the whole way."

The car bounced up over the top of the levee, and down the other side. In minutes they were headed back into New Orleans. Tree was quiet the whole way, doing math in his head. Or what passed as math. Titus had fucked him out of a lot of coin. And he wouldn't be seeing it again. Which was why nobody would be seeing Titus again. Still, he had a cash flow problem, and that shipment of ice from the swamp would go a long way to making things right.

Saturday. Things would be better.

At about the same time Tree and the Gang were heading back into the Ninth Ward, at the same hour the good folks of Alcide, Louisiana, were safely tucked into their respective beds, and the exact same time two star-crossed aliens were snoozing in the swamp, Tropical Depression Number 17 was moving up in the world. The rotating clump of thunderstorms in the southern Gulf of Mexico had found its mojo. It was matriculating into Tropical Storm Tammy, with maximum sustained winds of 50 miles an hour.

A big high pressure area over the western Atlantic had set up some nice steering currents of air that pushed the storm northward, and with no big cool fronts coming out of the Rockies, the National Hurricane Center had plotted Tammy's initial path right into the central coast of Louisiana. The Center was predicting Tammy could grow into a Category 3 storm before landfall, which would put her winds in the 111-130 mph area, what the experts called "devastating" and the coastal locals called "get the hell out of Dodge."

Within minutes of the storm's birth announcement, plans kicked in to evacuate the hundreds of oil wells along the northern end of the Gulf. Choppers from Lafayette south to Houma were spooling up to get the airlift moving. Fishing fleets were making plans for one last run before heading in to safer harbors. The rock stars from The Weather Channel in Atlanta were packing up to get their asses on the beach for the money shot of the stormy Gulf at their backs and concerned looks across their faces.

Somebody at FEMA in Washington got a wake-up call, only this time it was a literal wake-up call, versus the shittier kind of wake-up call that had come after Katrina.

At MacDill Air Force Base in Tampa, the crew of a NOAA P-3 Orion "Hurricane Hunter" aircraft began their briefing before heading southwest over the Gulf and into Tammy. They would give forecasters real-time measurements of pressure, humidity, temperature, wind speed and wind direction. This would give the coastal locals a fair approximation of when to get the hell out of Dodge.

The hot water of the Gulf was steadily feeding Tammy a potent dose of energy, and when the sun came up, the storm would get the meteorological equivalent of three cups of coffee with a Red Bull chaser to start her day.

The slow, simmering pot of hot, crazy September gumbo was about to really get stirred.

Chapter 7:
"Frogasaurus Rex"

Huey lay on his mat on the floor at the foot of Cam's bed. His eyes were wide open. The sun was still an hour away, and the only sound was the steady *whirr* of the ceiling fan and his master's slow, steady breathing. There was something out there. He could smell it. Over the span of his six years of life, he had catalogued just about every smell out of the swamp, and man, there was some weird shit out there. And he knew them all. But this new smell was different, odd. It was a living thing, that's for sure. And it was making a *sound*. Something only he could hear. But what was strange was *the sound was coming from a different direction than the smell*.

The thing was moving, too. Slowly but surely. Taking its time. The smell, and the sound, and Huey's own animal intuition told him the thing was big and dangerous. Like bite-your-head-off dangerous.

Another thing Huey was concerned about was the sounds and smells of the regular animals in the swamp. They were off, too. They were scared. All of them were scared. He'd never experienced anything like it before.

But what really freaked him out was the sense that the thing wasn't another animal like him. It was like the humans. But not like them. His dog brain couldn't work it out, but what it could work out was that it was headed this way.

His instinct told him it was time to run. But he couldn't leave his Cam. He had to protect him. And he had to warn him, too. But the message was kind of complicated, and he'd have to figure out a way to let his master know that the shit was about to hit that ceiling fan.

Lee Curtis's home was west of Alcide in a neighborhood called Acadian Trace. The small, gated enclave had a single street off the main highway that ended in a cul de sac. It held seven homes built by a single developer who had mimicked the local Cajun architecture: wide front porches with high-pitched roofs. The spacious homes each had an acre of land that fronted the bayou. The shady area was full of live oaks, with white cypress and willow near the banks of the narrow waterway. It was Alcide's Beverly Hills, if Beverly Hills came with alligators, water moccasins and mosquitoes big enough to shoot.

Curtis wasn't a native Louisianan. He was originally from Cleveland, a geologist for one of the many oil companies who had come to rape and pillage. They had thought sending an African-American geologist would make them look like enlightened people to the locals. And he would be in the company's annual report, too. A good way to check off all the equal opportunity boxes, add some color to the all-white "oil bidness."

The locals could care less what color Lee was. Blacks, Creoles, Cajuns, Spanish, French, Italian, Irish and all manner of human blood had been mixing together for some time on the bayou. The oil company HR people were way late to the party. In fact, Lee enjoyed working the area so much, he stayed around, met and married Deanna Mitchell, she of the green eyes, caramel skin and Creole heritage. They had four gorgeous girls. Now he called Alcide home and told his Cleveland friends he had gone all *Dances With Wolves* down in bayou country.

Lee walked into his bedroom carrying two cups of hot coffee. He wore gym shorts and an Ohio State t-shirt. Deanna was stretched out across the linen sheets, completely nude, with the sheet covering one leg and not much more. Her exposed breasts heaved steadily up and down.

"Damn, Lee Curtis." She shuddered with a post-orgasm aftershock. "I don't think I can stand."

"You look good just like that." He sat on the edge of the bed. Deanna sat up and pulled the sheet up to her waist. Lee handed her a cup.

"I didn't think that school bus would ever get here," she said. Lee had hung around instead of heading off to work early. He had a 10 a.m. meeting in Lafayette and decided to help see the girls off. And get Deanna off, too.

"Gotta do this more often, Mrs. Curtis," he said with a wink.

"Yeah, well, anytime you want to help get those girls out of the house without any drama, you're welcome here."

They talked for a while. Deanna finished her coffee and headed for the shower. While she did that, Lee walked out front and up the sidewalk to grab *The Advertiser,* Lafayette's daily paper and the closest thing Alcide had to its own newspaper. He went back inside, refilled his cup and headed out back, across the expansive yard and down to the small pier on the bayou. The water was still, with an occasional bass hitting on a bug. Lee grabbed a deck chair and sat down to read the paper. He loved this time of morning, being so close to nature. He was an inner city kid who had found a home way, way on the edge of the outer city.

He glanced at the paper and took a sip of the strong dark-roast coffee. Crap," he said. Right at the top of the page, above the fold, was the story about tropical depression 17, expected to become Tropical Storm Tammy. Probably headed for Louisiana. A lot of the oil rigs, both off shore and on shore, would be evacuated. But in general, the storm wouldn't affect him much on a professional level, but it sure as hell would on a personal level. Deanna had planned little Macy's birthday party Saturday, and he was in charge of the fishing tournament for the kids. He skimmed the story until he found Tammy's exact location in the Gulf, the distance from the coast and forward speed. A quick calculation told him things would start going to crap late Saturday afternoon, then totally shitty throughout that night.

Lee looked up and thought about it. They might be able to squeeze the party in Saturday morning. It would depend on whether any of the locals would evacuate, which they sometimes did for bad storms. As long as the first rain bands held off, it just might work.

The paper he held was already old news, probably put to bed around 10 last night. He pulled out his smart phone and found his weather app. Sure enough, Tammy had been born in the wee hours of the night. Maybe a Cat 3. Shit.

He sat back and took another sip, stretching his long legs. Something caught his eye off to the right, a change in the stillness of the water. It looked like a large ripple on the surface of the bayou. The little wavelets caught the morning sun and shimmered as they spread. His first thought was it must have been a huge bass swallowing a bream for breakfast. His second thought was the ripple was too big for that. Maybe a gar? No, bigger than that. Gator, probably. They liked to feed at this time of day. But the ripple was getting bigger. *Closer.* No, it wasn't a ripple, really. More like a bow wave of something swimming toward him.

Lee stood up and squinted his eyes. Whatever it was, it would pass right by him, from right to left.

"What the hell?" he said.

He still held the phone in his hand, and remembered it had a video camera. He found the controls for it, aimed the phone, and started recording. The little digital camera was remarkable, enabling him to shoot true hi-def video. He took his eye off the screen and glanced up as the thing came close. That's when he realized what he was seeing.

He counted at least six huge alligators swimming furiously in formation on the surface of the bayou. They were doing a steady clip, so much so that they created a single broad bow wave ahead of them. That's what he saw. He kept recording as the flight of gators sailed by. When they had gone, he switched off the camera.

"Where you boys headed in such a hurry?" he said. He had never seen gators do that in a group. Weird. Had to ask Cam about that later.

Roland Avant stood at the bow of his floating meth lab/ love boat and stretched. He wore a pair of faded blue Nike gym shorts and nothing else. The sun was already up into the trees, the humidity soaring and not a breeze in sight. A heron squawked in the distance.

He had moved the old party boat late last night deeper into the swamp, looking for cover. Not an easy thing at night, but the smart thing to do. Lexie Hot Ass Smith was zeroing in on him, and he made it a point not to stay in one place too long. Besides, he spent most of the night packing the meth for his customers in New Orleans, scheduled to arrive Saturday morning for the pick up. He hadn't figured out exactly where that was going to take place, but he was working on it. Thinking was getting harder. He was pretty sure the shit was fucking up his brain, and his already limited reasoning power was a bit muddled at the moment.

In the distance through the cypress, he could see the open water of one of the many diversion canals that cut through the swamp. The canals were man-made and the scorn of the greenie weenies. Most were created by oil companies for navigation, pipeline routes, or to get to drilling sites. Unlike the meandering bayous, the diversion canals were usually straight shots from point a to point b. Fishermen and hunters liked them for that very reason. It was easy and quick to get to the action.

Roland had taken one of the canals last night for speed, then cut into the shallow swamp to hide among the dense growth. His kick-ass camouflage paint job was working like a charm. Moments earlier, a gator fisherman had cruised by, looked right at Roland's little operation through the trees, and not seen a thing.

He figured he needed one more day to finish getting his shit together, then figure out how to get everything close to a road for the transfer. He nodded his head in satisfaction and smiled. His few, already-yellow teeth had taken on a distinctive orange hue from the three bags of Cheetos he downed during the night. Four Mountain Dews had kept his motor running pretty good, but he was pretty sure he'd have to hit the ice pretty soon to really get his energy up.

Roland yanked down his shorts and christened the swamp with a long stream of urine. He closed his eyes to enjoy the relief. He heard a splash in the distance, and his eyes popped open in alarm. It sounded like something was crashing through the shallow swamp.

Roland pulled up his shorts and looked around. Nothing in the immediate vicinity. Sounds did weird things out here, skimming across open water, then dissipating among the cypress and reflected in different directions. Something made that splash, though, and it was big. Had that gator hunter doubled back?

Then he saw it. Directly across the diversion canal. Some of the larger trees were moving. Not by the wind. Something was shaking them, the way a bulldozer might if it were trying to push one over. But there were no logging operations going on out here. At the top of the trees, he saw several big fox squirrels circling the branches in a frenzy of movement. Even from here, he could hear their agitated cries.

What the fuck? Roland thought. He climbed up the ladder to the top of the party barge for a better look. From there, he had a better angle. Something wet caught the morning sun's rays on the other side of the canal. It was moving, too. What Roland saw next changed his perspective on just about everything.

His first thought was *dinosaur.* A real, live fucking T-Rex thing walking among the trees. He liked the T-Rex. They were the bad boys of the dinosaur world, kicking ass and taking names. This one was tall, almost as tall as the trees themselves. It was holding one tree's trunk and shaking it furiously. This was what was freaking out the squirrels. Well, almost. What was really freaking them out was a long tongue sticking out of the dinosaur's mouth. It was zipping up into the tree's canopy, trying to catch one of the squirrels. But it wasn't a tongue, really. It looked like an arm, because it had some kind of grasping thing or hand or something at the end of it.

That's what told Roland that maybe this wasn't a T-Rex. They didn't do that. The wide mouth of the dinosaur, and the tongue-arm thingy, made him think of a frog. That's the only thing his little brain could conjure at the moment. A 20-foot-tall bullfrog, standing on its hind legs, trying to zap some squirrels for breakfast. But the color was all wrong. The dinosaur was blackish-gray. And those eyes! Man, they were huge.

Then, *zap.* It caught one of the squirrels and reeled its tongue back in. This caused even more chatter among the "chickens of the trees," as he called them.

Roland rubbed his eyes, looking all the world like a cartoon character who'd just seen a ghost. He was hoping the vision was a meth-induced hallucination, but nope, the thing was still there. His keen mind continued to roll through the options of what the creature was. Dinosaur. Frog. *Frogasaur.* Yeah, that's what it was. Some kind of prehistoric critter no one had ever seen before. No, wait. Maybe it was a mutant thing, caused by who-knew-what chemicals the oil companies had dumped in the swamps for years. Naw. He liked Frogasaur better. Except this frog had teeth the size of chisels. Lots of them.

Now wonderment turned to fear. If the frogasaur turned his way, would it see him? No sooner had that thought crossed his mind than the creature zipped its gigantic tongue back into its mouth and turned its head directly toward Roland.

He froze.

Chapter 8:
"Hips, Lips and Tits"

Damn, he was hungry. Again. The creature had gone for over an hour without anything to eat. The swamp animals were catching on that something very bad was moving around, eating everything in sight. And they weren't waiting around to see what it was. That's when he saw the squirrels. He had never bothered to eat them before. Too small. And quick. But he was starving now, and a little pissed. And a lot horny. So he went after them with a vengeance.

The little bastards were fast. He tried to shake the tree and get them to fall, but they were having none of it. They swarmed around the trunk and the branches, trying to jump to another tree. It took a moment for the creature to detect a pattern to what the squirrels were doing. This time, he anticipated what one of the squirrels was about to do. He shot his oral arm out ahead of one, and timed it perfectly. He grabbed the little furry creature and snatched it back into his mouth. Didn't bother to chew. This thing was headed non-stop into his acid-filled stomach.

The creature might as well have been eating air. What he needed was one of those feral hogs. Or a deer. An alligator. Or even one of those smart things he thought were kind of tasty.

His large nose caught the scent of something. It was one of those smart things, and it was close. He turned back toward the water and across the canal. Did the smell come from across there? He used his sharp eyes to scan the trees on the other side. Nothing. He took a deep breath to catch the scent again, but it was gone. The wind had changed direction.

The creature waited for a moment, this time listening. All he heard was the lapping of water against the trees and the distant cry of birds. He was pushing his luck being exposed like this, but he didn't give a shit. He had to eat.

He gave a great snort and dove back into the diversion canal. Maybe an unsuspecting gator would swim by.

Roland stood stock still on top of the love boat, his eyes transfixed on the specter of death, the frogasaur. He had resumed his urination, but this time he had failed to lower his Nike gym shorts. The yellow liquid ran down his leg and pooled beneath his feet. This would cut into his wardrobe options for later in the day.

The frogasaur dove back into the canal. Roland was sure he would come up on his side, but he saw the creature surface downstream, headed east. It was only then that Roland let out a deep breath. His heart was pounding against his emaciated chest cavity.

Roland climbed down the ladder, his legs all rubbery, the weird taste of adrenaline on his tongue. He hadn't noticed the bladder malfunction yet. He reached into the ice chest at the back of the boat and pulled out another Dew. He slammed it back in seconds, and the yellow drink dribbled down his stubbled chin and neck. He gave out a loud burp and tossed the can on the deck.

"Fuuuuccckkkkk!" he said and bent over to grab his knees. His breathing was beginning to settle down a bit. He had to get to work and in a hurry. He had to get the meth packed up and ready to go today. No way he was going to stay in the swamp tonight.

Fucking frogasaur.

Lexie Smith sat in her patrol car, enjoying a fresh beignet and café au lait she'd gotten over at Tookie's Bakery. Old Miss Tookie had been baking for centuries in her little shop next to her home. It was a regular stop on Lexie's patrols. After picking up the sweet little pastry, she'd driven to her breakfast stop under a copse of live oaks at the old cavalry fort. It gave her a nice view of the highway running into town, and any jackass who had their truck rolling over 45 coming into Alcide was in for a ticket. She checked her face in the rearview mirror and wiped a little powdered sugar off her lip. Her makeup looked good. She had spent a little more time with it this morning, maybe more dolled up than she should have been as a deputy with the St. Martin Parish Sheriff's Department. Carla had supplied the makeup, a few tips, and an unrelated device known as "King Schlong." $49.99. Much cheaper than a man. And easier to talk to.

She checked her watch and looked down the road. Cam usually drove by at this time of morning, on his way to Fort St. Jesus to open up. He was running a little late. If there was going to be a *real* man in her life, it was going to be Cam. She had always been a little sweet on him, even in high school. But he had been a year ahead of her, the all-everything quarterback, and she had been a dork. Or dorkette. Shy, gangly, a bit awkward. Of course, the next year, she had arrived at school smoking hot. Boobs had come in big time. "Hips, lips and tits" her momma had said. Unfortunately, Cam had moved on to college, and they had been out of step from then on out.

Lexie finished off the biegnet, dabbed at her lips, and took another sip of the fantastic café au lait. Miss Tookie made it better than they did over in New Orleans.

Men. She had met her husband a few years after college. A looker from Lafayette. He had been some kind of land man for one of the oil and gas companies. She had already started with the sheriff's department, working the dispatch and a couple of simple patrols. That's when she had stopped him for speeding along Herman Dupuis Road and he flashed her that charming smile. A year later they were married and the shit had started almost immediately. He drank more. Started being away more. The verbal abuse kicked in not long afterward. Always about her work. How it was beneath her, and him. He hated Alcide and everything about it. He wanted to move to Houston and get settled with the big boys. But Lexie had no interest in that. A year later, he had hit her the first time. As is usually the case, there was the crying and the apologizing. But he started in again, and she had made her own excuses about not leaving him.

And then there was "Machete Monday," as she now called it. He had taken the day off for a long, extended weekend of drinking. She couldn't get the day off, and when she got home from her shift that evening, he was waiting for her.

The fight had been a screaming fit. He had pushed her, hit her and called her some awful things. When he ran into the garage, she had thought he was leaving, but the idiot came back with the machete, coming right for her. And that was that.

Asshole. After that, she retreated into herself and got into her work more than ever. She had gotten a lot of support from the town, especially the women. But the men kept their distance emotionally. She didn't help the matter, though, completely shutting down any interest in the opposite sex. But Cam had been different. He had been nice to her, always checking on her. A free lunch at the Fort. Some handyman work at her house. But she still kept it cool. She hadn't been ready.

But now...she started to feel like maybe it was time. And if that didn't work, there was always King Schlong.

A flash of sunlight off of glass in the distance got her attention. It was a pickup truck. Cam.

Lexie sat up, checked her face and tried to act natural. *What if he was speeding? The ticket thing had worked years ago. Okay, maybe that didn't really work. Bad luck. No ticket, then,* she thought.

Cam slowed, saw her and gave a wave. He pulled off the road and parked next to her. "Hey, am I interfering with an official police activity?" he said with a smile. He got out and walked over to her window. Huey stuck his head out of the truck's window and gave a friendly bark.

"Not unless you're speeding," she said. "Especially if I haven't finished breakfast yet and you're speeding."

Cam looked at the empty bag on the seat next to her and the cup in her hand. "Ah. Miss Tookie."

"It's why I'll never leave Alcide," she said.

He nodded. "Same here. Look, my offer to do some scouting for Roland still stands. Troy can come with me."

Lexie took a deep breath and sat back, thinking for a moment. "Man, if he killed Floyd, that changes everything. Might be dangerous."

"It'll be the two of us. We'll take some guns. Just eyes and ears, though. Two guys fishing, that's all."

"Okay, I should go with you, but I gotta stay close to town. Mayor's still on vacation. That makes me the face of government." Lexie saw how he scanned her face with those gorgeous eyes. She felt a little chill. The good kind.

"That's cool," he said. "We'll go this afternoon and report back later. Maybe you can swing by the Fort. I'll have something to eat."

"Sure, just be careful. That little bastard's up to something. And I think he's starting to unspool a little bit. Didn't like the way he looked yesterday, you know?"

"Yeah, he's hitting the pipe, alright," Cam said. "Meth makes you feel like Superman, from what I hear."

"Superman with no teeth," Lexie said. She bared her own teeth and pointed to them.

Cam laughed. "Yeah, I wish he'd try to fly, right off the cell tower down by the river. Save us a lot of trouble."

Lexie nodded. "You hear about that storm in the Gulf?"

"Yeah, caught it on the news before I left the house. Cat 3 maybe?"

"Maybe," she said. "So much for a boring weekend. I was gonna have Saturday night off, too. Looking forward to cutting loose or something."

Lexie couldn't believe she just tossed up that softball to Cam. It was inadvertent. Maybe.

"Yeah, me, too," he replied. "Slow Joe and the Whatnots are supposed to be playing over at P Daddy's in Lafayette. If Tammy hooks a left to Texas, maybe we can go."

And there it was, Lexie thought. "Hey, sounds good."

"Great!" Cam said. "So I have a date with either you or Tammy." He gave her a crooked smile.

"You'd rather me," she said. "I'm a lot more fun, and I won't wipe out half of Louisiana. As long as you're buying."

Cam chuckled. "Good to know. Okay, let's watch the skies and pray for Slow Joe."

"It's a plan," she said. Her mood darkened a bit. "But be careful out there with Roland. Just take a look around. I'll catch up with you at the Fort later."

Cam saluted. "Absolutely, deputy."

Lexie watched as he got back in his truck. "And keep your hands and feet in the boat," she said. "There's something very big and very mean swimming around out there. Just ask Floyd Guidry."

Cam winked at her. "Yes m'am. I'll keep my boots attached to my ankles."

Chapter 9:
"Perfect"

Troy lay in bed, staring at the ceiling. He was trying to concentrate. Should he pull that engine first thing this morning, or just knock out those two brake jobs first and do the engine last? Cam wanted to run out into the swamp on a Roland-hunting expedition. They needed to be on the water no later than two. It would be tight. Troy smiled. *Tight.* What Cam really wanted was to get Lexie in the sack, and the one way into the heart–and pants—of a hot law-enforcement officer was to do some civic-duty shit for her. Maybe help her bust the Meth Kingpin of St. Martin Parish. Fucking Roland. He and Cam should just put that shithead down. That's the way the old boys would've done it back in the day. Some Cajun justice. Let the swamp cover up the deed.

Anyway, back to the day. He tried to think about that engine, but then the image of old Cam getting Lexie out of her uniform popped into his head. Man, she was getting hotter every day. The thought of that long tall blond wrapped around him got him all excited. Or maybe it was Carla Fontanelli, who sat astride him, head back, long black hair swaying, boobs bouncing this way and that, on her way to her third orgasm of the morning.

She was getting a good rhythm going, dragging him along for the ride. *Damn, she was hot, too.* Funny thing, he'd never had sex with her in high school. They hadn't hooked up till three or four years ago, after a church picnic. They had gotten a little drunk, he took her out on his boat, and they'd lit up the bayou for three hours. Since then, they'd kept it casual, consensual and constant. Neither was looking to settle down, but they sure as hell liked to *get down.*

She was close now, and so was he. He grabbed her hips and held on, and she took them both to Downtown Happytown.

Carla lay forward on Troy, panting. His heavy breathing matched hers and she rode up and down on his chest in a gentle rhythm.

"Okay," she said between breaths. "That should do me for the day. How 'bout you?"

Troy still held on to her tight little ass. "I don't know," he said. "Might need a little tune up this afternoon. Heard Felice Guidry is out one husband. Probably should pay her a visit."

Carla slapped him on the chest, but still kept her head down. "Troy Pitre, you are a man-whore, but I do love you."

"I know you do," he said. "How old is Felice, ya think?"

Carla closed her eyes. "I don't know. Late forties, early fifties, maybe?"

"She's still kind of hot," Troy said. "I'd do her."

"You'd do a wild hog."

"Not that great, trust me."

Carla laughed. "I believe you." She sat up and stretched like a cat. "I sold Felice some very interesting products last month. She wanted to bring a little sizzle back to the bedroom."

Troy smiled up at her. "Well, at least Floyd died a happy man."

Carla had a thoughtful look on her face. "Hmmm. Might want to pay her a visit after the funeral. She's gonna need an upgrade, what with Floyd out of the picture."

"Way out of the picture," Troy said.

Carla rolled off him and stretched out on the bed. The sunlight streamed through Troy's bedroom window. Somewhere a mockingbird squawked loudly. She always acquainted that sound to fall for some reason. Fall was a good time for her business. Fashion changed and so did makeup. She'd be showing off the new line of Mary Kay cosmetics this month as the ladies of the bayou took advantage of the lower light of fall to make themselves even more beautiful. Most of those women didn't really need that much makeup. But she sold that shit like crazy anyway. Troy was right. Felice Guidry was still pretty hot. So was just about every woman—and man— throughout the area. Weird. But good. She guessed it was like LA, but in this case, it was the other LA as in *Louisiana.* Pretty people made her feel better. And made her lots of money, too.

In the distance, she heard the squeak and gear grinding of a school bus making its rounds. A nice familiar sound that always made her feel at home. Sleepy kids finding a seat as they made their way to another day in the semester. Safe. Routine. Normal.

Kids. She'd have to decide pretty soon if there were to be any in her future. The thought didn't concern her that much. Some days she'd say hell no never. Other days, the Mom movie would play in her head and she'd like it a lot.

Of course, kids came with a man. Which was like having another kid, her mother would always say. Carla turned her head to look at Troy. He had his eyes closed, a dreamy smile on his face. He was one fine specimen, that's for damn sure. Boyish good looks, but with a little bit of weather on him. Totally ripped. A good man, but still lots of boy left in him. He ran a successful business with his garage, stayed out of trouble for the most part and had lots of good friends. She could do worse.

Her problem was that for as long as she could remember, all men were attracted to her. She never had to work it to get one. Hers was more of a sexual management issue. When to dole it out, when to keep it locked away. Her reputation far outpaced fact, though. She hadn't slept with half the men people thought she had. *But it appeared that way.* A few were still living in this town. And for the most part, they were discreet.

The good news was that she was generally well liked by men *and* women. When they saw her black Audi A6 driving up and down the bayou, they knew she was selling fantasies. Whether it was a complete makeover to help women be more than they were, or some sex toys to liven up an evening, Carla always delivered the goods. And sure, she'd taken her sales technique to some new heights on a few occasions. Like the time she sold some toys to a young couple over in Henderson, a lawyer and his cute debutante wife. What started as a presentation of her inventory turned into a very sexy demonstration on her part and an eventual three way on all of their parts. They were still two of her best customers.

Carla's sex gizmo business was growing faster than the makeup, which was already making her well-into six figures. She was seriously considering creating her own line of sex toys, with a web site and everything. She even had a name: "Carla's Bayou Boogie Toy Shop." She could go nationwide in three months, and global shortly thereafter. Her marketing angle was simple. Her brand would be "born out of the sexy, steamy bayous of Louisiana, where the bedrooms were as spicy as the gumbo and jambalaya cooking in the kitchen." Or something like that. Throw in her own line of sexy "Voodoo Princess" lingerie and she'd be set.

"Troy," she said.

"Huh?"

"You still like my idea of starting my own website business?"

"Hell, yeah," he mumbled, eyes still closed. "Means you could work right from my bed, so to speak."

"Uh huh."

"You could use me as a test bed, or guinea pig, or sex pig, or whatever. I could retire."

"Definitely a sex pig," she said.

"Are there tax deductions for having a lab animal?"

"Yeah, I could claim you. No one else will."

Troy's eyes opened wide in mock surprise. He rolled over onto Carla and started tickling her. She tried to fight him off, but he was too big and too quick. Her screaming laughter filled the house, and since Troy lived outside of town on a secluded three acres fronting the bayou, there were no neighbors around to come to her rescue. Which was fine with her.

The female creature had awakened just before dawn and had immediately dismantled her shelter. She had worked hard on putting it together, and it had taken some time. It was a good one, too. She was perfectly hidden. The only thing that could have found her was the male. Okay, maybe not *that* male. From what she could hear from his low-frequency signals, he was still moving haphazardly through the swamps, feeding when he could, trying to get his bearings on her location. She could feel his growing intensity and hunger, and his frustration. He wasn't the sharpest guy on the block, either. But he was the only guy on the block as far as she was concerned. And if they didn't get hooked up soon, she'd have to abort all of her young or face a slow, painful death. No female she had ever heard of had waited too long and succumbed to death by failure to give birth. But she wasn't looking forward to slicing herself open, that's for sure.

So here she was, moving slowly through the shallow swamps, working her way through the cypress and tupelo, trying to get back to some deeper water and a channel she could use. The sky was a bright but milky blue, and the sun was warm on her skin. On any other day, she would have enjoyed that. Today, though, she was irritable. And a little hungry, too. She'd have to stop frequently to feed, which meant lying beneath the water near the shore to snatch some unsuspecting native animal. She might even risk it and try for one of the smart creatures that lived in the swamp. They were so easy to catch, but they scared her some. The damned things were very bright and could surprise you. They could hurt you—or worse—if you weren't careful. She wasn't in the best of shape, and she wasn't as fast as she normally was, but she was pretty clever, too. More so than that idiot male out there who was trying to find her. He was young, and this was his first mating ritual. Her second, actually. The first being on her home world a very long time ago. Then she got captured and dropped here with the male. The first part of the mating had been a little awkward. Well, for him anyway. But she'd been patient and things worked out. Now, years later, he had to close the deal on his own. So far, he had been less than impressive. He should be closer by now. But no, he was thrashing about. Every minute he wasted, the hungrier, crazier and meaner he'd get. And dumber, too. A very bad combination of qualities when you wanted to start a family. So here she was, trying to close the distance between them, helping him out.

The young ones squirmed in her body. She winced. *Bastard.*

"Four dykes in a dinghy." There was a joke there somewhere.

Kathy Flynn laughed to herself at the thought. Something her dad might've said. She stood on the flying bridge of the small cabin cruiser and looked down at the rest of her "crew." Tess, her current partner and self-avowed "lipstick lesbian," lay on the back deck sunning herself, bikini top off and her brown skin glimmering with oil. Maddie and Karen, their friends and compatriots from New Orleans, sat on a nearby bench seat, being kissy kissy. Watching them was starting to get her a little worked up. That and Tess, who looked downright edible lying there on the sundeck.

Kathy's family had a large camp on the Atchafalaya River near Butte La Rose, and since her mom and dad had died, she had been the primary caretaker of the place. So whenever she could, she'd get the girls together, head out of New Orleans and hole up in the swamps for a few days.

Kathy was excellent with the boat, better than her two brothers, her dad used to say. Although the cabin cruiser was probably a little too much boat for some of the smaller bayous, it was spacious and well stocked with food and booze. She'd also brought some excellent weed, and she took a hit on the joint that continued to mellow her out.

They'd gotten in last night, had a sensational dinner of grilled redfish she'd prepared herself, and then they retired for a very sexy evening of fun. This morning, they all packed up for a day on the water and headed out by eight. After an hour or so of cruising and sightseeing, she'd anchored the boat near Bayou Chene. She found a good spot near the shore so they could do a little fishing and sunbathing. She'd cautioned the girls about jumping in the water, since the alligators would still be feeding this time of the morning.

"Hey, you two gonna fish or what?" she said. "Tonsil hockey's not gonna put dinner on the table."

Maddie looked up at Kathy and smiled. "I *am* fishing," she replied. She had her long red hair pulled back with a pair of $500 Gucci shades set atop her head.

"Hilarious," Kathy said.

Karen, Maddie's partner, laughed. She reached behind her back and unclasped her bikini top, then tossed it in her beach bag. Her full breasts seemed to expand when exposed to the air, the nipples hard due to Maddie's ministrations.

"Maybe we can do some noodling later. That's what those rednecks call it. You know, when they reach their hands in the water and catch fish by hand?"

"Uh huh. Whatever," Kathy said. "Hey, Tess. Don't fall in, baby."

Tess mumbled something and rolled onto her back. *Damn, she looked good,* Kathy thought.

The bayou was glass smooth, not another soul in sight. No cars, no jet noise, no nothing. Just quiet. *Perfect.*

The female creature floated submerged in the bayou, her arms and legs spread wide, enjoying the coolness of the water. She undulated her body every so slightly to give her a bit of forward motion. The channel was deeper here and she could stay underwater for over an hour if she had to. She enjoyed the comfort the neutral buoyancy gave her. Her pregnancy put great strain on her back and joints, so floating weightless was pure bliss. Even better, an unsuspecting creature might swim by and she could catch a quick meal without much exertion. And she was really starting to get hungry.

Her hypersensitive hears caught the sound moments later. It was that chattering noise the smart creatures made. As best she could tell, it was the way they communicated with each other. At first it was faint, but it grew stronger with each minute, which meant she was getting closer. To a meal.

Catching the things usually wasn't difficult, if the circumstances were right. That meant she'd have to take a quick peek above the surface. But carefully.

She changed her body shape ever so slightly and began to rise slowly to the surface so just her eyes broke the still water. Over the years, she'd watch how the alligators did this to sneak up on their prey. Her kind weren't normally that subtle, but the technique had proven to be quite successful over the years. Especially now when she was slower and fatter.

It took a moment for her eyes to adjust to the bright sunlight. That's when she saw them. Four of the smart creatures just ahead on that big floating object. Her years here had taught her that these were females, just like her. Well, not just like her. They weren't fat, pregnant and ugly. Well, they were a little repulsive with their tiny heads. But food that tasted good didn't always look good.

The creature spotted one of the females lying near the water, stretched out on its back. That meant it couldn't run once the action started. Should be easy for her. Slowly, she submerged again and moved closer to the boat. *Perfect.*

On any given day, there were all manner of boats that could be seen on the bayou. Bass boats, ski boats, party barges and the pirogue, the classic Cajun canoe. But rarely did one see a kayak.

Brad Parsons didn't give a shit. His small red kayak moved effortlessly through the still water of the bayou. With measured, even strokes, he rounded the bend.

This would make a great article in his favorite magazine, *Men's Health.* Kayaking the still waters of Louisiana's bayou country. He imagined the opening paragraph: *"Brad Parsons, young, handsome, successful stockbroker from Lafayette, Louisiana, glides bravely through the alligator and snake-infested waters of Bayou Chene. He is fearless. But that's Brad's outlook on everything he does."*

He liked that. Then he thought of the picture of himself that would go with the article. Chiseled jaw line, blond tips in his hair. His ripped chest and six pack were accentuated by a sheen of sweat that made his skin glow in the morning sun. He was glad he'd shaved his chest and arms, too. He was an Adonis. Of course, he routinely shaved every square inch of his body, but that wouldn't make it into the magazine. He was a manscaped pristine machine. The ladies liked it that way.

Brad smiled. His health routine was impressive. Five miles of road work each morning. Free weights. Some machines. A nice diet of protein shakes and other magical concoctions, but no 'roids for him. That shit made you crazy. And made your balls shrink. Can't have any of that.

He looked down in the water and caught his reflection. Total awesomeness. *Perfect.*

Chapter 10:
"The Sirens Call"

Kathy Flynn reeled her line in. Not much happening under the trees. Her dad had taught her how to work the artificial bait near the cypress knees where the big boys were. Not today, though. She was about to cast her line one more time when something downstream caught her eye. She could see it around the bend, through the trees. Something low in the water.

Shit, some asshole in a canoe or something.

She looked down at the topless Tess and the abundantly topless Karen, thought about telling them to cover up, then mumbled *fuck it* under her breath. She took a last hit on the joint and held the magic smoke in her lungs for a beat.

"Hey, ladies, check it out," she said. She pointed down the bayou.

All three looked that way.

Tess lay back down and said, "Don't want it. It's attached to a man."

"C'mon, a live one every now and then ain't so bad," Karen said. She rubbed her crotch and gave a fake "O-face."

They watched as the young man in the kayak came into sight. He seemed to sit up straighter and waved at the ladies.

Karen stood up and waved. Her large breasts swayed with the effort. "Hey, let's have some fun."

"Uh oh," Maddie said. "This should be interesting."

Brad Parsons couldn't believe his eyes. Four reasonably hot chicks on a cabin cruiser, waving to him. All in bikinis, two of them topless. One of them *fantastically* topless. A five-way? Yes, his superbly fit body could tackle that situation with no problem. Probably some great girl-on-girl action while he caught his breath between getting off. That would get him stoked up. And they looked older than him. The *U.S.S. Cougar? Oh, hell yes,* he thought.

Time for a little strutting, he decided. He rolled his body to the right, and the kayak rolled with him until he was completely underwater. He let the momentum carry him the other way until he rolled back onto the surface. It was a maneuver he often did while hitting the white water up in Colorado. He gave his head a little shake to get the water out of his eyes, pumped up his chest and let the water ooze over him.

"What a dick," Kathy said. "Asshole has no idea he's wasting the effort."

"He doesn't know that," Karen said. She grabbed her ample bosom and squeezed her breasts together. A nice slow lick of her lips finished off the performance. With any luck, the idiot would probably come in his pants.

Tess sat up again to join the fun. She gave the guy a wave. He *was* kind of cute. Blonde, smooth skin, kind of girl-like. She could go bi in a pinch, or when the mood suited her.

The guy waved back. They could see he was angling his way toward them for a closer look. They couldn't wait to break the news to the poor bastard.

The female creature continued her steady run toward the boat. The chattering continued to get louder. Were they chattering about her? Could they see her under the water? For a moment, she considered breaking off her attack. Her hunger, though, changed her mind. She needed to eat for the energy she would need to find the male, and to keep the young inside her fed as well. Every little bit counted.

She rose slightly to get a better view of her prey, but not so much that she would break the surface of the bayou. Her vision was extraordinary, with an exceptional ability to see in low light. The water was relatively clear closer to the surface, so she could see very well. Her chosen prey was still near the edge of the floating thing, but it had sat up and was looking at something to the right. They were all looking that way. This might be easier than she thought.

Her final decision would be whether to use her oral arm to grab the thing and pull it into the water or rear up and just grab it in her mouth and save all the trouble.

Decisions, decisions. Even in her present state of pregnancy, she thought she could use her forelimbs to grab the back of the floating thing and pull herself up, grab the smart thing and be out of there before anyone knew what was going on. But there was the slight chance she might miss, or cut herself on something. Or get bopped on the head by one of the other smart things. Maybe too risky. So she would use the oral arm, which normally allowed her to grasp prey from a distance. In her current condition, it just didn't have the zip or the distance. She'd still have to get close, but at least she could stay submerged. Better odds, anyway.

With her plan in place, she gave one last push and zeroed in on her breakfast.

If Tess had been looking to her right, instead of her left at the asshole in the kayak–she would have noticed a shadowy shape moving across the bayou directly toward the boat. To her eyes, it might have appeared as the shadow of a small, fast-moving cloud. But there were no clouds in the sky this sultry September morning. If she had been looking, she might have noticed a slight bow wave moving toward the boat. And as the wave got closer to the boat, she would have finally seen the faint coloration of something big, gray and black moving toward the boat, just under the surface of the water. She would have watched it all the way in. And then she would be in for the surprise of her young, semi-naked life.

But Tess wasn't looking to her right. She was looking to her left at the guy in the kayak.

As the guy got closer to the cabin cruiser, Kathy glanced down at the boat's throttle. If she had to start it and go in a hurry, she knew exactly what to do. She also looked down at the 12-gauge shotgun she kept up here, nestled comfortably in a holder to the left. Her dad had insisted she keep it there, especially when the ladies were on the water alone.

The guy was maybe 50 yards out, definitely angling toward them, with sure thoughts of a memorable sexual escapade in his head. The girls were still putting on the act, waving their arms, showing off their wares. Kathy laughed out loud and joined the fun. She unclasped her bikini top, pulled it off and waved it over her head.

Brad Parsons pretty much sailed through college, taking the minimum hours necessary to allow him to party and get laid on a regular basis. But right at that moment, he remembered something from a freshman class in Greek mythology. It was the story of the Sirens, the three daughters of some river god. They sat upon the rocks of shorelines, luring sailors to them with their beauty and enchanting music. The unsuspecting men would turn their boats toward them, or just jump in the water and swim. Their fate was always the same: death on the rocks. But some guy made it, Brad remembered. That Odysseus dude. He put beeswax in his crew's ears, and had them tie him to the mast of his ship so he wouldn't jump in.

Brad smiled. Old Odysseus would have loved to get in on this action.

Kathy, Tess, Maddie and Karen watched as the guy set his oar down across the small kayak and let his momentum carry him their way. He had a big smile on his face, and probably a bigger boner, Kathy thought. He was close enough now that she could say something to him, and in fact, was planning on apologizing and explaining the orientation of things. In particular, their orientation.

And then, the strangest thing happened. The whole world seemed to drop into slow motion, and all sound was dialed down. That's how Kathy would later describe it. Below her, her three friends had their backs to her, looking at the guy. He continued to drift toward them. The day seemed to get brighter, the colors more vivid. And then it happened.

A large, gray form breached out of the water right next to the guy in the kayak. Kathy's first thought was *gray whale.* She had seen them when she had gone out to California last year. Beautiful creatures. But something in her head said *no.* The shape was all wrong. The gray thing slammed right into the guy and took him and the kayak over in a great splash. *Were those teeth?*

She and the other three all let out a short, collective gasp. The sudden transition from glee to horror staggered them and seemed to freeze time.

The bow and stern of the red kayak popped up out of the water, but they were no longer connected to the middle of the small craft. They were ragged where they had been separated. The two pieces were carried into the shoreline by the violence of the event. There was something else red in the water, Kathy noticed. Not a solid. A liquid. Blood.

"What the fuck was that!" one of the girls shrieked. Kathy would never remember which one.

"Was that a fucking hippopotamus?" Karen yelled. "Was that a fucking hippo?"

They all stared into the churning water, now brown and red.

"Get the fuck away from the side of the boat!" Kathy yelled. "Get your asses up here!"

Karen, Tess and Maddie cried out and climbed up the short ladder to the flying bridge, huddling like scared puppies, holding on to each other. Tess was shaking and mumbling something.

The bayou had gone quiet again, and the four women looked around on all sides of the boat, trying to see whatever it was that had grabbed the guy. Maybe he would surface. Kathy had a pretty good idea he wouldn't. At least not all of him.

"Fuck," she said. She looked down into her beach bag and pulled out her cell phone. Her hand shook like she was freezing, but she managed to dial 911.

The female creature gagged a little under the water, and then spit the piece of kayak out of her mouth. Didn't mean to eat that. The smart thing was somehow attached to it, and she grabbed it when she grabbed him. He was mighty tasty. A big one, too. She hadn't even seen him at first, what with her concentration focused on the other thing on the floating object. When she did see him, she turned at the last minute and decided she could eat him with a lot less effort than the other one. Her belly full, she floated down to the cool bottom of the bayou and closed her eyes. *Perfect.*

Chapter 11:
"The Hungry Hippo"

Cam watched from the counter as Father Mike and Sister Joanie stocked up on some basic groceries. Looked like milk, bread and eggs–the usual crap people ran out of during the middle of the week. Joanie also grabbed a couple of six-packs of Coronas.

Hey, Cam," she yelled. "You got any limes?"

"Sorry, Joanie," he said. "Fruit truck doesn't run by here today. Have to get that up at the Piggly Wiggly in Breaux Bridge."

Cam shook his head and smiled. That Joanie was a piece of work. She wore jeans and a white denim blouse. She looked good. The only sign of nunnery was a large cross she wore around her neck that stopped right between her boobs. Mike did have his priest gear on, though. But if you didn't know any better, they were just another young married couple picking up some stuff. They even *moved* like a married couple. Casual. In-step. Voices low. That weird *comfortableness* that married people had with each other.

Except they were a priest and a nun.

Weird. Cam had heard the talk that maybe Mike and Joanie had hooked up, or were hooking up. He eyed them carefully and thought that one through. He could see it. Possibly. Maybe.

He and Mike had been in the same classes together in high school. Although not a jock like Cam and Troy, Mike was a popular kid with just about every clique. And although not in Troy's league as far as sexual conquests, he knew of at least four girls in the school that Mike had bedded in the back of his old van. Maybe five. There were unconfirmed reports that he and Carla had gone a few rounds.

Mike was "the nice guy." And he used that bullshit to great advantage. Well, he was a nice guy. *But he was a horny nice guy just the same,* Cam thought.

They walked up to the counter and put their stuff down. Cam began ringing them up.

"Heard you talked to Felice Guidry," Cam said. "How's she doing?"

Mike shrugged. "She was kind of numb. Don't think it's hit her yet."

"Wake's Friday night," Joanie said. "You know her?"

"Seen her and Floyd in a few times when they came up this way. I'll pass on the festivities, though" Cam said.

Cam and Mike made eye contact.

"Boots," Mike said.

"Feet," replied Cam. They both held it together for just a beat and burst out laughing.

Joanie looked at them both. "Really?"

"Sorry," Cam said and held up a hand in apology.

"What kind of thing could have done that?" Mike asked. "Must have been a huge gator."

Cam thought a moment about sharing his theory about Roland and decided to hold that one close to the vest.

The door slammed open and they all turned to see Lexie burst in and go to the cooler. She grabbed two bottles of Gatorade and headed immediately to the counter.

"Mike. Joanie," she said. She was a bit out of breath and looked a little flush.

"You okay?" Cam said.

"Gotta head down to Bayou Chene. Got a 911 call. I'm meeting the sheriff's boat at the ramps."

Joanie frowned. "What happened?"

"Some woman called it in. Guy in a kayak got eaten."

"A gator?" Mike said.

"A *kayak*?" Joanie said. "What kind of idiot would kayak on the bayou?"

"I hope it was a gator," Lexie said. She glanced at Cam. "Chick said it was a hippopotamus."

They all did the zoological math in their head a moment.

"A hippo? In Bayou Chene?" Joanie said.

"That's what she said. Cam, you want to weigh in on that one?"

"Ridiculous," he said with a snort.

Mike said, "Was there ever a report of a hippo getting loose from a zoo or something? Did the zoo in New Orleans lose one after Katrina?"

Cam shook his head. "No way."

"Hippo," Lexie said. "This ought to be good." She threw a five on the counter. "Gotta run. Give me the change later."

They watched as she ran out the door.

"That was weird," Joanie said.

Mike looked off for a second. "Bayou Chene? So where was *Floyd* killed?"

Cam spent the rest of the day with his usual routine. He manned the store by himself in the morning for a few hours, and when Zach, his helper, came in around 10, he walked next door to take care of his vet business. Zach was a 19-year-old kid who'd foregone college to help with his dad's fishing charter business. When business was slow, he'd earn a couple extra bucks helping out Cam with the store, and sometimes at the clinic.

His vet clinic was small but very profitable. It wasn't the dogs and cats mainly. His meal tickets were the horses, pigs and cattle around the parish. Cam kept them healthy, and their owners kept him in the black. Sure, he did his share of pet vaccinations, spaying and neutering, but Alcide wasn't Beverly Hills. Not a lot of Fifi's and Punkins sleeping in the parlor. Just porch dogs and big-ass tomcats that kept the rats and other vermin in check. Rabies was one of his biggest concerns, with all the outside pets and wild animals coming into regular contact with each other.

Cam walked into the small lobby and flicked on the lights. The place smelled of wet animal fur and disinfectant, both vying for dominance. He walked around the receptionist's desk, which was really his office, and checked the voice mail. Nothing serious.

He walked into the back room where he had cages set up for in-patient care. The only occupant was a calico with some kidney issues. The old girl was doing better, and he would probably have its owner pick her up tomorrow if she had another good night.

"Hey, Flo," he said, and gave the cat a scratch through the cage. The cat meowed loudly and rubbed her head against the cage to get closer. "How ya feelin' girl? Better?" He changed her water and gave her a little wet food to see if she could eat. She sniffed the food, but drank the water greedily.

"No eat, no go home," he said.

The cat looked at him as if to say, *"fuck you."*

"Whatever," Cam said.

He went out back onto the wide porch that looked out over the bayou. It was the same porch as the Fort's, with just a waist-high railing separating the two businesses. The sun was warm, and the air had the smell of fish on it. A slight breeze kissed the tops of the trees. Another great day in Sportsman's Paradise.

Something not-so-sporting was going on out there, Cam thought. Something got a hold of old Floyd and tore him a new one. The pictures Lexie had shown him were still with him. Those boots. With the feet still in them, sitting at the bottom of the boat. A few morsels of gator left behind, too. He wanted to believe Roland was involved, but the more he thought about it, the less he liked that theory. It was just too way over the top for even Roland.

Which meant something wild was out there. Something big and hungry. And now that 911 call about a hippo eating some guy. He couldn't wait to get the download from Lexie on that one. Was that what killed Floyd? Putting aside his doubts, he considered the hippo theory. He guessed one might have gotten away from a zoo or circus. And hippos

killed more people in Africa than lions. They were very terri-
torial, and the males could be very aggressive. But they didn't
eat people. They were herbivores. They'd kill you in a second.
But eat you?

He shook his head. Stupid. Probably a gator. The guy
was low in the water if he was in a kayak. And how did he
get way out there on Bayou Chene if he was in kayak? That's
a long haul, even with a motor.

Still, pretty aggressive, even for an alligator.

Cam heard a chuffing sound and saw Huey sauntering
down the porch. He had been sitting out back behind the
Fort, but when he saw his master, he walked down his way.
Cam knew Huey didn't like going into the clinic. The smell
of animal fear, disease and death was all over the clinic, and
Huey wanted no part of it. Plus, every now and then he got a
thermometer shoved up his ass, and that was pretty much a
deal breaker for the dog.

The big Lab came over for a scratch, and then turned
his attention back toward the bayou, ears up, low growl in his
throat. Cam followed his gaze, and like yesterday, couldn't see
or hear anything. But Huey could.

"What's out there, boy?" Cam said. This time, it wasn't
a rhetorical question. He really needed the dog to get into
some detail.

Huey whined a bit in response to his master. Cam was
no kind of dog whisperer, but he felt like he and Huey had a
connection. The dog was definitely trying to tell him something.

"Okay, boy, we'll figure it out," he said. "We're going
out there this afternoon and have a little look around. You

wanna do that?" He gave the dog's head another scratch. He could have sworn Huey gave him a look that said, *"No way in hell, dude."*

Cam walked down the stairs to the dock. His red-and-white Tracker bass boat was held up in the air in the boathouse. The black 125hp Merc motor glistened in the morning sun. He hadn't taken it out in over a week.

He used his key to unlock the electrical box on the side of the boathouse, hit the switch and watched as the winch lowered the boat into the brown water with a steady whine. He took a quick look to determine that all was well and stowed away.

Huey stayed on the dock while Cam stepped into the boat. He'd need to top off the tank before he and Troy headed out. That would mean a stop at the boat ramps, which had the nearest marine gas pump. Cam had thought about putting one behind the Fort, but the cost, environmental paperwork and general hassle of installing a gas pump soured him on that idea in a hurry.

Cam secured the line, stepped back onto the dock and looked at his watch. He was itching to get out on the water and do some Roland hunting, which now had turned into a monster hunt. He had wanted to go with Lexie, but she'd be with her sheriff buddies, and he doubted they would want a civilian on the trip over to Bayou Chene.

Cam hit the speed dial button for Troy. After four rings, he picked up.

"When are you going to be done?" Cam said.

"Uh, I don't know," Troy said. "Maybe one. One thirty? You want me to meet you at the Fort?"

"Yeah, just come here," Cam said. "The sooner the better."

Troy detected something in Cam's voice. "You got a lead on Roland?"

"Roland," Cam said. "He may be the least of our worries."

"What, you mean the storm?"

"That's the second least of our worries," Cam said. He gave Troy the shorter version of Lexie's already-short version of the kayaker's close encounter of the dead kind.

"What kind of idiot would go kayaking on Bayou Chene?" Troy said.

"The dearly departed kind. Something's eating the local gentry, buddy," he said.

"I'll bring a gun," replied Troy.

"The big one," Cam added.

Chapter 12:
"Doo Doo on the Bayou"

Troy finally made it to Fort St. Jesus at 1:45. Cam was waiting in the Tracker with Huey, both sharing a bag of Fritos.

"Sorry, had to wait for my guy to get back from lunch to cover for me," Troy said. He carried a gun bag that held a Remington 700 30.06 scoped rifle. He handed the bag to Cam and stepped into the boat. "You packin'?"

Cam patted his hip, where a 9mm Berreta was nestled in a holster.

"Bring any beer?" Troy said.

"Ice chest," Cam said, and pointed to the other end of the boat.

Troy reached in, pulled out a can and popped it open. "What's that storm doin'? he said.

Cam backed the boat out of the slip. "A high category one right now. About to go to a two. Got a bead right on us."

"Great," Troy said. He leaned back and got comfortable. "So which way we headed?"

"My guess is he started on the Atchafalaya, then cut into some back bayous or sloughs. He had to do that if he took that piece-of-shit houseboat he fixed up."

Troy eyed Cam. "You thinking down toward Bayou Chene? Where Lexie went?"

"Not that way," Cam said. He pushed the throttles to forward and idled away from the dock. When he got to the middle, he pushed it all the way and the powerful bass boat dug into the calm bayou, accelerated, and finally planed out.

Cam, Troy and Huey rode in silence. It was a beautiful September day, calm and bright. With the hurricane out in the Gulf, there was a sense of anticipation in the air, although the first clouds or rain bands had yet to make it to shore. It was as if the distant storm was sucking the air right out of the sky, making a hole for itself over land.

Cam made good time on the Atchafalaya River, which was unusually high for a September. He headed north for a while, and then slowed the boat and turned into a bayou that meandered back toward the west. The narrow waterway was a great place to fish, plus it cut through a huge swamp. It was an excellent place for Roland to hide.

Troy sensed where Cam was headed. "I would have thought he would have gone east. But this would be better, and closer to town."

Cam throttled down a bit on the motor. "Yeah. You could really get lost in here, especially if you wanted to."

"We looking for Roland or the hungry hippo?" Troy said. He handed Cam a beer and grabbed himself another one.

"Both."

Troy pulled the big rifle out of the bag, checked to make sure he had a full load in the magazine. He was cocked, locked and ready to rock.

"Ate a kayaker, huh? Troy said. He shook his head and smiled. "You really think it was a hippo?"

Cam just shook his head "no." He slowed the boat and eased it close to the bank. They ran parallel to the shoreline, peering deep into the swamp.

"No way he could get that houseboat in here." Cam said. "There's got to be a hidden slough or small diversion canal he got into."

"Bet he was towing something smaller, too," Troy said. He cradled the rifle in his lap. "He's got to have a way to get in and out of here fast, you know, to get back to town for supplies and stuff."

Cam had thought the same thing. Roland's family had hunted and fished these bayous for generations. He knew how to get around, how to get found and get lost. A small, fast boat would be perfect. The thinking was, no one in town had ever seen Roland in a small boat. Which meant he probably stashed it somewhere close to where he could get his truck near water. Sneaky little shit was up to no good. Bagging that little bastard for Lexie would definitely make her day, and improve Cam's love life. It was as simple as that. Throw in the killer hippo, and it would be a great day.

They spent the next half hour idling down the shoreline, seeing nothing but big blue heron, water moccasins and a couple of small alligators sunning themselves on what little dry ground they could find.

Troy broke the silence. "So, you and Lexie. You thinking you got a shot, really?"

"You know, yesterday I would've said maybe."

"I think you did."

"Yeah, well. Today, I'm feeling pretty good about it."

"Something happened?" Troy said.

"Stopped and talked to her while she was in her speed trap, over by the cavalry site. Something changed, I think. She was making small talk, and I think she had on more makeup, too. She knows I come by every morning."

"Well, at least you shaved," Troy said, and took another gulp of beer.

"And I asked her out and she said "yes." Over to Lafayette for some dancing." Cam gave Troy a wink.

"That's what I'm talkin' 'bout, brother," Troy said, and stuck his hand over to Cam for a fist bump.

"Yeah, I said I would have a date either with her or Tammy. She said she'd be more fun."

"Outstanding," Troy said. "I bet she would. I hope Hurricane Lexie is a category five."

Cam rolled his eyes. "Whatever."

Troy went back to staring out into the swamp, but Cam noticed he had that look on his face, like he was working something out.

"So, what do you think about Carla?" Troy asked. "I mean, you know, now."

"As opposed to what, high school?"

"Yeah."

"Some ways she's the same old Carla. Hot, sexy, a little too much mischief in those eyes," Cam said. "But she's pretty smart. Seems like a good businesswoman, saleswoman, whatever she is," he continued. "I think she's strong."

Cam stared at Troy, wondering where this was going. Troy nodded to himself, and tossed his empty in the cooler.

"I kind of like her," Troy said. "She's fun. Kind of independent, and I think she likes being around me."

"Around you, like in a proximity kind of way, or *wrapped* around you?"

"Well," Troy said, "Nothing wrong with that kind of around, but I mean just hanging around. Talking, you know. Feels kind of good."

Cam laughed.

"What's so funny, asshole?" Troy said.

Cam held his hand up. "No, no, not that. It's just that here we are, out on the bayou, heavily armed, and we sound like we're on Oprah or Dr. Phil or something. We're sharing our innermost feelings." Cam held his hand to his heart and made a swooning kind of face.

"You're kind of worrying me, Cameron," Troy said. He held the rifle up and took aim at a red-eared turtle that had come up for air about 20 yards away. He then swung the rifle around and scanned the opposite shore, using the scope as a monocular. Maybe if he caught sight of Roland, his finger might slip and something bad might happen.

"What the fuck?" Troy said. He pulled the rifle down, sat up and stared across the water. He brought the scope back up to his eye. "You see that? To the right of that fallen tree. Up on the piece of ground."

Cam squinted his eyes against the bright sunlight. He reached down and found his binoculars, put them to his eyes and found the spot. "What *is* that?" he said.

"Let's go," Troy said, but Cam was already ahead of him. He gave the throttle a little push and steered the boat across the bayou.

Cam's first thought as they neared the halfway part of the bayou was that they were looking at a carcass of some kind. A *big* one. Like a cow or horse that had bloated all up and got stripped by animals.

But the closer they got, the less is looked like that. Whatever it was, it looked tubular and long, but wrapped around in a circle, nearly five feet off the ground. It was red and gray and black and brown, all mixed together, like some weirdly flavored toothpaste that had come from a giant tube, squeezed onto the ground.

But toothpaste didn't have steam coming off it, the way this thing did.

"What the hell is that?" Troy said. "And is that steam? Or is it on fire?"

Cam cut the throttle and the Tracker drifted toward the shore. Ten yards out, it hit them.

"Oh, *mother fucker!*" Troy called out. He put his hand to his mouth, gagged, and leaned over the side of the boat and deposited his breakfast burrito, a ham-and-cheese po'boy, two cups of coffee and three beers into the bayou.

Cam gagged as well, but switched to mouth breathing a few seconds faster than Troy had and held his breakfast down.

Once Troy had barfed up everything but his right nut, he pulled his head up and stared back at the...whatever. One look, and he gagged again and tossed some unknown green liquid out of his mouth and over the side.

The Tracker kissed the bank, not 20 feet from the pile of stink.

Cam's veterinarian brain kicked in and he looked at the thing, trying to identify an organ, appendage, anything that would give him a clue as to what it was. Nothing matched anything in his data bank.

"What do you think?" Troy stammered through his hand, still attached to his mouth.

Cam didn't answer. He was staring intently at the tubular mass. Now that he was looking at details, things started to compute. He stepped out of the boat and approached the mass carefully, finally squatting down for a better look. Huey stayed in the boat. No one noticed what Huey was up to. The dog crouched low, his hackles way up, ears back, tail down. He let out a low, menacing growl, his teeth bared in a white snarl of sharp canines.

"Holy shit," Cam said.

"What?"

"Shit," Cam answered. "It's a big pile of fecal matter."

"Fecal what? You mean a giant turd?"

"Look," Cam said. He pointed at the pile, his finger just inches from the stuff. "There's hair in there. Probably a hog or deer. And look there. That's a scute. See the ridges? Hey. That's a piece of deer antler."

"A *scoot?*" Troy eased to the front of the boat and stepped out, but stayed back.

"Scute. That bony part on the back of a gator."

"That's a pile of shit? What the hell took a dump that big?" Troy said.

Cam stood up. "The real question is what the hell's out here that's big enough to make a pile of crap that big."

"A hippopotamus?" Troy asked. Cam noticed Troy's voice had gone up at least one octave. Or he really had barfed up one nut.

"You know, I don't think I've ever see hippo shit," Cam said. "But I'm pretty sure that ain't it. Hippos don't eat gators, deer or hogs. Especially at one sitting."

Troy held the rifle tighter and shoved the stock up against his shoulder, but kept the barrel down. He looked all around. "Dude, that's a *five-foot-tall* pile of shit. I'm six-four, and my pile of shit might be *five-inches tall*. I wasn't very good at math, but run some numbers in your head and this thing's gotta be *huge*."

Cam looked down at the pile of shit. He had a weird electric feeling in his hand. It was his nervous feeling, the kind he used to get before a test or a game. It was usually more of a warning than nerves. Shadows from the trees danced across the pile and the sunlight caught something embedded in the foul mess.

Cam looked closer. "Hey, there's something metallic in here. Hand me a stick or something."

Troy looked around and found a six-foot-long piece of white cypress that had washed up onto the bank. He handed it to Cam and stepped back.

Cam pried the metal out of the thick matter, releasing a fresh wave of stink that made his eyes water, despite the fact that he was breathing out of his mouth.

Troy turned his head away. "Aw, man, that is gross!"

Cam got the small piece of metal free. It was oval shaped, about six inches across at its widest, and it was covered in crap. He used the branch to push the thing into the shallow water, and then turned it over a few times to wash the gunk off of it. He reached into the water to retrieve it.

"Don't touch that thing, Cam!" Troy ordered. "You get that stink on you and it ain't ever coming off."

Troy had a point. The water was still discolored by the fecal matter. Probably a bunch of bacteria in there, too. Cam used the stick to push the metal upstream into fresh water. He then found a piece of palmetto frond to use as a makeshift glove. He carefully reached into the water and pulled the metal object up.

"What is it?" Troy said.

"I'll be damned," Cam said as he held it up. "It's a belt buckle."

Chapter 13:
"Momma, Don't Let Your Cowboys Grow Up To Be Eaten"

The male creature lay in the shallow swamp behind a pile of fallen trees. He could see through them to the bank of the bayou, where the two smart things were standing, looking at the massive dump he had taken just a few moments before.

What the hell were they doing digging in that? he thought. Strange creatures. They were both within easy striking distance. Even the dog was close enough to grab. He'd eaten some of them before, too. But there were a couple of problems the creature had to deal with. First, the smart things were carrying weapons. He'd seen them used over the years to kill smaller animals in the swamp. They could kill from a long way. He doubted they could harm him, but since he'd never been shot at and hit by one, he wasn't taking any chances. Still, his outer skin was thick and strong.

The second problem was that he felt a little queasy. He'd been eating so much, so fast for the last few days, his stomach was totally screwed up. The huge dump he took had helped matters. And he'd puked some stuff up earlier, too. The one-two punch of that had left him a little weak, though. He wasn't even that hungry at the moment. But he would be. And he had to get to that female soon. He could feel the chemical buildup inside him getting stronger. It wasn't at maximum yet, but it was getting there. He figured one more eating binge and he'd be good to go.

Cam used his iPhone to take some shots of the shit-pile, video included. He also took some close-ups of the belt buckle. He then used the handy little device to mark his GPS position, just in case they wanted to come back.

"You almost done," Troy said. He had his back to Cam, the 30.06 at the ready, scanning the bayou and the far shore. It'd been awhile since Cam had seen Troy so rattled.

"Got it," Cam said.

"Good. Huey's about to shit a brick. Something's really freakin' him out." The dog was still in his attack position, locked on to a point deeper in the swamp.

Cam took one more look around. He still had that feeling in his hand. Except now that feeling had become one that humans first felt thousands of years ago. That feeling that something was watching him. It was a prey sense left over in our DNA to always remind us that something bigger and bad-assier was lurking in the dark.

"Let's get the hell out of here," Cam said.

"Gladly," added Troy. He stepped into the boat. Cam pushed off and jumped in, letting the Tracker drift back into deeper water. They both looked back at the gigantic pile of crap. Now, from a distance, knowing what it was, they each compared its size to the surrounding trees. The scale was apparent. Big. *Very* big.

Cam sensed Troy's next comment and said, "There's nothing in these swamps that big. Hell, whale shit's not that big. Elephant shit's not that big."

Troy just stared back at the shore. "That turd was at least a foot in diameter. And long, too."

Cam looked at the belt buckle in his hand. There had been paint on it, but he could still read some of the raised lettering. "Hey, Troy. Whatever that thing is, it's from out of the state."

"Why do you say that?"

Cam held up the large belt buckle. "Says, 'Houston Rodeo' on it."

Troy rubbed his head. "Great, it ate a horse with a cowboy on it. Let's go."

Cam started up the boat and headed farther down the bayou.

"Hey, dickhead, home's that way," Troy yelled, pointing in the opposite direction.

Cam just nodded his understanding and pointed in the direction they were going. Troy shook his head and held onto the 30.06 even tighter. Huey continued to stick his nose in the air, trying to catch the scent of whatever it was that had freaked him out.

They rode for another 20 minutes, rounded a bend and saw a shirtless man in a small aluminum bass boat tied to tree. He was smoking a cigarette.

Cam slowed the boat down out of courtesy so he wouldn't make a large wake. Both he and Troy stared at the man before they recognized who it was.

"Fucking Roland," Troy said.

"Bingo," Cam replied. He cut the engine to idle and headed toward Alcide's resident drug lord and poster child for better living through chemistry.

Cam half expected Roland to run, but he just sat there, smoking. They pulled up next to his boat.

"What's up, Roland?" Cam said. "Engine problems?"

Roland took a deep hit off the joint and gave Cam a nervous look. "Dee-Sale. Troy Boy. Hey, Huey. Y'all lost or somethin'?"

"No, not really, Roland," Cam said. He took a quick look in Roland's ratty boat, half expecting to see all sorts of drugs. The only thing in there was about an inch of dirty bayou water.

"You look a little twitchy there, podnuh," Troy said. "Hittin' the merchandise?"

"Don't know what you're talkin' 'bout, asshole," Roland said. He flicked the last of his joint into the water. He waited a beat and let the smoke out of his lungs slowly.

Cam noticed how Roland kept looking around. He couldn't make eye contact. His left hand was shaking, and be bounced his right leg up and down like a jackhammer.

"Where ya headed?' Cam said.

"What, you the cops now, Dee-Sale?"

"Just a citizen."

"Just takin' a little ride, enjoying a nice sunny day."

"Uh huh," Troy deadpanned. "Where you got that meth lab...er...houseboat stashed?"

"My little secret spot. Nothin' illegal about that," Roland said. A big bass hit the water in the middle of the bayou. Roland jumped about a foot. "What are y'all doin' back up in here? And why is Troy Boy there bringin' the big guns?"

"Never know what you're gonna run into back here," Cam said.

Roland smiled and hung his head, shaking it slowly. "That's for damn sure."

"What do you mean by that?" Troy said.

"Nothin'. You're the one carryin' the artillery," Roland said. He looked around again.

Cam eyed him carefully. "You seen anything...out of the ordinary, Roland?"

"What's ordinary?" he replied and laughed. Cam noted it was his own private joke, a knowing but nervous laugh that said, *"if you only knew."*

"You know, stuff you don't normally see or hear back up in here," Troy added.

Roland looked at both of them. Cam was sure that for a moment, Roland's wise-ass, meth-clouded demeanor faded away, and there appeared what was once the original, somewhat-normal Roland Avant sitting in front of them. He definitely had something on his mind.

"Naw. Nothin' weird," Roland said. "Just the usual weird, you know?"

"Okay," Cam said. "We're out of here. And Roland, you better not be selling that shit around the parish."

"Whatever," Roland said.

"Hey, dickhead," Troy said. "Better watch the weather. There's a storm comin'. Wouldn't want to be on that houseboat during a hurricane."

Roland let out a hacking cough/laugh. "Yeah, there's a storm comin' alright. Better get ready to kiss your ass goodbye."

Cam started the boat and eased back in reverse until he was well clear of Roland's boat. He gave the motor a little juice and headed deeper into the swamp. Troy gave him a questioning look.

"We'll go this way for a while longer, then double back to see if Roland's still there," Cam said. "I'm guessing not, which means we're close to his shit."

"I think the little fucker saw something," Troy said.

"Me, too. He was more scared than jacked up on that shit. The weed wasn't really mellowing him out."

They both looked back. Roland was lighting up another joint.

Troy scanned both banks. Huey did the same. Cam steered the boat, but he was thinking more than looking. That pile of shit defied explanation. Even if a bunch of gators used that area for a communal toilet, it wouldn't look like that. The pile looked fresh and together, like it came out of one asshole. And if diameter of shit was in direct proportion to diameter of asshole, this thing was huge. And it was definitely a carnivore, judging by the bits and pieces of animal matter embedded in the pile. Then there was that belt buckle. He would lay odds that there was a human attached to that belt. He'd have to show it to Lexie. That would make interesting conversation.

Shit. Lexie, he thought. She was out there right now, completely unaware that something very dangerous was lurking in the swamps. Well, she *was* thinking "dangerous," just not completely-over-the-top-WTF" dangerous.

Floyd Guidry eaten. A kayaker eaten. A cowboy belt buckle and its owner eaten. Cam was starting to tally up the damage. What the hell was out there? Some unknown species? The Basin was huge, and still relatively primordial. It was possible a new species was out here. Scientists were discovering shit like that all the time, especially in places like the Amazon. But those were small toads, or lizards. Maybe a butterfly. Rarely a mammal. Something this big couldn't just hide for thousands of years. Somebody had to have seen it. But his family had lived around here for generations, and there were no urban legends or stories the old people had handed down. At least that he knew of. Sure, there were the stupid swamp monster stories parents scared their kids with. But no bayou Loch Ness monster.

Hollywood always got it wrong, too, Cam thought. They made some great monster flicks, but few writers bothered to do their homework. So you got giant sandworms, for instance. To him, that just never made sense. Things got big, from an evolutionary standpoint, because survival depended on being big. And to get big, you needed a lot to eat. What you ate had to be plentiful and big in its own way. There would be no reason to have a giant sandworm. There's nothing to eat in a desert that would produce a predator like a giant sandworm. An animal that big would need to eat a lot, and often. Which it couldn't in a desert.

Whatever was running around the bayou, though, was eating big—both in quantity and size. People, hogs, deer, alligators. How come no one had ever seen it? Was it the last of a dying species? And why would it be going extinct? There was a lot of food and cover in the Atchafalaya Basin.

Weird.

They continued west for a while longer, but saw nothing unusual. And there was no sign of Roland's houseboat. Cam looked at his watch and did the math. If they wanted to be back at the Fort in time to meet up with Lexie, and maybe make some dinner, they'd have to start heading back now.

He did a lazy 180-degree turn and pointed the boat in the direction they'd come. Troy said nothing, but gave him a thumbs up. It was time to go home. Huey looked at his master as if to say, *"It's about time. Let's get the hell out of here."*

Cam picked up speed, and soon Troy was pointing to the bank. He had found where Roland had been. There was no sign of him.

Cam pulled his phone out again and marked the GPS coordinates of this spot. He already had the pile of shit recorded. This would give him a good approximation of where Roland was holed up. If Roland was heading back home, the Tracker would probably overtake him.

Later, they passed the location of the giant pile of crap. There was still steam coming off it, which Cam found odd. The air wasn't cool enough to do that. In the winter, you'd see a pile of fresh cow patties steaming in the pasture, but never on a warm September day.

Roland watched Cam and Troy sail by from his hidden spot deep in the trees of the swamp. His camouflage skills were amazing. Those two assholes were back here looking for him. That's all he needed. He looked down at the bags of meth that were ready for transport. It was time to get them back to civilization. His buyers would be in town soon, and he didn't want to cut it close. He doubted those gangbangers had the patience to stick around Alcide waiting for him to deliver the goods. His original plan had been to spend the night back here and sneak into town in the morning. But the situation had changed in a big way. A big, hungry, frightening way, due to a rather surprising change in the fauna of the swamp.

"Fucking frogasaur," he said aloud.

Chapter 14:
"Hidey Hole"

"You sure he hasn't already gone home?" Troy said. He swatted a mosquito from his head.

Cam nodded. "I'm betting he hasn't."

They had been sitting in the Tracker for over an hour, shooting the shit and not much else. The boat was well hidden inside the swamps along the bayou, very near where it merged into the Atchafalaya River.

"I'd bet the farm Roland wasn't ahead of us. He's *behind* us. Up to no good," Cam added.

"Probably, but let's give it another five. It's getting late and I'm hungry again. Puked everything up."

"I'll fry some catfish when we get back to the Fort. Lexie will probably be hungry, too."

Troy made a face and waved his arms. "Oooo, a man who cooks," he said. "You're quite a catch."

Within a minute they heard the low whine of an outboard motor straining in the distance. At first, it was hard to tell what was coming due to all the trees between them and the bayou. Cam and Troy leaned forward and squinted. Huey had his front paws up on the gunwale, his ears up at attention.

"Told you," Cam said. They watched as Roland puttered by in the beat-up aluminum bass boat. "Hundred bucks says he's got the shit in the boat now, moving it on shore."

"Follow him?"

"Hell, yes. I want to see where he goes." Cam started up the Tracker and eased out of the swamp and into the bayou. By that time, Roland had rounded a bend and was out of sight. Cam estimated Roland's speed and matched it, putting enough distance between both of them so Cam wouldn't be spotted.

They followed Roland like that for 15 more minutes, until they saw him merge into the bigger Atchafalaya River and head back toward town. The river had longer straightaways, so Cam had to be careful to stay out of sight. He moved the boat out of the middle of the river and hugged the bank instead. Every now and then they'd see Roland far in the distance, but he never turned to see that Cam and Troy were behind him.

The sun was low over the west bank and cast long shadows on the trees across the river. Cam used the light to his advantage, staying in the shadows along the shoreline. He had to be careful, though, since there were occasional sand bars, submerged stumps and fallen trees along the bank.

For 25 minutes more they zigged and zagged along the river, and as far as Cam could tell, Roland never spotted them.

"Check it out," Troy said. He pointed toward Roland.

They were getting closer to town, at which point Roland had to hang a right off the river and into the bayou that ran along Alcide, or continue on south deeper into the Basin.

Roland took the right and headed toward Alcide.

Cam eased off the throttle and drifted toward the entrance to the bayou. Once there, he looked down the narrow waterway, but couldn't see Roland. They could see what was left of his wake, though, so they knew he was still chugging along.

"Stay sharp," Cam said to Troy.

Troy nodded. He had picked up Cam's binoculars and had Roland in sight, almost a quarter mile in the distance. "Well, at least the son of a bitch is leading us home," Troy said.

"Maybe," Cam said.

Five minutes later, Troy held his hand out toward Cam, signaling him to slow down. Cam cut the throttle.

"Where the hell is he going?" Troy said. "Look." He handed Cam the binos.

Cam got the focus and spotted Roland ahead, his boat now idling near the shoreline. He watched as Roland grabbed a willow tree that had fallen over almost parallel to the water. The tree was still alive and had a thick canopy of leaves. Roland was fidgeting with something on the tree, and then suddenly the "fallen" tree eased upward to an almost 45-degree angle. Roland guided his boat under it into a narrow, hidden canal. Before going any farther, he pulled the willow down again. Cam could now see that he was using a rope to secure it to a semi-submerged log at the entrance of the canal.

"Clever little bastard," Cam said. "Got him a secret little canal. You'd never see it with that willow in the way."

"Wonder what he's got back up in there?"

Cam let the boat drift into the trees for cover. He took out his iPhone and pulled up Google maps of the area. In a moment, he said, "Huh."

"What"?

"You know that old gravel road that goes to the abandoned well head on the other side of the bayou? Looks like it cuts near where old Roland is headed. I bet he's got a way back into there. And it leads back to a pasture. The pasture fronts the highway about a half mile past that."

"Think that's where he's got his truck?"

"Gotta be," Cam said. "I'm sure he stashes the bass boat in there, then walks to his truck. Might have him a little hidey hole somewhere in there, too."

Troy checked his watch. "Wanna follow him in?"

"Naw. Don't have to. We know where he went. Let's mark the spot, get with Lexie and give her the option of what to do. But I think we earned our deputy badges today." Cam gave Troy a big smile.

"Maybe she'll let you use her handcuffs. That might be fun."

"We'll see. Let's head back to the Fort."

In less than an hour, Cam, Troy and Huey had tied up back at Fort St. Jesus Bait and Tackle. Cam checked in with Zach to make sure all was well, and then told the kid to stick around for another hour or so. People were headed home from work, and business picked up a lot after five.

Cam dragged a burner and propane tank out back and went inside to season and batter some catfish fillets he had in the small fridge in the back. Troy took care of heating up the oil. In no time, Cam was back outside with a platter of plump fillets and dropped them into the sizzling oil.

"Make some hushpuppies, too," Troy said. He sat in a rocker downing a longneck.

"Yes, dear,' Cam said. He dropped some of the spicy battered corn meal balls into the pot. With dinner now on, he grabbed a beer and sat on another rocker next to Troy. Huey took his usual spot between the two.

They sat in silence a moment, enjoying the beer and the setting sun. A pontoon boat went by, occupied by three middle-aged couples out for a late afternoon booze cruise.

"Think they know there's something out there that can drop about a ton of shit at one sitting?" Troy said.

"They don't look too worried to me," Cam said. "But, I gotta tell you, that shit's kind of messing with my head. There were pieces of deer, hogs, gators…"

"People," Troy added.

"Maybe. Yeah. We might need to bring this to the attention of the seafaring population," Cam said.

"Serious, Cam," Troy said. "What do you think it is?"

"I don't know. It just doesn't fit with anything out there. Unless I'm missing something."

"Remember a few years back when they opened the spillway?" Troy said. "You think all the Mississippi River water might've let something loose? Or brought something down from up north?"

During the huge floods in 2011, the swollen Mississippi River had been bled off into the Atchafalaya Basin through the Morganza spillway. The goal was to save Baton Rouge and New Orleans from some major flooding downriver. It had raised water levels as high as 15 feet in some places in the spillway. Opening the gates was a rarity. The last time before then had been in 1973. It wasn't a catastrophe, since the area was designed for that, but it sure as hell was an inconvenience to people who rolled the dice and lived inside the levees of the spillway. The good news was that the Mississippi's water flushed out the swamps and left fresh water, and once the water receded, helped restore the marshes and bayous. The newly deposited soil also helped raise the land toward the Gulf, offering more protection during hurricanes. But other than that, it had been a major pain in the ass. Except for the good folks of Baton Rouge and New Orleans. They had been big fans.

Cam glanced over at Troy. "What, you mean released Godzilla from some underground cave he'd been living in? I think I've seen that movie." He took a big gulp from his beer.

"No, no, just displaced something. Something that would normally be hiding deep in the swamp."

"Fuck, who knows," Cam said. "Until we see it, we'll never know."

"I don't *want* to see it," Troy replied. "I've got a good feeling that if you see it, it might be the last thing you see."

Cam said, "Probably should have gotten a fecal sample, send it to the lab at the vet school at LSU," he said.

"That sounds like fun. Sorry I didn't remind you," Troy said.

Cam got up and checked the fish. They were golden brown and ready for the plate.

The back screen door squeaked open and Lexie stuck her head out, first one way, and then the other. She spotted Cam and Troy and walked over.

"Man, that smells good," she said. "Got enough for one more?"

"Got plenty," Cam said. He looked carefully at Lexie. Her blonde ponytail was a little askew, and the nice makeup she had on this morning was diminished to near nothing. Her eyes were a little red, too. "Rough day?"

She caught his comment the wrong way and tried to smooth her hair back. "I must look like shit," she said.

Troy leaned back. "You look fantastic, deputy," he said.

Cam ignored him. "No, I mean the kayaker thing. What's the word?"

"Let me get a Coke or something first," Lexie said. "We eating back here?"

Cam looked behind him at an old cypress picnic table where fishermen usually sat for lunch. There was a black metal ashtray on it, filled with cigarette butts. "Yeah. Right here. I'll get some plates."

Later, they sat at the table, digging into the fried catfish and hushpuppies. Cam let her eat a bit before pressing her. "So?"

"Dead and *gone*," Lexie said between mouthfuls. "And I mean gone. No sign of a body, or a piece of a body. Some residual blood on what's left of the kayak, but that's about it. This thing ate him in one gulp."

"Holy shit," Troy said. He stopped eating and just stared at Lexie.

"Guy's name was Brad Parsons, from Lafayette. Found his wallet and cell phone in a dry bag floating inside the biggest piece of the kayak. Good fish, Cam." She stuffed another piece of fish in her mouth.

"So somebody saw it happen?" Cam asked.

"Four Ladies of Lesbos on a three-hour cruise," Lexie said. "You know that chick from New Orleans that's got the camp on the river? Kathy Flynn?"

"Vaguely," Cam said.

"Her and her girl toy and another couple of women of that persuasion. Hot chicks, let me tell you," Lexie said and gave Troy a look. She had his full attention now.

"The guy was paddling towards their boat, then *wham*, something hit him like a bass hitting a worm."

Cam leaned in a bit. "What did they say it looked like? The...thing."

"All they could come up with was 'hippo,'" Lexie said.

"What do you mean, 'all they could come up with'?" Troy asked.

Lexie scrunched her pretty face. Cam thought she looked like a little girl doing that. "Well, they *thought* it was a hippo. But they all got the impression it wasn't quite a hippo. Something different about it."

"Like what?" Cam said.

"The head was all wrong. It was wider, and the eyes were bigger. And they said it had a mouth full of teeth. More shark-like than a hippo's. Pass the Tabasco," she said and grabbed another fillet. "But it happened so quick, those were all *impressions.*"

"Anything else?" Cam had stopped eating.

"Yeah, they said it had *arms*. Not the large legs of a hippo. Arms with hands. Finger-like things, too."

Cam looked at Troy. "Any sense of size?"

"They didn't say exactly. The forensics nerds carried off the kayak pieces for evidence. But it bit it clean in two. So big enough to do that and swallow a guy whole."

Cam just nodded his head, thinking to himself.

"You're the animal specialist around here," Lexie said. "Mind telling me what we're talking about?"

"Not a native animal," Cam said. "No way. Must've got here some other way. The Everglades are full of weird exotic things people had for pets then let go. Big-ass snakes, shit like that. But this takes the cake."

"And apparently a kayaker," Troy said. He got up to retrieve another beer from the cooler. "So we think this is the same thing that got a hold of dearly departed Floyd?"

"Maybe." Lexie just stared off into the bayou, deep in thought. "Of course, that brings up a bigger problem."

"What's that?" said Cam.

"The kayaker was killed southeast of here in Bayou Chene. Floyd died in the other direction. Probably a 15-mile difference. Within 24 hours of each other."

Cam sat up. "Shit. There are *two* of these things?"

Chapter 15:
"Just One More Day"

After they had exhausted all the weird talk about the hungry hippos, Lexie pinned Cam and Troy down on the comings and goings of Roland. They explained how they found him and finally tracked him back to his hidey hole.

"Outstanding, deputies," she said. She flashed Cam a smile that just about melted him. "I think I know where that is. I'll check it out."

"Not alone, I hope," Cam said. "Roland's one thing. Those hippo things are something else. Good place to hide up in there." Cam tried to sound civically concerned rather than emotionally. He was pretty sure he blew it.

"I'll get some backup," she said. She pushed her plate away and finished her Diet Coke. "And if I can't, I'll call you two bad asses."

"Deal," he said.

The screen door opened and Lee Curtis stepped outside. He had a plastic bag filled with some small items. "Hey, boys. Lexie, what's up? Zach said y'all were back here."

"Hey, Lee," Cam said. "You still having that fishing party Saturday afternoon for the kids?" He looked at Troy. "What with the storm and all." It was the "and all" that Cam was most worried about.

Lee grabbed an old bar stool and pulled it over. "Might have to move it up to Friday afternoon. Deanna's calling all the moms. We'll see."

Lee put the bag down on the porch floor and pulled out his phone. "I wanted to show you something." He pressed a few buttons and looked up at Cam, Troy and Lexie. "Some video I shot off my pier yesterday. Damnedest thing I ever saw."

Lee pressed one more button and handed the device to Cam. Lexie and Troy got up to look over his shoulder. They watched the video of the pack of gators swimming by Lee's pier.

"You shot this behind your house?" Cam said. "What time?"

"Around nine maybe. I was sitting out there having some coffee."

Lexie and Cam exchanged glances. "Your backyard faces which way?" Lexie said.

Lee thought a moment. "Kinda towards the south."

"So these guys were moving roughly west to east then?" she said.

"What does that have to do with anything?" Lee said. "Anybody ever see gators do this before?"

"No," replied Cam. "Not like that."

Lee said, "I mean, they were *motorin'* down the bayou. Like they were in a hurry. Or something spooked 'em."

Troy cleared his throat. "Play it again."

Lee played the video once more, and they all stared at the little screen. Cam said, "See anything else...unusual... around the yard?"

"Nope. I thought *this* was unusual." Lee pocketed the phone. "Anyway, you're the vet. Didn't know if this meant anything."

"Yeah, just email me that video. I'll do some research and make some calls to see what that kind of behavior is all about."

"Cool," Lee said. "I gotta go. Dinner's in 20." He looked at his watch and headed back inside and out the front to his car.

Cam stood up from the picnic table and walked to the railing and looked out over the bayou. He turned to Lexie. "So, we got something to the east and something to the west. Two incidents. Two…whatevers."

"I think so," she said. "The distance seems too great for the same animal to do both attacks. You think those gators know something we don't know?"

Troy made a sharp laugh. "They probably know *more* than we know," he said.

"We got a little report to make, too," Cam added. "Before we tracked Roland to his hiding place, we found something weird." He pulled his phone out of his pocket and handed it to Lexie. "Scroll through those pictures. The last one's a video."

Lexie frowned and stared at the images. She used her thumb to swipe from one shot to another. Cam watched her expressions change from curiosity to confusion as she tried to figure out what exactly she was looking at.

"I give up," she finally said.

"Feces," Cam said.

"Shit pile," Troy clarified.

"This is a pile of crap?" Lexie said. "It's huge."

Cam explained how they came upon it, the awful smell, and the bits and pieces of animals inside the crap. "And then there's this," he said. He pulled the big belt buckle from the pocket of his cargo shorts and handed it to her. "Know who this might belong to? Because I think this is all that's left of them."

Lexie examined the buckle and read the "Houston Rodeo" letters. "No, but I know who the first person is that I'll ask. Felice Guidry."

"You think that's Floyd's?" said Troy.

"Fits the area where he left the planet," Lexie said. "Worth a try, anyway."

"Jeez," said Troy. "What's left of Floyd's in that pile of shit? Man." He shook his head.

"I feel like I should warn everyone," Lexie said. "But of what, Cam? What the hell are these things?"

Cam leaned against a post, arms folded, staring down at the porch. "No idea," he said. "There's probably an explanation, I just don't know what it is at the moment. But I do know one thing." He looked over at Troy and winked. "We're gonna need a bigger boat."

Troy laughed. "Good one, Cam."

"Again with the movie lines," Lexie said. "Funny. Real funny." She looked at her watch. "Okay, I'm heading back to the office to type up this report. And maybe there's something back from the M.E. on what was left of Floyd. Check on the hurricane, too."

"And don't forget Roland," Cam said. "I think we got that bastard."

"Don't worry," she replied. "We're gonna pay Mr. Roland a little visit tomorrow I think."

Roland sat in his old truck, parked in front of his shitty little singlewide just outside of town. The sun had set, and a random thunderstorm was blowing across the parish from the south. It had not yet reached Alcide, but the strobing lightning flashes signaled its impending arrival. With each flash, the surrounding countryside was illuminated, revealing trees bent over from a steady wind coming in from the direction of the fast-moving storm.

Roland tossed his cigarette out the window and blew a large cloud of smoke out of his nose. He held his cell phone in front of him, thumbing in the number he had been given. He hit "dial" and waited through four rings.

"You ready?" was the answer he heard through the phone.

"Yeah, tell Tree I'm good to go. But hurry before that hurricane blows in."

"When? Where?" the gangbanger said in his most menacing street voice.

Roland took a deep breath. A lightning flash and near-instant clap of thunder signaled a very-close strike, and that the storm was damn-near on top of him. He winced and moved the phone away from his hear. He'd heard a lightning bolt could come through a cell phone and blow your head off. Or was that a regular phone? He couldn't remember but didn't want to take a chance.

He gave the banger the location of the transaction, careful to make sure they wouldn't get lost in the unfamiliar area. The shitheads had probably never been out of the Ninth Ward before. Well, except maybe that time it was under 15 feet of water after Katrina.

"What's the cop situation?" the voice said.

"Just one. A chick deputy," Roland said. "The rest of 'em are scattered around the parish or based over in St. Martinville. Just watch your speed and stay cool."

"Yeah, yeah. You just stay cool. My boss don't like no surprises."

"Well, neither do I," said Roland in a moment of rare bravura. "Just make sure the money is green and American."

"Tomorrow," the voice said and clicked off.

"Asshole," Roland said, and tossed his phone on the passenger seat.

He sat back as the thick drops of the thunderstorm peppered his truck. The world outside went gray and wet. He could feel the truck shudder in the strong winds of the storm. Just one more day and his bank account would be full. All the months back up in that stupid swamp, the mosquitoes, the sneaking around, watching out for Deputy Hot Ass. And the Frogasaur. Did he actually see that thing? His moments of clarity were a little sketchy. Maybe it was some hallucination caused by all the wonderful ice he'd been inhaling. Probably so. He'd been under a lot of stress lately. Nerves. He rubbed his eyes and looked in the rearview mirror. Whoa. He looked a little ragged. He knew he had to crash, chill out a bit, maybe eat something. But he wasn't sleepy or hungry. He had some shit in the trailer. That's what he needed. He opened the door of the truck, and its bent hinge squeaked loudly. The rain was a sold sheet of cold water now, loud and angry. Roland didn't give a shit. He stepped out of the truck as if it was a sunny day. He walked the 50 feet to the trailer at an easy pace. The rain was loud on the rusty aluminum roof of the singlewide. It would be leaking now in the bathroom, where the vent angled up to the roof. Fuck it. In a day or so, he'd be in New Orleans, in the penthouse suite at Harrah's, getting a blow job from two of the hottest hookers New Orleans had to offer.

Just one more day.

Chapter 16:
"Calling St. Michael"

The Sacred Heart of Jesus Women's Club met every Thursday evening at the parish hall for a simple dinner and fellowship. Or womenship, as Father Mike liked to say. He handled the invocation and grace before dinner, sat with some of the ladies—which was always a political thing to see who got to dine with handsome Father Mike–and generally mingled about after dinner when the ladies got into the real gossip. Joanie always showed up, but of course, she hated it. These were women who knew her parents, who'd watch her sometimes when she needed babysitting, who hired her to babysit some of their younger children, and a few whose sons she had sex with during high school. But now she was *Sister Joanie.* Which continued to amaze and stupefy the good women of Alcide and St. Martin Parish.

Mike was listening to a lively discussion at his table from a few of the women. Mostly about Felice Guidry, newly widowed wife of the newly eaten Floyd Guidry. They would all be at the funeral this weekend, of course, but the main topic was Felice. She was back on the market, and an attractive middle-aged woman back on the market made the ladies reassess their husbands' fidelity.

Mike smiled and nodded his head, but he wasn't paying that much attention. He looked over to the next table and watched as Joanie engaged in some chatter with her group of ladies. Joanie was holding court, and the women were paying rapt attention. This petrified Mike somewhat, because there was no telling what Joanie was talking about, but he was pretty sure it wasn't last Sunday's gospel. Judging by the looks on the ladies' faces, it was pure-gold gossip.

Joanie had dressed modestly for the ladies, thank goodness. Gray slacks and a simple white blouse buttoned up high. Her signature cross was around her neck. She'd left the make-up off, or maybe toned it down, Mike couldn't tell. Joanie looked great either way. She had her chestnut hair down and it gathered slightly at her shoulders. One of the ladies at her table took up the conversation and Joanie picked up her glass of tea and took a sip. She licked her lips slightly, nodded at the lady, and turned her head Mike's way. She gave him a quick smile and a wink.

Damn, Mike thought. *I wish she wouldn't do that.* The gesture made his heart beat a little fast, and there was a stirring down below that he quickly dealt with via a quick prayer to his namesake saint, Michael the Archangel. Mike was pretty sure St. Mike never had to deal with such things. Smiting his ex-old-buddy Lucifer and tossing him out of heaven had kept him pretty occupied at first. Running the angel corps was his full-time gig now, which was enough to keep your mind off things.

Mike wondered what was going through Joanie's mind. Did she flirt with him on purpose, just to get a reaction? Was that just her personality? Or was there something more? His heart kind of ached for her But was it just a strong platonic emotional bond, a shared connection between two young adults who had given their lives to Christ?

Mike had been in and out of love, and bed, with enough women in his life to know what was going on. At least, he thought he did. He and Joanie had known each other long enough now that they could talk, really talk, to each other. He didn't know her that well in high school, but after she had come over from St. Alphonse, they had made a connection. And they could talk for hours. About anything. And while she talked, he just stared at her, taking in everything about her. Her smile, her eyes, her lustrous hair. The shape of her nose, her long legs, the curve of her...

"Father?"

Mike heard his name, but it took a beat for him to readjust his concentration. It was Sandra Favreaux, a striking 47-year-old redhead with big green eyes and a big new rack across her chest, courtesy of a plastic surgeon in New Orleans.

"I'm sorry, Sandy," he said. "What was that?"

Sandra did the geometry on Mike's eyes, where they were now and where they had been a moment ago. She gave a knowing smile and glanced at one of the other women across the table. "You think Felice is gonna stay at her place or move to Lafayette, where her sister lives?"

Mike took a deep breath and adjusted his thinking. "Hmmm. I think she'll stay. The house is paid for. She said Floyd had a good insurance policy, so she'll be set. She likes it around here. Can't see her moving to the city."

Mike looked around the table at the women. It was not the response they had hoped for. They were thinking it would be best if Felice dropped out of the local scene. They didn't need any new Cajun cougars running around the place.

Mike couldn't resist. "You know, I wouldn't be surprised if Felice found her a new man pretty quick. Attractive woman like that. And, man, can she cook. I'd miss her around the parish." The truth was, Mike would miss the parish income. Felice and Floyd had been generous with their financial support. He had checked just to make sure.

The subject quickly changed to the hurricane and what precautions people were taking. The citizens of Alcide weren't fools. Experience had taught them what to expect from any category of storm. They knew which low spots would flood, which roads would be impassable because of fallen trees, how long the power would be out, and where to go until the storm passed. Most would leave to stay at relatives' homes to the north in Opelousas, Alexandria and beyond. Just an extra 50 or 100 miles north made a big difference in storm strength and destruction.

The ladies finished their coffee and the evening began to wind down. A few volunteers stayed to clean up. Mike and Joanie made the rounds and thanked the ladies for coming.

He retreated to his office, with Joanie trailing behind. It was spacious and orderly. A big cypress desk dominated the room, handmade by a local carpenter. Two leather chairs sat in front. There was also room in the corner for a couple of more chairs and a tiny coffee table. The window behind the desk looked out into the swampy woods, dimly lit now by a few of the spotlights on the outside of the rectory. The earlier thunderstorm had passed, and the foliage on the trees shimmered with moisture. A thin bit of steam hung over the scene.

One wall of the office had floor-to-ceiling bookshelves, filled with the requisite Catholic playbooks and how-to manuals. But there were also a number of books on hunting, camping and travel, a few of Mike's passions. The other walls featured framed photos of Mike with family and friends, from his high school years to the present.

Mike switched on a 32-inch flat screen TV that sat on a table to the left of his desk. Joanie plopped down in one of the leather chairs and put one leg over the chair's right arm. He flipped a few channels until he found The Weather Channel. There was Jim Cantore, in a blue windbreaker, microphone in hand, on the beach at Grand Isle. The windbreaker was being whipped by a steady breeze. Even in the darkness, the TV lights illuminated an-already-angry surf piling up on the low barrier island to the southeast.

The graphics on the screen revealed Hurricane Tammy as a category two, with winds over 110 mph. Mike and Joanie listened as Cantore rattled out weather data, possible storm tracks and evacuation notices. The current track had the storm passing just west of Alcide.

Joanie said, "Great, we're gonna get the right side." The right quadrant of a hurricane was always the worst for wind and rain. The forward speed of the storm was added to the actual wind speed to make that side a howling maelstrom that packed a hurricane's biggest punch.

"Gotta board up tomorrow," Mike said. "We'll get the men's club on that in the morning." He stared at the screen again, doing some math in his head. "We can probably sneak Floyd's wake in tomorrow night, but putting him in the ground is gonna have to wait. Felice will be pissed."

"It'll be safer there for him," Joanie said. She glanced away from the TV at Mike. "He'll have both feet firmly in the ground by Monday."

Mike didn't bite. "Funeral home will be fine. It never floods. Us? Who knows? Might be rough."

He tossed the remote on his desk and sat back. The insurance on the church was fairly substantial, so he wasn't worried about the money. The deductible was a little high, but they had cash set aside for that. "I'm staying," he said.

"I'm not going anywhere, either," Joanie replied. "We can hole up here."

"If it goes to a three, things might get a little interesting," Mike added.

"We'll be fine. This church is solid. Been through hurricanes since long before you and I were born."

"Except we're probably on our fifth steeple in 30 years," Mike said.

Joanie shrugged. "Gotta give something to the storm," she said.

"Maybe we should make book on the steeple this time," he said. "Could haul in some extra cash. I'm sure that's legal."

"Doubtful, but l like the idea."

Joanie sat back and put her feet up on the front of Mike's desk. She gave him a smile. "You ever notice how those women look at you?"

"The Women's Club women?"

"All women."

"Yes, with reverence and respect," Mike said. "They hang on my every word." He flipped through a stack of mail on the desk.

"They want to catch you when you fall." Joanie said. "And I don't mean down the stairs."

"Do I look wobbly?" he said. He gave her a level gaze.

"Hmmmm. Kinda solid. Maybe." She smiled again.

A moment of awkward silence passed between them. Finally, Joanie said, "Tell me the truth. You ever thought about hanging it up? Going civilian?"

Mike shook his head. "In it for the long haul." Mike didn't like where the conversation was headed. Okay, maybe a little. He felt his heart pick up a few beats.

"I think priests should be able to marry," she said.

"I think we've had this conversation."

She gave him a dismissive wave. "I know, I know. But really, you should be married, have some kids. Will that make you a lesser priest?"

"It would make me an even more tired priest," he said.

"Protestants got it figured out," Joanie replied. "They look happy."

Mike wanted to turn the tables. "What about you? You think nuns should marry?"

"Absolutely. I wouldn't mind a man and some kids."

"You need the Pope's phone number? I'm sure if you call he'd change his mind," Mike said.

She shook her head. "I mean, look at us. We're like a work-wife, work-husband kind of couple already. Without the perks, of course."

Mike thought it was getting a little warm in his office. He and Joanie had these talks before. At first they had been rhetorical, just some lively debate, even though they agreed on most things. The Roman Catholic Church wasn't a democracy. There would be no caucuses, no floor vote to change the rules. Over time, though, when their relationship had become more comfortable, the discussion seemed to have a hidden subtext that neither wanted to push.

"Okay, so if the rules changed, we could date, right?" Mike said. "But we work together. Most companies frown upon co-workers dating. Plus, I'm your boss. There's the whole sexual harassment thing to consider."

"My boss?" Joanie laughed. "That never stopped office hanky spanky before."

Distant thunder rumbled from the retreating storm. On the TV, Jim Cantore was getting excited about something that was just handed to him. Mike tried to concentrate on the screen. Joanie just looked down and smoothed her slacks against her long legs.

She said, "I'd date you if we could. You know, even though we work together. That kind of thing never bothered me."

Mike felt like he had to return the compliment. *That was a compliment, right?* "Same here," he said. "Boy, that would get the office ladies talking."

"You know, they already think you and I…are an item. You knew that, right?"

Mike sat forward. "What?"

"Really. Even the Women's Club ladies look at us like we're a couple."

"That's crazy," Mike said. *Crazy in a good way,* he thought. Truth was, he caught their knowing glances when he and Joanie were around each other. They did act like a couple and people noticed. They didn't seem to mind, either.

"So they're saying we're already a couple in every way except…"

"Right," Joanie said. "Except. Except I think they wonder about even that."

Mike was slightly appalled. "You think they think we're messing around?"

"Oh yeah. Most of the parish does."

Mike knew this, but chose to ignore it. This was the first time Joanie had ever broached the subject with him. "Crap. If this gets back to the Diocesan Office, we're screwed."

"I wouldn't worry about it," Joanie said. Again with the smile that tore at Mike's heart. "I think our parishioners like it. The good sinners of Alcide don't' feel so bad if their priest and nun are rolling around in the sack together."

Mike was getting that weird feeling again. Actually, it was that good feeling again. He tried to summon St. Michael, but he was pretty sure he was getting a busy signal.

Chapter 17:
"Cascade Effect"

The next morning, Lexie sat in Sheriff Gautreaux's office with the medical examiner, going over the prelim report on Floyd Guidry. She had driven over to St. Martinville very early, both to get the report and continue the discussion about the kayaker, Brad Parsons, recently eaten and passed from the planet.

The M.E., Larry Theriot, was a short, round little man with a monk's hairdo and thin little reading glasses perched on his bulbous nose. She had met him on a few occasions, mostly during teaching seminars the deputies took on crime scene protocols.

"So at first, it looked like the deceased's feet were cut off clean with a big knife, like a machete, or cut with a big boat propeller," he said, holding a large photograph of Floyd's feet, sans the boots. The photo had been taken in a clinical setting, Lexie noticed, probably on the autopsy table. She reasoned Larry didn't need a whole table for the autopsy. Might've just needed a dinner tray.

"At first," he continued, holding up an index finger. "But when you look at the cuts under magnification, you can see there's some tearing, a pattern to the incision. Like a serration. Not unlike a shark bite, which I've seen on more than one occasion."

Lexie doubted the landlocked idiot had ever done a shark-attack autopsy, but let it ride for the sake of harmony.

Sheriff Gautreaux sat like a sphinx behind his desk, feet up, arms folded, letting Theriot do his thing. Lexie, trying to impress the boss, sat next to Theriot and leaned forward more to examine the photo.

"So this happened at the time of death, or later, like after he had been dead in the water?" Lexie said. She glanced over at the sheriff to see if he reacted to her pointed question. No reaction at all. But his eyes did shift back to Theriot.

"No, this skin was cut ante mortem, not post," he said. "In other words..."

"It happened while his heart was still beating," Lexie said.

"Right. Whatever got him, pretty much ate him alive." Theriot's eyebrows shot up, as if this were some fantastic revelation.

Finally, Gautreaux spoke. "And this is what happened to that kayaker, according to those eyewitnesses?"

"Yes. Something came up out of the water and took him. One big motion," Lexie said.

"Hippo," the sheriff said. His tone was doubtful.

"Kind of," Lexie said. "At least that's what they said. It's in my report." She gestured to a manila folder next to the sheriff's big feet.

"But not a gator," he continued, his eyes now at Theriot.

"Not a chance," the M.E. said. "Bite's all wrong. If this had happened in the Gulf, I'd say maybe a big ol' bull shark or a great white. Those suckers can jump out of the water like nobody's business when they're hunting prey, like sea lions."

"Bulls have been known to swim up into rivers," Gautreaux said. "They can handle fresh water. But this far?"

Theriot and Lexie just shrugged and looked back down at the pictures.

"Okay, we'll go on the theory this could be a shark that's lost its way," Gautreaux announced.

"Two," Lexie said, holding up two fingers. "The distance and time between the two attacks make me believe it couldn't be the same animal. What are the odds?"

Gautreaux, already bored, said, "Uh huh."

"But that's not what they saw," Lexie continued. "A shark, I mean. She never said 'shark.' Never. The closest she could come up with was 'hippo.' But she said the thing's mouth was too big, and there were lots of sharp teeth. And it had *arms*."

"Arms." Gautreaux pulled his feet down and wheeled his squeaky chair up to his desk. "One, two, whatever. I'm gonna get some guys in boats with spotters and we're gonna have a lookie see. In the meantime, I'll tell the reporters we're treating these as probable gator attacks."

Lexie thought about the pictures of the big pile of shit Cam had taken. He hadn't downloaded them yet, and while she considered mentioning it to the sheriff, she decided to wait until the actual photos were developed. It would sound too weird to explain without some visual reference of a pile of crap five feet high, full of pieces of gator, deer and hog. And maybe a man. The belt buckle was still in her patrol car.

By the looks of Theriot and Gautreaux, the meeting was over. Lexie wasn't done. "What about Guidry? Whatever ate him, *got in the boat and ate four full-grown alligators*. I'm not a marine biologist, but I'm pretty sure a bull shark's not gonna do that."

"Who knows?" the sheriff said. "We'll go with the closest explanation until we get the real explanation. That's pretty much how we'll play this. So, gators to the press, bull sharks to the guys. We'll see where the chips fall."

And where the next ton of shit falls, Lexie thought.

Lexie turned to Theriot. "Uh, you ready to release the... body...to the family? I'm gonna see Mrs. Guidry today and I could tell her. The wake's supposed to be tonight. Might be nice to have something in the box."

"Sure, tell the funeral home to come get the remains," Theriot said. He put the photos back into a folder. "That's all I got, unless you find something else. Haven't had a weird one like this for quite some time. Kind of a mystery, don't you think?"

Gautreaux made a *harrump* sound, as if he didn't need any mysteries around St. Martin Parish. Lexie just nodded.

"Stick around, Lexie, I got something else," Sheriff Gautreaux said.

Theriot said his goodbyes, walked out of the office and shut the door behind him.

"What's up?" Lexie said.

"Missing person," Gautreaux replied. "Waitress over in Henderson. M'Lou Marchand, age 23. Works at Rex's Diner near I-10. Didn't come into work yesterday. Nobody's seen her or heard from her."

"Not I kayaker, I hope," Lexie said.

"Let's hope not," the sheriff said. "Anyway, I got everybody on it. Ask around your part of the parish. See if anybody knows her, saw her or knows anybody she knows. You know the drill."

"Sure," she said. "I-10. Lot of coast-to-coast freaks ridin' that highway. Think some transient got her, somebody like that?"

"Who the hell knows? Wouldn't be the first time. I got Jimmy and Frank all over the diner. Chances are, if somebody got her, they were eatin' boudin and eggs for breakfast there in the last week."

Jimmy Polito and Frank Granato were St. Martinville's two real detectives. Ex-New Orleans P.D. bad boys who decided to get out after Katrina and make a home in the bayous. Lexie liked them. They were smart, funny and tough. She would love to ride with those two anytime. And Frank was kind of cute for a middle-aged guy.

"What else is shakin' over in Alcide?" he said.

Lexie sat back and took a deep breath. "Roland Avant, our local meth chef, is up to something," she said. "Couple of fishermen spotted him going into a slough he had camouflaged outside of town. I'm gonna check it out. Might be where he's got his lab. I'm almost positive he's using an old houseboat for the kitchen. Might have it stashed back up in there."

"You need some backup, you call it in beforehand. Don't get up in this guy's business without some help. That meth shit messes up people's heads."

"Roland's an asshole, but I don't think he'd draw on me," Lexie said.

"Yeah, well, I've heard that before standing over cops in hospital beds and at funerals for cops," Gautreaux said. "Don't ruin my week, Lexie," he said. He pointed a finger at her.

"Yes sir," she replied. She liked the sheriff's fatherly tone.

"Looks like this storm's gonna screw up the weekend," Gautreaux continued. "Just make sure everybody's buttoned up over there. You know the places that'll flood. Make sure some dickhead doesn't drive into a bayou or something. Power's gonna go down, probably cell, too. Use the radio. If you need help, call us. We'll do the same. Otherwise, just cover your part of the world."

Lexie nodded.

Gautreaux fiddled with the folders in front of him. "I hate shit like this," he said, pointing to the reports in front of him. "When's the last time a gator bit somebody around here? What, ten years ago? And that idiot got too close to a nest."

"We'll figure it out, Sheriff," Lexie said.

"What's your theory?"

She shrugged. "It's the swamp. There's all kinds of things back there that'll mess with you. My guess is that it's not one animal, or just one kind of animal. I think it might have started with a gator, but some other things got involved. I don't know. When's the last time anybody's seen a black bear back up in there?"

"A while," the sheriff said. "Still endangered."

"And didn't there used to be panthers, or cougars, in the swamp?" Lexie said.

"Some guys spotted one near Lake Fausse Point State Park about 10 years ago," Gautreaux said. "I'm sure there are more out there, but not many."

"Right. So a few things. It's like plane crashes," she continued. "It's never the *one* thing, but a cascade effect of different things that all come together to cause the disaster. I think this is the same thing. Although we think it might be one thing—a gator, or a bull shark—it's probably several things that came together in a rare combination." She nodded to herself, happy with her logic. Gautreaux just stared at her.

"Cascade effect?" he said, and smiled broadly. "Damn, Lexie. Did you put that in your report?"

"No, sir. The facts are on paper. The theory's up here." She pointed to her head.

"Okay, let's keep it that way." He stood up to signal the meeting was over. "Have a good one, Lexie, and let's find this Marchand girl before the storm hits. Something tells me if we don't find her before then, we never will."

"Right."

"And be careful with that Roland dude. The thought of that makes me a little uncomfortable. Guy like that can turn your day into shit in no time."

"Got it."

Lexie left Sheriff Gautreaux's office and killed a little time mingling with some of the other St. Martin Parish deputies who happened to be in the building. There was a buzz in the place that usually came just before a hurricane. Lots of hallway chatter about preparations, who was going to do what, and predictions on how bad it would be. But there was also some growing chit chat about hungry hippos, monster gators and wayward sharks. She didn't envy the sheriff's job of keeping the weirdness out of the papers.

She checked her watch and figured she'd get back on the road. She took Highway 96, the old Catahoula Highway, out of St. Martinville and headed east across the wide flat plain of farmland between there and the western edge of the Basin.

The sky was overcast, with a gentle but steady breeze out of the southeast. The first telling signs of Hurricane Tammy, which continued to set her sights on the central Louisiana coastline. It would all be downhill from here, as far as the weather was concerned. The first rain bands would come late tonight or early in the morning, and the wind would pick up by Saturday afternoon. Saturday night and into Sunday morning would be an ass whipping of the first degree.

As the farmland rolled by, Lexie ticked off the things she had to do before all that happened. She wanted to get over to Felice Guidry's and show her the belt buckle Cam found. If her hunch was right, it belonged to Floyd. Then she wanted to check out Roland's little nest off the bayou, to see what the little shit had going back up in there. Despite Sheriff Gautreaux's warning, Lexie was confident she could handle Roland, even if he wanted to go gunslinger on her ass. She hadn't pulled her gun out of its holster since she killed her husband, professionally speaking. She mentally did the psycho babble math to see if she could draw down on another human being and take them out if necessary. *Oh, hell yes*, she thought. *Was that normal?* another voice asked inside her head. Shouldn't she be a little shaky after killing a man, especially her husband? The sheriff had made her go see a psychologist over in Lafayette after the shooting, and he had pronounced her A-OK. She had never told anyone about the nightmares she had then and still had occasionally. The ones with headless husbands begging for another chance at life. The thought of those dreams made her eyes water a bit, and she wiped them with the back of her hand.

"Fucking asshole," she muttered. Lexie's anger toward her dearly departed husband had not abated. He had caused all this, including his own death. Slap her around? Sure. But the fucking machete? What the hell was that all about? The bastard was gonna do it. He was going to take her head off with the thing. She had seen it in his eyes. Would he have killed himself after killing her? The classic domestic murder-suicide scenario? She would never know.

So if that shithead Roland tried anything, she was pretty sure she wouldn't hesitate to shoot the bastard. And if she did kill another man, bringing her total up to two, would Cam still be interested in her? Would she have the reputation as a real man killer? A mental case who was quick to draw her gun? Would the sheriff take her off the streets and stick her in the office somewhere?

A wild dog ran across the highway directly in front of her patrol car. She hit the brakes just enough to miss the animal. At first she thought it was a coyote, but it was a mutt of dubious heritage with no collar or tag. Its tail was between its legs and it was running flat out. Something had scared it. Probably a farmer had taken a potshot at it.

The dog snapped her out of her musings, and she hit the accelerator to make up time to get to the Guidry homestead. After that, a little check-in with Roland. With any luck, she'd catch him with the goods and be done with him.

Chapter 18:
"Skeezy"

The male creature sat on the bank of the swamp, chewing on a rotten log. Pieces of the spongy wood flew to either side of him. He spit a large chunk out and it went flying into the water. His mouth hurt. Just after waking up, he had seen a large alligator snapping turtle in some shallow water and rushed over for the morning appetizer. He knew he should have waited a second before grabbing the mean little thing to determine which end was which, but he went after it anyway. The little fucker had bit him on his oral arm. Right on the tip of it. Hurt like hell, too. Two chews later the turtle was history, but it had left behind a sharp little pain that pissed the creature off even more than he was already.

And, of course, he was still very hungry.

One of those hogs might wander over, he hoped, but he hadn't seen one in awhile. He'd have to get into the water and set a trap for one, but that meant wasting time when he could be moving closer to the female. But he had to eat. It was the great dilemma of males everywhere. Food or sex?

The signal from the female was stronger now. They were getting closer, and she seemed to be moving toward him, too, which helped matters tremendously. The problem was, he was seeing more of the smart things than ever. He was getting closer to where they all lived. A few years back, he had come this way to explore and watch the smart things. He wanted to learn all he could about them. Back then, when he wasn't wound up with crazy horniness and hunger, he had the patience and stealth to sneak in close and watch them. He wasn't compelled to grab one and eat. Back then, he ate at his leisure, usually waiting until food came to him. A hog or a deer would last him for days. Now, he could eat both in a single morning. And for this morning, all he had to eat was that damn little turtle, which had tried to eat him.

A hog would be awesome right now. A couple of those smart things would be even tastier.

Lee Curtis stood on the little dock behind his house and looked up and down the bayou. He had hoped to see some more weird alligator behavior, but the bayou was still. A fresh humid breeze out of the east made the warm morning rather pleasant, and it brought with it the heady aroma of the distant swamp and all its creatures, from the land and under the water.

He looked up at the sky at the high overcast, a dirty white that was surely going to get dirtier and darker as the weekend progressed. He glanced at his smartphone. The screen displayed the National Hurricane Center's app that tracked tropical weather. The map showed the storm in the central Gulf of Mexico, with its track plotted ahead of it. Little hash marks and dots indicated where it would be in multi-hour increments. The thing was a high Category 2, and it was headed right for south central Louisiana.

"Whatcha think?" his wife's voice said from behind him. It startled him a bit. Deanna Curtis stood on the bank in a blue terry cloth robe, arms folded.

"We're good," Lee said. "If we can get started right after school, maybe four or so, the kids can get in a little fishing. Rain'll probably hold off till after supper."

Their daughter Macy's birthday party and fishing tournament had been planned for months, and was originally set for late Saturday morning. The hurricane had changed all that. Now he and Deanna were trying to squeeze it in before the storm forced a lot of the people to move inland or hunker down.

"Kinda right on the edge," Deanna said. "All the parents are on board, but they want to get their kids no later that 6:30, before it gets too dark."

Lee put the phone back into his jeans pocket. "That'll be fine."

"I'll go ahead and set some tables up out here," Deanna said. "I'd rather them eat here than inside."

"And if it rains, we just move onto the back porch," he replied. "How many we got coming?"

"Eleven, last count," she said. "That's pretty firm."

Lee did the mental math in his head. "Okay, might need a couple of more poles, then. I'll swing by the Fort and see if Cam has any more."

"What about bait?" she said.

"Yeah. Bait." With little kids, bait was always problematic. The boys liked the worms. They were cool and wiggly. Crickets tended to affect their escape easier and ended up in the grass instead of on hooks. The girls didn't care much for touching either of them. He knew Macy wouldn't have a problem. She was going to be his little sportsman. Sportswoman. She'd touch anything. She even helped him clean fish on occasion.

"I'm not touching any of that shit," Deanna said with a shake of her head. "You're gonna have to bait those lines."

"Right, right," he said. "I'll see what's Cam's got. I'll probably go with worms."

"You gonna clean the fish they catch?"

"It's catch and release," Lee said. "All fishies go back to their momma and daddy."

"Good, you never know what they're gonna pull out of that bayou," Deanna said. She walked back up to the house.

Lee looked at the water again. The surface of the bayou rippled, and he thought for a moment that the gators were back, but it was just a breeze that kissed the surface. Despite the warmth, he shivered with a chill.

Roland Avant sat slouched on a rickety lawn chair out back behind his crappy trailer. About 30 feet of open ground separated the trailer from a stand of sweet gum, tupelo and pin oak. There was no patio, just a wide swath of dirt, a rusty barbecue pit and a small aluminum table. A dump of burned garbage marked the edge of the tree line.

Roland's chin rested on his chest and his eyes were closed. He held his meth pipe in his lap. He sensed something near him, a displacement of the air. But it was the voice that got his attention.

"Hey, what's that?" it said.

Roland opened his eyes and brought his head up. Man, he was feeling skeezy. He shook off the buzz and looked around. Then he wet his pants for the second time in one week.

"Motherfucker!" he yelled.

Sitting across from him was the male creature.

"Frogasaur! Frogasaur!" Roland yelled. His mind said, "run" but he was paralyzed with fear. His feet shuffled in a spastic version of running in place.

"Frog-a-what?" said the voice.

Roland squinted his eyes. He could swear the words came from the frogasaur, but he didn't think its mouth moved. Maybe a little.

"You're the frogasaur," Roland said. "Don't eat me!"

"Not in the mood at the moment," the creature said. "What's that shit in your lap?"

Roland looked down at the meth pipe.

"Yeah, that. I saw you inhaling it."

"This? This is some prime product," Roland said. He was confused. Was he having a conversation with this thing? It sat on its haunches. He could plainly see the arms and long fingers with claws on them. A flash of memory coursed through his brain and he remembered the long tongue it had used to catch squirrels.

"Can I try some?"

"Really?" Roland said.

"Hell, yeah," said the creature.

Roland handed the pipe to the creature. It grabbed it with surprising finesse for something so large. Even sitting down, the creature was 15 feet tall. It held the pipe up and inhaled the toxic meth smoke.

Roland watched for a moment as the thing's huge eyes widened and then closed. A few seconds later, it opened them.

"That's fucking amazing," the creature said.

Roland was pretty sure he was hallucinating. It was kind of like an acid trip, which he had taken on numerous occasions. Bad 'shrooms sometimes had the same effect. But still, the damn thing looked real. And he could smell it. Or maybe that was himself.

Roland smiled. "Take another hit," he said. The creature obliged.

"Why'd you call me frogasaur?" the creature said.

Roland took the pipe back and took a hit. "You look like a frog dinosaur," he said.

"The name's 'Gaston,'" it said.

Roland sat up. "Your fucking name is 'Gaston?' That was my great uncle's name."

The creature nodded. "Yeah, well, nobody ever told me my real name. I heard one of your kind use that name many years ago, and I decided to use it for myself."

Roland laughed. "Dude, you don't look Cajun."

"Maybe, but I've eaten enough of them," the creature said. It laughed, or what Roland thought was a laugh. It was a deep baritone, and its wide mouth opened so he could see the plentiful teeth.

Roland also thought that was immensely funny. When he stopped laughing, he said, "You're not from around here, are you?"

"What was your first clue?" the creature said.

Roland smiled. "I mean, no one's ever seen you before. You can't be native to the swamp."

"No. I'm an immigrant. And not of my own choosing. Some assholes dropped me and my friend here a long, long time ago."

"Friend? There's another one like you?" Roland rubbed his eyes, but the creature was still there.

"Female. We're kind of a couple, but we haven't seen each other in a while. We're about to hook up, and it can't happen soon enough. I need to get laid in a bad way."

"I hear that," Roland said. "I could use some action myself." He watched as the creature nodded his understanding. Man, his mouth was huge. His head did kind of resemble a toad frog. Skin was different, though. The nose was wide, and instead of it being just a couple of holes like some snake, it actually had a shape to it. But it had four nostrils. No wonder it liked the meth. Probably got a major hit with that breathing apparatus.

"One more," it said, eyeing the pipe.

Roland passed it over and watched the thing inhale. If this was a hallucination, it was pretty fucking real.

"This shit kills my appetite," it said. He handed it back to Roland.

"Yeah, it does that, Gaston," Roland replied. This was excellent news, as far as Roland was concerned.

Gaston took a deep breath and looked around. Roland sensed he was pondering something. "You okay?" Roland asked.

"I'm cool. But I got a ways to go. Even though I'm not hungry, I should probably eat something now just in case I don't have time later."

This was terrible news as far as Roland was concerned. Urgently, he said, "Dude, you shouldn't eat anything for a while after hittin' this shit," he said, holding up the pipe. "Might make you sick. You might puke or something." Roland had no scientific proof of this theory, and he had no personal history of such a thing, but at the moment, he was selling it like his life depended on it. Which it did.

"Really?" Gaston said. "I felt like crap earlier. Don't want to go there again. If you say so. I'll wait a bit."

"Good idea," a relieved Roland said. "Where ya headed?" He thought it a good idea if Gaston left. A really good idea.

The creature pointed to his left. "That way. She's back that way somewhere. I can smell her now."

Roland looked that way. "Oh, okay. Good luck with that."

The creature stood up to its full 20-foot height. Roland let out a small groan as he looked up at the thing. Shit, it was big. "Alright, I'm outta here," Gaston said. He walked towards the street on two legs, and then switched to four as he crossed it, headed into a marsh and into the bayou.

Roland remained in the chair. He shook violently. That sense of skeeziness had returned. He needed some more shit. But those asshole gangbangers would be in town soon, and he had to go get the stuff from its hiding place. Okay, one more hit.

Chapter 19:
"Miss Nettie's Cow"

Lexie held the belt buckle out for Felice Guidry to look at. The two sat in a couple of cypress chairs out back of Felice's house, under a young live oak. Felice put her coffee cup down next to Lexie's on a small wooden table. She took the shiny metal in her hand and examined it closely. Lexie watched as Felice's lip trembled slightly, and a single tear escaped from her eye and rolled down her cheek.

Felice nodded once. "Yes, it's Floyd's. He wore it that day. Got it last year when we went to Houston for the rodeo. We go every year with a few other couples, stay at a nice hotel. You know, paint the town and all that."

"I'm sorry, Felice," Lexie said. "You can keep it if you want to." She thought a moment about some of her dearly departed husband's things. They were gone from her house within a day after she killed him.

"Where'd you find it?" she said.

"Cameron DeSelle found it…while fishing. He gave it to me. For some reason, I felt it was probably your husband's."

"Thanks, Sweetie," Felice said, and wiped her eye again. "That man caused me some grief, but he loved me, and I loved him."

"Grief?"

"Honey, I know your history, so I don't have to tell you about men. You meet one guy, you fall in love with another and you marry a third. 'Cept it's all the same man. You gotta love all three, including the third."

Lexie was pretty sure she loved the first and the second. The third was another story.

"That Floyd was a handsome man. Looked 10 years younger than he was. When I met him, he had his pick of any woman in the parish. But he fell for me."

Lexie smiled. "Felice, from what I've been told, you were smokin' hot yourself, and you're pretty smokin' hot now." Lexie wasn't lying. The woman looked a lot younger than she was, too. Dark hair, probably with the help of a bottle, dark eyes, smooth creamy skin, with just a hint of some crow's feet around the eyes. Her French bloodline was showing through. Lexie was sure Felice wouldn't be a widow for long.

"Nice of you to say, Lexie," she said, and brushed her hair back. "I'll probably have to bring my game up a bit now, don't you think?" She laughed a bit, and Lexie thought she was even more beautiful because of it.

Lexie knew just to let Felice talk.

"He cheated on me," Felice continued. "A lot. It's weird, but I don't think the word 'cheated' is right. That sounds mean and harmful. Floyd was never mean to me, never laid a hand on me." She eyed Lexie for a moment. "And he didn't sleep around because he was mad at me. Or because I didn't screw him enough. Let me tell you, that man had an appetite, if you know what I mean. And I ain't braggin', but I'd give as good as I'd get. That boy was wore out after I was done with him. And we got after it pretty good. He needed that Viagra, not because he couldn't get it up, but because I wanted it up a lot longer."

Lexie felt her cheek flush a bit. *Awkward conversation.*

"So he fucked around, so what?" Felice said. "He just liked some variety every now and then. He didn't love them. He loved *me*," she continued, and tapped her chest with her finger. "I can forgive a man for that, long as he comes home and takes care of business."

"Did you know any of...Floyd's women?" Lexie asked. She never knew if her husband was a philanderer. Probably was, but she was too focused on his violence to pay it any mind. Asshole.

"Some," Felice said. "A few of the ladies at church," she said. "I'll hold on the names," she said, and winked at Lexie. "Father Mike knows 'em, though. You'll see 'em lined up at the confessional. They keep Father busy with that, for sure. Floyd might've done it with that Carla Fontenelli, but every woman in the parish says that. Which probably means he didn't. That girl needs to park that thing somewhere, though."

Lexie agreed. She thought back to a few days ago when she found Carla at Fort St. Jesus Bait and Tackle, sitting there having lunch with Cam. She had felt a twinge of jealousy.

Felice put her index finger to her chin and looked up. "I think the latest was a little young hottie waitress he was banging. I never caught him, but he was eating a lot at that diner up in Henderson. Apparently he was having a lot of dessert with his eggs and bacon, if you know what I mean. And a couple of my spies told me they'd seen the two of them in Floyd's truck."

Lexie sat up. "Did you know her name? Was it M'Lou Marchand by any chance?"

Felice thought a second and said, "Don't know her name, but I heard she was young and pretty. Why?"

Lexie explained about the girl's disappearance. "Did they have a little spot they'd meet?"

"Who knows?" Felice said. "I'm sure they shacked up in some motel somewhere. Probably had some fun in the truck, I guess."

Lexie asked, "You think he ever gave her a ride in his boat? Took her out there with him?"

"Gator hunting?" Felice said. "Shit, that'd be a first. Come to think of it, that would be a great place to fool around. Quiet, secluded. He'd have to sneak her out there without anyone seeing them at the dock. But Floyd was quite the sneaker."

Lexie let that roll around her head for a few seconds. Could it be that what got Floyd had also gotten M'Lou? There was no evidence anyone else had been in the boat with Floyd. At least, she didn't think so. Shit, something ate *two* people and four alligators in one sitting? She thought of the huge pile of shit Cam and Troy had found, a pile that contained Floyd's belt buckle and presumably random pieces of undigested Floyd. She looked at the buckle that now rested in Felice's lap. What kind of stomach had that been in?

"Felice, did they return Floyd's stuff to you yet? Stuff that was in his boat or truck?"

"No. I figured your people still had all that. They will return it, right?"

"Once the full autopsy report is done and an official cause of death is determined." She was pretty sure there would never be anything official about Floyd's cause of death.

"What about...the body?" Felice said.

Shit, Lexie thought. She had forgotten about that. "Coroner already released it. Somebody just needs to let the funeral home know and they'll take care of the rest. I'll try to be at the wake tonight, but with the storm coming, I don't know if I'll have time."

Felice looked down at the buckle. "I understand."

"You going to stay through the storm?" Lexie asked. She gave the home a once over. It looked pretty solid, but it *was* a double-wide, just the same. The term *mobile home* took on a different meaning in a category three hurricane. With winds that high, everything was going to be mobile.

"Going over to stay with my sister in Hammond," she said. "Probably get up and go Saturday morning. She and her husband will be here tonight. The funeral mass and cemetery's gonna have to wait till Monday, maybe later, depending on the damage."

Lexie nodded her understanding. "He'll be fine at the funeral home," she said. "Some of the highest ground we've got. Pretty solid, too."

Felice smiled and let out a short little laugh. "I wouldn't worry about him," she said. "For once, I'll really know where he'll be overnight."

Cam held the gray piece of four-by-eight plywood up to one of the windows that constituted the front wall of Fort St. Jesus Bait and Tackle. Two eyelets had been screwed into the top of the wood, and he hung it vertically on two matching hooks above the window. The sheet of plywood covered the window completely.

He stepped back for a better look. Although the wood was a little warped with age, it was still solid. Young Zach, his helper, held a power drill in his hand and examined the wood.

"Looks good, Cam. Step back," he said. The teenager began to screw the wood in place.

Cam went around the side of the building for another piece of the plywood. He and his dad kept the plywood in a shack out back, pre-drilled, with eyelets already on it, ready anytime a nasty hurricane blew in. To date, he had used the wood at least four times.

His cell phone rang and vibrated in his pocket. He pulled it out and looked at the screen image. It was a picture of Nettie Carson. Gray hair, dark brown skin and a big brilliant smile courtesy of some nice dentures. The old woman lived by herself on a small farm just outside of town.

"Hey, Miss Nettie, what's up?" he said into the phone.

"Cameron, it's Miss Nettie," she said.

He ignored the fact that he already had greeted her and smiled. "Hey. Miss Nettie," he said again. Her youngest son, Lincoln, had played defensive end on Cam's high school team. He had gotten a scholarship to the University of Houston, graduated and now was regional VP for an oil-field equipment supply company.

"Cameron, I need you to get out here," she said in her high, shrill, old woman voice.

"Okay, what's up?" She had five head of cattle, some dairy cows, two horses, various chickens and the proverbial old mule that didn't do much of anything. She was a good customer, although she usually paid him in eggs and a very good meal, which he was fine with.

"Cameron, sumpin got a holt of one of my cows," she said.

Cam took a deep breath. When something got a "holt" of something, it could mean many things. It could mean you had a cold, and it had gotten a hold of you. Or a spider bit you, which could also mean it had gotten a hold of you. It was just one of those wonderful southern expressions that made his world that much richer. Except, there was something in the way she said it that got his attention. "Got a hold how, Miss Nettie?" he said.

"Well now, Cameron, if I knew, I wouldn't be callin' you, would I? You should just probably run over here and take a look."

Cam looked at his watch. He had to get the Fort boarded up today. It would probably be raining in the morning, then downright apocalyptic by afternoon. And he had to get all of the animals out of his clinic and back home. Their owners would be coming by throughout the day.

He stuck his head around the corner. "Hey, Zach! I gotta run an errand. You cool?"

"Sure. You got me till about four."

"Okay, keep putting the boards up, and keep an eye out if anybody comes by the clinic. Call me on the cell if you need me."

Cam thanked the stars he had Zach around. The kid was responsible as hell for someone his age. And you never had to tell him twice to do something. He reminded himself to mention that to Zach's dad next time he saw him.

Cam went inside, grabbed his keys and woke Huey up from a nap he was enjoying on the floor behind the counter. The dog had been up most of the night whining and whimpering, pacing around the house. He'd checked the dog out but couldn't find anything wrong with him.

Huey followed Cam outside and jumped into the truck. Cam started it up and looked over at the dog. "You all right, brother?" he said.

Huey looked over at him with tired, bloodshot eyes. A slight wag of the tail said, *"I'm cool."*

Cam grabbed Huey's Zepellin CD and slipped it into the player. He found the track he thought Huey might like. The sounds of "Black Dog" burst through the speakers. Huey put his head out the window and away they went.

The sky was a solid overcast now, and there was a permanent breeze brushing the tops of the trees. Traffic was heavy, at least for a rural parish deep in the Louisiana bayous. Pickup trucks packed with household items were headed out of town, many pulling bass boats and other types of aquatic craft. Shopkeepers were boarding or taping up windows on their stores. There was a line four deep at Troy's gas pumps. *Good for Troy,* Cam thought. He caught a glimpse of him in one of his garage bays under an aging Ford Taurus. He looked like he was in a hurry.

Cam tapped the top of his steering wheel to the blazing guitar riffs of Led Zeppelin. Huey seemed fascinated by all the activity around town. The dog would see someone he recognized, either human or canine, and wag his tail in delight.

Once through town, Cam hung a right off the main highway and drove another few miles down a crappy parish road out to Nettie's little farm. There wasn't much back here, and Cam worried about the old woman who lived alone. Her husband, William, had died about 10 years ago.

He pulled the truck into a gravel turnaround in front of a neat three-bedroom ranch home. It had 1959 architecture written all over it. Low, sprawling design. High windows. Red brick. A two-car open garage looked like a gaping mouth off to the right side of the home. An old brown Thunderbird was parked inside. It had to be 20 years old, and surely only had about 10,000 miles on it.

Nettie came out the front and waved. She was tall, close to five-ten, Cam guessed. Her son, the defensive lineman, had taken from her side of the family. He ended up around six-five, 260. Cam got out and Huey bounded out with him.

"Come here, let me see you," she said, arms out. Cam smiled and walked up to the old woman. She gave him a surprisingly strong hug. She reached up and put both hands on his face. "Well, you been eatin', at least," she said. "Look good, too. You got a girl yet? I am available, you know." She gave him a sly wink.

"Miss Nettie, that's a powerful offer, but you know I don't date customers."

"Well, you could make an exception. Come on, I'll show you my little problem."

Rather than walking into the house, she led him and Huey around the side of the home. A hundred yards back was a small barn, shed and pens for some of the animals. The smell of cattle dung and chicken shit hung heavy in the air. The damp east wind helped the fragrance along.

Nettie opened a gate and led Cam and Huey into a pasture. Off to the left, huddled in a corner, were a few cows. Cam noticed their tails were moving this way and that. They were agitated. To the right, under a large pecan tree, he could see a few turkey buzzards pecking at something in the grass.

"Get outta there, ya nasty little bastards!" Nettie yelled. She waved her arms. The buzzards looked her way, unafraid. They took a few more bites, looked up and flapped away on heavy wings.

Cam had a sinking feeling of dread. He thought Huey did, too, since the dog hung back a little and whimpered.

"Whatcha make of that?" Nettie said, pointing to the ground.

Cam looked at what had one time been a cow. There wasn't much left. Most of the head, a flank, a couple of hooves. The ground was matted with dried blood. Whatever "got a holt" of the animal did it here. Caught it and ate it where it stood.

"Damn," was all Cam said. "How long has the carcass been out here?"

"Found it this morning," she said.

"So it looked like this? Other animals been eating on it? Coyotes, wild dogs or wild hogs?"

"Nope," she replied. "It's pretty fresh. Might've happened just before dawn."

Cam walked around the carnage and took a closer look at the head. "And you didn't hear anything?"

Nettie folded her thin arms and shook her head. "Nothing. Slept like a baby. Hearing's not as good as it used to be, but still, you'd have thought I would have heard something."

Cam didn't do many necropsies, but if he had time, this would have been a good one to do. Something had bit the hell out of this cow and ate most of it. He stood up and looked around. The wind changed directions and he caught a familiar stench in the air. Not the cow. It was more like the giant pile of shit he had seen before. And there was something else, too. A slight chemical odor that was noxious and hard to place.

"What the hell did this, Cameron?" Nettie said.

"I honestly don't know, Miss Nettie." Which was kind of the truth. "But you need to stay in the house, not wander too far. You staying for the storm?"

"Yeah, but Lincoln's driving over to ride it out with me."

"Good," Cam said.

Nettie looked at the mess. "Whatever it is, it sure as hell is big."

Cam had squatted down on his haunches and looked at the ground. "Yes, m'am, it is. Very big."

There, on the ground in the soft earth, was a huge imprint of a clawed paw print. It was like nothing Cam had ever seen.

"Holy shit," he muttered under his breath.

Chapter 20:
"Roland's Summer Home"

The humid September air lay over New Orleans' Lower Ninth Ward like a giant piece of plastic sheeting. The heat and moisture were trapped low to the ground, with no wind to move the moldy smell that permeated the area situated just east of downtown. There was a sheen of condensation on the streets, the sidewalks and just about anything that wasn't protected from the sky. It hadn't rained. Yet. But everyone in the Crescent City knew a storm was coming without having to turn on the weather station.

The tough Lower Ninth Ward was now the official poster child of hurricane awareness. Wind. Water. Devastation. Years after Katrina, the area had been rebuilt, to an extent. But you didn't have to look far to see the scars on the homes and buildings, and the mental scars on the faces. People had died here. And badly. The area had been impoverished before the storm. It still was. There remained many vacant lots that held only a slab of concrete where a home had been, now overgrown with weeds.

Trey "Tree" Taylor stood behind his big, black Town Car that was parked in a narrow alleyway between two abandoned buildings off of St. Claude Avenue. He looked down into the open trunk as his driver, Raymond, lifted up the floor where the spare tire should have been. Now it was a secret compartment that held a different kind of spare.

"Fully stocked, Tree," Raymond said, and grinned at his boss. Inside were assorted pistols, sawed-off shotguns and automatic rifles, plus spare clips of ammunition.

The big man just nodded. He unconsciously reached behind his back and felt under his shirt for the pistol he always kept there.

"Cool," he said. "Close it up and let's get the hell out of here." He looked at his watch. "What ya think? Two hours over there, two back?"

Raymond squinted and did some calculations. "Prolly more, Tree." Gotta get through traffic here and in Baton Rouge first before we even get to the Basin."

Tree frowned. "Alright, get the crew and let's roll. You talk to that cracker?"

"Yeah, got directions and all. I know where to meet him."

"Got the cash?"

"Under the guns," Raymond said.

"Okay. Let's get this over with. Got that storm movin' in. Wanna be back before then."

"Nuthin' to it, Tree," Raymond said. "Gonna miss us a bit, anyway. We'll be in and out of there before that."

Tree looked around and up at the overcast sky. "Let's just get that shit. I can turn it in a week and we can cash in pretty good. Bank account's a little lean."

"Should be a breeze, Tree," Raymond said and gave his boss another sycophantic grin.

Cam got back to the Fort in time to see Zach put up the last sheet of plywood. *Damn, that kid was good.* Cam decided he'd throw in a little spot bonus for him before the day was out.

"I changed the street sign, too," Zach said, and pointed to the portable yellow sign that sat perpendicular to the street. In black letters, it said, *"Still open. Stock up. Head out."*

"Good thinking, buddy," Cam said, and slapped Zach on the back. Cam was thinking the whole town needed to board up and stay boarded up. Hurricane Tammy would come and be gone, but something very big and nasty was running around that might stick around.

"Anybody come get their pets?" Cam said.

"Yep, I checked 'em out. The hotel is vacant."

Cam looked around and thought a moment. "Okay, check that box," he said. "How's the ice situation?"

"Been selling pretty good, but we still have half a load."

"It'll do," Cam said. "No way I can get another delivery before tomorrow. Ice is gold right now."

"Where you gonna ride out the storm?" Zach said.

"Probably right here. Me and Huey will stay open as long as we can, then hole up inside. Got everything I need to eat and drink in there."

"Want me to fill up the ginny?"

"Yeah, good idea. I think it just needs to be topped off."

"I'm on it," Zach said and gave Cam a salute. He walked off to get some gas cans Cam had stored out back.

A horn blew from behind Cam out on the street. He turned to see Lexie in her patrol car. She pulled in and got out. Huey wagged his tail and went right for her. *The dog had good taste,* Cam thought.

"Deputy," he said.

"Got 'er boarded up already, huh?" Lexie said, surveying the front of the store. "You win the Deputy Lexie Take-Care-of-Your-Property-Before-The-Shit-Hits-The-Fan Award."

Cam smiled. "What do I get?"

"I don't know. I'll think of something."

Cam was thinking of something, too. There was probably some discrepancy between what she was thinking and what he was thinking. Or maybe not, he hoped.

"You make it out to Felice Guidry's?"

Lexie nodded. "Yep. The buckle's Floyd's. Kind of tough to give her that, knowing where it had been."

"You didn't tell her, did you?"

"No, no. Just told her you found it while fishing. Jeez."

"Okay, good."

Lexie stepped a little closer to Cam. "You know if Floyd was messing around with a waitress?"

He shook his head. "Really didn't know the guy that well," Cam said. "Why?"

Lexie explained the situation with M'Lou Marchand.

Cam nodded throughout. "I think I know who that is. I've eaten at that diner before. Cute girl."

"Gone girl," Lexie said. "Got a bad feeling, too. She might have been with Floyd when...you know."

Cam stared at her hard. "In the boat? Was there any evidence of that?"

"Not that I know of. I'm gonna check it out again, though." She glanced at her watch, then up at the sky. "What's the word on the storm?"

"About to go to a three, I heard," he said. "Nasty. Some think it won't be that bad at landfall. Still."

"Whatever it is, it's gonna ruin my weekend plans."

"One other thing to put into the hopper," Cam said. "Something ate one of Miss Nettie's cows. Just got back looking at it."

"What kind of 'ate' are you talking about," she said.

"The worst kind. One sitting, couple of bites, not much left."

"Oh shit," Lexie said. "Like the kayaker thing?"

"Sounds like it. But it can't be the same one. Too far away. Unless it flies."

Lexie grimaced. "Flies? Let's just assume there's more than one. Can't get my head around something like that flying around."

"Right," Cam said. He pulled out his phone and selected a picture. "Check this out. It left a track."

Lexie took the phone and stared at the image. It was almost like a giant handprint. Maybe two feet long, a foot wide. There was a clear pad, long fingers, indentations where there appeared to be claws. The thumb looked to be opposable, like a primate's. "Is that a credit card next to it?"

Cam nodded his head. "Yeah, so you can see some scale and size."

"This was around the cow?"

"That one and more. Look how deep those tracks are. The ground was soft, but not wet. Whatever that thing is, it's heavy."

"Hippo," Lexie said.

"Uh huh," replied Cam. "Not."

"I don't even know how to report this," Lexie said. "A hoax?"

"Doubtful. We got two guys who were on the wrong end of lunch. One with witnesses."

Lexie rubbed her hand through her head. "Man, now we got this to worry about. According to the sheriff, the official line is 'it's unexplainable until it's explainable.' Or something like that." Lexie sighed. "Okay, I'll just keep my eyes open."

"You do that," Cam said.

"Yeah." She kicked the gravel-and-oyster-shell ground with her feet. "Hey, I'm gonna check out Roland's little spot. Think you can show me exactly where it is?"

"Sure? Am I still a deputy?"

"I'd say so. You found the place, you need to show me."

"All right, then," Cam said.

Cam left the Fort in the capable hands of Zach, who was on his way to a single-day record for cash bonuses. He and Huey hopped in his truck and pulled ahead of Lexie's patrol car. Traffic in town was still pretty steady. By tomorrow morning, the streets would be empty and so would most of the houses. They headed east, then north on the parish road that paralleled the river. Cam called up from his memory the gravel track he had seen on Google maps on his phone. There was an abandoned wellhead back in there, and it wasn't far from the bayou itself.

They drove for 20 minutes along the winding road. There was some traffic, more than usual at least, as people did what they had to do before the arrival of a hurricane. Cam kept one eye on the road, the other off to his left to see if he could spot the gravel track.

He saw it, but was going too fast and passed it. "Shit," he said. The entrance was already overgrown. Easy to miss. He hit the brakes, Lexie close behind. Cam stuck his hand out the window indicating the entrance was behind him. He saw Lexie put it in reverse and followed her to the entrance.

She stuck her head out the window. "Can we get back there with these or should we walk?"

Cam answered with a "follow me" wave and turned into the track. Once away from the road, the gravel opened up more and there was less overgrowth. The road was high, built to take big drilling equipment and trucks, so it sat above the marshy ground on either side. It winded its way for about a third of a mile until it ended in a big wide turnaround. The old gas head was capped off and surrounded by a high chain link fence.

Lexie got out and walked over to Cam's truck. "You sure this is it?"

He was staring down at his iPhone, looking at the Google map he had called up yesterday. "Yeah, the slough looks like it's about 50 yards that way."

Lexie looked off to her left, but didn't see a clear path through the woods. "Okay, deputy, let's go," she said.

Cam and Huey got out of the truck. Huey stopped a moment and put his nose into the air. The steady breeze out of the east carried local smells, but also things from far away.

But he didn't get a whiff of the creature for some reason. That got a tail wag, but was still a bit worrisome to the big dog.

"C'mon, Huey," Cam said and patted his thigh.

He and Lexie walked to the tree line and searched for a way into the underbrush. They split up to save time. He kept looking over at her, admiring her thoroughness. And her ass. She looked great, even in her uniform of black pants and grey shirt. He figured her pants were a little tight for regulations, but he wouldn't complain to the sheriff.

"Over here," she said.

Cam and Huey walked over to her.

"See? Someone's been through here," she said. "Look at the grass pressed down, and that broken palmetto. Follow me."

Lexie walked into the swamp and Cam and Huey followed. Once into the trees, the path was clearer. They followed it for about 20 yards until it forked.

"Which way?" Lexie said. A gust of wind, stronger than the steady breeze, whistled through the tops of the tupelo and cypress.

Cam looked down at both paths. Huey even stuck his nose down, trying to ID whatever came through here last. "Left," he said. "Footprints." He pointed to obvious imprints of tennis shoes.

"Nice," Lexie said and smiled. "Walk around them. Crime scene guys might want to come back and take casts of them."

Cam looked up at the gray overcast, which seemed to be darker than earlier in the day. "Doubtful. We'll probably get 10 inches of rain in the next couple of days. This'll be underwater."

"Crap," she said. "You're right." She took out her phone and snapped some pictures of the ground and close ups of the tennis shoe tracks.

"After you," Cam said.

Lexie continued down the path, which began to slope downhill. They came around a large pin oak and stopped.

"And there she is," Cam said. They looked down at the narrow slough, which was about 20 feet across. The brown water was still, covered by a solid canopy of overhanging willows and vines. The waterway ended to their left, and continued out to the bayou towards the right, too far to see. Cam knew that's where Roland had bent the old willow down to create some camouflage at the entrance.

"What's that?" Lexie said.

Cam had missed it. A small wooden shack sat to the right. It was nearly invisible, its weathered brown-and-gray wood perfectly blended into the environment. Whoever built it didn't know a thing about carpentry. The low-pitched roof was slanted and leaning. There were gaps in the sides. It reminded Cam of something he and Troy had built behind his house when they were kids.

"My guess is it's Roland's summer home," Cam said. "Let's take a look."

Lexie nodded, and Cam saw her unsnap her holster cover so she could pull her gun out if necessary. *Badass. Hot badass.*

Thirty yards away, through the thick foliage, Roland Avant watched. "Motherfucker," he muttered under his breath.

Chapter 21:
"Swamp Boogie"

"Smells like piss around here," Cam said. "Human."

"Yeah," Lexie said. She moved slowly toward the shack. Although there were cracks in the walls, she couldn't tell if anyone was inside. She pulled out her gun. "Stay back."

Cam had never seen her draw her weapon. She held it in two hands, pointed toward the ground. He noticed she thumbed the safety off. She was going in hot. *Hell, yeah, she was.*

He looked over at Huey. The dog had his ears up and tail down, but looked curious rather than locked onto a hidden Roland. Good sign that no one was home.

Lexie got to the door of the shack. "Crap." A padlock held the thing closed.

"Hmmm, wonder why anyone would padlock a piece-of-shit place like this?" Cam said. He walked to the side of the shack and looked at the construction of the wall. He reached up, grabbed a plank and pulled hard. The board squeaked loudly as nails were wrenched. Cam pulled again and the board came loose. He took a quick peek inside. "Empty," he said. He grabbed another plank and pulled it off until they had easy access to the shack's interior.

"What a dumbass," Lexie said. "He puts a padlock on the place but it's built like a four-year-old did it."

"That's our boy," Cam said with a smile.

Lexie pulled her flashlight from her belt, flicked it on, and stepped inside. It was dank and smelled of body odor and chemicals. Cam followed her in. He used the bright display of his phone to add to her flashlight.

The shack was barely 10 feet by 10 feet, with a planked floor that was about as level as a big washboard. It was strewn with candy-bar wrappers and assorted other paper trash. A couple of yellow-and-white lawn chairs were folded up against one wall. Along another wall was a crude wooden table that leaned precariously to the left. On the floor along the wall to the right were two large black garbage bags, full of something.

Lexie looked at Cam. "That's either garbage or gold," she said. She opened one bag and looked inside. "Gold."

He looked closer. The bag was filled with gallon-sized Ziplock bags packed with a white-powdery substance. He reached in to grab one.

"Hey! No, no," Lexie ordered. "Put these on." She handed him a pair of surgical rubber gloves she had pulled from her pocket and put on a pair herself.

Cam snapped on the gloves, held them up and wiggled his fingers like he was going to stick his finger up somebody's ass. Lexie just shook her head. "Your time will come," she said.

He reached in and pulled one of the bags out. On closer inspection, the white stuff looked more crystalline and rock-like.

"That would be your Grade-A meth," Lexie said. "Jackpot."

"Man, that shithead has been cooking up a storm," Cam said. "This whole bag is filled with this stuff."

Lexie looked in the other bag. "Same thing over here. Oops. Wait a minute," she said. She pulled out another plastic-covered thing, except this one looked like a white brick. "This isn't meth. Looks like booger sugar. Son of a bitch."

"Where'd that asshole get that?" Cam said.

"Who knows, but there's a shitload of street value here," Lexie said.

"Congratulations, deputy," Cam said. "Looks like your career just took a big leap."

She nodded with a sly smile. "Hells yeah," she said and put her hand up for a fist bump. "Thanks to my assistant deputy."

"Always a pleasure," he said. "What now?"

"Gotta get this shit out of here, call it in."

"Yeah," he said. "And find Roland."

Roland Avant rubbed his face and head vigorously, like he was trying to get a bunch of tiny bugs off of himself because they were biting the hell out of him. Truth was, he thought there *were* a bunch of weird spiders all over him. He'd seen them early this morning, not long after Gaston left his trailer. The frogasaur *had* been there, right. He was pretty sure.

Fuck, now this!

That fucking Hot Ass Lexie Smith and Dee-Sale just found his shit. They were in the shack now, probably jumping with joy over what they had found. And man, was he feeling super skeezy now. Like he wanted to jump out of his skin.

He'd hit the pipe big-time before coming out here in his bass boat. That's where he sat now, just near the bank where the slough cut out from the bayou. He was about to pull in when he saw Lexie and Cam and Huey walk up on the shack. Two minutes earlier, he would have been right there.

Motherfucker! He had to think. Those gangbangers were on their way from New Orleans to pick up the stuff and pay him in some much-needed cash. Hell, he'd already reserved a suite at Harrah's. What was he supposed to tell them? The shit got stolen by the cops? He wasn't sure, or maybe he was, that he'd get the shit kicked out of him. Probably worse. Those dudes sounded like death on wheels. They would probably think he'd found a better deal with another buyer and cut them out.

Roland lifted up his stained green T-shirt and looked at the old revolver he had stuck in the waistband of his filthy jeans. He fingered the handle and looked back toward the shack. Man, nobody would hear the shots way back up in here. He could just sneak up on them while they were in the shack and...leave the bodies there. It would be weeks before anybody would find them, if then. He'd be long gone to New Orleans, deep into his own little witness protection program in the Big Sleazy. The cops would probably pin it on him. Probably fingerprints all over that shack, but what the hell. He didn't have any choice.

He pulled the pistol out and popped it open. The cylinder was full. He clicked it back into place and took the safety off. The boat wobbled a bit as he eased toward the bow and onto the bank. He'd have to be really quiet. Lexie and Cam wouldn't hear him, but the dog would. Have to shoot the dog, too, he thought. Whatever.

He was probably 20 yards from the shack. The going was slow, both because of his attempt at stealth and the tangle of briars, vines and palmetto. At least the ground was soft, so his footsteps wouldn't be heard.

Roland wondered which one of them he should shoot first. Usually you'd shoot the guy. More dangerous. Best to get him out the way. But Lexie had already blown her husband away. And she was a cop. She would definitely have a gun. He didn't know if Dee-Sale had one.

So it'd be Lexie.

But Dee-Sale was a big dude.

And the dog might bite him.

Shit, he needed a grenade. That would be pretty cool.

Aw, hell. He'd just stick the gun in there and start blasting away.

He could hear them talking now. They were excited. They were about to be *really* excited. Roland smiled at that. He almost laughed out loud.

Man, he was like a fucking ninja. He made it to the shack and eased around the side with the door. It was still padlocked. How the hell did they get in there? He eased around the next corner and saw the wall planks on the ground and a gaping hole in the side of his little abode.

This was gonna be a breeze. He was about to graduate into the elite club of stone-cold killers.

Lexie put the brick back into the bag. She looked around for anything else they might have missed. "Don't see any trap doors or anything?"

Cam smiled. "That would be one flooded basement."

"Yeah, guess so. That was a joke, you know."

"Right. But if any dumbass would try to dig a basement in a swamp, it would be Roland."

Lexie laughed at that one.

Cam noticed Huey wasn't paying attention anymore. The dog's ears were back up and his head was cocked to the left. He heard the low growl in the Lab's throat. Cam thought of big things with big feet and sharp claws. He thought of eaten gator hunters and swallowed-whole kayakers. He reached over and touched Lexie's arm.

"What?" she said.

He pointed down at Huey and put his index finger to his lips.

She looked around, her hands tight around her pistol. Huey barked. It was a warning bark. Cam knew it well. The sound was almost painful in the small enclosure.

Then the light changed. Something moved outside, and the shadow danced across the cracks in the wood.

Cam and Lexie turned that way. Huey let out a series of barks that said, "Something bad is out there."

Lexie stuck her head and torso out of the hole in the wall and looked to her right. Roland was to her left, five feet away, gun up and pointed right at her.

Huey now had locked onto Roland from the inside of the shack. The animal's acute hearing, smell and low-light vision had picked up his shape through a few cracks in the ancient wood planking. Huey jumped up on his hind legs and put his big front paws on the wall and simultaneously let out a series of aggressive barks. The dog's weight made the flimsy shack rattle and shake.

Just as Roland was about the fire, the wall he was leaning on shook violently, and the dog's bark scared the shit out of him. His finger continued its motion on the trigger, his drug-addled brain unable to stop the signal it had sent just nanoseconds earlier. The gun fired.

Chapter 22:
"Good Day for the Resume"

Lexie heard the commotion to her left, but she didn't turn quickly enough. Roland's gun shattered the quiet of the bayou with a loud pop. His round went right into the mud two feet in front of Lexie. She turned to see Roland's crazed face surrounded by a blue haze of smoke from his pistol, now pointed down at the ground.

Lexie's instincts kicked in and she swung her gun around toward Roland and fired. The bullet grazed the top of his left shoulder and he let out a scream.

She ducked back into the shack and fell backward onto her rump. "Fucking Roland!" she yelled. "Get down!"

Cam squatted down and tried to see Roland through the walls. He didn't have to. Huey still had his big paws up on the wall and was barking like a maniac. Roland must have moved, because Huey walked farther down the wall.

Lexie recovered and got back up, headed out the hole in the wall. She led with her pistol. "That motherfucker," she said through gritted teeth.

"I think he's moving," Cam said. He felt naked without a gun, completely helpless. Okay, maybe not. He had one-pissed-off deputy with a cute ass there to defend him and his dog.

They both heard a loud crash and a splash of water. In the distance, they heard Roland say, "Fuck." Then more noise as something heavy moved quickly through the underbrush.

Cam was about to say something, but Lexie was already out the side of the shack, followed by a barking Huey. He jumped out with them.

"Freeze, asshole!" Lexie shouted. She had her gun pointed in the distance. Cam could see Roland crabwalking through the thick brush, making his way toward the bayou. Lexie squeezed off a round. The bullet hit a sapling and the little tree trunk exploded. Roland didn't stop.

"He's got a boat back there, I bet," Cam said. They lost Roland in the thick vegetation, and moments later heard the wet, throaty sound of a small outboard kick in. In a flash, Roland was gone.

Lexie stood there, her breaths quick and shallow, listening as the boat's sound faded into the distance.

"You okay?" Cam said.

She holstered her pistol and took a deep breath. "Fucker shot at me," she said. "Piece of shit."

"Well, at least we got the goods," Cam said.

"Yeah, but I want that little fucker," Lexie said. She turned to face Cam and was about to say something, but it caught in her throat.

Cam noticed her eyes were watering up. She took a step toward him, and was still trying to say something. Finally, she put her head down and Cam realized what was happening. Without thinking, he put his arms around her and she put her head on his chest. She made a couple of deep, gulping sobs and her whole body shook.

"It's okay, it's okay," he said and rubbed her back. "You did good. It's all right." She didn't respond, and continued to sniffle and shake. He decided he better just be quiet. He remembered something his father had told him about women. Something like, "When they're upset, just shut the fuck up and wait."

Lexie did a huge sniffle and lifted her head. "Awww, fuck," she said, more embarrassed than upset now. She wiped her eyes. "If you tell anyone I just lost it, I swear, I'll shoot you."

"Deal," he said. He still had his arms around her. It felt incredibly good.

"I'm sorry," she said. "Not very deputy-like."

"An adrenaline dump," he said.

"What?"

"Back in Iraq, after a firefight, or a near-miss from an IED, I saw guys shake like crazy for five minutes and cry. A big surge of adrenaline, then you come down off of that. Body's way of balancing out. Did it a couple of times myself."

She wiped her leaky nose. "I thought you just did vet shit, take care of the dogs?"

"Most of the time. A few times I went in on the big operations, with the human doctors, to do field triage, in case a dog got wounded in the field. Just like the regular soldiers. Couple of times it got very interesting."

"Oh, okay," she said. She was slowly getting her composure back.

Cam looked at her and wondered how she had handled the adrenaline dump after her husband came at her with a machete and she shot him dead. Best not to ask that question. He was enjoying the moment, arms still around her.

"Thanks," she said, and kissed him on the cheek. She gave him a hug, too.

"You're welcome. None of my buddies back in Iraq ever kissed me, though." He gave her his most dazzling smile.

"Lucky you," she said. Her liquid eyes had locked onto his, and they were still in an embrace. Seconds ticked by.

It was hard to tell who initiated what happened next. If they had asked Huey, who sat next to them, watching the whole thing, he would have said Cam went in first. But that was a dog. And he always voted for his master. A baseball fan would have said a tie goes to the runner, and that was pretty much what it was. Both Cam and Lexie leaned in, met half way, and locked lips right there in the swamp, next to Roland's summer home, moments after they had both been nearly killed. They melted into each other's arms, hands roaming, tongues probing, hearts pounding. After a few moments, they separated.

Lexie had a dreamy look on her face, but stared directly into Cam's eyes. "I could arrest you for assaulting an officer," she said in a breathy, husky voice.

"Hmmm," he said. "I was going to say the deputy used excessive force."

"You call that 'excessive force'? If you only knew."

Cam was left speechless at that one. A series of images flipped through his mind, each better than the last. They all involved various scenes of undress, handcuffs and the reading of his Miranda rights. He was pretty sure he was going to waive his rights to representation. He had no problem being roughed up by the arresting officer.

They still held each other, bodies pressed together. Her nightstick had turned and was now between them. His nightstick had also gotten in the way a bit.

"We'll have to get back to this later," she said.

"I'm planning on it."

"I gotta deal with this shit." She looked off in the direction Roland had run.

"Of course." He still had both of his hands on her ass.

For about 30 seconds Cam ran through a couple of scenarios in which both of them could have some spontaneously combustible sex right here in the swamp. The shack. The ground. His truck. He flipped through them all, ran the computer simulations in his head and pronounced all of them suitable. The truck was voted best, due to comfort and a distinct lack of ants and mosquitoes joining the party. Back here was more private, assuming Roland had already put some distance between them, but it was still a swamp. There was shit back here that could eat you—either slowly or very quickly. The clearing where the truck was parked was also fairly private as long as somebody didn't pull off the highway, or some oil company guy didn't decide it was a perfect day to check on a capped well. Cam wanted to lay some new pipe of his own.

She must have known what he was thinking. "I'm still *on* duty," she said.

It sounded almost like a question to Cam. *Crap.* "Okay, let's get out of here. They separated. She adjusted her night stick. He, his.

"Grab the bags," she ordered.

They went back into the shack, gathered up the big plastic garbage bags full of meth and coke and carried them back to her patrol car. While Cam put them in her trunk, she got on the radio and called the dogs on Roland. He heard some radio squawks, some excited chatter from a man with a slow drawl, probably the sheriff, and some official-sounding code numbers and words. *One-Adam-12 shit,* Cam thought.

When she got off the radio, he asked, "You taking this shit back to headquarters?"

She looked at her watch. "Eventually. Got some things to check out. Might try to get that way late this afternoon."

"You're just gonna leave it in your trunk?" Cam said.

"Got nowhere else to store it," she said. "It'll be fine."

"What about Roland?" Cam looked back toward the swamp.

"That's gonna be tricky, what with the storm coming," she said. "Most of the patrols are going to be busy with traffic and emergency stuff. Roland's getting a nice head start to wherever he's going."

"I say he's gonna hole up in that houseboat he's got hidden out there. Ride the storm out there," replied Cam.

"Good luck with that. Let the storm take care of him." She looked up at the overcast. The air was heavy with Gulf moisture. She could smell the salt water.

Cam stepped toward her and gave her a tender kiss. "Be careful. I've got to get the Fort battened down. Might run over to the church and see if Father Mike needs any help, too."

Lexie blushed a bit and smoothed her blonde hair back toward her ponytail. "You, too."

"Come by for supper," Cam said. "To the house. Last night there. Me and Troy'll probably spend tomorrow night at the Fort during the storm."

"Yeah. I'm probably going to be driving around tonight and tomorrow as long as I can, then hunker down at the house during the worst of it."

"Okay," he said. "Nice haul, deputy." He gestured toward her trunk. The one behind the car.

"Yeah, good day for the resume."

Cam and Huey got in the truck, Lexie in her patrol car, and they headed back down the gravel road to the highway. He followed her all the way back toward town, grinning ear to ear, jammin' to some more Zeppelin.

It had been a good morning, even though there'd been some gunplay and the potential of death. At any other time, he'd be shaking a bit, going through his own "adrenaline dump." But another hormone was racing through his body, one that trumped adrenaline any day: good old-fashioned testosterone.Probably some other thing, like endorphins, too. He was feeling pretty damn good.

He looked out on the bayou as the road ran parallel to it for a few miles. The surface was agitated a bit by the steady breeze, and the willows were turning their back to him, changing from one shade of green to another.

Huey had his head out the window, digging the music and the random fragrances of the swamp. Suddenly, he yelped. Cam thought a rock or a fat bug had hit the dog in the face. Huey jerked his head back into the cab of the truck and barked loudly. There were teeth involved, and he had his hackles up again. He jumped into the backseat of the truck and went from one window to the other.

"What's the matter, buddy?" Cam said. He turned down the music. "Smell something?"

Huey jumped back into the front seat and stared at his master. Cam called it the "Jedi Mind Trick," as if Huey were trying to telepathically tell him something important. Cam knew that if he were a dog, he'd know exactly what Huey was trying to say. Dogs relied on a number of things to communicate with each other. Eyes, teeth and tail were just a few.

Cam looked out on the bayou again. Something important was scratching at the back of his brain, trying to get inside. He felt a chill and a sudden moment of fear. The same kind of fear humans got when walking outside in the dark. It was primal and very real. The image of the large footprint in Miss Nettie's pasture flashed through his head.

And something else.

Chapter 23:
"Unidentified Eating Objects"

Cam pulled his truck in front of Fort St. Jesus Bait and Tackle. The small parking lot was crowded. He watched as a couple walked back to their car with bags and ice. Well, at least people didn't think he was closed, he thought, which is what the place looked like with all the windows boarded up.

He and Huey sat in the truck for a moment. Cam couldn't shake a feeling of anxiety and dread. But was it the storm? Roland? His concern for Lexie? Or that unknown thing lurking in the swamp, eating the locals? He knew he should be thinking about that more. But he was distracted by a lot of things. At the top of that list was Lexie, followed by the storm and crazy-shit Roland. The vet in him was really puzzled, though. Something weird was going on. Something had eaten a couple of guys, a bunch of gators, one unfortunate cow and who knew what else. It had laid a turd the size of a small house out in the swamp, too. No animal out there could do that, at least not one that had been catalogued by zoologists. Could it be there was an undiscovered species in the swamp? Cam was a realist, and knew that anything was possible. But it just didn't make sense. Something that big and hungry would have shown itself a long time ago. Why now?

It was all those things, but there was something else. He decided to not force it, just wait and let it come to him when it wanted to come to him. He and Huey climbed out and went inside. People were grabbing supplies off the shelf, mostly water, bread and what few can goods he stocked. Zach was behind the counter ringing up a few people. He gave Cam a wave, but stayed focused. The kid was probably relieved Cam was back to help.

He said hello to everyone in the store, and then went into the back to bring what little inventory he had out onto the shelves. There were a few cases of canned goods, about ten cases of bottled water and more batteries. Shit was going fast. He spent the next hour or so stocking shelves, helping customers and discreetly listening to see if anyone was talking about seeing something unusual in the area. The only topic of discussion was Hurricane Tammy.

He relieved Zach from behind the counter and let the kid grab some lunch in the back. Zach had turned on the little flat screen behind the counter to the Weather Channel, which was totally focused on the storm. Customers watched the latest updates as they came to the counter. There were frequent shots of some dumbass with a microphone standing on the beach at Grand Isle, getting his ass sandblasted by the approaching storm. The consensus was that the storm would pass just west of Alcide, which was bad for Alcide, not so bad for New Orleans and Baton Rouge.

Good times.

The Fort St. Jesus Catholic Church Men's Club, as they were unofficially known, had shown up at the parish office that morning to board up the facilities. They had found Father Mike already hard at work, putting plywood on windows, storing some exterior lawn furniture and otherwise getting ready for the impending meteorological apocalypse.

Joanie was inside, putting important paperwork in the safe and locking down anything in the office that might want to go airborne if the roof suddenly did the same. She had gotten permission to miss teaching her classes at the elementary school, which was going to be let out at noon anyway. Mike thought she looked pretty good in her shorts, hiking boots and tan canvas work shirt. She had her standard red kerchief on her head, to at least give a nod to her locked-away nun's habit.

Mike was also in full work-wear: jeans, blue flannel shirt and an LSU baseball cap. He directed the men to their tasks, which was pointless. They knew the drill already, but let Mike take command.

He looked up at the steeple rising above the small church. The morning overcast had been replaced with more-defined gray clouds that were moving quickly from east to west. The cross at the top of the steeple was framed nicely against the ominous sky. A white beacon of hope in the storm. Or so he hoped.

"Doubt it's gonna make it, Father," a voice said behind him. It was Joe Girard, a lean, gray local carpenter of 60. His steel-colored hair was tousled by the breeze.

"Well, if anyone would know, it would be you, Joe," Mike said. "You built the damn thing."

"Yeah, well. Even I can't beat a category-three hurricane. But I'll put another one up for you, no problem."

"Thanks," Mike said. "I've got a feeling she'll hold."

They both looked at the steeple in silence. Joe thinking about the odds of his craftsmanship beating the storm. Mike, the odds of his faith beating the storm.

A truck door slammed by the road. They both turned to see Cam walking over with Huey.

"Huey's here to help," Cam said. He gave Mike a handshake and Joe a nod.

"Good, we could use four more paws," Mike said, and scratched behind Huey's ear. The big dog wagged his tail and smiled.

Joe walked off to help the rest of the Men's Club.

"You seen Roland today?" Cam said. He also looked up at the steeple.

"No. He got himself into something?"

"You might say that. Took a shot at Lexie."

Mike stared hard at Cam. "No shit?"

Cam explained the morning events to Mike. "Don't think he's long for this world, Father," Cam continued. "You might want to get him prepped for the next life. He's gonna need it."

Mike rubbed his face. "Meth."

"Yeah. Rhymes with 'death,'" Cam replied.

"Where'd he go?"

"Probably hiding in the swamps. Gotta come out sometimes, if he survives the storm."

"Any more on the two deaths in the swamp—Floyd and that kayaker?" Mike asked.

"And Miss Nettie's cow," added Cam. He explained that one to him, and the tracks.

"Okay, that kind of creeps me out now," said Mike.

"Yeah. Got pictures, too." Cam pulled out the phone, showed Mike the giant pile of crap and the tracks around the cow carcass.

"You think some kind of circus animal got loose, a tiger, some lions?"

"Well, there's the hippo theory going around. And the bull shark. Which last I heard, couldn't run down a cow in a pasture, but what do I know?"

"Land *and* water," Mike said.

"Yep."

"We'll probably laugh when we find out what it *really* is."

"I doubt it. Have *you* seen anything weird?" Cam said.

Mike shook his head. "No, not really." He thought a moment. "The weirdest thing was not what I saw, but what I *smelled.* The other day driving to Felice Guidry's. Some mud had been tracked across the highway, grass pushed down. Thought a tractor had come through there. But when I passed over it, I almost puked it smelled so bad. Kind of chemically, kind of shitty, all mixed together."

That got Cam's attention. "That's what that pile of shit smelled like. Troy lost his breakfast and lunch when we got close."

They both thought a second before Cam continued. "Lexie thinks there may be two of them. What with the distance of the two attacks."

"Two of *what?*" Mike asked.

"Unidentified Eating Objects–UEO's," Cam said with little humor.

"Great." Mike looked around. "Well, let's get this finished up. One crisis at a time."

Mike was happy for the extra help. Cam joined the Men's Clubbers and they got busy. Joanie came out and helped move some flower pots off the patio and into the two-car garage next to the rectory. In an hour or two, they'd be done.

Mike had to get ready for Floyd's wake over at the funeral home tonight. They had moved it up to six, on account of the storm. He'd mingle with the crowd for a while, comfort Felice, and then do a rosary. After that, the funeral home would be locked up tight, along with just about everything else in Alcide. Joanie would go with him, of course, which made the unpleasantness of the evening a little more tolerable. She was much better at these things than he was.

There'd be a casket, closed of course. No one thought it a good idea to look at Lloyd's feet. It would make for lively conversation, though, if they did open it. But they wouldn't. There wouldn't be a person in the room who didn't know what was in there, though—and what *wasn't* in there.

Poor Felice. She'd have to endure it all. But he wasn't too worried. She was still a fine-looking woman. He was pretty sure he'd be marrying her to someone new within six months.

That made his mind drift into marriage mode for himself. He ran a little computer simulation in his head, where the Pope would announce tomorrow that priests and nuns could marry. Suddenly, he and Joanie could date. But would they have to? They were already "dating" in a way. Should he just go ahead and ask her to marry him? Man, that would be great, he thought. He really loved her. Loved her in a "spend the rest of our lives together" kind of way. He'd had his crushes as a young man, but this, he felt, was the real thing.

But the Pope wasn't going to announce that tomorrow, or the next day, or the next year. This was the 2000-year-old Roman Catholic Church. Decisions were made in geologic time. Over centuries. *We'll get back to you on that in...oh, say...300 years.* If he and Joanie were going to get married, it would be after they started working for the other side of the street. The Protestants.

Hmmm. That was a thought.

"What the heck are you daydreaming about?"

Mike turned around and saw Joanie standing there.

"The Pope.

"Uh huh. He sent you a text or something?"

"Yeah. He's moving me to corporate," Mike deadpanned.

"Whatever," Joanie said. "We're basically done here. I'm gonna take the car and ride around, see if anybody needs any help. Might run over to Miss Nettie's and check on her."

"Miss Nettie's?" Mike said with some concern, remembering Cam's photos.

"Yeah. Old lady who lives in a shoe by herself out in the woods?"

"Something ate her cow."

Joanie just stared at him. "Okay, kind of random. Coyotes? Wild dogs?"

"They don't know. Pretty much ate the whole thing, left some strange tracks." He explained what Cam had told him and showed him.

"This got something to do with Floyd and that kayaker?"

Mike shrugged. "Who knows? Just keep your eyes open. Don't give any rides to a monster or anything, okay?

"Got it, chief. We riding over to the funeral home together? I'll swing by and clean up and we can go."

"Try to wear something decent," he said.

Joanie rolled her eyes. "Yes, sir, boss."

Chapter 24:
"Roland's Plan B"

Roland sat in his bass boat shaking like he was freezing, despite the warm, thick humid air. He was hidden under some thick willow along the bank of the Atchafalaya, near where an old gravel road ran close to the river. It was another gift from the oil companies, a way cut through the thick vegetation for crews to service a big natural gas pipeline that ran through the parish.

He had pulled off his t-shirt to look where the bullet had grazed the top of his shoulder. The wound was still bleeding a little bit. The round from Lexie's gun had left a nice little crease that took off enough layers of skin to sting like hell. Roland looked at the entry point, and then tracked a line down to his heart. That bitch was dead-on with her aim as far as which side of his body she wanted to hit. Her angle was just a bit high. Unless she was aiming for his head, in which case she was off by a lot less. Either way, he had used up at least one of his nine lives for sure.

He looked down at his watch. There was a pretty good chance he'd burn through his remaining eight lives in just a few minutes. Those gangbangers were scheduled to arrive at any moment, with a bag full of cash, looking for their stuff. Which was now in the hands of Lexie Hot Ass Smith.

Motherfucker!

He had thought about just holing up at the houseboat and blowing off these guys. After all, he had shot at a cop, and they'd be looking for him, probably after the storm blew through. He'd be long gone by then. The gangbangers would be pissed, but at least they'd still have their money. No harm, no foul, except for gas money to and from New Orleans.

But he wanted that big money, probably just like they wanted the meth and the coke. Shit, he had a room and a couple of hookers waiting for him in New Orleans. And so he had hatched a plan inside his meth-mashed brain. But he'd need the gangbangers help. They'd either agree with him, or just blow his head off. Either way, he was pretty sure he'd be doing some of the most intense negotiations of his young life. Man, he needed another hit.

He heard a big splash somewhere in the river behind him. He also thought he heard a grunting sound or something. Was that Gaston? He wondered what that big ugly fuck was up to. Maybe he needed another hit, too. He was now pretty convinced that he did have a visit from the thing, that it wasn't a hallucination. Pretty sure, at least. He could use a little muscle right now, what with those assholes from New Orleans on their way. He'd love to see the looks on their faces with big ol' Gaston at his side. *"Hey fuckers, say hello to my little friend."* That made Roland laugh.

He looked out at the water but didn't see Gaston. Crap, he thought. He'd have to go it alone.

Before long, he heard the distinct crunch of tires rolling on gravel. Whatever it was, it was moving slowly. Taking its time. Not a bad idea, he thought. The gravel road was narrow, and a wrong turn of the wheel would have you sliding down the bank into the Atchafalaya.

The vehicle was definitely getting closer, because now Roland could hear the throaty rumble of a big motor. Not a truck. Not diesel. It was a car. Must be them. Or a patrol car. Roland figured he'd play it safe. He eased out of his boat and stepped out onto the bank. He nearly fell on his ass and into the water, but caught a vine hanging from a tree and steadied himself. He was feeling shakier and shakier by the minute.

The bank was steep, and Roland had to get on all fours to make his way up to the road. He had to get up there and find some cover, before the car came around the little bend. A few more feet and he was up and the car was still nowhere in sight. He scampered across the narrow gravel road and into some tall weeds.

The tires-on-gravel sound was more pronounced up here. He ducked down even more and found a narrow sight line in the direction of the approaching car. If it were Lexie, he'd just lay low and let her go by. He guessed he could try to shoot her again, but he wasn't up to it at the moment, and his hands were shaking something fierce. She'd probably blast him out of existence, since she was certainly pissed off by his last attempt at killing her.

The car that approached, though, wasn't a sheriff's patrol Crown Vic. It was a black Lincoln Town Car, windows tinted to near black, with badass spinners on the wheels. The big chrome grill was polished, and even in the flat gray light of the overcast sky it shimmered like pure polished silver.

Roland took a deep breath, stood up and walked out into the road. The Lincoln stopped with a lurch about twenty feet away. He held his hand up as if to stay "stop." Nothing happened for about a minute. Then he heard the electric whine of a window going down. A head eased out and looked at him.

"We lookin' for Roland. You him?" It was Raymond, Tree's driver. He wore aviator sunglasses. Roland could see his reflection in the lenses.

"Yeah, that's me."

"Jess keep those hands out for a minute, slick," Raymond said. "Be cool."

Roland was feeling anything but cool at the moment. They could pop him right now and his body would never be found. He had to go with the flow, though, and put his arms out to the side. He swallowed hard, and noticed there wasn't any spit in his mouth.

Four doors opened at once, and five young African-American men got out. Every one of them had a pistol drawn. It wasn't hard to figure out who was in charge. There was a guy that looked seven feet tall to Roland. He wore what looked like a black leather duster and a black leather beret, a bit out of place for September in Louisiana, especially in the swamp. Roland thought it best not to comment on the fashion faux paus. After all, he was wearing nothing but dirty faded jeans.

Two of the men came around Roland and patted him down. They found his gun stuck in his waistband in the back. They took it out and stepped away from him. "You get it back in a minute. Security," one of them said and looked back at his boss.

The big guy stepped forward. "You Roland?" he said with a deep baritone that sounded vaguely affected.

"Yeah, you must be Tree." Roland stuck his hand out for a shake, but the big man didn't reciprocate.

Tree looked around. "Where's the stuff?"

Roland nodded in a herky-jerky fashion. "Well," he said. "There's kind of a problem."

That got everyone's attention. No one spoke, so Roland kept going.

"That deputy I told you about, the chick, she found my stuff and took it. Got it right now."

Tree looked slowly up at the sky. Roland didn't really want to consider what options were going through the big man's head at the moment.

Tree's head slowly came back down and he stared at Roland for a second. "Hey, motherfucker. We just drove a long way for this pickup. Don't fuck with us."

"I'm not fucking with you," Roland pleaded. "I got nothing, but I think I know how we can get it back."

"We?" Tree said. "Ain't no 'we' about this. I want that shit and I want it now." Suddenly he had his Glock up, pointed directly at Roland.

Roland held his hands up. "No, wait. We can do this, but I need your help. We all benefit here. You get your shit, I get my money. I'll even take a little cut, in good faith, you know?" Roland just made that offer up in the moment. The Glock was fucking with his negotiating skills.

Tree looked at his troops.

"Fuck this dude, Tree," one of them said.

Roland was pretty sure he wasn't going to get fucked. That would have been a whole lot better than what the guy really meant.

Tree stared out at the river. The slow-moving brown water looked like a giant snake slithering through the lush swamp. He turned back to Roland.

"Fucker, we drove a long way for this shit. You messin' up my plans."

Roland tried to muster some backbone. *"Your* plans?" he said. "Shit, I been cookin' up that shit for months, workin' my ass off. You think I'm gonna sit by why some bitch of a deputy takes my shit? Hell, no! I'm goin' after it. You can buy it, or I'll sell it to someone else."

Tree took a deep breath, but never took his eyes off Roland. "What kind of plan?"

Had Roland's body been hooked up to some medical monitors, which was a frightening thought in his current state of meth-addicted willies, doctors would have seen a distinct drop in heart rate and blood pressure.

Roland put his arms down at his sides. "It'll be easy. She's still got the shit somewhere in town. Probably in her trunk. She's the only cop around here. The rest of 'em are way over in St. Martinville. Storm's got everybody focused on other shit."

"Still don't hear a plan," Tree said.

"I know where she lives," Roland said. "We can hole up there, wait for her to come home and grab her. Get her to tell us where she's got the stuff. We get it and haul ass outta here."

"Grab a cop?" Tree said. "Fucker, you crazy, man."

"Hell, yeah. Ain't nobody gonna know. Shit, after we get the stuff, you can leave her tied up or something till we get outta town. Or pop a cap in her ass if you want." Roland wasn't sure if "pop a cap in her ass" was still current street language. He may be a decade or two off. "And it's a nice ass, by the way."

Tree thought about that for a moment. He turned and walked to the edge of the gravel road. He looked down on the river. A large log floated by on its way to the Gulf. His lieutenants stared at him expectantly. Whatever his decision, they'd stand with him.

He turned again to Roland and pointed a giant finger at him. "This how it gonna go. *You* gonna grab her at her house. If you lock her down, you gonna call us and we'll come by for the shit. We take care of business and we roll. You're on your own, then. If she fucks you up, ain't my problem. We outta here anyway."

Roland nodded. He would have preferred all this muscle, but at least they were on board with the plan and he was still alive. Not a bad outcome, all things considered.

"I got a little problem, though," Roland said. "They're looking for me. I can't drive around town, you know? Can you drop me close to her house? I can hoof it in from there."

Tree rubbed his big hand across his face. "Man, I'm already getting' tired of your problems. We kinda tight in there." He pointed back at the Town Car.

"It'll be just for a few minutes," Roland said.

Raymond, Tree's driver and the intellectual top of the class as a far as Tree's posse was concerned, smiled and said,

" Hey, Tree. We can put his ass in the trunk. Plenty of room in there."

Roland's eyes went wide. Most people riding in trunks had holes in their heads and wore duct tape as a fashion accessory.

Tree nodded. "That'll work jus' fine. What you think, dude?"

Roland swallowed hard. "Yeah, yeah. That'll work."

"Then let's roll," he said. They all turned to walk back to the car. The trunk lid popped open remotely and Raymond escorted Roland to the back of the car.

"Plenty of room in here, fucker," Raymond said. He gestured at the inside of the trunk like a car salesman.

Roland looked into the cavernous trunk, wondering if this would be his last few moments on the planet. It looked like a large, gaping mouth, ready to swallow him. Raymond still had his pistol out.

"Just get in," Raymond said.

Roland took a deep breath and climbed into the trunk. He gave Raymond directions on where to go.

"Got it," the gangbanger said, and slammed the trunk closed.

The world went black for Roland, and he curled into the fetal position. The shakes started again, but at least he was still alive.

Lexie Hot Ass Smith, however, might be living her last day, he thought.

Chapter 25:
"Girls Just Wanna Have Fun"

The fate of M'Lou Marchand continued to weigh on Lexie's mind and soul. Female victims of violence were near and dear to her heart. The thought of a young woman like that, lost or missing, dead or kidnapped, just plain messed with her head. She knew she had some real trouble out there with Roland loose, but for some reason, she wasn't too worried about that idiot. She knew she'd find him, and if she was lucky, send his ass packing for Angola. Or points farther. But the missing young woman had filtered to the top of her to-do list. If her body was in some ditch somewhere, or in a shallow grave, the storm might bury her forever. She figured she had 24 hours to learn the truth.

The connection to Floyd Guidry was troubling, which was why she was on the phone with Scotty Melancon, back at headquarters in St. Martinville. Scotty was a skinny kid, with red hair and freckles, just six years out of UL and in charge of evidence lock-up at the sheriff's department. On the surface, a scary thought, but the guy was a born bureaucrat if there ever was one.

Lexie sat back in her patrol car, her cell phone to her ear, parked about two miles out of town along the highway that led north to I-10. It was just a small gravel pull-in that served as a rest area. One 55-gallon drum sat to the side as a roadside waste container.

"Scotty, you pulled all of Guidry's possessions for me?" she said.

"Yeah, Lexie," he said.

Lexie picked up the eagerness in Scotty's voice. Eager as in, *"I think you're hot, Lexie."* Fine with her. "Okay, so just tell me everything you're looking at."

"Sure. There's not too much. A thermal lunch box. A zip-lock dry bag with car keys, a cell phone and a wallet that were inside. I got 'em out now. A sweat shirt. A pair of deck shoes. Not what he was wearing, by the way."

"Right," she said. "I saw what footwear he had on." 'Footwear' was about as accurate as you could get, as far as Floyd's earthly remains were concerned.

Scotty continued. "A water jug. Looks like a light blue windbreaker. A Bass Pro hat, and a small backpack. That's about it."

Lexie mentally checked off the items, visualizing each. "Nothing that looked like it would belong to a woman?"

There was a pause. "No, not really. Backpack's a little strange, though."

"In what way?" Lexie said.

"I dunno. These gator hunters don't strike me as the backpack kind of guys. That and it's pink."

"Anything in it?"

Another pause. Lexie could hear him pick the backpack up.

"Hmmm. Kinda light. Don't think so. Might be."

"Scotty, did anybody look inside the thing?" Lexie figured that'd be about par for the course.

"I didn't. It's tagged, though. Beats me."

Lexie said, "Jeez. Open it up, Scotty, and pull out whatever's in there." *Unbelievable.*

Lexie could hear a zipper being opened, and some rustling sounds. The wait was a little too long. "Scotty, you there?"

"Uh huh," he said.

"Scotty," she said, the way a losing-patience-by-the-moment mother would say a child's name. "Find anything?"

"Yeah. Clothes. I got a pair of cut-off jeans. A Breaux Bridge Crawfish Festival T-Shirt. A pink bra. A pink thong. Pair of flip flops. Pretty sure Floyd couldn't fit into any of these."

"Ya think?" Lexie said.

"Oh, there's a little wallet coin-purse thing. Hang on. Driver's license says 'M'Lou...'"

"Marchand," Lexie said.

"How'd you know?"

"Okay, Scotty. Thanks. Lock it up and I'll call the Sheriff."

"Sure thing, Lexie. Let me know if you need anything else."

She hung up and figured Scotty enjoyed handling the bra and thong. Probably made his morning. She called the sheriff and let him in on the little surprise from Floyd's boat. She listened as he railed on his investigators for not looking in the backpack.

"So Floyd's banging this chick?" he said. "You sure?"

"Pretty sure. Felice thinks so."

"So she's in the boat during the attack? Crap," he said. "Gotta get the lab boys to look at all that blood trace again. See if any of…her…is left on the boat. I swear, we didn't see anything that let on someone else was there."

"A very hungry hippo," Lexie said.

"Bull shark," said the sheriff.

"Bull shit," Lexie thought.

Carla Fontanelli was having a so-so day. She had the Audi unspooled down the parish highway, flying low to the ground. She had some deliveries to make. Makeup, mostly. A few party-toy orders that had come in. The lesbians over by the river, the ones from New Orleans, were some of her big customers. They always let her know when they'd be in town, and she'd delivered some goodies to them, and showed them the new stuff.

They also showed her some new stuff, too. She'd just come from there. Well, to be honest, she'd just *come while she was there.* Several times in fact. She wasn't gay per se. But she did love what a talented, hot woman could do to her. Or several women, for that matter. They'd been hittin' the weed pretty good by the time she got there. Maybe some other pharmaceuticals, too. Having themselves a little pre-hurricane party. Blabbin' on about the thing that ate the kayaker.

That sales visit burned through a couple of hours, but she managed to ring up some new orders while she was there, work out a few kinks, so to speak, and move on. Most everyone was headed out of town, but women didn't like to travel without the face paint, so she was picking up some incremental business, too.

All in all, a so-so day.

She thought about Troy. No doubt she liked the men better than the women. That boy was pure fun on a stick. Maybe she'd get him to join her at her place for the hurricane. Lights out, storm blowing, buck-ass nekkid for a couple of days. She smiled. Not *naked.* That just meant you weren't wearing any clothes. She wanted *nekkid.* That meant you weren't wearing any clothes *and* you were up to something.

She expertly downshifted around a curve, and then planed out along a long straightaway. The trees were swaying now, slowly but regularly. They knew the shit was coming for sure. She caught a glimpse of the bayou through the trees. The water looked murkier in the gray overcast light. Little wavelets were forming as the steady wind kissed the surface. A couple of fish hit the top of the water.

She almost didn't see them. While her attention was focused on the bayou, four deer emerged from the bank, slick with water, and bounded towards the highway. They were moving fast. Her eye caught the flash of gray and she turned her head just as the deer crossed the road. She hit the brake and downshifted at the same time.

"Shit!" she said. The Audi was an exceptional car, but it began to fishtail a bit as the tires locked up, before the anti-lock brake system kicked in, enabling Carla to maintain her steering. And steer she did. Instinctively, she tried to avoid the deer, all females and maybe a yearling, too. The car went off the road into the soft gravel shoulder and slid some more. The small rocks peppered the underside of the car like machine-gun bullets. Carla did what most people did in such situations. She overcorrected as she tried to get back onto the highway, and the Audi went down the grassy slope toward the waterway. The softer ground served to both help and hurt her. It slowed the car down as the wheels sank into the waterlogged earth. But once it stopped, she was pretty sure she wouldn't be going anywhere.

The car slid to a stop, at an angle, pointed more toward the bayou. Maybe halfway down the slope. She had avoided hitting any trees, since most were on the bank, so she sat in her car in the tall Johnson grass and tried to get her breathing under control.

At least she hadn't killed any deer. Or destroyed her front end.

Carla collected her wits and shifted the car into a low gear and gave it the gas. The wheels spun and dug her deeper in the soft earth.

"C'mon, c'mon," she said. The wheels dug in deeper. She was stuck.

She looked at her watch. Still a few more deliveries to make. *Dammit.*

Carla dug into her purse for her cell phone. She flipped through her contacts until she found Troy's number and called him.

"Hey, babe, what's up?" he answered.

She explained the situation.

"Where is this?" he said.

"Shit, I don't know." She looked around for landmarks. Just swamp, bayou and more swamp and bayou. "Along the straightaway. You know."

He paused and said, "Okay, I got an idea where that is. Let me tank up the tow truck and I'll be there in about 20 minutes or so."

"Okay. Just hurry up. Got a few more calls today before the storm hits."

"Yes m'am," he said and hung up.

"Crapahola," Carla said. She tapped her fingers on the steering wheel like they were the keys on a piano. She took the time to call her next deliveries to let them know she might be late because of car trouble. That done, she looked around. Not a car passed her. Not unexpected on this stretch, since most people had already left because of the storm.

The car was starting to get a little stuffy. She opened the door and put her foot out, but stopped. She took off her high heels, a pair of Christian Louboutin's she had no intention of getting mucked up. While she was at it, she rolled her pricey jeans up a few inches.

She stepped out of the car and looked around again. She caught the full, wet, earthy smell of the bayou. The overcast had kept the temperature down into the low nineties, but that was exactly where the humidity level rested, too. So it was pretty much a wash on the comfort scale.

A bullfrog croaked in the distance. Various birds cried and chattered. They were the sounds of the swamp, all familiar to her. She was a bayou girl through and through, although she usually dressed and looked more like she had spent the afternoon on Fifth Avenue. That was just part of her own personal *cha cha*, but she was a local girl just the same.

Carla walked down to the edge of the bayou to have a look. She knew her snakes, her bugs, her poisonous plants, and had a healthy respect for the gators, and was otherwise comfortable in the outdoors.

If she had her rod and reel in the trunk, she thought, she might cast a few to while away the time before Troy got here. It wasn't a good time of day to fish, and the changing weather and wind was probably giving the fish the fits at the moment. But you never knew what was out there. You might get lucky.

Or you might not.

The male creature was rubbing his head on a low tree branch a few hundred yards from where Carla was standing. He was on the other side of the bayou, and had been sniffing out those deer all morning. They tended to lay up in a thicket during the day, and if he was patient, he could sneak up on them from downwind and grab one.

But he was neither patient nor sneaky today. He was too hungry and too horny. And the wind was swirling among the trees, so the deer got a whiff of him before he could grab one, and they hightailed it out of the swamp and swam across the bayou and ran across the road, and were probably still running. He chased them for a bit, but the thickly wooded swamp worked in the deers' favor, slowing him down as he tried to navigate the watery terrain.

So he stopped and let them go. He was kind of pissed off. Now he would have to get back in the water and lay a trap for something that came along. That took time, and he was in a hurry to get to the female. But he had to eat. And man, he felt really *twitchy*. He stopped to scratch for a second.

And that's when he got a whiff of something even tastier than a deer. It was one of those smart things, and it was close. They were so easy to catch.

He might grab a meal after all.

Chapter 26:
"Boudreaux and Thibodeaux and the Mardi Gras Float"

Carla noticed it almost immediately. The sounds of the bayou flipped off like someone hit "mute" on a TV remote control. Birds, frogs, bugs, and squirrels–the whole bunch just shut down. Even the wind seemed to stop for a moment.

It made the hair on the back of her neck stand up, and she shivered a bit. *Weird.*

It was that absence of sound that enabled her to hear the approaching rumble of a truck of some kind. She walked up the slope, past her car, all the way to the side of the two-lane. In the distance she could see the truck coming. Looked like Troy's tow truck. *Finally.*

She unbuttoned the top three buttons on her yellow silk blouse, revealing her ample cleavage in all its glory. As the truck got closer, she stuck out her hip, hooked her thumb out and smiled.

Troy's tow truck slowed and then stopped even with her.

"I could use a little help with my front end, sir," she said.

Troy said through the passenger side window, "I can see that. I need payment up front, though."

Carla caressed the top of one exposed breast. "I think we can work something out."

"I bet we can, ma'm," he said. "Let me get my tool... my *tools*...out."

Carla cracked up at that one. "That was fast."

"Not much traffic," Troy said. "Everybody's heading out." He got out of the cab and looked down at her car. "What the hell happened? You fall asleep or something?"

"A bunch of deer came out of the bayou, ran up the hill and over the highway, right in front of me. Moving *fast.*"

"Deer? This time of day? They were swimming across the bayou?"

"Yeah, weird," she said. "I hit the brake but slid off the road. Ground's kinda mushy down there."

Troy looked down at the Audi and got the plan in his head. "Okay, let me turn the truck around. Go get her out of gear."

While Carla went back to the car, Troy climbed into the tow truck, hit the rooftop hazard lights and backed the truck just off the highway. He winched the cable out and pulled it down the embankment. In minutes, he had the Audi hooked up.

"Doesn't look too bad," he said. "The front end looks way out of line, though. I can get her straight back at the shop. Won't take long." He walked back to the road and hit the switch, and the powerful winch motor engaged. It slowly pulled the car up the slope and behind the tow truck.

Carla looked closely at the front of her once-shiny car. It was covered with mud and weeds. "Shit. Need to wash it now," she said.

"That'll cost you extra," Troy said and gave her a wink.

Before she could answer that, a large splash caught their attention. She and Troy turned as one and froze in their tracks.

The male creature emerged from the water on his back legs, standing at his full 20-foot height. His arms pushed a couple of willow trees apart to make room for the rest of his body. His slick, gray-black-white skin shimmered with moisture, and his thick muscles undulated with every movement.

He stared right at them with his huge eyes and grinned, displaying an impressive set of teeth. His nostrils flared as he took a deep breath. The huge mouth opened and the long, gray oral arm shot out toward Carla.

Thirty or forty years ago, if Troy and Carla had been standing there under similar circumstances, they would have immediately jumped into the truck and driven off. The sheer horror of the situation would have tapped into the prey instinct and driven them to move out. Just like the deer that had run across the road earlier.

But this was the second decade of the 21st century. Movie special effects had come so far that people were immune to the weird and the wonderful. They had been there and done that, as far as monsters, aliens, zombies, dinosaurs and what have you were concerned. Especially in 3D. People weren't amazed anymore. Weren't *scared*. They just watched and ate their popcorn and said something like, *"pretty cool."*

Carla and Troy were kind of in that moment. Kind of. They weren't consciously aware of it, but their minds were flipping through past movie references. *Jurassic Park? The Thing? Cloverfield?* No, no and no. Not quite any of those. This, of course, was happening in nanosecond time. Right until the reality of the moment kicked in, reminding them that this *wasn't* "only a movie." This was "shit-in-your-pants-get-the-hell-outta-Dodge" scary.

Carla got things moving with a piercing scream. It caught in her throat the moment the giant, long, tongue thing hit the side of the Audi, thumped across the hood, and grazed her arm. She saw the hand-like gripper on the end as it sailed just past her.

Troy, who was standing next to Carla, instinctively dove to his right onto the hard surface of the highway. He looked up in time to see the tongue retract quickly back toward the thing.

"What the fuck is that what the fuck is that what the fuck is that?! Carla shrieked. Panic had a way of screwing with coherent enunciation.

Troy got up and looked over the hood of the Audi. The thing was walking up the slope right at them.

"Get in the truck! Get in the truck!" he shouted. He grabbed Carla and shoved her toward the driver's-side door of the tow truck. She almost tripped, but gained her balance and leaped up into the cab.

"C'mon!" she yelled.

Troy, still mesmerized by the weirdness of the thing, shuffled sideways toward the door and watched as the creature dropped down to all fours, made a grunting sound, and leaped toward them.

Troy was in the truck in flash. He started the engine and hit the power windows to "close." The *whirring* sound of the window motors sounded like a scream to him. No, wait. That was Carla.

Suddenly, the truck shook violently, rocking back and forth. Troy looked in the rearview mirror and saw the thing perched on top of the Audi. It was bouncing up and down on it, like it was playing with it or something. For some reason, he thought of a documentary he saw about polar bears, and how they had tried to break into a house.

He put the truck in gear and hit the gas. The back wheels were in the gravel shoulder. Add the extra weight of the Audi, still attached, and the tow truck didn't move an inch. He looked in the mirror again, and saw the creature was gone. That respite lasted only a second before his driver-side window blew open, followed by a claw-like hand that was opening and closing rapidly. Troy ducked his head back and the claw went by, right toward Carla. She jerked to her right and got as far over to her door as she could. Her screams filled the cab.

"Get the fuck outta here!" she yelled.

His foot was all the way to the floor and the big engine of the tow truck was howling. It sounded more like a scream to him, but Carla and the engine were both fighting for attention in the noise category.

The creature's arm turned and tried to grab anything it could, and in the process, ripped the ceiling fabric loose, grabbed the sun visor and ripped it clean off. It had it in its grasp and pulled it out the broken window.

Finally, the rear tires of the truck found purchase and it lurched forward onto the highway, dragging the Audi and the creature with it.

Troy thought he heard another sound. A deep, throaty howl. Definitely not Carla. Except maybe when she was having an orgasm, which she wasn't having at the moment. It was the creature, now firmly on top of and attached to the tow truck.

"Drive! Drive!" Carla shouted.

Troy had the truck accelerating down the highway. At first he thought he was hitting pothole after pothole as the truck bounced this way and that. Then he realized it was the creature on the truck, banging away with its claws, shaking the truck back and forth as it flew down the highway.

"What is that? What is it?!" Carla yelled.

"Fuck if I know!" Troy shouted back. "Hang on!" He swerved the truck back and forth, zigzagging across the two lane. There was still no traffic coming. Troy was hoping an M1 Abrams tank might come by for an assist.

Carla was still up in the corner of her side of the cab, watching out the broken window next to Troy. She was anticipating another claw coming in, so she didn't see the other hand of the creature come down her side of the truck. Its hard, sharp claw tapped the window once, then reared back and broke the glass. The pieces shattered and fell inside all over Carla's lap and into her hair. She screamed again.

This time, the hand was more purposeful. It felt around for something and went right over her thigh. It closed around it and pulled hard.

"It's got me! It's got me!" she yelled. She grabbed the thing's arm and tried to get free.

Troy was still trying to maintain control of the tow truck, now flying down the highway at about 80 miles per hour, weaving back and forth, pulling the Audi and one hungry whatever the fuck it was on his roof. He saw the thing's hand close around Carla's leg and start to pull. He reached over and grabbed its arm and tried to pull it loose. It was cool and still wet, and for the first time, he caught the smell of the thing. Like nothing he had ever smelled. Well, until recently, anyway. It was pungent and a little chemically smelling. For the first time, he thought of the big pile of shit he and Cam had found.

Troy was a big guy, and strong, but he couldn't get the thing's arm loose from Carla. The claws were sharp and he feared they would rip into her thigh and tear her femoral artery. She'd bleed out in minutes.

He let go of the creature's arm, despite Carla's desperate screams. With one eye on the road, he reached into the center console and felt around for a utility knife he kept in there. There was all kinds of crap inside the small box: a couple of empty beer cans, a phone charger, coins, an opened bag of beef jerky and other unidentified stuff. Finally, he found the sheath the knife was in, pulled it out of the console and got the knife out.

"Move your hand!" he yelled.

Carla let go, and Troy could see the tears streaming down her face. It was hurting her. He reached over, and with a slashing motion, cut the creature's arm just above its huge clawed hand. For the first time, he noticed it looked more like a human's than an animal. The thumb was opposable, like a primate.

There was a high-pitched howl from outside the truck. He'd hurt the thing, and Troy watched as it pulled its arm out of the truck. But it was still on the roof.

A mile down the highway, coming toward Troy and Carla, was a blue 1973 Ford pickup. Inside was Tommy Thibodeaux, a short, wiry man of 75. A cigarette hung from his lips. He had the local Zydeco AM station on the radio, and was rocking out, tapping the wheel with his finger. Next to him sat his lifelong buddy, Sonny Boudreaux, also 75. Sonny was a big guy with a slight paunch. He also had just lit up a smoke.

Sonny sang along in a heavy Cajun accent, to the patois French lyrics of the Zydeco band. To these guys, it was sweet music. To the uninitiated, it sounded like someone skinning a cat alive.

"What dat asshole doin'?" Tommy said. He leaned forward over the wheel and squinted into the distance.

Sonny noticed the oncoming tow truck, too. "Guess he tryin' to find a lane to use. Only got two to choose from." This was highly funny to Sonny, and he laughed out loud.

"Dass a tow truck," Tommy said. "Pullin' a car. And what the fuck is dat on the roof?"

"Look like some half-ass Mardi Gras float or sumpin'," Sonny said. "You know, like ya see in New Orleans."

Tommy grabbed the wheel with both hands. "Well, dat fucker better pick a lane or he gonna lose his decoration, dat's fo' sure."

"Look like he got a motor in dat ting, too," Sonny said. "Look, it head movin'. Dat's kinda funny."

Tommy didn't comment on that last statement. He was pretty sure there was an even chance he and the Mardi Gras float were going to collide head on.

The creature's basic thought, as he sat atop the tow truck, flying down the Louisiana road at 80 miles per hour, was that this day was getting shittier and shittier. First, he missed his chance with those deer back in the swamp. Then had a sure shot at a good meal right alongside the bayou with the first smart thing. And when another showed up, it looked even better. But they had been just a step quicker.

He knew he should've just let them go. Or maybe just chased them down the highway. But no, he had to be a total asshole and jump on top of the machine. For a moment, he thought he had a chance to pull one of those things out of there. He got a nice cut on the arm for that thought. So here he was, going faster than he had ever gone. Almost like flying. Kind of cool, really. But a terrible idea just the same.

He had some decisions to make. Actually, just one. How the hell to get off this thing without killing himself?

Misters Boudreaux and Thibodeaux, they of the old blue pickup and Zydeco music, were about to solve that problem for him.

Chapter 27:
"The Big One Gets Away"

The thing on the roof was pissed. Troy felt the truck rocking even more, and it was bouncing up and down, too. But that wasn't Troy's biggest concern at the moment. The creature had slid forward, covering most of the windshield of the tow truck and blocking Troy's view of the highway. He could've sworn there was something coming his way, too.

Troy wanted to stick his head out his now-shattered window, but the creature's hand was right there, holding on for dear life. The other hand was doing the same on Carla's side. One swipe of that clawed hand and he'd lose his head.

"Can you see the road?" Troy yelled.

Carla moved from side to side, trying to look around or through the thing that covered the windshield. "No! I can't see."

"Fuck," Troy said. He wanted to slow down, but if he did, they were going to be lunch, or whatever mealtime it was.

They had reached a sort of stalemate. Despite the weaving back and forth across the highway, the creature was firmly attached to the roof. He still couldn't see ahead. The thing pretty much covered the entire windshield. So he looked to his left for the edge of the road as it flew by, and used that to keep him on the highway.

Carla was damn near hyperventilating now, scrunched closer to Troy. She kept looking at the creature's right claw, which held fast to the top of the door and onto the ceiling of the car.

"Stick your head out there and see if anything's coming!" Troy said. "I can't see shit."

"*You* stick your head out there," she shot back.

Troy figured she had a good point. *Crap. What the hell.* He stuck his head out the driver's side window as far as he could. He was practically standing up, with one foot on the accelerator and one planted firmly on the floorboard.

"Holy shit!" he yelled and cut the wheel hard to the right.

"Sonafabitch," Tommy said. The tow truck/float whatever-the-heck-it-was, was right on him, seconds from impact. He cut the wheel hard on the old Ford, and its balding tires squealed in anguish from the sudden movement. They went into the soft gravel shoulder and kicked up a meteor shower of debris as they did. That's when Boudreaux and Thibodeaux got a good look at the Mardi Gras float.

The old pickup and Troy's tow truck zipped by at a combined closing speed of 150 miles per hour. NASCAR speed. Troy estimated they missed each other by a foot. He didn't have time to celebrate. The physics involved were way beyond his comprehension, but a tow truck pulling a car with a giant monster thing on top of the cab makes for some squishy handling. The vehicle also slewed onto the opposite shoulder, but instead of the noisy clatter of soft gravel, it hit a pothole big enough to swim in.

The jarring effect made little Carla bounce completely off her seat. Troy bit his tongue, and he immediately tasted blood.

The creature's head slammed onto the hood of the tow truck from the force. For a moment, he thought he was going to slip off and get run over. It was time to get moving. He pulled himself back off the hood and the windshield, found good places to anchor his legs, crouched down and sprung to the right into the tall grass along the bayou. The natural slope down from the highway to the bayou helped reduced the effects of his landing. He skidded through the grass on his stomach for nearly 50 yards, and then rolled a few times before coming to a stop on his back. He rolled over, shook his head violently, and ran like hell into the water. The cool liquid helped soothe the grass burns on his underside, and the cut on his right arm.

Now he was hungry, horny *and* hurt.

And really pissed off.

Tommy got the old Ford back on the highway and back to a reasonable speed. The cigarette still hung from his mouth. He gave a quick glance at the review mirror to make sure the tow truck didn't wreck. It didn't.

"Whoa," he said.

"What?" Sonny replied. He noticed Tommy looking back, and turned his whole body around to see what he was looking at.

"The Mardi Gras float decorations just jumped off dat truck."

Sonny turned to his friend. "You mean it *fell* off?"

"Not exactly. Look like it *jumped.*"

"How you know dat?" Sonny said.

"Cuz it got up and ran into the bayou."

Sonny smiled. And went along with the story. "That was some ugly float, though."

"Wouldn't want any beads they'd be trowin'," Tommy said.

Troy and Carla rode in silence for a while. With the windows blown open, the thick, humid air swirled throughout the cab with a loud roar. Carla's dark hair flew this way and that, and she fought valiantly to keep it out of her eyes. Her mascara had run with her tears, and she had the classic raccoon face to show for it.

They would occasionally shoot each other a glance, but no words were spoken. It was as if they both sensed it wasn't quite time to start assimilating the facts of the situation.

Finally, Troy spoke. "Your leg okay, where it grabbed you?"

She nodded. "Hurts some. No blood, though."

"Me and Cam found a pile of shit out in the swamp yesterday that was five feet high. Had pieces of deer and hog in it. A belt buckle, too."

"From *that* thing, you're saying?"

"Probably. What else around here could take a dump that huge?" Troy said.

Finally, the question. Carla said, "You have even a reasonable idea what the fuck that was?" She pointed out the window.

"It wasn't native," he replied.

"No shit," Carla said.

Troy looked at her, like a schoolboy about to try and explain a difficult concept to an adult. "Okay, maybe a mutant? Chemicals in the water? Maybe some radiation? Maybe it started off as a big hog and just *changed*."

"That's ridiculous," she said.

Troy nodded. It did sound like a movie he had seen. "Alright. Some weird government project gone wrong, maybe? Cross breeding animals, mixing DNA, shit like that. It gets loose. Bam."

"Okay, let's go with that," Carla said. She could always count on the U.S. government to be up to something, usually not in a good way. Like being *nekkid*.

Troy tapped the steering wheel with the palm of his hand. "Damn, wish I had time to grab a picture. Cam needs to see this."

"Draw him a picture. I'm not going back on this road. Ever."

"Need to tell Lexie, too," Troy continued. "Get it up the chain to the sheriff's department and the wildlife boys. See if they can catch it."

"Wow, that sounds like a spectacularly terrible idea," Carla said.

"Well, at least let's tell Cam. He being a vet and all."

"Yeah, maybe he can fit that thing with a collar and some tags," she said. "Teach it to catch a Frisbee."

"It'd win the ugliest dog contest, for sure." Troy gave her a big smile. She couldn't help but laugh, despite her current state of mind. It came out like a bark, though, half a laugh, half a sob.

The backyard of Lee and Deanna Curtis was a bustle of activity. Little Macy's birthday party was in full swing. A long folding table had been set up, its pink plastic tablecloth billowing in the humid breeze. Presents were piled high on one table, and a big homemade banana cake with six candles on it sat on one end. But all that was for later. Right now it was time for Macy's Big Fishing Rodeo.

Twelve kids were stretched along the bank of the bayou, some sitting, some standing. Each one held a simple cane pole with a line connected to a red-and-white bobber and a small lead weight. Lee had set the hooks shallow, and depending on preference, they held either worms or crickets.

Lee surveyed the contestants. Seven girls, five boys. The wind, changing weather and time of day would certainly cut down on their fishing success, which was fine with him. There was a "most fish" prize and a "biggest fish" prize, and he was pretty sure the take would be slim. His job was mainly to keep the lines from getting tangled.

"Got one! Got one!" a boy yelled. Lee hurried over to watch the kid reel in a hand-size bream. Not bad, really. That event pretty much garnered every contestant's attention, and all eyes were on the fish as Lee hoisted it out of the water and measured it. He got the hook out without killing the thing and released it back into the water.

"Alright!" Deanna Curtis said, and clapped her hands. She looked over at her husband and then at the darkening clouds. He held up crossed fingers.

"So far so good," he said. "I'll let 'em fish for about 30 more minutes, then we can cut the cake and open presents."

There was a splash in the water, and Lee and Deanna turned that way. Two of the boys had found some old bricks and were tossing them into the bayou. A big splash was like an explosion to a boy. Noise. Drama. Destruction. Fun.

Lee yelled, "Hey, guys. You're scaring the fish away. No throwing."

The two boys looked back with sheepish expressions, wiped their dirty hands on their jeans and picked their poles back up.

"Keep an eye on those two," Deanna said. "Next thing you know they'll jump in for a swim."

"Fantastic," Lee said.

"And watch for gators," Deanna added. "Looks like a damn buffet over there with all those kids along the bank."

Lee nodded. On such things, he deferred to her bayou sense, since he wasn't a native. Suddenly images of crocs in Africa snatching baby gazelles from the shoreline shot through his brain.

"Right." He grabbed a beer from an ice chest and walked to the bank. Lines were still untangled. A few of the kids were getting little nibbles, probably from shad or minnows. That was great. Gave the kids some hope, but no chance of anything on the line.

Deanna freaked him out about the buffet comment, especially after he'd seen that group of gators swim by yesterday. He peered into the murky water. Hard to see anything, even a foot below the surface. A gator could swim up under water and be *right there* and no one would see it until it was too late.

He decided to stick close to the bank. "Hey, kids, take a step back from the water, okay?" he ordered.

The male creature swam submerged down the bayou. His effort at trolling had netted him one small alligator, a couple of turtles and a good-sized bass. Just appetizers for him. For the moment, that was all he would be getting. His little adventure on the highway had left him a bit drained, and the cut on his arm was just now beginning to feel a little better. It wasn't a bad cut. He had skin like thick, dense rubber. But it had hit a few nerves and felt like shit, just the same.

He felt closer to the female and could sense the resonating call she was putting out. It was louder than before and more distinct. It wouldn't be long now. Maybe tomorrow. Then he'd be done with her and could get back to his bachelor ways deep in the swamp. No more chasing cows in pastures. No more car hopping. Just a quiet, laid-back lifestyle that would suit him just fine.

But that was later. Now, he had to eat, and he used all of his senses to find, target, kill and eat prey. So it was with his ears that he found a very rich opportunity for an afternoon meal. A *substantial* afternoon meal.

The sounds were high-pitched, not unlike the birds that flew in the swamp. At first, he thought it might be one thing making all the noise. But the more he listened, the more he understood that there were a group of things chattering away. Right on or near the bayou.

The creature, still under water, cocked his head to the right to help locate the direction of the sounds. They weren't coming from the water, but rather above it, on the bank. He kicked his powerful legs and swam faster under the water. A school of bream shot right in front of him, split and regained its original size.

He was definitely getting closer now. The chattering became more identifiable. It was the sound the smart things made, but somehow different. And there were a lot of them.

Time for a peek.

The creature let himself float toward the surface of the bayou, like a submersible rising from the depths. He let himself get just below the surface, so only his large eyes came out of the water. The wind was steady and caused little wavelets on the bayou, which washed into his eyes. He had to blink regularly so he could see.

And there they were. About 100 yards down the bayou, on the bank. A large group of the smart things. Most were young ones. But there was one big adult standing nearby, and one farther up the bank. The creature assessed the situation. He was pretty sure he could grab a couple of the young ones, or the adult by the water, without any problem. What gave him pause, though, were the things in the hands of the young ones. He couldn't tell exactly what they were. The smart things weren't very strong, and they couldn't swim very fast, but that had *things* that could hurt him. Things they usually held in their hands. He didn't have a word for *guns*, but he had seen them in action. Loud. And capable of killing things. He himself had never been hit, or shot at for that matter. Still, it was something to think about.

He went deep. Moved closer.

Lee, who had been staring intently at one kid's bobber that jerked underwater a few times, thought he saw something on the bayou out of the corner of his eye. Like it was there and gone. Something on top of the water. Whatever it was, it was gone now. He scanned the bayou left and right, but all he saw was the breeze brushing against the water. A brilliant white egret flew in and perched delicately on a cypress branch across the water.

He went back to watching the lines. Some of the girls were getting fidgety, now bored with the concept of fishing. The boys were hanging tough, especially since one of their own had landed the big one. And the only one. Their young competitive natures had taken over now.

Lee noticed the surface of the bayou had changed about 20 yards out. The little wavelets the wind had been creating had become more pronounced in a small area. And that area was now moving towards them. He thought it might be a rogue gust of wind that had fallen out of the sky, counter to the prevailing winds.

The disturbance in the water moved closer and closer, but Lee noticed it held no accompanying wind gust. It wasn't the wind at all. It was something in the water.

One of the little girls let out a high-pitched scream.

Suddenly the water right along the shoreline shook and shimmered and boiled up into a tempest. There was a loud *sssssssssssinggggg* sound. Lee saw what the girl had seen.

A good-sized bream had jumped out of the water, right onto the bank, and right onto her feet. But a half-second later, before anyone had time to comment on that sight, the whole shoreline erupted into a riot of jumping fish. Bream, crappie and a couple of small bass. Most were jumping in and out of the water, but some had miss-timed their leaps and were now flopping in the grass by the kids. The boys were going crazy now. They had put their poles down and were trying to pick up the biggest fish they could. The girls collectively screamed and stamped their feet and ran up the yard to the party table.

Lee had never seen such a thing. Well, he did remember something on the Discovery Channel about invasive Asian carp on some river up north, who leapt out of the water when they were agitated, but these weren't carp. They were local fish.

Deanna ran down to the edge of the water to watch. "Holy crap," she said. "I've never seen that before."

Lee bent down to pick up a couple of the cane pools that were in danger of being dragged in if a fish hit the hook. "Kind of cool, but what would make them do that?"

Deanna looked at the crazy spectacle. "Something's scaring them," she said. "Might be a big gar close by. Might have run them right into the shallows."

Lee thought back to the gators yesterday who seemed to be fleeing something. They weren't afraid of a gar. What would scare *them?*

"Okay, guys, let's head in!" he said a little too loudly. He gave Deanna a look.

"What?"

"About to rain. Grab the cake and let's go in."

Deanna looked up. Cloudy, breezy, but it wasn't raining. "I think..."

Lee shook his head and grabbed one little boy by the arm. "Just drop the poles there. C'mon. Time for cake and ice cream in the house!"

The remaining boys, Lee and Deanna walked up the slope to herd the girls back into the house. Suddenly, a tremendous splash echoed across the water. Lee and Deanna turned to see something gray, white, black and very big breach the surface of the bayou, and then flop over onto its side.

"Look at the whale! Look at the whale!" little Macy screamed. She pointed at the water.

"What the fuck was that?" Lee said.

"F-bomb!" one kid said, but Lee ignored him.

Deanna's jaw was somewhere just above her breasts. "C'mon kids, cake and ice cream in the house!" She started running, herding the kids with her arms.

"Lee, grab the cake."

The creature sank to the bottom of the bayou and lay in the cool mud. He shuddered in frustration and anger. He had moved in on the group of smart things on the bank, going in for a capture and kill. Then everything went to shit. First, a school of fish he had frightened had exploded onto the surface and alerted the smart things. Then, he had noticed the big adult had picked up something in its hands, which may or may not have been able to hurt him. The young ones had scampered farther up the slope. And just like that, everything had changed. The adult was in protective mode and was preparing to attack him. He didn't want to take the risk. So he did a U-turn while underwater and headed back out into the middle. He was so pissed, he had jumped nearly out of the water, and angrily slapped the surface with his body.

While he sulked on the bottom, he tried to calm himself again. It was getting harder to do, though. With any luck, this time tomorrow he would find the female and get down to business.

Chapter 28:
"Gunslingers"

The black Lincoln Town Car pulled into Fort St. Jesus Bait and Tackle and parked between a mud-caked 4x4 and a blue Honda Civic. Cam was on the front porch, emptying a 55-gallon drum that served as a trash can. He'd never seen the car before. Maybe somebody's relatives in town to transport them out of here before the storm.

The motor on the Town Car switched off, but no one got out. Cam couldn't see through the blacked-out windows, but he was expecting some old guy and his blue-haired wife to ease out. It looked like that kind of car. A rolling living room. Big cushy suspension. Quiet ride. A retirement home on wheels.

To his surprise, a young black guy got out the driver's side, looked around, then tapped the roof of the car. At that, the other three doors opened and four other black dudes climbed out, including one big guy all dressed in black, with black shades. Cam thought for some reason, *Mr. Big.* Seemed to fit.

Definitely not locals, Cam thought. Didn't recognize them at all. Could have been someone's relatives. *Ms. Nettie?* Grandkids? No, too old for that. Her son was Cam's age, and these guys looked to be in their twenties. The math didn't work.

Cam's alarm bell went off in his head. Wasn't sure why. Probably the look of these guys. Punks. They had that vibe about them.

The five of them sauntered toward the front steps, taking their time, looking around. Like five gunslingers in town, walking into the saloon. Getting the lay of the land.

They walked past him, and Cam said, "Guys" and continued his trash duties. But he kept an eye on them just the same. Zach was inside, still busy ringing up the local citizenry as they stocked up for the storm. Cam tied up the garbage bag, walked around the side and tossed it into the dumpster. He came back quickly, put a new bag in the drum, and stepped inside the store.

A quick glance and he saw that the five gunslingers were at the back of the store. Two of them were at the cooler, the rest were spread through the handful of aisles. Zach was busy at the counter, but he, too, was watching the five guys. The kid was smart, and wary for someone so young. He gave Cam a look, and Cam nodded. They were on the same wavelength.

Cam stepped behind the counter and helped bag a few items while Zach rang up the order. What he was really doing was getting into a defensive position, with the counter between him and potential trouble. That and getting within arms length of the shotgun he had in a sheath under the counter. He could have it out, cocked and ready to rock in just under two seconds.

He and Zach got the two customers rung up and out the door in a couple of minutes. Now it was just the two of them and the five gunslingers.

Zach said under his breath, "Don't know those guys."

"Me either," Cam replied. He arranged a couple of items on the counter, but he was looking at the visitors. "Stay sharp. If it goes to shit, get down."

"Okay," he said. He sounded a little shaky.

After a few minutes, four of the guys walked up to the counter and dropped their goods down. Some Red Bulls, chips, jerky, various candy, a roll of duct tape, some rope and a pair of work gloves. The fifth guy, Mr. Big, hung back and scoped out the store some more.

None of the guys said anything. They were *cool*. Indifferent. As if Cam and Zach were invisible. The help. Cam thought about striking up some conversation, if nothing more than to get a sense of what they were doing in town. But they didn't look like they were in a talkative mood, so he blew it off.

They paid in cash and walked out, Mr. Big still hanging back from the others. It was like they were security that always walked in front.

"Assholes," Zach said. He made sure they were out the door and gone before making this insightful comment.

"Yeah, they need to keep going," Cam said. "Bad dudes. Sure'd like to know what they're doing around here. Long way from I-10."

"Looked like a gang or something," Zach said. "The big guy was the boss, like the Godfather."

"Yeah, the boss," Cam added. "Still a bunch of punks, though. Might've been scoping out the place. We'll keep an eye on them. Might give Lexie a heads up, too."

Tree and the guys got back in the Town Car and eased back out onto the road. Roland had given them directions on how to get to the drop-off point, and part of those directions included passing Fort St. Jesus Bait and Tackle. They were on their way.

Roland, still in the trunk and still debating his time left on the planet, heard the crunch of gravel, the opening of doors and the passing of cars on the road. He figured correctly they'd stopped at the Fort. No one had bothered to get him a soda or some smokes or a beer, though. Whatever. He just wanted out of the trunk, which now began to feel smaller and smaller. And he had to pee. Maybe puke, too.

After a few minutes, his new friends returned to the car and they drove on. Roland tried to get a sense if they were driving in the right direction, but his skeezy brain couldn't handle it, so he just closed his eyes and waited.

Fifteen minutes later, after a few turns, some starts and stops and some heated exchanges from the front, the Town Car came to a stop. Roland heard one door open and listened to footsteps coming toward the trunk.

With a *click* and a *thump,* the trunk lid opened on its own accord. Roland opened his eyes and saw Tree standing above him.

"This it?" he said in his booming baritone.

Roland sat up and looked at his surroundings. Lots of green, and a few birds chirping. He climbed out of the trunk on shaky legs, brushed the back of his dirty jeans as if that would help, and surveyed the area.

They were on a narrow dirt road, with thick woods on either side. He could see the highway about 100 yards back the way they came.

"Yeah, yeah, perfect," Roland said. He smiled. Tree didn't.

Tree looked at his watch. "You got two hours."

"That'll work," said Roland. "I'll have her locked down by then. You know how to get to the house, right?"

"Yeah, saw it when we came in."

"Good. Give me a call just to make sure. Then pull around back when you get there."

"Don't fuck up," Tree said. He pointed a huge long finger at Roland.

"Not a problem. I owe this bitch."

"You owe *me,* motherfucker," Tree said. "Find that shit."

"Count on it," Roland said.

"I am," Tree said. He handed Roland a bag with the duct tape, rope and gloves inside.

Troy and Carla rolled into his garage/gas station just as a wind-blown light rain came up and peppered the gravel parking lot and corrugated tin sides of Troy's garage. He pulled into one of the two empty bays, just far enough to get Carla's Audi out of the rain. The tow truck was now completely through and outside again in the back. They both jumped out and ran into the garage. Troy's mechanic, Odell Landry, walked out of the garage office to meet them. Odell was a slight, thin, semi-retired oil-field roustabout who did double time at the garage. He had a short buzz cut of silver hair. The guy could fix anything.

"What happened, Carla?" he said.

Carla ignored Odell as she opened the trunk. Troy was already lowering the front of the Audi onto the concrete floor of the garage. He looked over at Odell and said, "She spun out after some deer ran across the road."

"Storm must be spookin' 'em," Odell replied.

Carla looked up at Troy, then over to Odell. "Yeah, spooked," she said. She continued to gather some of her "product" from the trunk, consolidating some things into one canvas bag.

Troy got the Audi down and unhooked. He ran back out to the tow truck and pulled it into the other bay.

"What happened to the windows?" Odell said. He stepped closer to the passenger side of the tow truck and carefully placed his hands on the jagged glass that still remained.

Troy hesitated a moment. "Uh, hit a couple of limbs when I went down off the road to get to her car."

Odell just looked at the glass on the seat of the truck. "I can fix this soon as we can get some glass in here."

"Good," Troy said. "After the storm blows through." He looked back outside as the rain continued to fall. "Could you go ahead and shut the bay doors? Let's lock it down for the weekend. Keep the gas pumps on, though."

"Sure thing," Odell said, and went to close the big doors.

Troy walked over to Carla, who still stood by the trunk. "What are you going to do?"

She put some boxes of makeup into the bag. "Got to drop some things off for a couple of customers. I promised them I'd have them today. Let me borrow the pickup."

"You're shittin' me, right?" Troy said. He looked over to Odell, then back at Carla. He said in a low whisper, "Who knows where that thing went to."

"Not going that way," she said. "Back toward Henderson. Couple of stops to make and then I'm heading back."

Troy ran his fingers through his wet hair. The loud clatter of the big bay doors going down made it too hard to hear. "Just stay away from the bayou. Any bayou, river, mud puddle, whatever."

"You gotta tell Cam," Carla said. "We should warn people."

"Oh yeah," he said. "That'll sound great."

"Yeah, maybe not," she replied. "Everybody's leaving anyway. But at least tell Cam. He'll believe you."

"He saw the shit," Cam said. "He'll have to believe it."

She finished with her bag. "Okay, that's it. Should be back in an hour or two. You'll be here?"

"Here or over at the Fort. Call me when you're heading back."

Carla stood on her tippy toes and gave him a little peck on the cheek. "Thanks for rescuing me from the dragon, Sir Knight."

"That wasn't a dragon," Troy said. "That was a certifiable Grade A, government science experiment gone bad."

"Then call them and tell them their pet got loose."

"I got a feeling they already know that," he said. "But there's no fed facility around here, is there?"

Carla thought a second. "Fort Polk," she said.

"But that's an army base. Can't be any labs up there."

"Maybe that's what they want you to believe," Carla said. "Thousands of wooded acres. I mean, how much of that is needed to train troops? Just a part. Bet they've got some science lab hidden in the woods."

"Could be," Troy said. He squeezed his lips together with his thumb and forefinger. "But we'd see army trucks around, you know, looking for it."

"Nah, too obvious. Probably disguised as regular guys in regular trucks. Fishermen, hunters, that kind of thing."

"Huh. Might be. Hadn't seen that much traffic, though."

"Maybe," she said. "Maybe they're looking in the wrong place."

Troy sighed. "Shoulda got some video or pictures."

"Sorry, I was too busy screaming my fucking head off," Carla said. "You seemed a little preoccupied at the time, too."

"Yeah, but still."

"Give me the keys." She held her hand out.

Troy dug in his pockets and gave her the keys to his pickup truck. "Try not to get it eaten. You either."

"Sounds like a plan," she said. She grabbed her bag of goodies and ran out into the rain to his truck. A deep, rolling thunder shook the garage. It made Troy jump.

Chapter 29:
"Easy Breezy"

The female creature was heading in from the east. She had been making steady if slow progress, thanks in part to very little boat traffic and the fact that she was a big fat pregnant thing with a growing anger problem. It had been hard going through the swamp, so she stuck to the bayous, sloughs and canals. Some had her heading in the right direction, while others took her off course. She had to stop frequently, to rest and to get her bearings. The young inside her were now squirming around almost constantly, and it made her a little nauseous. Plus it hurt like hell. She knew the little bastards already had teeth, and it gave her the willies to think they might just take matters into their own hands—or mouths— and eat their way out. But that was her imagination, what little she had. The young had to be chemically altered before they would start heading down the birth canal. It was how their kind did things. And that meant the male needed to get his ass over here as fast as possible, which for her wasn't fast enough. Which was why she was slogging through the Basin, looking for *him*. Closing the distance. Helping him out.

She was seeing more and more of the smart things. Mostly near their dwellings along the bayou. At first, it had been wild country, but now she had begun to see the places where they lived. They were handsome structures, well made and close to the water. But also close to the pathways their mechanical things traveled on. Those things were *fast* and big. Some bigger than her. The smart things got inside them and went long distances. Very efficient. She could use one now. But she doubted anyone would give her a ride. It would most certainly be their last.

There was something else, too. The weather was changing, and not for the better. She sensed the pressure dropping, and she could see the wind picking up. She'd seen these storms before over the decades. They were violent things that altered the landscape and caused the indigenous animals to burrow into their holes and nests and wait it out. Under normal conditions, she had done the same. But these weren't normal times. She was already taking big chances moving through the swamps in her condition. And it looked like she and the male would be meeting up the next day, and judging by the number of dwellings she was now seeing, it would be right in the heart of where all the smart things lived. Dangerous, but she and the male would have no choice. She'd have to beat him to a good place, wait him out, guide him in, get it on and get the hell out of there. After that the young would be on their own. And despite their relative small size they would be hungry. A single young one might have trouble bringing down a full-grown smart thing, but fifty of them? No problem at all.

Roland moved through the thick hardwood forest that backed up to Lexie's house. It was relatively high ground, compared to the surrounding swamps, so it was easy to travel in a straight line. The woods were made up of a ridiculous variety of trees, including sweet gum, pin oak, and ash. There were occasional briar patches, but Roland was able to easily navigate around them. The distance from where Tree and his gangbangers had let him out and the backyard of Lexie's place was a half mile, and it wasn't long before Roland could make out the shape of her place through the trees.

A light rain began to fall, and Roland could hear distant thunder. He figured this was the first salvo from that hurricane in the Gulf. He hadn't really had time to track it, or listen to the news for that matter, so he didn't know if the thing was about to make landfall or was still way out there. His gut told him this was just some early stuff. He had lived through enough hurricanes to know when the hammer was about to drop, and this didn't look like it. Good for him. Bad for Miss Hot Ass.

Roland switched into stealth mode the last few yards before the tree line. He crouched low and moved from tree to tree, like some meth ninja. His heart was really pounding in his chest, and sweat poured down his face. Or was that rain? He thought both. And he was still twitching like bugs were crawling all over him. But other than all that, he was feeling pretty good. Well, at least for Roland.

He settled behind a huge live oak, which gave him plenty of cover. The old tree's near-black trunk sat right on the edge of the woods and Lexie's back yard. Roland peeked around it and surveyed the place. The yard was about 40 yards deep, from tree line to her small back patio. The yard was fairly open, broken only by a good-sized plum tree, a young magnolia and an ancient willow. Her patio was small, only about 10 feet square, and held a round glass table with a closed blue umbrella and four blue cushy chairs. Off to one side in the grass were a bunch of clay pots of varying sizes, some half-filled with potting soil, some with unidentified plants in them. There was a sliding glass door off the patio that probably led into her kitchen.

The place looked quiet. But Roland couldn't see the front yard and the driveway well enough to know for sure that no one was home. He could risk it by scampering across the yard, and then moving along the house to the front. But if she was there, she might see him. He went to plan B.

That entailed staying along the tree line but moving to his right another 50 yards or so. The woods weren't perfectly perpendicular to her yard, but curved around a bit that way, giving him a good angle on the front yard.

In a few minutes he had the angle and smiled. No car out front. Better yet, there was no traffic on the narrow road that led to the place. The nearest house was about a quarter mile down the lane, and there was a "for sale" sign in front of it. Overgrown grass in the front confirmed it was empty. Even better.

Roland stayed in the woods until he was directly behind Lexie's house. He took a deep breath, coughed, and ran across the yard until he reached the patio. The effort had him breathing like he had just run a mile, thanks to his current health conditions, or lack thereof. He grabbed his knees and tried to control his breathing.

The rain lashed his face and he stepped under the shallow eave for protection. The curtains on the sliding glass door were open, and from this close he could plainly see that all the lights were out. Getting better by the minute.

Now he just had to figure out how to get in. He wasn't worried about style points. A broken window or a kicked-in door would do fine. What he was worried about was an alarm. There was an even chance a sheriff's deputy would have the place wired. He looked on the sliding glass door for a sticker from an alarm company, the kind that was supposed to serve as advertising and a warning, but he didn't see one. He moved over to the high kitchen window, then down the back of the house to two other longer windows, presumably ones for bedrooms. A smaller, higher frosted window was probably the bathroom. No stickers there, either. He took a chance and went to the front, quickly surveying the windows there, but there were no stickers. He ran around back again and tried to catch his breath. His heart was flipping over in his chest, and it took him a minute to calm down.

"Shit, only one way to find out," he said out loud. He found a brick next to the assorted potted plants, walked over to one of the back bedroom windows, knelt down and broke the glass with three quick hits.

A mockingbird in the woods let out a loud squawk and nearly made Roland crap in his pants, but no alarm went off. He carefully reached through the broken window, unlatched the lock and slid the window open wide enough for him to go through. He was about to step into the room when a very important thought went through what was left of his brain.

"Fucking silent alarm," he said under his breath.

He stood up and ran back into the woods, far enough to find cover in the undergrowth. He squatted down again and waited, listening to the tympani drum in his chest.

Irony was a skill lost on Roland's intellect, so it took him a moment to put it all together. *If* Lexie had a silent alarm, it would go off on some asshole's monitor at a security company, probably in Lafayette. *That* asshole would call the nearest law enforcement entity, which in Alcide's case was the St. Martin Parish Sheriff's Department over in St. Martinville. Then some asshole *there* would dispatch the nearest patrol car, which in the case of Alcide was...Lexie.

"Fuck," Roland said. The mockingbird squawked his agreement.

He looked at his watch, and tried to figure out how long it would take this high-tech process to play out and for Lexie to get here. *If* she would get here. There was still a chance there was no alarm.

Roland moved from a squat to sitting on his ass. He let his head drop between his knees and looked at his watch again. *Can something please go fucking right?*

He sat that way for 30 minutes. He might have dozed off. Might have passed out. He was finding it harder and harder to tell the two apart. Either way, nobody showed up at Lexie's house. And that was long enough for the cavalry to get here.

Roland took a deep breath, stood up and brushed off his ass, as if he would be wearing these grimy jeans to church on Sunday. He quickly moved out of the woods to the back of the house, straight to the broken window. He duck walked his emaciated form through the window and found himself in one of Lexie's spare bedrooms. It had a single bed with a frilly pink duvet over it and an abundance of pillows on top. There was an old blue chair in one corner, a four-drawer white chest in the other. There were a few prints on the wall, all flowers or outdoor scenes. The room smelled faintly of lavender, but the house also had the smell of a dinner cooked or reheated from maybe a day before.

Roland turned into Meth Ninja again and moved haltingly out of the room and down the hall. He found Lexie's master bedroom. There was a double bed in there, the covers all messed up. The dresser was bigger, a faux walnut thing with a large mirror above it. There was a big cushy chair in one corner with a floor lamp next to it. Some old clothes were thrown over the chair. Roland walked over and looked at the pile. He picked up a black bra and held it up, imagining Lexie still in it. This got his blood pumping and his brain a-thinking. *Hmmmm.*

He refocused, dropped the bra and went back into the hall. He stopped to listen. The rain had picked up again and he could hear the water sluicing off the roof and into the gutters and downspouts. A low rumble of thunder shook the house.

Roland followed the hall into the living room, where he stopped to survey the lay of the land. Typical setup with a sofa and loveseat, some assorted chairs and a TV and stereo system. A kitchen table and six chairs sat next to the sliding glass window toward the right. A pass-through bar gave him a view of a nice-sized kitchen. A short hallway led from there to a utility room with washer and dryer and out into the covered garage.

This was where it was going to happen. She'd walk in that front door and he'd put a gun to her head and start the evening's festivities. He'd have to call Tree and his thugs first, when things were buttoned up. He figured it wouldn't take long for her to tell them where the drugs were. Or maybe they'd just go out to her trunk and find it all there.

Roland walked to a front window and carefully pulled back the curtain. He took a quick peek outside. Still not a soul in sight. And it was getting harder and harder to see anyway. The day was quickly ending, helped along by the dark, threatening skies.

He had to think. He sat on the love seat and stared at the front door. Would she come in that way, or pull into the garage and come through the kitchen? He voted for the kitchen. It would be raining when she got here and she'd park in the garage. Check.

She would be armed, of course, and probably still a little pissed off about him shooting at her earlier in the day. But she wouldn't be expecting him. She'd be distracted, and that would work in his favor. But where to hide and get the drop on her? He stared at the kitchen. It would have to happen in there, just as she was coming in. The longer she was in the house, the harder it would be for him to get into position to take her. And he had to do it from behind. If she saw him, even if he had his gun out first, she was more than likely to just draw on him and shoot. May the best shot win. And he figured she was the better shot.

He looked at the kitchen for a few minutes more. Then he saw how he was going to do it.

Easy breezy.

Chapter 30:
"Mike and Joanie Go On a Date to the Funeral Home"

Father Mike looked at his watch and continued to pace inside the rectory. His cell phone chimed and he pulled it out of his pocket. On the screen, the text message read, "Meet you in the car. Relax."

He shook his head and put the phone back in his pocket. He grabbed his prayer book and a big black umbrella and headed out into the light rain to the Caddy. It was parked in the driveway, not the garage, so he jogged the few feet without opening the umbrella. Despite the gray dusk, the car's vivid pink color didn't lose its luster.

He hopped in and tossed the umbrella onto the back seat. The car was warm and smelled of leather. Once he got the car started and the wipers on, he switched on the radio to listen to the weather. No big surprise, it was all about Tammy, on its way to Louisiana and now a powerful category 3 hurricane. Landfall expected tomorrow night. 24 hours. And already the weather was turning to crap.

The passenger door burst open and Joanie jumped in and slammed it shut in one fluid movement.

"Nice," he said.

"Shut up."

She had her full nun's habit on. Water droplets made the black habit shimmer in the fading light.

"No umbrella?"

"Couldn't find it." She brushed some of the water off of herself and checked her face in the mirror.

Mike noticed that despite the habit, Joanie still had her face made up. She looked good, even in the uniform. He continued to stare at her.

"What?" she said.

"You. You look pretty good."

She gave him a smirk, but there was a smile in the look, just the same. "Are you being facetious?"

He shook his head. "No, no. Wasn't talking about the habit. Just your face."

"Right. Ain't much else to see. Does this habit make my butt look big?"

Mike laughed. "What butt?"

"Exactly. I'm doing this for you, you know."

Mike put the car in gear and backed out of the rectory's gravel driveway. He continued to smile.

Once on the road, he turned off the radio and settled in for the drive to the funeral home. Joanie folded her hands in her lap and stared out her window into the gloomy dusk.

"See many people out earlier?" he finally said.

She sighed. "Some. Most have bugged out. Hope there's a good turnout for the wake."

"Yeah. From what I hear, it'll mostly be Floyd's old and new girlfriends. That'll make it a crowd."

Joanie smiled. "Heard he was quite the horn dog."

"Tell me he didn't hit on you," Mike said. "That'd be stepping way over the line."

Joanie didn't say anything. She just stared out the window.

"Really?" he said.

"No, he never hit on me," she said. "C'mon, if I was gonna cross that line, I'd probably do it with you. You being on the same team, so to speak."

"I'm so relieved," Mike said. He was. And very happy, too. His heart raced a bit, and there was some stirring down below. He hit the speed dial for St. Michael, but no one was home.

"Does it make you uncomfortable when I flirt with you?" Joanie said.

"Does it make *you* uncomfortable when I flirt with you?" he shot back.

"Unfair question. And you don't flirt with me," she said.

"I do. I'm just more subtle than you are."

"Huh," she said. "Whatever. Answer my question."

A flash of distant lightning illuminated the car interior. "No, it doesn't make me uncomfortable. To be honest, I like it. I shouldn't, but I do."

"You're a man," she said. "You're supposed to like it."

Silence for a moment. Finally he said, "But are we playing with fire? I mean, we've both been around, so to speak. We know where talk like that leads. It's how relationships start. It's fun, provocative. It's meant to...lead somewhere."

"And where would you like it to lead?" she said.

Mike shook his head. "Joanie, I swear. You're something else. If we weren't all vowed up, I'd be all over you. I like you a lot."

She smiled. "See. *That's* what a woman wants to hear. I like you too, Mike."

"We're looking at some big-time sinning here, Joanie. The vows, the out-of-wedlock thing. We could do some serious time for what we're thinking about."

She put her hand on his right hand, which was resting on his thigh. Her touch sent a jolt of electricity through him. "But what if it's meant to be? We wouldn't be the first."

He let her hand stay on his, and he moved his fingers so they intertwined with hers. "Let's stay focused on the wake. For now."

"Okay," she said.

They rode to the funeral home in silence. But their hands stayed together.

Lexie cruised the parish road, watching the wipers on her patrol brush the rain from her windshield. It was nearly full dark now. She had the wipers set on "slow." The rain wasn't that bad. Tomorrow, though, they'd be on "fast." Or "hurricane," if there was such a setting.

There wasn't much traffic on the highway. Most people had left, or were in their homes enjoying supper. She wasn't hungry yet, but she would be soon. She'd make the loop around this part of the parish, then head over to the funeral home and pay her respects to Felice. She couldn't stay long, what with the storm moving in, and Roland running around. After that, she'd stop by her place and re-heat some lasagna she had in the fridge. She tried to remember if she had some garlic bread, too. That would be great. A beer with that would be even better, but she was on permanent duty for the time being, so no booze, and she would have to leave the house after she had a quick bite and get back to work.

She mentally checked off some other stops she'd make through the night. Most of the closed businesses. Some of the outlying neighborhoods and camps. The church. And certainly she'd stop by The Fort to see Cam. She smiled at that thought. She was definitely feeling it for him. She thought it funny how timing was so crucial in a relationship. For months she'd seen Cam, but there was nothing there. Or if there was, she couldn't see it. Then *wham,* a certain look from him and she was toast—in a good way.

She sighed and filed away those good thoughts. There were other things to think about. She looked into the dark swamps and thought about M'Lou Marchand. The poor girl was probably dead. Eaten by whatever got Floyd. Probably nothing left of her, either. But still. Lexie had a funny feeling. A cop feeling. Maybe M'Lou got out. Got away. Maybe she was still alive. The thought of her lost back up in there with a storm coming kicked her in the gut. There would be no way to send people back there until the storm passed.

And then there was the thought that something much scarier than the storm was out there. Something *out of the ordinary.* That was as far as Lexie was willing to go with that theory. She had long dismissed the hungry hippo theory. And the bullshit bullshark theory. It creeped her out so much she hit the roof lights on the patrol car and immediately the red and blue strobes bathed the cypress and willow with otherworldly light. *That* creeped her out even more and she switched them off.

She rode at a slow, steady pace, so she wouldn't miss anything. Or hit anything. The rain eased off and eventually stopped, leaving a steamy haze over the formerly hot roadway. She suspected that wouldn't last long. This wasn't really the hurricane yet, but it was weather being created by the storm as Tammy pumped thick humid air off the Gulf and over land. The real fun wouldn't start until tomorrow.

She put her mind on idle for a while and listened to the dispatcher on the radio. It was Tricia Laurent, a petite, fifty-something bottle redhead who'd been with the sheriff's department for almost 30 years. She was a chain smoker whose gravelly voice and Cajun accent made for an interesting combination over the airwaves. She was chatting it up with the roving patrol cars around the parish, sending them here and there, mostly for minor stuff, but there was one pickup that had slid off the road into a ditch near Catahoula. Probably some asshole starting to get liquored up early for the weekend who took a curve too fast. Didn't sound serious. Her part of the world was running pretty smooth, if you could discount Floyd Guidry, the idiot kayaker, M'Lou Marchand, Roland Avant and something weird roaming around the bayou. On second thought, maybe her world wasn't running smooth at all. It was running way too hot for her.

She turned around at the parish line at a wide part of the road and headed back in to Alcide. The rain continued to hold off and she made good time. There was more traffic here, mostly people getting off work and heading home. These would be the ones staying for the storm. She couldn't see their faces in the dark, but she knew them by their cars and trucks. Some she had grown up with, some were the parents of people she had grown up with. There was a bit of comfort for her in seeing those cars and people. It was home.

Lexie slowed down along the main drag of Alcide. All of the businesses were closed. A video rental store, the one with the room in the front with all the best sellers, and the room in the back that sold the best-selling porn. Which were all pretty much best sellers. A little jewelry store. The city offices, empty with the mayor out of town. The blowhard was probably feeling guilty about not being with his people during their crisis. Probably not. A feed and hardware store, a semi-competitor of Cam's. The local burger joint–not a chain. Just a walk-up window. Pretty good, too. The popular clothing shop, small–but saved some folks a trip into Lafayette for certain things. A craft store that got a lot of business from brave tourists who ventured way off of I-10 and spent a quiet drive through the swamps. The local CPA/lawyer office—run solely by the slick Wayne Babineaux, who really had his main office in Lafayette, but made a few trips to his Alcide office during the week to soak up some cash from the locals. Finally, there was Paran's Country Store, which stocked more groceries than Cam, since that's what it was really. The light was still on, and Paran himself could be seen taking a couple of bags out to a woman's car.

All in all, a nice little smattering of commerce for the little hamlet of Alcide. Some towns needed their own businesses. And sometimes, a couple of towns shared a few, like the funeral home.

She passed Troy's Garage. The garage itself looked closed, but the little office that served the gas pumps was manned by Troy's helper, Odell Landry. No sign of Troy. *Probably banging Carla somewhere*, Lexie thought.

Next there was the Church. Looked closed up. She glanced at her watch and figured Father Mike and Sister Joanie were already on their way to the funeral home. It was really closer to Butte La Rose than Alcide, and pretty much handled the earthly departures of people in this part of St. Martin Parish. Again, a shared business.

Finally, on the edge of town, and on the edge of the bayou, was Fort St. Jesus Bait and Tackle. Only one truck graced the parking lot. It looked like Troy's tow truck. She knew Cam kept his around the side. She pulled in next to Troy and shut her down. She got out of the car and breathed the heavy humid air filled with the smell of the salty Gulf and the earthy swamp. She suddenly had a craving for some good hot coffee.

Inside, she found Cam and Troy shootin' the shit. Cam was behind the counter sitting on a stool. Troy was on the other side, also on a stool and slamming down a canned beer. No customers were around.

She didn't like the look on their faces.

"What's up, boys?"

Cam and Troy gave each other a look. They both looked a little pale and a lot distracted.

Troy coughed and spoke first. "Oh, you know. A hurricane blowing in. A fucking mutant monster tearing up the swamp. And my tow truck."

Lexie held up her hand. "Whoa. What?"

Cam said, "I think we've ID'ed whatever's eating the townsfolk. And cattle."

Chapter 31:
"Be Careful Out There"

Troy gave a rather impassioned accounting of his and Carla's adventure on the highway. Cam sat in silence and munched on a bag of chips. Lexie just stood there, her mouth open and her eyes blinking in a near comical way.

Troy's story ended with a nice beer burp. "And there you have it," he concluded. He popped open another one he had ready on the nearby counter.

Lexie looked at Cam as if to ask, *"Is he bullshitting me?"* Cam just shrugged.

"I...I...don't know what that is," was all she could say, as if she were the one who had to come up with an explanation.

"Me and Carla think it's a government project gone bad," Troy said. He was getting comfortable with this theory. "You know, switchin' out DNA from different animals, creating something new in the lab. Shit like that. Probably got loose. We're thinking Fort Polk." He nodded his head, agreeing with himself.

Again she looked at Cam.

"Hell, who knows?" he said. "Something like that's not going to come along naturally. But from a scientific standpoint, combining all kinds of DNA like that and making a new animal is really, really hard. Mother Nature doesn't like us doing that shit. Only *she's* allowed to do that shit."

"Could it be something that's evolved for millions of years, like us?" Lexie said. "Been here all along and we just haven't seen it?"

Troy snorted. "You mean like the Loch Ness Monster?"

"Yeah, like that," she said. "Maybe it's the last of its kind."

Cam shook his head. "Couldn't be the last of its kind. It's not like we've hunted the thing into oblivion. And there's enough food around for it to eat all it wants. Hell, whatever the oil companies have been doing around here hasn't killed off anything yet, either, despite what the greenie weenies might say."

Lexie scratched the back of her head, and her blond ponytail swung back and forth. "What if it's not...native?"

Troy said, "To the swamp?"

"To Earth," Cam said before Lexie did.

Troy put his beer down. "A fucking alien?"

"Why not?" Lexie said.

"Cuz I couldn't see that thing flying a fucking spaceship, that's why. It came across as an *animal*, not E.T."

"What, you didn't see *Predator*?" she replied.

"It didn't have a fucking laser," Troy said. His voice went up an octave. "It had fucking teeth. And a fucking 20-foot long tongue. With a fucking *hand* on the end of it."

"Shit," Lexie said.

"Yeah, take a look at the tow truck when you get the chance."

A rumble of thunder shook the Fort. They all looked up.

"Unfuckingbelievable," Lexie said. She paced around a bit. "Whatever it is, the storm takes precedence right now. Afterwards, we'll all spend some time with the sheriff on the monster thing. That should be a fun conversation. Cam, you'll have to take point on that one. You're the closest thing we have to a scientist around here. He might even believe you." She looked at Troy. "Mr. Hot Shot Mechanic here, not so much."

"I love you, too," Troy deadpanned. "But it did try to eat me. I'd say that makes me an expert."

"He's got a point," Cam said. "When something tries to have you for lunch, it kinda helps your bona fides."

"Okay, okay," Lexie said. She had both hands up. "And Carla's driving around out there? She's got some balls."

"Actually, she's got some dildos. To deliver," Troy said. Cam couldn't help but laugh at that one.

"Glad you two yuk monkeys are enjoying yourselves," she said. She imagined the thing Troy had described eating Floyd Guidry in one bite. The gators and M'Lou, too. And it fit with what the lesbians saw when the kayaker was attacked.

The door burst open. It was Lee Curtis.

"Did y'all know there's a fucking whale living in the bayou?"

Lexie, Cam and Troy turned as one. Curtis, a bit wild eyed, went on to tell them about the thing that had breached the water in the bayou behind his house.

"At Macy's birthday party?" Cam said. He felt his stomach drop. *That's* what had been bothering him. After seeing the cow carcass and hearing about the attacks on the water, he had felt anxious. Lee had told him about the party earlier, and Cam would have paid Lee a cautionary visit to tell him to keep the kids in the house. If he could have remembered the party. Which he didn't. "The kids okay?"

"Yeah, yeah. Whatever it was scared the fish right out of the water. Damnedest thing I ever saw. At least where fish are concerned. Explains those gators the other day getting the hell out of there. Can there be a whale in the bayou? Could it have swum in all the way from the Gulf?"

"Not a whale," Troy said. "Trust me. I had kind of a close encounter of the shit-in-my-pants kind earlier today." He proceeded to fill Lee in on the particulars.

"Holy shit!" he said. "What the fuck is it?"

Cam said, "Don't know yet. But it's aggressive. What time did you see it?"

"Late afternoon, during the party," Lee said. "Why?"

Cam walked around the counter and to the wall near the coolers. He had a map of the parish with all its waterways. "Lexie, show me where Guidry was attacked."

Lexie walked over and squinted at the big map. "About here," she said.

"Troy, you and Carla got hit about here, right?"

Troy nodded.

"And Lee, you're right here," Cam said. "And the cow got eaten right around here." He grabbed a marker out of a drawer and marked the four spots. "And we found that big pile of shit somewhere in here." He marked that, too. He then drew a line through all four points.

"Son of a bitch," Lexie said. "It's moving this way."

"Show me again where the kayaker bit it." Cam said.

Lexie found that spot, and Cam marked it. All the spots he had just marked were west of Alcide. This one was much farther east. He looked at Lexie, then Troy. "There are definitely two of them."

"What?" Lee said. "You're shitting me?"

"He shits you not," Troy said.

"Fuck, I gotta get back to the house. Cam, you got some 10-gauge shells?" Lee said.

Cam nodded. While he went to get a box, Lee pulled out his cell phone and called his house. His orders were short and direct. *"Lock it down and stay in the house."*

Lexie stared at the map again. *Where was the thing going? And would the storm affect its travels? And is the other one moving, too? And which way?*

When Cam got back to the front, Lexie said, "Cam, that thing is following the bayou. Heading this way."

They all turned and looked out the back door into the gloom, towards the adjacent bayou. For the first time, they all noticed Huey, sitting next to the door, already focused on the waterway. He had his ears up, and they could hear the low, resonant growl coming from his throat.

"I think Huey's been on to this thing. He's been doing that off and on for the last few days."

"You should listen to your dog more," Lee said. He paid for the shells and said, "I'm outta here. Stay safe." And he was out the door in a hurry.

"This is some crazy shit," Troy said. He finished his beer with one long pull. Again with the burp.

"If that thing knows what's good for it, it'll hunker down during the storm like the rest of us," Cam said. "We should be good for the next few days. Then we can deal with it."

"Deal with it?" Troy said. "That fucker wasn't in the mood to talk."

"I mean catch it or kill it," Cam replied. He looked over to Lexie, who was still staring at the dog. "What do you think, deputy?"

Lexie snapped out of her monster musings. "What? Yeah. We'll do something after the storm. Gotta warn everybody. That's going to be hard for the next 48 hours. Most people are gone, and the rest are all locked down. I guess I could go door to door."

"Not enough time," replied Cam. "The storm's gonna help you out there. Wait till after."

Lexie sighed. "Yeah. You two cowboys going to be okay in here tonight?"

Cam and Troy shook their heads. Even Huey broke his concentration and looked at her. Cam said, "This place is rock solid. Got a ginny, got food, water."

"Beer. Guns," Troy added.

"Got the Huey early warning system," Cam continued, with a nod to the dog. "I think he smells and hears that thing, from a long way. If it gets close, we'll know about it."

"We better hope so," Troy said. "I gotta call Carla." He got off the stool and walked to the back of the store, cell phone in hand.

"What about you?" Cam said. "Where you headed now?"

"I'm gonna run by my house, make sure everything's buttoned up. Grab a bite, then head out."

"Eat with us. Got some jambalaya I'm heating up," he said.

She thought for a moment and did some inventory of what she had in the fridge back home. Meager at best. "Okay, but let's make it quick."

"Yes m'am," he said, and headed back into the kitchen.

While Cam and Troy were occupied, Lexie paced a bit. She went over to Huey, knelt down, and scratched the big dog's head. "You smell it, Huey? Where is it, boy?" The dog whined and gave his big tail a couple of half-hearted wags. Lexie thought he gave her a sad look. Or maybe it was a "I'm scared shitless" look. She wasn't a dog whisperer. Huey stood up and put his head to the back door. He sniffed a couple of times. "You want out, boy?" She opened the screen inner door, then the wooden outer one. She held them both open for him. He looked out, sniffed, and looked back at her. But he didn't go out. This time she was pretty sure he sent her a message that basically said, "No way in hell am I going out there." She shut the doors. Huey sat down again.

Lexie got up and grabbed a stool by the counter and waited for Cam to bring the food. She could hear Troy in back talking to Carla on the phone. She couldn't believe Carla was out in this weather, delivering party toys to the hot and the horny across the parish. Then again, with the power going out pretty soon, probably for days, sex might be the only entertainment. Truth be told, she was feeling a little needy herself. That kiss with Cam earlier had opened up some real possibilities. But she'd be busy for a while. Maybe when things calmed down she could see where it would all lead. Bed would be a good start.

"What you thinking about?" Cam said. He carried out three bowls of steaming jambalaya and put them down on the bar.

Lexie looked up. "Hell, what's not to think about? Monsters. Hurricanes. The usual." She grabbed one of the bowls of jambalaya and dug in. The rice, chicken and sausage mixture was just the right level of spiciness for her. A nice tingle, but not enough to hide the flavor. "You should open a restaurant, Cam. This stuff is good."

"Thank Mrs. DeSelle. Mom can cook like nobody's business." Cam's parents were retired and living on the east shore of Mobile Bay. He watched Lexie wolf down the food. "So you're on patrol all night?"

She nodded with her mouth full. "Pretty much. I'll keep it close to home. Watch for flooding, trees down, jackasses running around and getting hurt."

"And a monster. Or two."

"Yeah, that."

Cam said, "Keep your cell phone handy. Might call you during the night. Wake you up."

"Hah. I could use the company," she said. "Shouldn't be too bad tonight. Tomorrow night's gonna be a bitch." She pointed back at Troy, who was still chattering on the phone with Carla. "He staying here tonight or tomorrow night?"

"Slumber party starts tonight. I'm staying open late, and then I'll just bunk in the back on a cot. Troy will sleep next to the beer, I think. He's kind of freaked out by what happened anyway."

Lexie looked at her watch. "Shit, I keep forgetting. Gotta run by Floyd Guidry's wake tonight, too. I'll do that before I swing by the house."

Cam nodded. "Cool. Drop by anytime tonight or tomorrow. I'll open up early in case anyone needs anything at the last minute."

Lexie finished her dinner and slammed down a bottled water. "Thanks, Cam," she said. She wiped her mouth on a paper towel napkin and started to turn for the door. She looked back at Troy, then to Cam, and leaned across the counter and gave him a kiss on the cheek. She didn't pull away, but kept her face close to his and said, "See you soon."

Cam smiled and returned the favor on her lips. "Be careful."

"Always," she said, and walked out into the night.

Chapter 32:
"The Dearly Departed"

Lexie pulled out onto the empty road and headed toward the funeral home. It was a few miles out of town, toward Butte La Rose. The road ran along the bayou for a while, and later veered away for a few miles around a thick swamp before linking back up with the waterway. With little traffic on the road, she hit her high beams to illuminate the darkness on both sides. If anything came out of the woods, she'd see it immediately, and pretty much blind it with her bright headlights. They did catch a few eyeballs on the edge of the swamp. Possum, a couple of gators and maybe a wild pig or two. Nothing that would eat her car, though.

Still, she was on edge. There was something out there that wasn't normal. But then, that described half the women and pretty much all of the men in the area. She figured she'd put herself in that category, too.

With no traffic, and no car-eating monsters, it didn't take her long to get to the funeral home. The place just appeared out of nowhere. It sat on a couple of acres cut out of the woods and swamp. It was designed to look like a large, French-planter-style home, with a high pitched roof that covered a long front gallery and lots of tall windows running the length of it. If you didn't think too much about what went on in the kitchen and back rooms of this particular home, you'd say it was fairly inviting. The parking lot was surprisingly full, considering most people had bugged out of town. That made Lexie happy for Felice. A good turnout for a funeral was a good thing for the living. Lexie didn't know if her late-great husband had a decent gathering for his funeral. She didn't attend, considering she was the one who sent him on his celestial way.

She pulled the cruiser into the lot and did one circuit before finding a parking spot around the side. She walked around to discover three or four gatherings of people at different points of the deep porch. Most were smoking and shooting the shit, letting out some nervous laughter, the social way of dealing with death. With a couple of long strides, Lexie was up the steps and moving to the front door. She heard a couple of, *"Hi, Lexie's,"* acknowledged them with a nod or a quick point of the finger, and headed inside.

The foyer of the place was huge, well appointed and comfy. Deep Persian rugs covered an oak floor. There was a big round table with a marble top that was set with a giant vase of gladiolas. A couple of doors on either side probably led to offices. The place smelled like all funeral homes: nauseating floral. The real scent of death.

A sign with a black felt front and white letters announced the only service in the place tonight. It simply said, "Guidry," and "East Chapel." That indicated the direction to her right, and she walked the long front hallway and found the doors to the East Chapel. A couple of 12-year-old girls sat outside, their heads buried in their phones, texting furiously. Probably texting each other. Neither looked up to acknowledge Lexie's presence.

She pulled open one of the two wooden doors and looked in. The small chapel was fairly full. Father Mike was up front at the podium, leading everyone in the rosary. A silver, brushed-metal casket sat behind him, surrounded in a semi-circle by wall-to-wall floral arrangements. She debated for a moment on whether to go in. She listened to see where they were in the rosary.

Mike said, *"Pray for us, O Holy Mother of God."*

The crowd answered, *"That we may be made worthy of the promises of Christ."*

Lexie thought, *Wrapping it up.* Then Mike and the congregation said a short prayer she couldn't remember and that was it. Rosary over. Mike made the sign of the cross and walked over to the front row where Felice and her grown children were sitting. He said a few words, shook a few hands and worked the crowd. People got up, some walked to the front, others to the back. The wake continued.

She got some welcomes and nods from people headed to the kitchen for coffee and food. She waited for them to pass and walked in and down the short aisle to where Felice was sitting. Mike had moved off to talk to some rough-looking men in suits that looked like they had been bought in 1972.

"Hey, Felice," Lexie said. She extended her hand to Floyd's newly minted widow and Alcide's future most-eligible catch. Felice looked stylish in a simple black dress. Her hair was pulled back behind her shoulders. Despite some redness around her big eyes, Lexie thought she looked pretty good. She couldn't help but notice a few middle-aged men scattered about the vicinity. She recognized them all–divorcees, widowers and some momma's boys who never grew up. Felice was about to get a lot of attention. *Good for her*, Lexie thought.

"Thanks for coming, Lexie," she said with a weak smile. "Any more on what happened?"

"Not really. Storm's got everyone moving in different directions. We'll figure it out." *Might have already done that*, she thought.

Felice sighed. "I know you will, honey. Just be careful."

Lexie nodded. The casual line from Felice had struck her for some reason. There was a sincerity to it that gave Lexie a little chill. Cam had just said the same thing 30 minutes ago.

She said hello to the rest of the family and chatted up some of the other locals who were milling about. She eyed Father Mike, who was now cornered by some blue hairs in a corner. He was nodding and smiling at their comments, but it was apparent he needed some help.

"Excuse me. Father Mike? Got a second?" she said. She gave it an official sheriff's-business tone. Combined with her uniform and holstered gun, it was enough to get the old ladies away from him.

"You looked like you could use some assistance, Father," she said.

Mike looked around. "These things creep me out a little," he said. "Don't tell anyone."

Lexie laughed a little. He might have been joking. Might not.

"Joanie's supposed to be my wingman at these things, but she's no where to be found. Probably in the kitchen stuffing her face."

"You heard about Troy and Carla?" she said in a conspiratorial tone.

Mike leaned closer into her. "That they're banging their brains out?"

"No. Yeah, that, too," Lexie said. "What happened to them today. There were attacked out on the highway just outside of town."

"What?" Mike said. "Are they okay?"

"Yeah."

"Who attacked them?" he said.

"Not the proverbial who, but the proverbial *what*," Lexie said. She grabbed his arm and moved him away from a group of people that had moved within earshot of them. "The thing that probably got Floyd." Lexie nodded at the nearby casket.

"What kind of *thing?*" Mike said.

Lexie proceeded to recount Troy's tale from earlier. She noticed Mike's Adam's apple bobbed a few times. The silent "gulps." When she was done, Mike just stared at her and didn't say a thing.

"It's real, Mike. No matter how crazy it sounds, or weird, the fact is that it's out there. Along with a friend." She had failed to mention the theory that there were two of the things, and chances are, at least one was heading down the bayou toward town. Mike gulped some more.

"Sounds...*biblical*," Mike said.

"Sounds like bad news," she replied. "Be careful heading back to church. That thing attacked a tow truck, for goodness sake."

Mike nodded. "You gonna tell everyone?"

"Here? Now? No way," she said. "I wouldn't know where to begin. I haven't even told the sheriff yet. People think I'm half crazy already. The storm's gonna keep everyone locked up at home for a few days anyway. When all that's over, and the rest of town gets back, we can have a little sit down, I guess."

"Have to," he said.

Lexie scrunched her face, with a kind of disgusted look. "Nobody's gonna believe it unless we catch it."

"That sounds like a completely crappy idea," Mike said. "Remind me to be out of town when you look for volunteers for that little expedition." A couple walked by, and Mike gave them a smile.

Lexie looked over at the coffin. Closed, of course. An attractive middle-aged woman Lexie didn't recognize knelt on the small kneeler in front of it. Her head was bowed in prayer. Probably one of Floyd's old girlfriends, saying goodbye. Lexie glanced over at Felice, who had her eye on the woman. Felice had her beat by a mile, in Lexie's opinion.

"What's in the box?" Lexie whispered to Mike.

"Not much," he said. "They tell me the coffin is as light as a feather. I'm guessing the feet. Seems to be what the good money is on."

"Jeez."

Lexie visualized the thing Troy had described. The size of it. The mouth. The teeth. The tongue. All of it leading to the demise of one Floyd Guidry. At least it left something to put in the coffin. But what about M'Lou? Did it get her, too? Lexie had that funny feeling that no, it didn't. But if so, where was the girl? Too much to think about.

"Okay, I'm outta here," Lexie said. "How late are you and Joannie going to be?"

Mike looked at his watch. "About another hour and then we'll head back home."

"Watch yourselves," Lexie said. "No shortcuts home through the woods to granny's house."

"Good idea," Mike said. "You be careful, too."

Lexie headed back outside. More people were on the porch, talking and smoking. A light rain was falling again, and she jogged to her patrol car. She got behind a few cars that were heading out of the parking lot, no doubt their obligations to the dead and the living fulfilled now that the rosary was over. She didn't blame them for getting home early, what with the weather changing.

She would go by her house for one final check-in before her non-stop shift began. There was no telling how long it would be before she could check on the place. She wasn't too worried about it, though. It sat on relatively high ground, far from the bayou. There might be some street flooding in the neighborhood, but she doubted it would get into the house. At least she hadn't seen that happen since she'd been there. But if Tammy dropped 10 inches of rain in the area, all bets were off.

The power would go off for sure, and she had some meat in the fridge she'd throw into an ice chest to save it. She had grabbed some ice from the Fort before she left, and would put it to good use.

Within 10 minutes she pulled into the street that wound through her neighborhood. *Neighborhood* wasn't the right word. That would entail her actually having neighbors. There were just a couple of houses in the development, hers being the only one occupied at the moment. The developer who had built the neighborhood had big dreams, but they never panned out. There just wasn't that big of a population explosion in Alcide, and it wasn't like a new plant or factory had been built that would attract jobs. Anyway, she had gotten a good price for it. So there was that.

The shallow drainage ditches on either side of the street already had an inch or two of water in them. Not a good sign. By tomorrow night, this whole area might be a lake. She hoped Casa Smith would at least stay high and dry.

She pulled into her short driveway, illuminated by the front porch light and the dome light in her carport. No monsters about. Still, she was wary when she shut the motor off. The back yard of her house was dark, and led to even darker woods. She chided herself for not installing some motion-sensor floodlights back there. She always thought about that when it was dark, but forgot when she made her trip to the Home Depot over in Lafayette.

Lexie sat in the car for a moment and listened. She could hear the *tick tick* of the car's engine beginning to cool. There was the dripping of rain off the eaves. A pleasant sound at the moment, sure to become angrier as the weekend progressed. And that was it. Pretty quiet.

She opened the car's door wide and waited a beat before stepping out. No weird noises that she could tell, and least nothing unnatural for her part of the world. There were the sounds of various bugs and tree frogs crying out in the night, but no monsters. Of course, she didn't know what this particular monster would sound like, but she was pretty sure she'd know it if she heard it.

She took a deep breath and got out, walked around the patrol car toward the door that led into her laundry room and the kitchen. A quick glance at the doorknob revealed no one had tried to force the lock, or that she had forgotten to lock it. She slipped the key in and opened the door into the laundry room. Immediately she was greeted with the smell of laundry detergent and fabric softener. It reminder her that she had forgotten to take some laundry out of the washer and throw it into the dryer.

"Crap," she said aloud. She flicked the light switch on.

She knelt down and opened the front-loading washer and the door of the dryer. After a couple of quick tosses, she had everything in the dryer. She hit the power button and the warm, comforting sound of the oscillating dryer filled the tiny room.

Lexie took two steps into the kitchen and instantly knew she was in trouble. But it was already too late.

Chapter 33: "Visitors"

It was the smell.

Sour. A couple of degrees of funk greater than your average body odor. Your basic gag-a-maggot stink.

Roland.

Her hand went to her gun.

"Uh huh, bitch. Freeze."

Lexie heard the hammer go back on a pistol. It was so close to her ear it sounded like a giant manufacturing machine. She held her hands out.

"That's right. One move and you're fucked," he said.

She felt his hand reach to her side and pull her gun out. Its weight had been comforting, and now the absence of it made her heart skip a beat. He also removed the pepper spray in her duty belt.

"Put your hands on your head and take a step forward," he ordered.

She did as she was told.

"Now, turn around."

She now faced her attacker. Roland looked like hell. He held his old revolver out by one shaky hand, and he had it pointed right at her chest. He wore a grimy t-shirt, soiled jeans that may have been blue at one time and muddy old running shoes. His face seemed even gaunter than before.

Eyes sunken into the sockets. Black rings around them. His blonde hair was now so greasy and dirty it appeared almost brown. And then there was the smell.

"Now, drop that belt off of you and kick it over here."

She slowly undid the belt and let it fall to the floor. Without looking, she kicked it his way. He moved it over more with his foot. Quickly he reached down and picked it up. He put it on the nearby counter.

"Hands back on your head. And don't try any shit. I owe you one."

Lexie watched as he examined her belt.

"Cool, a Taser," he said. He pulled the device from Lexie's duty belt and examined it closely. "Always wanted to light somebody up with one of these."

"Roland, you are so fucked right now," Lexie said.

"Huh, you wish," he said.

Lexie didn't like the way he said that. Like there was more to it.

"Here , put these on and tight," he said. He handed her the speedcuffs that were attached to the belt.

Lexie slipped the cuffs around her wrists and locked them.

"Now sit over there on that sofa and don't move. We gonna have us a little talk."

Lexie complied. She didn't like Roland's demeanor. Not one bit. He was seriously on the edge and way too twitchy to be holding a gun. A few days ago, she would have thought there would be no way in hell he could kill somebody. He was just a freaking meth addict. But after the events of late, including the little shootout at Roland's cabin, she was pretty sure he could do just that. She had to stay cool. The little bastard needed something or she would have already been dead.

"Where's all my shit?"

"The stash we found at your little cabin?" Lexie said. "At headquarters in St. Martinville. Locked up tight."

"Bullshit," Roland said. He rubbed his face as if trying to get a spider or two off of it. "No way you made it over there yet."

Lexie shrugged.

"Stand up," he ordered. "Turn around."

He came up behind her and slipped his hand into her right pants pocket and dug out her car keys. "Sit back down."

Lexie watched as he pulled his crappy little flip phone out of his pocket and pressed some numbers into it. He waited a beat and then said, "Got her. Get over here now. Park around back if you can." He flipped the little phone closed and looked down at her with a shitty little grin. "Now it's gonna get interesting," he said.

This really got Lexie's attention. Who the hell did he just call?

"My associates are on the way. Some real assholes from New Orleans. You see, you fucked up a little business transaction between us. And now they want the goods they came here to buy. And I want to get paid. So you better tell us where you hid our stuff."

Oh fuck, Lexie thought.

Roland paced around for 10 minutes before he heard the big engine of the Town Car as it pulled into the driveway.

As he suggested, they drove around back. He let them in the back sliding glass door.

Tree walked in first, practically ducking to make it inside. He was followed by his four minions. They each had a gun drawn.

"Dat her?" Tree said.

"Deputy Smith," Roland said.

"Where's the shit?"

"She ain't talkin'," Roland said. "Well, she's talkin', but she's lyin'."

Tree walked around the living room and examined the house. He was thinking, and everyone just let that big scary brain do what it had to do. He finally sat down in the love seat across from the sofa where Lexie was sitting. He pulled out his Glock and laid it on his huge thigh.

"Look, bitch," he said. "I don't give a fuck that you're some kind of half-ass coonass deputy whatever. I deal wit dem badass New Orleans cops all the time. You ain't shit, you hear me?

She just stared at him.

"What I need is what I came here to buy. Where you got it at?"

"Like I told dumbass here, it's back at headquarters in St. Martinville," she said.

"That's bullshit, Tree. It's probably in her trunk. Got the keys right here."

Tree looked at him with a *Well, what the hell are you waiting for?* look.

"Right," Roland said. He went out into the garage.

While Tree waited for Roland's return, he looked Lexie over. "You a fine piece of ass for a cop." He grinned at her. His four minions snorted their approval. Within a few minutes, Roland returned from the patrol car.

'Nothin'," he said. "I swear, Tree, she ain't been over to St. Martinville since she took it. Been drivin' around checking on shit before the storm blows in."

"Ain't no deputy's office or anything?" he said. He continued to stare at Lexie, who held his gaze without blinking.

"Shit no. Not in little puny Alcide. You're sittin' in the deputy's office. Or her car. That's it."

Tree sighed deeply. It was as if he sucked in half the air in the room. "Well, then. It's somewhere, and she knows." He pointed at her with the gun.

"Hell yeah, she knows," Roland said. He walked around the room like a lost chicken. "Have to get it out of her."

"Or put it in," Tree said. This time the grin directed at Lexie had a bit more lasciviousness to it.

"Look, jackasses, the drugs are at the sheriff's office," Lexie said. "Gone. No way in hell you can get at them. You can slap me around all you want, but when it's over, I still can't help you. If you want my advice, I'd get the hell out of here and get back to New Orleans before the storm hits. And take Roland with you. It's your only chance."

"Shut the fuck up," Tree said. He stood up and stretched. He looked at his team. "Take her in the back bedroom, get her ready," he said. "Time for some waterboarding, or some other shit. What they call that shit? 'Enhanced interrogation?'" His guys laughed at that one. "Get dat rope and duct tape. Gonna need it," he ordered.

Roland and one of the gangbangers walked out back while Tree and the remaining three thugs encircled Lexie. Her head went from one to the other.

"Man, you are making a big mistake," she stammered out. "End this now before you get too deep."

Tree laughed. "Oh yeah, bitch, it's gonna get *real* deep here in a second." He grabbed his crotch. "You better get your story straight in a hurry."

As scared as Lexie was at the moment, she was also pissed. Pissed that she didn't make a move earlier when it was just Roland. There had been a narrow window of opportunity when it was just him, before she had been handcuffed. Sure, it would have been risky, but she had a chance. Now, she was totally fucked. And would be totally fucked, by the now appropriately named gangbangers who stood around her. And there were pretty goods odds they'd put a bullet in her head when they were done with her. Her only advantage was the information she held in her head—the location of the drugs she and Cam had taken from Roland's camp. As long as she kept that knowledge in her head, the longer she would live. Once they got it out of her, she was done.

"Got some stuff," Roland announced. He and one of Tree's guys walked into the kitchen. Roland held a large roll of silver duct tape. The other guy had some white nylon rope.

Tree nodded toward the back of the house. The three guys around Lexie grabbed her and pulled her up to a standing position. She gave them some token resistance, but it was futile.

Lexie was pushed down the hall. They stopped at the two guest rooms, but kept going until they found the master bedroom. They pushed her inside and removed the hand-cuffs. Roland and the fourth gangbanger joined them. Tree remained in the living room.

"Strip, bitch," one of them ordered. He held the gun to her head.

Lexie hesitated.

"Or you want us to do it for you?" said another. He, too, pointed his gun at Lexie.

She unbuttoned her shirt and removed it. This was met with whistles and catcalls.

"Sexy Lexie," Roland said in a singsong way. "Sexy Lex-ie," he repeated.

Lexie sat on the bed and removed her shoes and socks. She stood up and undid her pants, letting them drop to the floor. She stepped out of them.

The sight of her in panties and bra left the five young men speechless. They had never seen anything like it, at least in real life. Roland's jaw went slack. He had fantasized about this for a long time.

"All of it," he said. His voice was now raspy.

"I swear, Roland, if I make it out of here alive, my sole mission in life will be to see you die. Right after I cut your balls off." Lexie was surprised at how strong and determined her voice sounded. At the moment, she was neither of those things.

"Whatever," he said. "Keep going."

She unclasped her bra in the front, and her breasts fell free. She tossed the bra at one of the gangbangers. She gave Roland another look of defiance and slipped her panties down her legs and kicked them away. She folded her arms across her breasts.

"Dayummm," one of the gangbangers said. "On your back, on the bed," he said. Lexie hesitated, and two of the young men grabbed her and threw her on the four-poster bed her parents had bought for her. And then they got to work with the rope.

Chapter 34:
"Storm's a Brewin'"

Father Mike and Sister Joanie rode back to the church in silence. A light rain had begun to fall, and the darkness had deepened as the gray clouds had descended closer to the earth.

Mike stole glances over Joanie's way. She stared out the window at nothing, lost in whatever thoughts Joanie's agile mind had slipped into. Even with the nun's habit on, she looked beautiful in the pale headlights that reflected off the slick road and nearby trees. They had held hands all the way to the funeral home, a tender gesture by any standards held by single or married couples, but scandalous by those set forth by the little country that sat in the middle of the city of Rome.

Mike wanted to hold her hand now. "What's on your mind?" he said.

She hesitated a moment and looked his way. "Floyd and Felice. Married for decades. Now she's alone. How people stay together, despite their own failings. What the heck could've eaten Floyd. Stuff like that."

"Let's start with that last one," Mike said. "Any theories?"

"Probably aliens," she said, as if this sort of thing happened all the time. "No other explanation."

"Aliens."

"Right."

"Okay, let's talk about the other stuff. Relationships," Mike said. "They happen. People fall in love, they get married, they weather the storms, but stay together."

"Sounds like Felice was doing all the weathering," Joanie said. "Floyd got the better end of that deal."

"Probably. But he had his own sense of right, in a way. He didn't *love* those other women. He loved Felice. He just needed some *strange*."

"A lot, apparently," Joanie replied.

"Still, a sin."

Mike had his right hand resting on the seat. Joanie reached over and held it.

"I think this is where we left off," she said.

"Yep."

Like before, they rode like that without a word. Each one mulling over the consequences. Mike drove a little slower than normal. He thought of Floyd, a kindred spirit in the world of cheating. After all, that's what he was thinking of doing. Not cheating on a wife, but the Church. Capital "C." The one he vowed to be faithful to for the rest of his life. And that other "C." Celibacy. One and the same. But Floyd remained faithful to Felice, despite his wanderings. By all accounts, she was his one true love. He took care of her, they had children together, shared so many secrets. Well, most of them, anyway. Some were better left hidden away. So could he be like Floyd? Still faithful to his "wife," the Church, but also have a little something on the side? He glanced over at Joanie. She didn't look like "something on the side." She looked like the real deal.

Mike had always believed a Catholic priest could be married and still do his duties for the congregation. The Protestants had proven that. Sure, they had fooled around on their wives some, too. They were human. He could easily see himself married with kids, living at the rectory, taking care of his pastoral duties and tucking his children in at night. Of course, the hours would be long, but doctors did it, right? He could handle it. And if some priests chose to be celibate, that was cool with him, too. Make it optional.

Mike sighed. *Never gonna happen.* So he could choose to quit the priesthood—and hope Joanie quit her order, too—or just live the double life of Floyd. "The Life of Floyd." Mike smiled. Wasn't there a "Life of Riley?" He couldn't remember the details, but he thought it was a good thing, too.

A few minutes later they pulled into the garage next to the rectory. The rain was really coming down now. Mike wondered if the hurricane had picked up speed and intensity and was arriving a full day ahead of schedule. He shut the motor off and looked at Joanie.

"Take that thing off," he said.

Joanie did a double take. "What?"

"The veil."

She gave him a look.

"I can't kiss you if you're wearing that. It'd be like kissing Sister Lucinda from third grade."

Joanie removed the black veil, then the white wimple that surrounded her face. She undid her hair and it all fell to her shoulders. She gave her head a shake. "Whew, that thing gets hot."

This is where there'd be some poetic staring into each other's eyes, the sound of the rain being drowned out by the beating of their hearts, or possibly some swelling theme music if this had been a movie. Or some such shit. What happened was Mike leaned over, Joanie met him halfway, and they kissed. At first, there was no lip lock, no tonsil explorations—just a sweet, tender kiss, soft and a bit hesitant, like middle school kids.

At first.

"Really coming down now," Troy said. He had the back door of Fort St. Jesus Bait and Tackle opened a bit, his head just sticking out. The back porch was cleared of all furniture in preparation of the storm. The heavy rain on the bayou sounded as if there was a big waterfall out in the darkness instead of a slow-moving bayou. A distant flash of lightning lit up the scene. The surface of the bayou was dancing with the heavy drops.

Cam didn't hear him. He stood near the counter, looking up at the flat-screen TV. The Weather Channel guys were nearly orgasmic in anticipation of the storm slamming into Louisiana. On screen at the moment was a continuous loop of Hurricane Tammy as seen from space. It was a giant white pinwheel spooling round and round as it edged ever closer to the coastline, although it had slowed a bit. It was staying true to everyone's predictions, a fact repeatedly mentioned by the weather people. For once, they were getting it exactly right.

Tammy was still barely a Category 3, sustained winds around 115 miles per hour, although they were measuring gusts at up to 130. There was some talk it might drop to a Cat 2 when the eye hit the coast.

"Anything new?" Troy said. He sat down on a nearby stool and looked at the TV.

"Looks like landfall will be early tomorrow night now," Cam said. "It's slowing down."

"Slow and strong," Troy said. "Bad combination."

"We're gonna get a shitload of rain," Cam replied. He looked over at Troy. "You set up back there?"

"Nice and cozy." Troy had unfolded a cot back in the storeroom. He'd put a sleeping bag on top of it and an electric Coleman lantern on a stack of beer cases nearby. Cam's cot was back there, too, along with an old horse blanket on the floor for Huey. The big Lab was curled up on the floor behind the counter at the moment, dreaming of slow, fat squirrels.

Cam looked around. The store was buttoned up. He planned to be open for just a few hours in the morning, but now with the storm slowing down, he'd probably keep the place open for most of the day tomorrow. Still, he wasn't expecting a lot of business.

"You heard from Carla?" he said.

"Yeah, she's back at her place now. Got all her deliveries done. Got my truck, though. She says she might bring it back tomorrow if she can."

"No woman. No truck," Cam said. He smiled. "A double shot of loneliness."

Troy shrugged. "Got a whole room full of beer to sustain me. I'll make it."

Cam fidgeted with his cell phone. He pulled up Lexie's number on the speed dial and touched it. Seconds later, it was dialing her. There was a click, then her recorded voice telling him to leave a message.

"Crap."

Troy stuffed his face with a Twinkie. He mumbled, "Dude, she's too busy for chit chat."

Cam said, "Don't forget to pay for that." He looked at his watch. Getting close to nine. "I'm gonna lock up." He walked to the front door and bolted it. He did the same with the back, and set the alarm, leaving the motion sensors off since he, Troy and Huey would be bunking in for the next few days.

"Okay, nobody open the doors. Alarm's on," Cam said.

Huey looked up as if to say, *"As if. Ain't got no thumbs anyway."*

Cam wondered if the alarm went off, the security company would call it in and Lexie would show up. Interesting thought. He kind of missed her at the moment. Truth be told, he was worried about her. Storm brewing. Something extremely weird running around attacking cars, people and cattle. And she was out there by herself. Nothing he could do about it at the moment.

He pulled up his stool and watched the giant buzz saw heading right for him and Louisiana.

The male creature had made pretty good time during the day. He hit a long stretch of the bayou without incident, making a fairly decent angle toward the female. They were definitely getting close now.

The weather had changed, and a lot of game had gone to ground. And that meant he was extremely hungry. Most of what sustained him at the moment was in the water: gators, large turtles and fish. But what he was really hungry for was one of those wild hogs. A fat one. Or a deer. A cow would be great, too, but he would have to backtrack to that pasture, and he didn't want to lose any more time or distance. He would just have to suck it up and go in lean and hungry. Once he was done with the female, he'd go on an eating binge, then hightail it deep into the swamp. His body would be back to normal then, and he'd eat at a slower pace.

But that would be later. Right now he pushed easily beneath the water, surfacing occasionally for a breath of air. Each time he did, he thought he could smell the female even better. The rain probably helped that along. But each time his head popped onto the surface, he could see more and more signs of the smart things–their dwellings, the roads they traveled on, their watercraft. That was going to be a problem for both he and the female if they hooked up right in the middle of where the smart things lived. They'd have to get things taken care of quickly and get out of there.

Another thought went through his head and he smiled, or what passed for a smile for a creature like him. If there were smart things around, he'd feast like crazy before heading out. He could have sex and a great meal all at the same time and place.

That would be awesome.

Chapter 35:
"Lexie Goes Commando"

Lexie lay on her back, butt-naked, spread-eagled on her four-poster bed, tied with rope to each post. She was pondering her hoo-hoo. Her lady business hadn't had much attention in the last few years. Okay, it hadn't had any attention, except for the sporting equipment supplied by Carla. But as for men, well, no one had entered into the Magic Kingdom in a long time. She was hoping Cam might do her the honor pretty soon. In fact, she was planning on it. But there was a good chance that wasn't going to happen. Because in a few minutes, she was going to be gang-raped by a bunch of thugs, forced to tell where she had hidden Roland's drugs, then shot in the head. The irony was, she had always hoped she'd die in her own bed. But that was supposed to be of old age, with her family surrounding her, not like something out of a slasher movie.

Lexie wondered who'd be the first person to find her. One of her fellow deputies? She hoped not. The story of how she died would be spread around like old-woman gossip. Would Cam find her? That thought tore at her gut. She wanted to be alive when he saw her naked.

She sighed. *Fuck this shit.*

She could hear the gangbangers talking in the living room. After she had been tied up, and groped pretty thoroughly, they had left to report back to their boss. He would have first dibs, she figured, and the thought of that giant on top of her made her shudder. The discussion probably had to do with the pecking order after he was done. Roland, of course, would probably be last, and the thought of that filthy piece of shit humping away on her really got her focused.

She looked at the ropes binding her hands and feet. The knots were nothing but granny knots. She doubted any of these jackasses had been Boy Scouts. No bowlines or half hitches, the kinds of knots a Scout would know. The knots her Daddy had taught her.

She looked at the one binding her left wrist. It was pretty tight, painfully so. The knot on her right wrist, though, had a little play in it. She curled her long fingers inward and used her index finger to scratch at it. Her nails were short, but she had enough of one that it found purchase in the nylon rope. Lexie knew she would never scratch through it in time, but she hoped she could wiggle it loose. And that's exactly what was happening. She leaned to the right as much as possible to give her more slack, and when she did, the knot loosened even more. Finally, she had the entire tip of her index finger through the knot and was able to untie it completely.

Her right arm was free.

Lexie leaned over and got to work on the tight knot binding her left wrist. Same kind of crappy knot, but much tighter. She tore at it with her free hand, tugging, pushing, wiggling, doing everything she could to get it loose.

A deep laugh emanated from the front of the house, followed by a chorus of chuckles. *Sounds like the pecking order deliberations are winding up*, Lexie thought.

Finally, the knot loosened and she got her other arm free. With two hands, it didn't take long to get her ankles untied. Within one minute she was ready to go. She gave a quick look at the bedroom door. No one was coming, but it wouldn't be long. Her only means of escape was through the bedroom window, which looked out onto the backyard. She went to it, pulled the curtains back, unlatched the lock and eased the window up. She was relieved it didn't squeak. When she had it up as far as it would go, she sat on her bottom and kicked the screen out. She looked at her long legs hanging out into the rainy darkness, and was reminded she was seriously naked. Under the circumstances, she would put survival before modesty. But there was the practicality angle, too. She would have to escape into the woods and the swamp beyond. Wet, cool and full-on dark. Her body would take a beating, especially her feet. And even though it was still a warm September, the cool, wet night would bring on mild hypothermia.

Lexie looked back into the room and saw her uniform scattered around the floor. Did she have time to get dressed? Should she just grab what she could and hit the road, so to speak?

She pulled her legs back inside and compromised. She grabbed her pants and slipped them on, sans panties, all the while watching and listening to her captors in the living room. She was going commando. Same with her top. No time to fiddle with a bra. She got her shirt on and buttoned the top two buttons. Her shoes? Where were they? She frantically looked around the floor and around the bed. Finally, she spotted them on the other side of the chair. She passed on the socks and slipped the boots on and did a quick knot to keep them on.

Lexie then heard the words that sent a chill up her spine. From the front of the room, the deep bass of the giant's voice was very clear, "Okay, let's get this party started."

Since she was to be the party favor, Lexie decided it was time to make some hay. She scooted to the window, dropped down and went through in one fluid motion.

Just as the party boys entered the room.

Lexie wasn't sure, but she thought she heard a distinct, *"Motherfucker!"* She wasn't waiting around for clarification. She was running full stride across her backyard. The rain was falling pretty good now, but she didn't really notice. She was making a beeline for the tree line.

"Get that bitch!" a booming voice yelled from somewhere behind her.

The backyard grass was like a soaked sponge, and in seconds, Lexie's boots were filled with water. It didn't slow her down in the least. In fact, she sped up, cut to her left slightly, and found the old deer path that began at the edge of the woods. It was hard to see, even in the daytime, but she was familiar with it, framed by two pin oaks that marked the way. She was in the woods.

The sound of the rain seemed to increase in volume, but it was the pattering sound of the heavy drops hitting the canopy above her that changed the pitch. It at least slowed the rain as it fell through the trees, but it didn't matter much to Lexie. She was already soaked.

More yelling from behind her, but it sounded much farther back than before. She was gaining ground. The woods were pitch black, but she ran full on anyway. She knew the trail by heart, at least for a hundred yards or so. She often walked back this way looking for blackberries, which grew in some of the sunnier spots. But she was rapidly approaching the end of the trail and slowed a bit. A branch from a small tree slashed across her chest and part of her face. The impact caused her to stumble and fall into the wet leaves on the trail.

Instinctively, like prey being chased by a predator, Lexie turned toward her pursuers, even as she slid across the trail on her side. She was prepared to fight, and figured she had a chance in the darkness. But no one was behind her. In fact, she could still hear the gangbangers, but they seemed to be far to her left, yelling at each other. Maybe 50 yards away. Not far under normal circumstances, but in the dark woods, it was as good as a mile.

She stayed on the ground and caught her breath. She had to be careful that she didn't stumble right into those assholes' path. With no moon, no stars and no compass, she would quickly lose her sense of direction. Her house was still behind her. She could see the faint glow of her houselights through the trees. That meant she was heading north. But once she lost sight of those lights, all bets were off. Her survival training told her that most people who were lost walked in a big circle, since one leg was always longer than the other, causing the wayward traveler to lean one way more than another. Hence, the circle.

Lexie got up, brushed off her wet pants, and walked quickly through the woods. She was off the trail now, or it had ended. More branches lashed at her face, and she had to keep one arm up to protect it. She kept one ear focused on her noisy pursuers, angling as much as she could away from them. But the deeper she went, the more the darkness seemed to deepen, and she could feel disorientation creeping into her psyche. Lexie tried to get a mental image of an area map into her head. If she headed due north, which she still believed she was walking, there was probably 10 miles of woods and swamps ahead of her before she reach I-10. And if she did reach it, the highway would be 30 feet above her as it began its elevated span across the Atchafalaya Basin towards Baton Rouge. No way up for help.

In the map in her head, she could see the parish highway, but it was off to the east, maybe three miles, so she would have to take more of a right turn through the woods to make it there, and presumably, a ride back to town.

Lexie stopped walking and listened. She could hear faint voices in the distance, and the *crunch snap* of stupid people moving awkwardly in the woods. But the sounds were definitely far away and getting farther. They'd never find her back up in here. She turned back where her house should be, but didn't see lights anymore. The deep woods obscured them, and she had lost her last directional landmark. Above her, the rain continued to fall from low gray clouds. There was nothing to guide her. She even tried to listen for the steady *whoosh* of high-speed traffic on the distant interstate, or the occasional horn of an 18-wheeler. If she could lock in on that, it would tell her where true north lay. But there was nothing. The sound of rain drowned out any such noise.

Shit! Lexie turned in a complete 360-degree arc. She could still hear the diminishing sounds of the gangbangers. They had to be behind her and to her left. So southwest. She lined herself up, with the distant voices along that heading and her eyes facing what should be north.

She turned right, tried to find something ahead in the darkness to fix on for dead reckoning. Nothing. It was just too dark. She walked ahead anyway.

Tree, his gangbanger posse, and Roland, stood in the darkness of the woods, looking in all directions. Raymond, the boy genius of the bunch, had pulled out his smartphone and hit a flashlight app that created a brilliant white screen that served as a pretty good light in the darkness. The others had done the same, and the combined light illuminated a small patch of woods around them. Just not in the distance.

"Who the fuck tied her up?" Tree bellowed. "I might just shoot your ass right here and let the ants eat you." Tree indeed pulled out his gun and waved it around him. The others flinched. This was no idle threat, they knew. The crazy son of a bitch just might do it.

"They was tight, Tree," one said. "I checked. Bitch must've had a knife hidden or sumpin'."

"Yeah," somebody seconded.

"Fuck!" Tree howled. "We ain't gonna find her back here. Where she go?" He directed this at Roland.

"Whole lot of nothin' this way," Roland said. "She's fucked if she don't find the road. It's back that way. Long ways, too." He pointed to what he thought was east.

Tree put his hands on his hips and looked around. "Let's get the fuck out of here."

They trudged back toward the distant light of Lexie's house. In 10 minutes they emerged from the tree line and made their way back inside, totally soaked and muddy. One of Tree's men got some towels out of the hall bath and tossed them around to everyone but Roland. He was standing by the bar, looking at something in his hand.

"Hey, motherfucker," Tree said to him. "What you doin'?"

Roland didn't look up. "It's her cellphone," he said. "It must have gone off while we were out."

"So?"

"So look who called her." Roland looked up at Tree and smiled. "Cam DeSelle."

"Who the fuck dat?" This from one of Tree's guys.

"*Dat,*" Roland said, "is a big fat clue."

"To what?" said Tree. He walked over to Roland.

"To where I think she hid all your drugs."

"What?"

"Fort St. Jesus Bait and Tackle. Where you stopped today for those snacks. DeSelle owns the place. He and the deputy are buds. *That's* where she stowed the stuff to get it out of her car."

"How you know?" Tree said

"Well, she didn't go back to St. Martinville. No way she had time for that. They ain't in the car. We searched the house. It makes sense. She left your stuff with him, till maybe after the storm."

"You sure?" Tree said.

"Yeah. Gotta be where it is. Should have thought of that before."

Tree shook his head and looked around the room. He was in thinking mode. Everybody got quiet. Roland continued to thumb through Lexie's cell phone.

"Okay, let's get the fuck out of here," Tree said. "We do a drive-by of this place again tonight, scope it out. You find us a hotel to crash at and we'll come back with a plan for tomorrow." He pointed a finger at Roland. "You sure that bitch gonna be lost back up in there for a few days?"

Roland shrugged. "Not a few days. Maybe one. She's gonna be lost in there tonight. Might take her all day tomorrow to get out, *if* she gets out. There's some weird shit back up in there that can eat you." He thought about his big buddy, Gaston. *Wonder where that big fuck was hanging out tonight?* Again, he refrained from bringing this up with his new city-friends. Might freak the brothers out.

"She get out and makes a call, we're fucked, Tree," Raymond advised.

"Yeah, yeah. Timing's everything," he said.

He looked around again. "Let's go. And we'll take that road you was talkin' about. Maybe we get lucky and catch that bitch after all. I wanted some of that."

Roland thought, *If only we could be so lucky.*

Chapter 36:
"Disconnected and Dislodged"

Lexie continued to make her way through the dark woods. The rain had let up some, but it was a small consolation. She was thoroughly soaked, and her arms, legs and face had taken a beating from all the low branches and briars she had stumbled into. But under the circumstances, she was feeling pretty good. She had had time to process the evening's events, and realized how *really* close she had come to a truly shitty death. She had calmed down some, after what Cam called "an adrenaline dump"—the second in as many days—and now just tried to figure out how to get back to civilization. For a while, she had contemplated backtracking and returning to her house. Her theory was that the gangbangers had probably left, thinking she was trying to get as far away from them as possible. But she had been ambushed once already tonight, and she didn't want to go for another. She figured her best bet was distance, and she had attained that.

Except she was pretty sure she was now lost.

Lexie had a sinking feeling she had strayed from her original eastern course, toward the road, and was now heading west, or north. Maybe even south toward her house. She wasn't sure of anything. Her survival skills told her to stop and hunker down, wait till first light when she could get some sense of direction. So that's what she did.

All those smug survival guys on TV would say build a shelter and get a fire going. No way in hell she could get a fire started in this rain. And everything was wet anyway, never mind she had no matches or flint or whatever they used. But she might be able to build a crude shelter.

Her eyes had now grown accustomed to the darkness. There was some ambient light, probably coming from the city lights of distant Lafayette toward the west. It was enough to do what she had to do. First, she found a long branch on the ground and propped one end of it inside the fork of a tree, about four feet above the ground. Then she gathered shorter branches and laid them on either side of the longer one, creating the walls of her "tent." Most of those branches still had dead leaves on them, but still attached. It created decent cover. She added more leaves from the floor of the woods, starting from the bottom and working her way to the top of her tent. In ten minutes she had a pretty good leaf-igloo shelter. It looked like a blind. She crawled inside and was at least out of the rain. Her new home smelled of rotting wood and wet leaves, but it was the coziest place in town at the moment. She felt safe and hidden. Even if those assholes were still on her trail, they'd probably walk right by her and never see her new camouflaged dwelling.

With that somewhat comforting thought in mind, she eased down on her side and curled up in a ball. Her exertions had kept her warm, despite the wet clothes, but now she was beginning to cool off. She figured the outside temperature was probably in the sixties—still warm—but her wet condition would result in a miserable night. She hoped her shelter would at least capture some of her body heat.

Lexie closed her eyes and thought about a hot bowl of Cam's gumbo. And a hot bowl of Cam.

The male creature surfaced again and took a deep breath of the rainy night air. It was filled with the usual stuff—the swamp, various animals, both land and aquatic, and that faint unnatural smell that seemed to be everywhere these days. He attributed it to the smart things and their machines.

But he got a whiff of something else. Something he hadn't smelled the last time he had surfaced. He held his position on the surface and took another, deeper breath. And there it was. It was the smell of one of the smart things. Not the distant smell of the place where many of them lived. No, this was distinct, individual, and *close.* He kept his nose in the air and turned a complete 360 degrees in the water, honing in on the direction from which the smell was coming. It seemed to be from the woods to his left, not that far away. Could it be he could grab a quick midnight snack? That sounded like an excellent idea to him.

The creature swam toward the bank of the bayou and eased his massive body onto the land and up the gentle slope. At the top of it was the hard surface that the smart things traveled on. He had seen those machines, and in fact, had ridden on one today. He filed that experience away as something not to try again. You could get hurt doing that.

He looked left and right, but didn't see any oncoming vehicles. With three big leaps, he was over the road and down the other side. The woods on that side were thick, and there was no water in them. He'd have to walk through there, which was no easy feat for something his size. But he smelled food, he was ravenous, and he had the time. What the hell. Go for it.

His big eyes gave him excellent night vision, and he scanned deep into the woods. Nothing moved from his vantage point, but he was pretty sure something would be soon. When he walked into the swamp, *everything* usually moved. He took another deep breath, got a lock on the smart thing, and started to hunt.

Roland got the gangbangers to drop him off at his trailer. No chance Lexie would be picking him up there, since she was kind of occupied at the moment. He thought about her out in those dark, rainy swamps, all alone and lost. He didn't give a shit. He was free of those crazy fucks, if just for the night.

He had directed them to drive over to Henderson and stay at the Holiday Inn Express right there on I-10 at Grand Point Highway. Closest decent place, and he figured the night manager would be quite freaked when all those shitheads walked in looking for a room. They'd probably shoot the guy and just grab some keys, just for the fun of it.

Speaking of fun, Roland was really pissed Lexie had gotten away. He had come so close to getting a chance to ride that fine piece of ass for a while. Even if he had to wait in line behind five other guys. Whatever. He just wanted this weekend to be over, get his money and hightail it out of town for good.

He kept the lights off in the trailer, just in case somebody was still looking for him. He doubted it. Everyone was hunkering down for the storm. He was the least of their worries. Roland wondered if his little mobile home would become truly mobile sometime tomorrow, picked up by Hurricane Tammy and dropped off somewhere miles away. He could care less. He was about to become a citizen of New Orleans anyway.

He dug around for some food in his small fridge, found a stale bag of opened Cool Ranch Doritos, two Twinkies and a flat Mountain Dew. He scarfed it all down in a couple of minutes. The food rush felt good, but he really needed something a bit stronger. He reached under his bed, found his emergency stash of meth, cooked it up and inhaled the magic smoke.

"Oh yeah," he said, and leaned back on his bed like a lover finished with some great sex.

Roland closed his eyes and thought about tomorrow. He and the bangers were going to have to pay Mr. Cameron Dee-Sale a little visit. That sneaky Lexie had for sure hidden his drugs there. Where else would she put them if not in her trunk? They'd have to get there before Lexie did, which was pretty much a certainty. Even if she made it out of the swamps, she would still be miles from Fort St. Jesus. That gave him some pause. She might still get there before them. Maybe he'd recommend he and the bangers lay a little trap for her along the road. Wait for her to pop out and take care of some business. A little insurance.

Yeah, that would work. Roland mellowed out completely as the sound of rain beat against the thin aluminum roof of his trailer.

Five miles away, Cam, Troy and Huey had bedded down for the night in the back storeroom of Fort St. Jesus Bait and

Tackle. There was now some wind with the steady rain, and it lashed against the side of the building and the rusted tin roof.

Huey was out cold on the floor, stretched across the thick horse blanket. On one side of the room, Troy lay on his back, hands behind his head, staring at the ceiling. On the other side, Cam lay reading a paperback to the weak light of the electric Coleman lantern.

"What you reading?" Troy said without looking over at Cam.

"*61 Hours,*" Cam said, also not looking up from his book. "Lee Child book. His character's name is Jack Reacher. Ex-army MP who roams around the country busting heads and saving people's asses."

"Sounds like fun," Troy said.

Huey whimpered, but his eyes remained closed. A fitful dream.

"You ever read science fiction shit?" Troy said.

"Not lately. More when I was younger."

"What about horror?"

"Read some Stephen King thing last year," Cam replied. He turned a page in his paperback. "Good stuff. Don't read it all the time, though." He glanced over at Troy. "Why?"

Troy sighed. "We got some sci-fi horror shit going on right now, for real, right here in little Alcide."

"Sounds like it," said Cam.

"Dude, I keep seein' that thing in my head. Can't sleep."

Cam had put Troy's and Carla's little experience out of his head at the moment. What they had described and what his rational, scientific brain told him couldn't get reconciled.

They had seen *something*, but what? Some mangy bear with no fur? Mixed with a little hysteria?

"You need to talk it through some more?" Cam had a quick Iraq flashback. He had this conversation plenty of times with guys who had gotten a good whiff of their own deaths, only to escape unharmed. They had to talk about it.

"I just can't figure out what it is, where it came from. I mean, it was surreal, dude. Right out of Jurassic Park or something."

"So you think it was a dinosaur?"

"Kinda," Troy said. "But it wasn't scaly or anything."

"I don't think dinosaurs had scales. You're thinking of dragons."

"Oh, yeah. Right."

"But dragons *really* really aren't real."

"Right. But you think maybe some leftover dinosaurs have survived all these years back up in the Atchafalaya?"

"Man, there are all kind of theories about stuff like that. But mostly it's things deep in the ocean. Lots of places for shit like that to hide for millions of years. But back in those swamps? I don't know. Guess it's possible."

Troy shuddered. "And to think all these years how much time I spent back there, fishing and hunting, and that thing was roamin' around. Shit, that gives me the willies."

Cam tried to focus on his book. Then he started thinking about the big pile of shit they found. He thought about the pieces of animals in it, animals that had been eaten. And then there was Floyd's belt buckle, and presumably some undigested pieces of Floyd in there, too. That was no hoax or illusion. It was the real shit. Literally.

Cam looked over at Troy, who now had his eyes closed. The big guy was supremely shaken by what happened to him today. No doubt about that. Usually, Troy was pretty even keeled. He didn't let things bug him too much.

He started to have that weird disconnected feeling he had when he was in Iraq. It was like living in multiple realities at the same time, with the same body. Except he was never completely in one or the other. He sort of felt *dislodged*. It was the only way to think of it. Like experiencing different story lines at the same time. In one, he's finally cracked the ice with Lexie. In another, getting ready for a hurricane. And, of course, there's the sci-fi movie he's living in, with weird dinosaurs or mutant creatures eating their way through the swamp.

Cam turned to his left and looked at a stack of beer cases. On the floor next to them was a pile of meth, cocaine and some weed. Roland's stash, earlier confiscated by Lexie, and now hidden in his storeroom. He was now part of the biggest drug bust Alcide had ever seen.

Yeah, there was that bit of weirdness going on at the moment, too.

Chapter 37:
"Dreams and Nightmares"

Lexie pulled herself into a tighter ball and tried to make sleep come. She had no idea how long she had been in her little leaf shelter. Despite building it in the dark, it was working. The steady rain couldn't penetrate the dense leaves she had packed on the side and on top. She was still wet, though, from her run through the woods, and the fabric of her shirt and pants was rubbing her the wrong way. One more reminder why Mom always said to wear underwear. If she could at least nod off some, it would make the night more bearable.

Suddenly, she had a realization. She had dreamed strange dreams. Snippets of weirdness and jumbled plot lines. Something about Cam and Huey. The classic monster chase, where her legs felt like lead and she couldn't move fast enough. Then one brief encounter with that survival hunk on one of the cable shows, who was throwing palm fronds on a bamboo hut on a warm beach, while Lexie lay completely nude inside on the sand. That one was actually pretty good, but she didn't know how it ended. And weirdest of all, her dead husband, carrying a machete and walking in circles all night through the woods, looking for her little shelter.

I did sleep!

The rain continued to fall outside, and its pattering sound was somewhat comforting. Had she been in her bed, snuggled under her thick duvet, it would've been fantastic. But there was another sound, like a rhythmic hissing, breaking the cadence of the raindrops. And it was close.

Lexie opened her eyes but remained completely still. When she did, she realized she could see more detail inside her little home in the woods. Leaves below her, leaves above her. A leaf cocoon. She saw the thicker brown branches that made up the framework. At first, she thought her night vision had improved to its maximum. But this was too much. It was dawn, or daylight. She had no idea what time it was. Her watch was back at her house, probably now in the possession of those assholes from New Orleans.

But the steady hissing sound persisted. No, not hissing. *Breathing.* It was coming from behind her, at the entrance to the shelter. Just feet away.

With a start, Lexie flexed, turned over on her back and prepared to fight. But what she saw looking into her woodsy home left her speechless.

A voice said, "I thought you were dead."

Lexie stared wide-eyed at the young woman who just spoke to her. Whoever she was, she had squatted down on her haunches to look inside the shelter. Her dark wet hair was matted to her scalp. There were scrapes on her pale face, and a small cut over her right eyebrow that had started to scab over. She wore a yellow raincoat that looked three sizes too big for her, and nothing else. Lexie could see her pale knees and ankles, also full of scratches and insect bites. The girl wasn't wearing any shoes either. Or panties for that matter. *A kindred spirit,* Lexie thought.

"We gotta get the fuck outta here," the girl said. Lexie noted how her big green eyes shifted to the left. There was fear in those eyes. And something else. A haunted look. They looked a little dilated, too. The girl was in mild shock.

Lexie rubbed her eyes and tried to shake off her own shock. "Who are you?" she said. The moment she did, she knew the answer.

"Mmm….M'Lou," the girl said.

"M'Lou Marchand?" Lexie said.

The girl didn't reply. Something caught her attention. There was a new noise. It was the distinct *crack* of wood breaking. Lexie's first thought was the storm had moved ashore and was beginning to re-landscape the woods and swamps of south Louisiana.

"It's coming. Please, get up!" M'Lou said.

A shiver worked its way down Lexie's spine. M'Lou didn't say *they're* coming. No, it was that fear-inducing, shit-in-your-pants *it's coming*. Lexie scooted on her ass across her leaf bed toward the entrance of the shelter. There was a real drop in temperature once she was out, probably due to her trapped body heat inside and the falling rain outside.

"What?" she asked. She brushed off her pants and looked around.

"There," M'Lou said. She was pointing behind them.

Lexie turned around and looked into the woods. At first, her vision was overwhelmed by the vastness of it. Greens and browns, big tree trunks like nature's own columns in a vast temple. Gray moss and vines hung everywhere. The entire scene was muted gray by the rain and the low clouds. Tall trees swayed in the increasing winds of Hurricane Tammy.

The leaves were still green, faded slightly by the summer heat. They wouldn't turn brown and drop until late November and December. This was Louisiana, after all. She was amazed that she had come through all that in the dead of night without running head on into a tree.

Lexie was about to turn back to M'Lou and ask again what she was talking about when she saw a tree move in the distance. Its swaying was out of sync with the other trees in the woods that were moving left and right with the rhythm of the fast-approaching hurricane. It looked like something had a hold of it and was shaking it.

Then she saw *it*.

Like everyone else who had seen the creature, her mind flipped through all the known animals of planet earth, past or present, to find a match. In about two seconds, Lexie's brain came to a simple conclusion: *no match. Get the fuck out of here.*

"What the hell is *that?*" she said, more to herself than to M'Lou.

"Monster," was all she heard from behind. "Run!"

Lexie started to run, but she was mesmerized by the thing coming toward them. It was maybe a hundred yards away. It was huge, standing on its hind legs. Looked to be half the height of most of the trees, maybe 20 feet or more, she thought. Hard to tell from this distance. It was grayish-white, with streaks of black on its skin. There was no fur. She wasn't sure, but she thought it had a tail. Its head was huge, with giant brown-gray eyes. The mouth was as wide as a hippo. A *hungry* hippo. She now knew why some thought there might be one loose back in the swamp. But it wasn't a hippo. The head was all wrong. Its features were more angular, sharper.

And when it opened its mouth, the teeth were long and pointed. More T-Rex like, but also different. *Sharper.*

"Holy fuck," she said. The thing pushed the tree down and looked directly at Lexie and M'Lou. It saw them.

"Go, go," Lexie said, and she gave M'Lou a little push. There was no trail, just short stretches of open pathways through the underbrush and around giant oaks. It was more like a maze. Sometimes they ran directly away from the thing, other times it seemed they lost ground and had to move almost toward it to find another way. Lexie noticed the thing didn't have this problem. It just walked over the underbrush. At times, it had to stop and squeeze between trees, and occasionally go around a thicker stand. When the overhang was too low, it just went on all fours and slinked under the growth like a giant, hairless rat.

Lexie could outrun M'Lou easily. The poor girl didn't have any shoes on, and there were sharp sticks and pieces of briar all over the floor of the woods. The classic line, *"I don't have to be faster than the bear, I just have to be faster than you"* ran through her mind. But Lexie was in "Protect and Defend" cop mode now, and no way was she going to abandon the kid just so she could survive. But she had a little voice whispering in her ear also. It said, *"Bullshit. When it gets down to survival, your ass is outta here."* Survival of the fittest. And the fastest. The one wearing shoes always survives.

Well, except for Floyd. He died with his boots on.

Lexie heard another *crack whoosh* and turned to see a big ash tree hit the ground. The thing was gaining on them. It was deceptively fast.

"Watch out for its tongue," M'Lou said through gasps. "Long, fast, like a frog. It can grab things with it."

Lexie looked back again, but the thing's tongue was still in its mouth, but she could see its teeth. "Run faster," she said, and helped M'Lou along. Lexie looked up at the low gray clouds. A big raindrop hit her square in the eye. She wiped it and looked again. The flat light was all around them, and she couldn't tell where the sun was in the sky. She had no idea which way they were headed now. But navigation wasn't important anyway. They just had to outrun this thing.

Lexie heard M'Lou whimpering between gasps for air. She was also making a weird animal noise that sounded like a series of short, staccato screams. *It was the sound of prey just before it died,* Lexie thought.

So this what the thing Troy and Carla had seen. It had attacked them inside his truck and gone along for a short ride, too. Probably what Lee Curtis saw in the bayou behind his house. Surely the last thing Floyd Guidry had seen before he died. Lexie tried to process what it might be. She went through all their earlier theories: man-made, alien, last-of-its-kind dinosaur. Nothing made sense, and at the moment, it wasn't a big priority on today's to-do list.

M'Lou hit a low tree branch and went sprawling. Lexie's momentum carried her forward and she tripped over the girl's fallen body and landed hard on some tree roots that ran across the ground. She saw stars for a moment, closed her eyes and shook it off. When she opened them, M'Lou was still on the ground, curled up in the fetal position and crying like a baby.

Lexie scambled to her feet and glanced back to locate the thing. It was still picking its way through the thick woods, but it had made up ground. She shook M'Lou hard.

"C'mon, M'Lou. Get up. Let's go!"

"Cccca…can't," she said. She was still in a ball, but shaking furiously. Lexie figured the girl was just out of gas. As tired as Lexie was from her night of adventure, this girl had been out in the swamps for days and nights, certainly since Floyd was killed. What was that? Three, four days ago? Lexie couldn't imagine being lost for that long in the swamps, never mind being pursued by that thing back there. It was amazing that M'Lou was still alive. Snakes, gators, insects and other weird shit made a stroll through the Atchafalaya a bit problematic. Despite M'Lou's present physical and mental shape, she was a tough kid. Lexie couldn't imagine letting her die now.

"Get your ass moving, M'Lou!" Lexie pulled the girl to her feet. She half hung from Lexie's powerful grip, but managed to put her bare feet into the soggy ground and stand. "We can do this. It can't catch us in these woods," Lexie said. She didn't believe it for one second, but she was giving M'Lou the halftime locker room speech. *"Hey, we're only down four touchdowns. We can win this thing!"*

With no further urging, M'Lou started to trot. Lexie followed and they were on the move again. There was a loud hissing sound from somewhere behind them. Like air being released from a huge tire. Lexie knew it was the thing. She kept expecting it to roar like a dinosaur or a lion or something, but all she got was a big hiss. Lexie took another look back and saw what caused the thing to make the noise. It was its tongue, now darting in and out of its mouth. Not like a snake, but more like a frog. The tongue was ridiculously long, shooting out this way and that. It finally shot almost straight up, into a big tupelo tree. When the tongue retracted, it had a big fat raccoon attached to it. The little furry bandit disappeared into the thing's gaping mouth. That snack complete, it turned its attention back on Lexie and M'Lou.

"Son of a bitch," Lexie muttered.

The rain continued to sluice down out of the trees. The wind caused them to move back and forth in a kind of slow dance that any other time would be fascinating to watch. Lexie didn't know when the hurricane was supposed to make landfall. The last time she had heard a report was last night, just before she got home. There was talk of it slowing down, so maybe the shit wouldn't hit the fan till late this afternoon or even tonight. The problem was, the shit had already hit the fan for Lexie, beginning last night and continuing on to this very moment. Hurricane Tammy would be the last pile of doo-doo to hit those wonderful rotating blades.

Lexie noticed the ground was sloping downward a bit and it helped with their speed, despite their constant dodging of tree trunks and limbs. The palmetto was starting to get thicker, too. The sharp fronds ripped at her legs, but at least she had pants on. M'Lou was catching the worst of it, though. But what really had her worried were the sounds coming from behind them. The thing was tearing up the woods, pushing more trees down, and now throwing branches as well. It was like a bulldozer and stump shredder going full force. Lexie got the distinct feeling the thing was now royally pissed.

But that worry was quickly supplanted by a new one as she and M'Lou skidded to a stop after rounding a huge magnolia tree.

It was the edge of the swamp, where the low land of the woods met the water. As far as they could see was water, full of cypress and tupelo. Raindrops peppered its surface.

"Crap," Lexie said. She bent down and grabbed her knees, trying to catch her breath. M'Lou just staggered around in a small circle.

Lexie had lived around here long enough to know that the swamp's depth ranged from a few feet to ten or more. Even if they wanted to wade into it, they'd be over their heads in minutes. And the thing chasing them was apparently well familiar with swimming in the bayou. It would catch them in seconds. She wished she had a compass, or the damn sun could be located through the rainy, swirling gray clouds. Her choices were simple, left or right. Straight was sure death. She looked up again at the clouds. They were moving from her right to her left at a pretty good clip. What did that tell her? She thought a second. Most weather moved west to east, but today the weather was dominated by Hurricane Tammy. The storm rotated counterclockwise, and was still probably just offshore. That meant the prevailing winds were blowing *east to west,* pushed by the motion of the giant, spinning storm. And that meant she was looking north.

"Let's go!" she said, and grabbed M'Lou by the arm and turned to her right. There was some comfort for her now that she had some sense of direction. The road was ahead somewhere, how many miles she didn't know. Could they actually stay ahead of this thing for miles? She doubted it.

Lexie and M'Lou scurried along the edge of the swamp. It was a little more open here, and they made quick time. She glanced back at the thing and saw it too was fast approaching the water's edge. At any moment it would turn and follow them. But it did something entirely unexpected.

It jumped into the water.

Chapter 38:
"Water World"

Cam stared out the back door of Fort St. Jesus Bait and Tackle. The rain was pounding the old tin roof of the place, and water was cascading down like Niagara Falls over the eaves. The porch area, although covered, was completely wet from the blowing rain. The surface of the bayou danced like a boiling pot of water. Despite being late morning, the day seemed to be getting darker, as if the sun had said, *"screw it"* and decided to set early rather than battle the oncoming hurricane.

Huey had his big nose stuck out the door, too. He sniffed heartily, turning his head from left to right, trying to get a read on what was out there. Cam looked down at the dog.

"Smell it, Huey?"

The dog's ears went up in response to his master's query. He took another sniff and whimpered a bit.

Troy came over to look, too. "How's our early warning radar doing with the monster?" He rubbed Huey's head.

"I don't think it's out there," Cam said. He stared out over the water into the deep swamp on the other side. "Huey ain't getting anything."

The dog turned and walk back into the store. He went behind the counter to his favorite spot and plopped down with a big dog sigh. Cam shut the door and followed the animal inside.

He, Troy and Huey had slept late, what with the dark skies and rain delaying dawn. After Cam had cooked up some boudin sausage and eggs for breakfast, they all sat and ate at the bar, watching the latest on the storm on the TV. It looked like the show would really start after sundown today.

Cam had checked his cell phone to see if Lexie had called or texted during the night, but the only message was from his parents over on Mobile Bay. It was his dad, who wanted to know if he had the place buttoned up. Cam had tried to call Lexie on her cell, but it went to voicemail again. He also tried her home phone and also got a recording.

Cam had paced around for a while, trying to occupy his time with little chores around the store. There were no customers, but he would stay open as long as he could. He looked at his watch.

"I'm going for ride," Cam said. "Watch the store."

"You got it," Troy said. "Gonna look for Lexie?"

"Yeah, kind of weird she being off the grid like that. I know she's busy, but she should have returned my call."

"Should have," Troy said. "Stay sharp out there. Radio said they already got high water on the road, in the low spots back toward Catahoula."

Cam nodded, grabbed his rain slicker, and headed for the door, Huey obediently following his master. They ran for his truck and hopped in. Even though it was a short distance, they were both soaked. The dog jumped into the back onto his old blanket on the seat and gave a quick shake. Water droplets flew all over the cab.

"Thanks, buddy," Cam said. He wiped water off his face and started the truck. East or west? He decided to go east, toward the big swamp, and see if Lexie was patrolling that area. There were mostly camps out that way, but it was prone to flooding, so he would have to be careful.

Cam hit the wipers to "high" and drove off into the blowing rain. The winds were only about 20 miles per hour, but they were steady. In another 12 hours, they'd be up to 100 plus. Shit would be flying everywhere.

He drove for a mile or so, out of town and onto the parish road. There wasn't a single car to be seen. The bayou was to his right, woods and swamps to his left. He'd pass an occasional camp, but no one seemed to be home at any of them. The drainage ditches on the side of the roads were full of water, and they flowed like a torrent, eventually ending up in the bayou. It was an irony not lost on him. Get the rainwater out to avoid flooding by dumping it into the bayou, which would rise even more and flood everything anyway. In another hour, the drainage ditches on either side would merge right in the middle of the road, and the northern way out of town would be blocked.

Cam drove on for another fifteen minutes. He had reduced his speed because the wipers couldn't keep the water off the truck's windshield. He looked left and right for any sign that Lexie had run off the road, but there was nothing. Before long, he had gone through Butte LaRose and later saw the elevated Interstate 10 in the distance, marking the northernmost edge of where he wanted to look. He made a quick U-turn and headed back south again. He went past Butte LaRose and kept heading south.

Cam hadn't gone a few miles farther when he heard a deep growl coming from the backseat. He slowed the truck and stopped.

"What's wrong, Huey?"

The dog ignored him. He was up on all fours, staring out the window into the woods. His ears were back, head low, hackles up. If there had been another dog in front of him in a stare off, Cam knew the attack was about to begin. But Huey was focused on something out there in the wild.

"You smell it, boy?" Cam said. He looked out through the rain into the woods. With the downpour and the swaying trees, there was no way to tell if anything was out there in the tree line.

Huey barked his warning bark. Cam knew the big Lab's language by now, and this was the *"something bad's coming"* bark. Now the hair on the back of Cam's neck was standing up. Suddenly he had no spit in his mouth. Troy's description of his encounter with the thing flashed through his head and it got him thinking bad thoughts. Was that thing about to burst out of the trees and hop on his truck, too?

Cam had a thought. A more coherent one. He pulled out his iPhone and got the GPS coordinates of his location. That done, he turned back to the barking dog. "We're out of here, buddy."

Cam hit the accelerator a little too hard, and the tires of his truck spun on the liquid pavement. He settled down a bit, and then the truck settled down a bit, and the tires finally dug in. His heart raced, and he drove back through town again, passing the Fort and heading west. Everyone seemed to be at home. Not a soul in sight. He passed the church and was glad to see Mike's pink Cadillac still parked in the garage. Wasn't going to be a mass tomorrow morning, that was for sure. He'd make it a point to check in on Mike and Joanie to see if they needed anything.

He drove on for another 15 minutes to the outskirts of town and turned off onto the road that led to Lexie's neighborhood. It looked like a lake. The water had backed up pretty bad here as the drainage ditches overflowed, unable to handle the three inches of rain they had had since yesterday. Probably seven or eight more inches to go, too, he thought.

Cam's truck was set high, so he had no trouble getting through the water. He slowed the truck down when he could finally see Lexie's house. Most of the front and back yards were still high and dry. Well, not dry, but certainly not underwater. The lots had been graded high, and her house was in no danger at the moment of going under. Lexie's patrol car wasn't in the carport. Cam thought for a second where she might be. Did she have to go to headquarters back in St. Martinville? Maybe she couldn't get back because of the flooded roads. Was she patrolling farther west, maybe helping some people get out of their homes?

Cam looked at Huey for suggestions. The dog just gave him a *"beats me"* look. So Cam carefully turned the truck around at a stop sign and headed back the way he came, leaving a wake that rolled across the open pasture-now-lake. He decided to continue on west as far as he could go. If he didn't see her soon, he'd begin to really worry.

West took him over towards Catahoula, but before he even got to the bridge that would take him over the bayou, the road ended right into another brand-new lake. It was a notorious low stretch of the old two-lane that ran for about a mile, and it was now under three feet of water, and growing deeper by the minute.

"End of the line, Huey," he said. He slowed his truck and stopped right at the water's edge. No way out to the west. No way out to the north. Whoever was left in Alcide was now committed to riding out the storm right in their homes.

"So where the hell are you, Lexie?" he said aloud.

Raymond, Tree's official driver, sat up on the seat of the big Lincoln Town Car and periscoped his neck up to see over the hood. "Fuckin' water's getting' deep, Tree. We should probably turn back."

"Fuck that shit," Tree said. "Keep your ass movin'. Looks clear down that way." He pointed down the parish road that led into Alcide. Five minutes earlier they would have seen Cam's truck do a U-turn and head back to town. Now they plowed through six inches of water over the road.

Raymond saw the clear stretch ahead and goosed the gas a bit to get them there faster. His hands were almost white he was gripping the steering wheel so tight. Rising water freaked him out. A little residual post-traumatic stress disorder after Katrina. It didn't take long before they were on the hard surface again, and Raymond let the big engine spool up some more. They were headed back to Roland's trailer and needed to get there fast. They had big plans for this fine, hurricane-filled Saturday.

Raymond almost missed the turn-off for Roland's trailer, a pockmarked, narrow street that ran into a few acres of high ground that had been in Roland's family for a hundred years. He pulled into the gravel drive out front and blew the horn. When no one appeared for a minute, Tree leaned over and held the horn down. Finally, Roland appeared, wearing the same jeans he had worn yesterday, and probably the day before that, plus an old blue flannel shirt under a brown windbreaker. He ran out to the car in the pouring rain and tapped on Tree's window.

Tree let it down a crack. "Get in the trunk, motherfucker. We gotta get our shit together. Where we go?"

"Y'all can come in here," he said, and gestured to his crappy trailer.

"Fuck that," Tree said. "I ain't goin' in that shithole. Where else?"

Roland wiped some water from his eyes. His greasy blonde hair was losing its battle with the elements and was now dark brown, plastered to his head. "Shit, man," Roland said. He looked around and thought about it a second. "Most places probably closed. Maybe down to the dock. Got a covered pavilion down there. Ain't nobody goin' fishin' today. Probably deserted."

"Which way?" Raymond said.

Roland gave his some quick directions.

"Get in the trunk," Tree said again.

Roland now officially hated that trunk. It could be his coffin at any time, and he was a little claustrophobic. Never mind that he would be laying on enough firepower to blow his brains out a thousand times over. He had no choice. Raymond popped the lid and Roland climbed in. He pulled the lid down over him. It partially latched, then a mechanism kicked in and automatically sealed it the rest of the way with a *thunk.*

They drove down to the dock and pulled into the oyster shell parking lot. It was completely empty. The rain continued to slash the air, and the steady wind created individual airborne waves of water that moved across the landscape as if it were an ocean. Raymond pulled the car as close as he could to the big pavilion Roland had talked about. It was about 30 feet by 40 feet, with three sides covered with aluminum walls. Inside were picnic tables, places to clean fish, and some kind of serve-through kitchen bar that was closed by a pull-down screen.

Tree and four of his guys, plus Roland, ran into the pavilion and found a dry spot in the far corner. Raymond stayed in the car and pulled it around a big shed to hide it from anyone passing on the road. He joined the gang a few minutes later.

They sat around the large picnic table for a little pow wow. Tree looked around at his men, and then leveled his gaze at Roland. "Okay, shithead, how we gonna do this?

Roland smiled his orange-toothed jack-o-lantern smile. "Well, I had all night to think about it," he said. "Here's how we gonna pay Mr. Cameron Dee-Sale a little visit today and get our stuff."

Tree listened and nodded his head.

Cam and Huey got back to the Fort, and the rain had let up a bit. He figured it was a brief respite between some of the outer rain bands of the hurricane. It wouldn't last long.

They walked inside and found Troy at the counter, reading a *Field and Stream* magazine and eating another Twinkie. The TV was on above him. Governor Bergeron in Baton Rouge was holding a press conference. Rumor had it he was thinking of a run at president in the upcoming election. He had the official "Katrina-worried-look" on his face. Grim. Determined. In charge. Trying to look engaged. Whatever.

"Anybody come by?" Cam said. He took off his jacket and threw it on an old deer antler coat rack by the door.

Troy shook his head. "Nada. I don't even think a car went by, except for you. The good folks are buried in deep." Troy closed the magazine.

"You pay for that?" Cam said as he walked behind the counter.

Troy slapped a dollar bill down on the counter. "Any luck with Lexie?"

Cam shook his head. "There's nothin' out there, except for a lot of water. We're cut off, by the way. Water about to go over the road to the north, completely over to the west."

"Really?" Troy looked at his watch. "Carla said she's on her way. She better get her ass in gear. I want my truck back."

Cam tried Lexie's cell again with no luck. He thought about calling the sheriff's department over in St. Martinville, but changed his mind. That might make Lexie look bad if one of the citizens of Alcide couldn't find her at their time of need.

"I think Huey picked up that thing's scent up on the north side, back in the woods towards I-10," Cam said. He walked over to his wall map and used his phone's GPS to mark the location.

He and Troy looked at the map.

"Huh," Troy said. "Looks like that sucker changed course. Thought it was headed this way."

"Yeah," Cam said. "Wonder what got its attention?"

Troy took the last bite of his Twinkie. "Probably saw something it wanted to eat. Or someone."

Cam didn't like the sound of that.

Chapter 39:
"Don't Mess With Lexie"

Lexie didn't wait long to watch the thing swim away into the swamp. The moment it jumped in, she grabbed M'Lou's arm and pulled her along.

"That's a good sign," she said. "Maybe it's lost interest."

M'Lou looked back and then at Lexie. "It likes the water," she said.

The two women moved faster as they found more open ground along the banks of the swamp. The palmetto was still plentiful, but they managed to weave in and around the clumps of the squat green fronds of the plants. Lexie nearly crapped in her pants when a young alligator, not more than three feet long, splashed the water to her left. Probably grabbed a fish, she thought. Gators seemed like poodles to her at the moment. A bigger predator was out there.

Lexie looked through the cypress trees in the water and tried to see if the creature was out there anywhere. The surface of the water was still being pinged by the rain. It shimmered like quicksilver, but there was no sign of the thing. Maybe it really had found something else to do.

She stopped for a moment to check on M'Lou. The girl was still in shock, with a strange near-catatonic look on her face. She seemed unfocused on reality. Or was coming into and out of focus.

"M'Lou, look at me," Lexie ordered. "M'Lou!" She gave the girl a shake.

M'Lou shook her head a bit and focused again on Lexie. "It likes the water," she said.

"I know, I heard you the first time," said Lexie. "That's great. You gotta stay with me. The road's ahead somewhere. We'll get there and flag down a car, okay? We're gonna be fine."

M'Lou nodded her head and looked over Lexie's shoulder, out into the swamp. "Okay. It got Floyd, you know."

"Yeah, I know," Lexie said. "How'd you get away?"

"It got to eating Floyd's gators, the ones in the boat," M'Lou said. "I freaked out, and just jumped into the water and kept going. Don't remember too much after that. I think it was full or something. Wasn't hungry anymore. For me, anyway."

Jeez, Lexie thought. M'Lou had been right there in the boat when Floyd bit it. Or it bit Floyd. Had it not been for the gators in the boat, served up as some easy dessert, M'Lou would have been the second course.

"Okay, let's keep it that way," Lexie said, and gave M'Lou her best reassuring-confident-deputy smile. "Let's move it."

The male creature swam along the bottom of the swamp, in an old channel that was deep enough for him to stay submerged. He was probably swimming a little too fast, and occasionally hit a hidden stump or trunk of a fallen tree. It didn't matter. He was so pissed and hungry and horny that he wasn't thinking straight. This little diversion for a quick breakfast had turned into one big cluster fuck for him. He was now off course, away from the female, and wasting time. It had seemed like such a great idea earlier. He'd picked up the scent of the smart thing, thinking it wasn't too far in the woods. And then things really got better when he smelled *another* one in the same direction. Breakfast was definitely going to be filling. When he finally saw them, together no less, it was just too damn good to be true. And it was.The damn trees hindered his progress, and he had to really work his way carefully. The two smart things had run, but they weren't making such good time either, and he actually closed the gap a bit. But he could never quite catch them. When they came to the water, they turned, and for a moment, he decided to follow them. But the water gave him a better idea.

Lexie and M'Lou wound their way along the swamp for another hour, making steady if slow progress. The foliage had thickened again, and they had to make a diversion back into the woods before they could circle over to the water's edge. Lexie was thirsty as hell, but she knew better than to drink the stagnant swamp water. The parasites in there would have her puking in an hour or two, and then a nice week or so in the hospital after that with a severe case of the runs. The rain was helping, though. She let the water cascade down her face and caught it with her tongue. It wasn't filling, but it was something. She wondered what the hell M'Lou had been eating and drinking for the last few days in the swamp. She didn't want to think about it for long.

A new threat emerged, too. Lightning. The steady rain had turned into a thunderstorm, probably embedded in one of the hurricane's outer rain bands. The woods lit up with every bolt, and the thunder shook the soggy ground under their feet. Lexie saw one old tupelo tree take a direct hit somewhere off to their right. The exploding superheated tree sap sounded like a bomb going off.

Both women cringed and dropped to their knees from the concussive sound of the thunder. The world began to flash and rumble as the entire parish took lightning strikes. The only good thing about the lightning was that it lit up the deepening gloom of the woods and helped guide them along.

They made good time in open areas, and then lost it when they stumbled into briars and deadfalls. There was backtracking, sidestepping and crawling, all in an effort to get to the road as fast as possible. There were no landmarks to let them know they were getting close, either. Lexie figured they'd know when they got there if they saw a stretch of asphalt under their feet and a center stripe. Until then, it was full steam ahead.

Lexie's feet were killing her. With no socks on and her shoes completely soaked, her feet were being rubbing raw. At least she had shoes. She looked down at M'Lou's delicate, porcelain-white bare feet and wondered how they felt right about now. M'Lou was probably so numb, she didn't notice.

Lexie's greatest fear—well, her second greatest fear—was that M'Lou would pass out. She figured she could carry her a ways, but it would be slow, until she could go no farther. Stopping was not an option. That thing was still out there, even if it had gone in another direction. And the hurricane would be in full force soon. Another night in these woods was totally out of the question.

Shit. Where the hell was that road?

They had run-walked-tripped-stumbled for another half hour when M'Lou stopped, stood straight and refused to move. Her eyes were wide with terror.

Lexie looked at her intently. "M'Lou, what's wrong, honey? You need to rest?"

The girl mumbled something and turned this way and that. Finally, she said, "Smell that?"

Lexie had been running so much she had been breathing out of her mouth for the last hour or so. Her sense of smell was non-existent. "What?" she said, and sniffed the air deeply. A few drops of water went into her nose and she sneezed. "What is it?" She took another deep breath through her nostrils and stopped half way through the process. "Whoa. What the hell is that?" The only thing she could smell was a near-nauseating chemical stench. It reminded her of some of the big refineries and chemical plants over toward Baton Rouge and New Orleans.

"That's...that's...what *it* smells like. When it's close," M'Lou said.

A rolling chill went up and down Lexie's spine. She slowly turned 360 degrees, scanning through the thick trunks of trees, low-hanging branches and moss. The last arc of her turn included the swamp, which had few trees, but was as gray and washed out by the rain and clouds as the rest of the woods. She saw nothing. No trees were being pushed over, at least not by a 20-foot tall monster. Nothing looked out of the ordinary.

"You sure?" Lexie said. "I don't see anything."

M'Lou nodded quickly, almost comically, with her head bouncing up and down like a cartoon character. "It stinks, weird like that," she said. "The last time I smelled that it was 10 feet away from me."

Lexie was certifiably about to lose it, but she knew she had to hold it together for the girl. She looked all around again, but couldn't see anything that looked like the creature. The smell was pungent, chemical *and* organic, all mixed together. Strange. She had never smelled anything quite like it. The odor seemed to come from all around them. The prevailing winds were out of the east, but they were swirling down at the floor of the woods. There was no way she could tell which way the smell was coming from.

"We have to keep moving, M'Lou," Lexie said. "We can't stop. We can't stay here."

At first, Lexie thought M'Lou would remain anchored to the ground, but the girl took a tentative step. Her head was on a swivel, sweeping back and forth as she scanned the woods. Lexie noticed she was shaking more, and at first thought M'Lou was getting hypothermic, despite the relatively warm day. But no, judging by the girl's face, she was scared shitless.

They both walked no more than 10 yards when suddenly the leaf-covered floor of the woods rose up, like the ground would do in an earthquake. But the ground didn't shake. It now had a huge mouth with very sharp teeth, though.

M'Lou screamed first. Then Lexie let one go, but it wasn't so much a scream as it was an extended "oh shit." The thing went from being on all fours to standing on its hind legs. She noted, briefly, that the legs weren't like any other animal that could walk and run on four legs. The hips weren't as pronounced. This thing looked like it was very comfortable on two legs. Like a car or truck that could switch from two-wheel drive to four-wheel drive with just the flick of a switch.

It let out that hissing sound again, and out came the tongue, right toward them. The thing dropped back to four-wheel drive and planted itself firmly on the ground. A flash of lightning and an almost-immediate peal of thunder didn't faze it. Its huge eyes never left the two women.

Before either of them could run, the long tongue-like thing had attached itself to M'Lou's right ankle and began to retract. The girl fell to her ass and was dragged toward the thing's gaping, tooth-filled mouth. Lexie dove towards her in an attempt to grab an arm or something and prevent her from being eaten by the thing, but she was a second too late and M'Lou skidded on her backside right for the thing. The rain slicker she had been wearing was now up over her shoulders, and Lexie could see that she was completely naked underneath. M'Lou's pale skin looked deathly in the gray light of the woods, and the girl's screams were something Lexie was sure she would never forget as long as she lived.

Lexie, now flat on her stomach, watched as M'Lou was pulled toward the thing. She had never felt more helpless in her life. There was nothing she could do.

M'Lou, however, wasn't going to go without a fight. She tried to dig her heals into the soft ground, and that at least slowed her imminent death. And then she did something that made the breath in Lexie's throat catch. M'Lou hooked her left leg around a small ash tree, and then reached out and grabbed it with both hands. The force of the creature's pull bent the little tree over, but it didn't break. M'Lou let out another higher-pitched scream, and she stopped dead in her tracks. Or her ass, actually. She wrapped herself around that little tree and held on, literally, for dear life.

The sudden resistance caught the creature by surprise, and it staggered back a step and opened its mouth wider. And that's when Lexie sprung into action. She grabbed a five-foot-long log that was about twice the circumference of a baseball bat. In one fluid movement, she was up on her feet and next to M'Lou. Lexie swung and hit the thing's tongue as hard as she could. Nothing happened. She half expected it to wail in pain and let go, but it did nothing of the sort. So she hit it again. And again. But it wouldn't let go.

"Get it off me!" M'Lou screamed.

"I'm trying!" Lexie yelled right back, and swung again with the same result. She looked back at the creature. Its huge mouth was open wider now as it tried to dislodge M'Lou from the tree. She could see how focused its two eyes were on its prey. It didn't seem to be even looking at Lexie.

That's when she had her next brilliant idea. Brilliant only if it worked. If it didn't, she would be having coffee with Jesus in less than 30 seconds.

With a banshee scream, she charged right at the thing. For a second, she thought it glanced at her, but then focused again on M'Lou. It must be really hungry, Lexie thought, or it had no fear of her. Probably both. But Lexie ran headlong right at the thing, the log in her hand as if she were a pole vaulter with a very short, stubby pole. Her initial plan was to whack the thing on its head, or in the eye. But seconds before she got to it, she had a change in plan. Instead of grabbing the log like a bat and swinging it, she put her right hand on the end butt of the log and her left farther up the trunk. With a great heave, she sent it flying right at the thing and into its mouth. That gaping, sharp-tooth death trap was still wide open, maybe more so, as it tried to retract its tongue with M'Lou on the other end. The log sailed true and went right into the creature's mouth and down its throat.

And creature or no creature, it shared one thing with just about everything else in the universe: it had a gag reflex. Immediately it let go of M'Lou and retracted its tongue into its mouth with a rubbery *snap*. It let out a huge gasp, and then a cough. Or what sounded like a cough. Lexie wasn't waiting around long enough to do any scientific research. She turned her attention back to M'Lou, who was writhing on the ground, holding her ankle.

Without a word, Lexie grabbed the young woman and yanked her to her feet, and then pulled her forward and they both began to run. The thing was blocking their original route, so they zagged farther into the woods around it, and then resumed their original course. They also caught a lucky break. The woods really began to thin out, with the trees more widely spaced and fewer deadfalls and briars. They had an open field of sorts to run through. And run they did. Lexie looked back at the creature. It was now back on two legs and it started to make that loud coughing sound again. It was also using its hands to reach into its mouth. She was pretty sure it was choking. *Fuck you, you bastard*, she thought.

She and M'Lou had run for a hundred yards when Lexie saw something that made her heart sink. A wide swath of water. They had run right into the edge of the bayou. It was almost 100 yards across. But how could that be? She was sure she had been heading east. The road should be around here somewhere.

"Son of a bitch!" Lexie yelled. Just when she thought they had caught a break, it all turned to shit again. And then something rather extraordinary happened. A big pickup truck came cruising by in the middle of the bayou, casting a wide wake as it plowed from left to right. The weird apparition confused Lexie, and she let her jaw hang slack.

That's when she realized what she was seeing. It wasn't the bayou. It was the road. The *flooded* road!

"Go, go!" she yelled to M'Lou, and they both plunged into the water that had been a shallow drainage ditch six hours ago, but was now a wide, flowing creek that covered the road in about a foot of water.

Chapter 40:
"Breakfast on the Run"

Carla eased Troy's big pickup truck along the centerline of the submerged road. She had both hands locked onto the steering wheel and sat forward to help her see where she was going. The rain was really coming down now, and the wipers could barely keep up. The wind was picking up, too, and the thick drops sounded like gravel being flung at the truck. Thank goodness she had the pickup. If she were driving the Audi, her feet would be wet by now.

For a brief moment this morning, she had thought about staying home to ride out the storm. And then she thought about being locked in Troy's bedroom for three days making some serious mischief, and she had a change of heart. Plus, she had his truck and boys being boys, he wanted it back. So here she was risking life and limb driving down the parish road on her way to Alcide. The high-set truck had no problem with the water. As long as she stayed on the asphalt. One wrong turn left or right and she'd be in the flooded drainage ditches, which were probably five feet deep by now and deepening by the minute. It was getting harder and harder to see the painted centerline or edge of the road. An occasional speed limit sign or mile marker were her only guides. That and her own memory of this road. Somewhere down the highway it would make a long curve to the right, so she'd have to be careful there.

Something caught her eye to the right. An animal of some kind came out of the woods and jumped into the water. Her heart skipped a beat for a second as she thought it might be the thing that had attacked her and Troy earlier. But this was too small. Probably a deer or a hog. She kept plowing ahead.

Lexie saw the pickup pass to her right and continue on to Alcide. Whoever was driving hadn't seen her and M'Lou. She half swam, half walked across the flooded ditch in an effort to get to the road in time and wave the truck down before it had gone too far. If she tried to stand up, she could easily touch bottom and keep her head out of water. But it was an inefficient way to move through the ditch, so she resorted to a classic swim stroke. M'Lou was doing the same. At some point the bottom would rise up and they'd be moving up the slope to the road. Somewhere behind them was the thing, either choking to death or extremely pissed and on it way to eat them. What did M'Lou say earlier? *It likes the water.*

Lexie's hands touched the bottom and she realized they were close to the asphalt now, so she stood and realized the ditch was now only two feet deep. M'Lou also stood up. A big flash of light and pounding thunder made them both flinch. For a moment, Lexie was afraid they'd be electrocuted if a lightning bolt hit the water nearby. But so far, so good. She slogged up the slope, followed by M'Lou. A quick glance back revealed no monster.

Once they were both safely on the road, Lexie began to wave her arms, hoping the truck driver would glance in the rearview mirror and see them. M'Lou joined in, and the two women high-stepped down the middle of the flooded road, waving their arms frantically. Lexie began to whistle, too, as if that sound could pierce the roar of the rain, the wind and the thunder. The truck kept going, and even though it was going only about 15 miles per hour, it seemed to be speeding away. Along with their chances of survival.

One sound did break through the storm. That hissing noise, now coming from the woods. And the distinct *crack* of wood breaking. The thing was coming.

Carla was sweating now even though she had the A/C cranked. It was that tense, nervous sweat that had nothing to do with heat. A drop rolled down her forehead and along her nose. It tickled and she wiped it with the back of her wrist. The effort pulled some of her dark bangs over one eye and she tried to blow the hair out with her mouth, with no luck. She took a quick peek in the rearview mirror to adjust herself. Her focus was on her face, but the moment she was about to turn her attention back on the road, she got a glimpse of something moving behind her on the road. The water on the back windshield obscured any details, and at first she thought it was the deer. She took another look in the side mirror and realized this deer had human arms and legs.

"What the fuck?" Carla said. She stopped the truck and put it in park. She turned around and squinted through the back windshield. It was definitely two people, running her way, waving their arms, footfalls splashing in the water over the road. She put her window down and stuck her head out for a better look. The rain assaulted her, but she confirmed they were human. What the hell were they doing out here?

She rolled the window up and put the truck in reverse to help close the distance. Backing up straight, even in dry conditions, was not one of her strong suits. Now, in the rain, in this big truck, it could kill her if she overcorrected and went into the deep water. So she took it very slow. Her reverse lights would let the two people know she had seen them. They would have to make up the distance themselves.

Carla was so focused on the people behind her, she almost didn't see something else coming down the road behind them. Her first thought was that it was another car, but the asshole didn't have his lights on, so it appeared as a gray shape, moving way too fast. And it seemed to bounce a lot, as if it had crappy suspension.

Lexie was actually smiling. She was out of breath, dog-tired and was miserable, but salvation was at hand. The truck driver had seen them and was backing up. They were going to make it. Something splashed behind her, and a quick look revealed the thing loping behind them on the road. Its head was down, and the big eyes were lasered in on her and M'Lou.

"Run, M'Lou, faster!" she said.

M'Lou caught the fear in Lexie's voice and turned around. She let out another scream. The truck was in reverse, but it wasn't moving fast enough, Lexie noticed. She and M'Lou would have to cover the ground themselves. It was now a death race. Loser got eaten.

The truck was now no more than ten yards ahead, but the red brake lights came on and it stopped as the driver put it into park. A woman's head poked out of the driver's side and looked their way. It was Carla Fontanelli.

"Hey, hop in," she yelled. Then her face went slack.

Carla recognized Lexie but didn't know who the other girl was. She had a million questions, but they could wait. Especially after she noticed the gray car behind the women wasn't a car. It was the thing.

Carla screamed. "Jump in the back, hurry!" she yelled, and got herself back in the cab.

Lexie noticed the brake lights go off on the truck. Carla had put the pickup in "drive."

"Jump in the back!" Lexie yelled to M'Lou. They both reached the bed of the truck at the same time. With one hand each on the tailgate, they planted a foot on the bumper and launched themselves into the pickup's bed. Just as they did, there was a loud *thwang* as the creature's tongue hit the back of the truck. The two women were thrown back as Carla hit the accelerator. She punched it too hard, and the truck's wheels spun in the water. It slewed to the left, and for a second Lexie thought they were floating. Carla let her foot off the gas, and then eased it down, and the big off-road wheels dug in and the truck moved forward with a lurch and gathered speed. They were moving too fast for the conditions, but under the circumstances, no one cared. A high plume of water arced away from both sides of the pickup as it sailed down the flooded road. Lexie risked a quick look back and saw that the creature was still running their way, but was slowing down. They were putting distance between them and it. The thing stopped, stood on its hind legs, and let out that hissing sound again.

Lexie didn't know what the creature's language was, but she was pretty sure it said...

"Motherfucker!" the creature thought. Well, that wasn't the literal translation, because it didn't have that uniquely human combination of words in its vocabulary. But if a linguist had the time, that's the best word he could match with what the creature was saying.

He stood there in the rain, on his hind legs, staring forlornly down the road at his breakfast receding from his view. He looked like a jilted lover. Another flash of lightning and its corresponding booming peal of thunder snapped him out of his pining.

He smacked his lips together and tried to settle himself down. All he wanted was a decent breakfast for goodness sake. He had a big day ahead of him. He needed his strength to properly service the female. A couple of those smart things would have fit the bill. Shit, he *had* them. They were out in the open, slow, defenseless, with nowhere to run. Sure, the woods were a bit of a challenge for him, but he'd done it before. He thought the chase might last a few minutes. But *hours?* Crap. Then, when he had laid that oh-so-sweet little trap, that crazy one damn near choked him to death with a stick. Ran right at him, too. Didn't give a shit. What was that all about? Couldn't they just give up and let him eat them?

The male creature sighed and looked to his right at the woods. He was way off track as far as the female was concerned. He had to make up time, and going back through those thick trees would just kick his ass, and he'd lose more time. The female might be pissed. He didn't need that in his life at the moment.

So he decided to do something he'd never done before. He looked up and down the road but didn't see any more of the smart things' vehicles. In one fluid motion, he dropped down to all fours and began jogging down the flooded road. He was going to follow it right to the female. And maybe a snack or two if he was lucky.

The female creature surfaced on the bayou at the edge of Alcide. The weather was getting worse, but she felt worse, which was worse for everyone. Her stomach roiled with the movement of the young ones, eager to be free and fed. She sniffed the air and let all her senses go to work. She also sent out the vibration, the call to the male to help him hone in on her position. In a moment, she had a fix on him, too. The bastard was way off to the north, farther away than he had been earlier. What the hell was he doing? She was here, ready to rock and roll, and he was off doing who knew what. Probably chasing food. She knew he would have a voracious appetite, but still. There was plenty to eat right here. If he had just stayed on course, he could take care of her, grab something to eat, and be on his way.

The wind and rain were heavy, and the skies continued to darken. She floated on the surface, turning slowly to get a lay of the land. Obviously, there was no boat traffic. The smart things wouldn't be out in this weather. But she could see their dwellings just around the bend in the bayou. Some were on the water, some were near it. This is where the majority of those things lived, in a little community. That was odd to her and her kind. Being in such close proximity to each other. She preferred solitude for most of the time.

The first dwelling was a long, low one, with a wide porch in the back and a small pier with a boat there, inside a boat house. There was another small building next to it. Something else caught the female's attention. To the right was another small dwelling, but it was different. It had a roof and two walls along its length, but it was open on the other sides. There didn't appear to be anything inside. It might be a perfect rendezvous point for her and the male. Their little sexual ritual couldn't happen in the water. She would need to be on land, high and dry, so he could take care of business. And since he was a young male, he'd need all the time and help he could get. The little building would keep them out of the weather somewhat, and give them a measure of concealment, but she doubted the smart things would be out tonight. The weather was getting much worse.

It was still light, though, and she didn't want to risk crawling up on land and being seen. If one of the smart things happened by the bank of the bayou, she might grab a quick bite, since she was pretty hungry herself. But otherwise, she'd stay in the water until night.

The female, satisfied with her plan, slipped under the water and dropped to the bottom of the bayou. She hoped that idiot could find her. She was done with traveling. He'd have to come to her.

Chapter 41:
"Saturday Night's Alright for Fighting"

Cam refilled Huey's water bowl and put it down on the floor. The Lab looked at him and then began to lap up the fresh water in big gulps. He turned back to the TV and turned up the volume. The racket of the rain hitting the tin roof was making it harder to hear. Huey's gulps ended abruptly, and Cam turned back to the dog to see what was up.

Huey had stopped, mid lap, and was staring toward the back door. Water dripped from his mouth onto the floor, but the dog didn't bother to lick it away. He was hyper-focused on something out there, on the bayou. He growled for just a second, and then began to bark his "intruder bark." The something-bad-is-close bark. It scared the shit out of Cam.

Troy had been in the back and walked over. "He hear something?"

"Something's out there," Cam said. "He did that a while ago when I was on the road north of town."

Troy looked in the direction the dog was looking. He gulped, and Cam could see his Adam's apple bob up and down. "You think it's that thing?"

"Pretty sure," Cam said. "In both cases. But it can't be the same one. Too far. Too soon."

Troy looked at the map on the wall, and the marks Cam had made earlier when they were tracking the potential path of the monsters. "You said there were two of them. Could this be the one that was out east, the one the lesbians saw eat the kayaker?" Troy pointed to that very spot on the map.

Cam eyed the map, too. "Could be."

They both jumped when the front door burst open, caught by the wind and slammed against the wall. Father Mike and Sister Joanie came in, heads down. Joanie grabbed the door and shut it against the wind. They were both drenched. Mike was wearing jeans and a grey sweatshirt. Joanie was also in jeans, with a long-sleeved blue T-shirt with "Pensacola Naval Air Station" written across the front.

"Man, glad you're still open. Got any ice left?" Mike said. "We forgot to stock up. Got a ton of deer meat in the freezer. I don't want to lose it if the power's out for a week."

"Plenty still left," Cam said.

"Water, too," Joanie said. She was already headed back to the cooler. She went over to Huey and gave him a scratch. He continued to let loose with his warning bark. "What's wrong, Huey?" she said.

Troy said, "Pretty sure one of those things is right out there somewhere. Probably in the bayou."

Joanie looked over at Father Mike. "That's what you were telling me about?"

He just shrugged.

Troy filled them both in on his and Carla's adventures of the last 24 hours. They both just stood there, wide-eyed.

"Sounds like an alien to me," Joanie said.

Troy said, "I'm thinking an Uncle Sam science experiment that got loose."

"You don't think it was an alien?" Mike said.

"I don't know," Troy said. "It was huge, weird-looking and very hungry. Never seen anything like it."

"And it's out there?" Joanie pointed towards the back door. She was starting to look a lot concerned. Huey's barking didn't help matters.

Cam jumped into the conversation. "Not that one. We think the same kind of thing got that kayaker over by Bayou Chene. But it's too far in the other direction. Has to be two of them."

"Crap," Father Mike said. "And that's what the dog's barking at?"

"Maybe," Cam said. He bent down to try and calm the big Lab.

Again, the front door opened, and the wind, rain and pressure change got everyone to turn that way. Cam stood up and recognized them immediately. It was the black dudes that had come in earlier. The last in was the big one, the boss. He easily pulled the door closed, while the rest of his guys sauntered around the store.

Cam and Troy exchanged looks. Huey stopped barking and focused on the new humans who had just walked in. His nose was in the air and he was alert. Father Mike and Sister Joanie nodded to the newcomers but got no response. Joanie went towards the back to grab the things she needed. Mike walked to the big ice cooler and started to pull out bags and place them on the floor.

Cam was having one of those bad Baghdad Bejeezie feelings. The kind he and the guys used to get on patrol, walking down some narrow street in lovely Iraq. It was that hinky feeling that you were about to get your head blown off, or a parked car was about to explode. Or that dude with the coat on in 110-degree heat was packing a suicide vest. Altogether, a rather unpleasant feeling that caused a drop of sweat to roll down his back.

He stood up from Huey and walked around to the back of the counter. He gave Troy another look, not too dissimilar to the look he gave him when he was quarterback and Troy was a wide receiver in high school. It said, *I'm about to change the play here at the line—an audible—and the ball is definitely coming to you.*

Troy gave Cam an almost imperceptible nod, and walked slowly back toward the counter as well. They both watched to see what Mike and Joanie were doing. If they felt something was amiss, they weren't showing it.

On the TV, the weather guys were doling out the news of Hurricane Tammy. It sounded more like play-by-play commentary from a football game than a weather report. The eye was just offshore of the central Louisiana coast, still maintaining category three status. The state was about to get another ass whipping. They didn't put it that way, but everyone knew that's what they meant. As if on cue, lightning flashed outside and the thunder made the tin roof shake with a metallic *clang*. And for the first time, everyone inside Fort St. Jesus Bait and Tackle could hear the wind whistle through cracks in the doors.

Cam made sure Troy saw him glance at the shotgun behind the counter, then the 9mm Beretta handgun on an open shelf under the counter, near Troy. Cam saw Troy sigh in resignation.

Other than the TV talking heads and the storm outside, it was a bit too quiet, and the tension in the room was spooling up. Cam said, "Anything y'all looking for in particular?"

At first, no one answered. Then the one nearest to Cam, who stood in front of the chips rack, turned and said, "No, man. Just grabbin' sumpin' to eat."

Cam didn't like the dead look in the kid's eyes. He'd seen that look in Iraq as well. In both the enemy and some of his own guys. That look generally preceded some serious shit.

Out of the corner of his eye, Cam noticed the big guy move back toward the front. He appeared to be looking for something on that aisle, but Cam noticed he kept flicking his eyes back toward him.

Finally, the big guy was 10 feet away from Cam, back turned to him as he also eyed the potato chips. Suddenly, with one quick movement, the big guy turned and leveled a Glock right at Cam. Simultaneously, the other guys had pulled their weapons. They swept them across the room, passing Troy, Mike and Joanie in their sights.

"Whoa, whoa, whoa," Cam said. He raised his arms. Not over his head, but shoulder high. "Take it easy, dudes."

Troy, Mike and Joanie also raised their hands. Joanie gasped.

The big guy took another step closer to Cam. "Shut the fuck up. We come for the shit. Roland's stuff the cop took. I know she left it here."

"What shit?" Cam said. "This is a bait shop."

The big guy fired his pistol. Cam thought he was dead, but the round passed just to the right of his head and into the wall behind the counter.

"Hey, fucker," the guy said. "Next one's in your head. Where is the shit?"

Cam ran the scenario through his head. He tells the intruders where he put the drugs after Lexie dropped them off. They take them, then they line he, Troy, Mike and Joanie up on the floor and shoot them all in the back of the head. Huey, too. That thought made his next decision easier to make.

"Okay, Okay," Cam said. "It's locked in the back." He looked over at Troy again and said, "Troy, you *did* lock it up in the safe back there, right?"

Troy nodded. Since he had done no such thing, and Cam didn't even have a safe back there, he understood that Cam was about to do something very, very rash. And that he, Troy, was going to join him in the rashness.

"Alright, let me get the key," Cam said. "Down here." He began to bend at the knees slowly, but kept his hands up.

"Careful, motherfucker," the big guy said. He let his gun trail Cam all the way down. "You come up with a gun, you dead."

"Not coming up with a gun. No gun. Just keys." Cam got down all the way on his knees, below the big guy's line of sight. He reached below the counter, grabbed his keys to the vet clinic with his left hand and held them up. When the big guy's eyes locked on the key ring, Cam grabbed the 10-gauge shotgun with his right hand and lowered the barrel straight ahead. There wasn't much on the shelf, and it was protected on the customer side of the counter only by a half-inch piece of plywood. Cam had a round chambered already and wouldn't have to slide the pump action. All he had to do was flick off the safety, which he did in one quick motion. He figured the big guy was expecting Cam to stand up if he had a gun under the counter, but Cam wasn't going to do what the big guy expected. Another little lesson from Iraq.

Cam pulled the trigger and the shelf exploded outward, right at the big guy's ankles.

What happened next was pretty much chaos, and no one would quite remember exactly what transpired exactly. But the gist of it was this: the big guy had taken a step to his left, just before Cam fired the shotgun. The big double-ought pellets missed his ankles, which was fortunate for him, since they were still in a tight pattern and at that close range would have amputated a leg. But he was still close enough for wood shrapnel to penetrate some of his leg and he let out a scream and fell backward.

Cam heard the *pop pop pop* of automatic pistols going off, and it sounded like someone had lit off a bunch of firecrackers inside the store. Off to his right, he saw Troy duck behind the counter, grab the pistol that was there and come up shooting. He squeezed off three quick shots before he dropped back down behind the counter.

Cam ratcheted another round in the shotgun and fired through the hole he had made in the counter. He was going for more shock and awe and less for accuracy. Through the hole, he saw the big guy still on the floor, but he had his pistol pointed right at the hole and let loose with a few rounds. Cam dodged to his left just in time as a couple of rounds went hissing right where he had been only seconds before.

Tree got up and backed out the store, still firing his pistol. His four goons were doing the same, concentrating their fire at Cam and Troy. The sound, the smoke, the smell of cordite and the taste of adrenaline assaulted Cam's senses. He took a quick peek and saw the last of the gangbangers retreat out the front door. The last one out was holding his left arm, high, near his shoulder.

Cam waited a beat, and then turned to Troy. "You okay?"

"Yeah, yeah," Troy said, clearly out of breath as if he had just run a mile sprint. "You?"

Cam nodded. He eased up and raised the shotgun, using it to scan the rest of the store in case one of the gangbangers was still inside. He saw nothing except Huey, who had survived the firefight unscathed. The big dog barked once.

"Mike? Joanie?" he yelled. "Are you hurt?"

Cam didn't hear anything. He had a sinking feeling they had been hit, maybe even by his or Troy's return fire. But he caught some movement at the end of one of the aisles and saw Mike moving toward the coolers. He went over to Joanie, who was just beginning to stand up.

Father Mike yelled, "Yeah, we're good. We're good." He and Joanie walked up front with a wary eye on the front door. Cam understood, and quickly moved to the door and locked it.

Mike waved his hand to part the acrid smoke. "Who the hell were those guys?"

Joanie coughed. "And what were they talking about? Drugs in here?"

"Lexie and I found a big stash of meth and coke Roland had hidden in a fishing shack off a slough by the river. He damn near killed us before Lexie ran him off. She didn't have time to take it back to St. Martinville, and she didn't want to keep it in her trunk."

"So she hid it back there," Troy added. He pointed to the storage room. "We've been sleeping next to it."

"They must be here for the pickup," Joanie said. "But where's Roland?"

"Who knows?" Cam said. "But I doubt they'll be coming back now that they know we're armed."

"I doubt that," Troy said. He had moved back to the door and looked out the small head-high inset window. "Take a look."

Cam came over and looked out. Across the street in the gray, wet, wind-swept gloom, he saw a black Lincoln Town car parked in front of a closed-up Dairy Queen under a big red awning out front. The five gangbangers had piled out of the car, pistols drawn. One walked around back, opened the trunk, and Roland got out. They all ran to the front door. Someone shot the lock off and they stepped inside.

"Crap," Cam said.

Chapter 42:
"Lights Out"

"I do believe they're gonna make another run at us," Troy said. He explained the situation to Father Mike and Sister Joanie.

Cam frowned. A strong gust of wind shook the bait store, and there was a loud screech overhead. Everyone looked up.

"Tin roof," Troy said. "Tammy's gonna peel it like a can of soup."

"Least of our worries now," Cam said. He moved to the back of the counter and looked around. He pulled out a box of shotgun shells. "Troy, I got more ammo for that back in the pantry of the kitchen. There's a .22 rifle in there, too. And a Colt. Bring 'em."

He looked at Father Mike. "Still as good a shot as I remember?"

Mike shook his head. "Yeah, but you got anything bigger than a .22?"

"Nope. Make it count."

"Great," Mike said. "Joanie, you take the .22. I want the Colt."

"You two cool with shootin' somebody?" Cam said.

"Stone cold cool," Joanie said. "Father Mike can hear my confession later." She stared at him. He looked away.

"Yeah, I'm good," Mike said. "I can go Old Testament on their asses. I'll sort out the consequences later."

"Good to hear," Cam replied.

Troy came out with the firearms, and the four of them spent the next few minutes loading their individual weapons. The rain outside had gotten heavier, and it was pounding the roof. There was also a rhythmic shudder to the place, as big gusts of wind tried to find a way inside. It was like Tammy was using a giant finger to probe weak spots in the structure. The lights flickered on and off.

"Our visitor from the Gulf is almost here," Troy said.

Suddenly there was another series of sounds from out front. There was the slide of a big vehicle in the gravel, and then the sound of rapid gunfire.

Cam, Troy, Mike and Joanie all crouched low and turned to the front.

"Troy, back door," Cam ordered.

Troy nodded and turned his attention that way. Huey joined him.

Everyone else trained weapons on the front door. Rounds pinged the side of the building, but the thick plywood covering the windows absorbed the hits. Barely. Splinters poked through on the inside.

"Stay down," Cam said.

Just then someone tried the knob on the front door. It wiggled as they tried to open it. Cam put the shotgun up on his shoulder and prepared to fire. There were a few rapid hits on the door and what sounded like a woman's voice yelling.

"Cam! Open up!"

Cam looked at Mike. He ran to the door and listened again. "Lexie?"

"Open the fucking door!" she yelled.

Cam quickly unlocked the door, and three women fell inside in a heap. He slammed the door shut against the rain, the wind, and the incoming rounds.

Troy looked down at the three women on the floor. Legs, arms, wet clothes and disheveled hair everywhere. It was quite possibly the biggest pile of hot women he had ever seen. Two of them he recognized.

"Damn," he said. He reached down and pulled Carla to her feet.

Cam helped Lexie up as well. She was soaked to the skin, her deputy's uniform was dirty and torn, revealing tan skin underneath. Whatever makeup she had been wearing had long since washed away. Her blonde hair was still in a ponytail, but it was dark and filthy. He could see a couple of small leaves embedded in it. As an added treat, the top two buttons of her shirt were missing, and he could see she wasn't wearing a bra. Her headlights were also on high beam.

"Hey, Cam, eyes up here," she said.

"Right," he said. Despite her condition, she looked great. He looked down on the woman who was still on the floor. She was wearing a rain slicker and not much else. "Who's that?"

Lexie bent down and helped M'Lou up. Cam thought she looked worse than anyone. Her pretty face tried to shine through dark, sunken eyes. She had insect bites on her cheeks and neck, and she was shaking uncontrollably.

"M'Lou Marchand," Lexie said. "She was on the boat with Floyd."

"Shit," Cam replied.

Lexie said, "You need to check her out. I think she's been in the swamp for days."

"Where've you been?" Cam asked. "I've been trying to reach you all day."

"Kind of an eventful night and day," Lexie said. She gave him the quick rundown of her last 24 hours.

Troy looked at Carla. "You saw that thing again?"

"In my rearview mirror," she said. "I think it's headed this way."

Lexie looked toward the door. "I see you've met my friends from New Orleans."

Cam filled her in on his last few minutes. "They know the stuff is here."

"Fantastic," she said. "They set up shop across the street. When we pulled in, they started shooting at us the moment they recognized me. We gotta call it in to the sheriff, get some help out here."

Cam shook his head. "Not going to happen. Both roads are underwater. No way in or out for a while."

Lexie looked around and took some mental inventory. Four of them had weapons, they had power, at least for now, and a reasonably sturdy shelter from the storm. "Okay," she said. Let's get M'Lou cleaned up and taken care of. She needs food and water, too."

While the others kept watch, Cam led Lexie and M'Lou through the back kitchen and down a short hallway that led into Cam's vet clinic. Having the kitchen connected to the vet clinic had produced no shortage of jokes in town about what

Cam was cooking on any given day. Tonight, that connection proved a godsend.

There was a small stand-up shower in the clinic's bathroom. Cam had put it in for whenever he had to spend the night there caring for a seriously ill or injured animal. Lexie and M'Lou got out of their wet clothes and took turns showering under the hot water. Lexie had never enjoyed a shower more. For M'Lou, it really was a life saver. Her body temperature returned to normal, and her hypothermic shakes subsided.

Cam didn't have much in the way of women's clothes, so he gave M'Lou one of his white lab coats to wear, which hung down to her knees. Lexie got one of his Saints jerseys that fit her like a dress.

While the storm raged outside, he sat M'Lou on one of the exam tables and took a look at her. Lexie stood by and watched. M'Lou gulped down a bottled water and ate a power bar.

Cam eyed her closely. "Okay, as if everyone doesn't know this already, I'm a veterinarian, so take that for what it's worth."

"Close enough," Lexie said.

"That's okay" M'Lou mumbled, her mouth now full of the energy snack.

Cam applied antibiotic ointment to the scratches on M'Lou's body, at least the areas where he was allowed to go. He didn't have M.D. privileges. He had Lexie take care of the off-limits areas while he turned his back.

"Take these," he said, and gave M'Lou two pills. "Antibiotics. God knows what's going on inside you. Just to be sure."

"These for people?" M'Lou said.

"They are tonight," he replied. "All I've got at the moment."

M'Lou shrugged and took the pills.

Cam looked at her swollen ankle. It was red and bruised. "What happened here?"

"That's where that thing grabbed her with its tongue," Lexie said. "I swear, Cam, that was the freakiest thing I ever saw. What the hell *is it?*"

He just shook his head. He was getting tired of the question, and was slightly annoyed that he was the only one who hadn't seen the thing. He applied more ointment to the wound, and then gave M'Lou some Tylenol for the pain. He sent her into the clinic's small lobby to have her lay on the sofa.

"Your turn, deputy," he said.

Lexie jumped up on the table. "I'm okay," she said. "Couple of scratches."

"Uh huh," Cam replied. He put some of the antibiotic cream on a scratch across the side of her neck, and on a couple of places on her arm where a briar had caught her. There was also one on the top of her thigh, right above her left knee.

He put a dab of the ointment on his finger and started to rub it in. "May I?"

"Sure," she said.

He delicately traced his finger along the scratch that ran from the top to her inner thigh. She spread her legs slightly to help matters, and held the jersey down over the Magic King-dom in a show of modesty.

Cam probably took a little longer than normal to dress the wound. She wasn't complaining, and he was in no hurry.

"There," he said. He sounded a little hoarse. "Anyplace else?"

"Not at the moment," she said. Her smile just about made Cam fall over.

"I was worried about you," he said.

"There was good reason to be. Thanks." Again with the smile. "So how are we going to get through this? I seem to remember we had a date."

Cam looked up at the storm raging just above their heads. The clinic was also creaking under the onslaught of wind and rain, even though the brunt of the storm was still some hours away. "Hurricane Tammy should keep those ass-holes quiet for awhile," he said.

"Let's hope so. They had some wicked-looking auto-matic weapons when we drove up. And there's no cavalry to come to our aid." Lexie had called St. Martinville to explain the situation. She had spoken to the sheriff himself. Like Cam said, there was no way anyone could reach Alcide in the im-mediate future. Maybe not for a day or so. They were on their own. The sheriff sounded particularly distraught. He didn't want to leave Lexie alone. He promised he would think of something. She thought he had sounded like her Daddy, and it had brought her some comfort.

With everyone patched up and fed, Cam, Lexie and M'Lou rejoined the rest of the crew inside the bait and tackle store. Cam didn't want to leave M'Lou alone at the vet clinic.

It wouldn't be long before the gangbangers realized it was another way in. They'd have to figure out how to defend that end of the building.

Troy was keeping watch by the front door now, taking careful glances out the small window. Night had fallen, and with the rain coming down, it was impossible to see across the street. The exception was the lightning, which gave him a quick snapshot of the situation.

Debris was beginning to fly through the air as well. Small branches with leaves still attached, the occasional soda can, paper and other light objects. Soon, it would be lawn furniture and garbage cans. As the storm got on top of them, the air would be filled with roofs, boats and any people stupid enough to be out in 110 mph winds.

Carla, who had brought along a bag for her stay at Troy's, had changed into another pair of jeans and a pink cotton shirt. Her hair was still damp. She sat on the counter, drinking a Diet Pepsi from a can.

Father Mike and Sister Joanie sat in stools nearby, watching the TV. Huey stood at the locked back door, looking through it as if he could see everything outside. His low growl was now mixed with a whine.

Cam had M'Lou go in the back storeroom and lay down on one of the cots. Although bathed, fed, watered and doctored, she still was suffering from exhaustion and exposure. He wanted her off her feet for now.

"Landfall," Mike said without taking his eyes off the TV. "Category 3. New Orleans and Baton Rouge are gonna get whacked by the eastern side. Looks like the thing jogged a little more east than they thought. The eye is headed straight for us."

Cam stole a look at the screen. Lexie surveyed the firepower in the room.

"Cam, you got anything else to shoot with?" she said.

"That's it. My Beretta. The Colt. The .22 and the 10 gauge."

"Mike, no offense, but I might want to commandeer your piece there," she said.

He looked down at the Colt in his hand and back at her. "Sure. You're a better shot anyway. I'm a 30-30 man myself." He handed her the gun.

Lexie now felt much better. She had forgotten how good it was to be armed. She had been so defenseless for the last 24 hours, the gun felt like a surge of power and energy in her hand.

Mike looked back at the TV. "Winds outside are already 85, with gusts to 100," he said. As if on cue, the building vibrated as a heavy gust assaulted the old wooden structure. There was an ominous roar, too.

Then the lights went out.

Chapter 43:
"The Hits Just Keep On Comin'"

The male creature, as big as he was, was no match for the storm's onslaught. He slipped and slid along the road, which was now higher and not underwater. He continued down the middle of the road, rain lashing at his body and random pieces of debris peppering his thick hide. Even though it was completely dark now, he could see quite clearly with his excellent night vision. The only problem was the random flashes of lightning, which screwed up his pupils as they tried to adapt to deep dark and bright white.

He was making excellent time, despite the conditions. The open road suited him, and with no traffic to worry about, he had no concerns about having to dash into the woods for cover. In fact, he was kind of hoping someone would come by. Food sounded good right now.

His big nose continued to get a good fix on the female. He was zeroing in on her, somewhere straight ahead. Sometimes her scent was strong, others weak. But when it was weak, he could also feel the vibrations she was sending out. She had locked on to him, too.

Man, was he horny. And hungry. And still a little pissed off.

The female creature continued to spend most of her time underwater, just behind the structure where a number of the smart things were. She suspected they were sheltering from the storm, too. Every now and then, she would float to the surface and get a fix on the male. His scent was strong. Finally, the idiot was heading her way, and fast. This deal might actually get done.

At some point, she would have to get out of the water and head for the small structure. That's where they'd hook up, out of the storm. If she was lucky, he'd do his job right and the young would begin the birthing process. Once he had finished, it wouldn't take long for the chemicals to induce birth. She'd deliver the young ones, lead them back into the water and deeper into the swamps. They didn't suckle off her, thank goodness, like some of the creatures she had observed in the swamp. The little bastards were ready to hunt the moment they were born. They would start eating anything that moved. It was kind of scary to watch. After that, she was done. Back to her old haunts. No male to deal with, no children to worry about. Just a big swamp to hide in and lots to eat.

But first, she had to get through this night. Before she left, she might grab a quick bite of some of the smart things that were so close. A nice snack before the trip. The male might even join her for the meal. After that, they'd go their separate ways.

The young ones squirmed inside her again. This time, it really hurt. *Come on, come on,* she thought. *Get your ass here now!*

Across the street from Fort St. Jesus Bait and Tackle, inside the abandoned old Dairy Queen, Tree paced back and forth in the darkness. He had exchanged his Glock pistol for a wicked and highly illegal AK47 automatic rifle. Just one of the many toys they had stashed in the trunk. The rest of his guys had upgraded to various other high-caliber weapons. Even Roland had found an Uzi he became enamored with.

Tree no longer felt the sting in his ankle where shards of wood had embedded themselves from the earlier shotgun blast. Wasn't shit to him. One of his guys, T-Roy, had caught a round in his upper arm. In and out. They had wrapped it up in an old towel they found. T-Roy sucked it up and was ready for some payback.

Tree, too.

"I'm gonna fuck them *all* up," he said to the room. He paced quicker now. His posse understood the moment. It was speech time. Tree was at the podium. The next words would be important. Maybe life altering. "How many they got in there now?"

T-Roy, jacked up on adrenaline and feeling a little agitated himself after being shot, chimed in, "Those two white boys up front, and some dude and a chick was in the back, shoppin' or something. Four. Then the three chicks just went in. Seven, Tree. Seven."

"One of them was that cop, huh, Roland?" Tree bellowed. "I wanted some of that ass, and you shitheads let her get away."

"Got her now, Tree," Roland said. Roland was pretty sure that wasn't going to happen. Lexie would end up dead before anybody got a piece of her ass. She was gonna shoot somebody or die trying, and it sure as hell wasn't going to be him that got shot. The moment to get a piece of Lexie had passed. He just wanted to get the drugs, get his money, and get the hell out of here. Problem was, he'd lived around here all his life, and he was certain the two ways out of Alcide were under water. Nobody was going anywhere.

Rain and wind lashed the front window of the abandoned DQ. The old building shuddered.

Raymond, Tree's driver, and the Einstein of the group, had the cojones to say, "Tree, man, we ain't doin' nothin' till this storm's done. That's some shit out there." He pointed in the general direction of meteorological Armageddon that was just outside the door.

Tree pondered this a moment. "Fuck that," he pronounced. "That's what they thinkin'. Gotta surprise 'em. Catch 'em when they ain't lookin'."

Raymond thought about his rebuttal for about a half second, and then thought better of it. "What you thinkin', Tree?"

"Got a little plan, workin', Raymond. Got a little plan." He smiled and thumped the side of his head with his giant finger.

The lights were out for a total of three seconds before the ginny kicked in automatically, and suddenly there was power. Cam was relieved that his little investment was paying off. He could barely hear the generator outside, its engine noise drowned out by the howling storm.

The TV powered up, but it took a second for the signal to unscramble and bring the Weather Channel back. When it did, they got a glimpse of one of the barrier islands on the coast completely underwater, whitecaps blowing under old houses on stilts. By morning, the stilts would be the only things left.

"Wonder what idiot is shooting that video?" Troy said.

"Dead man walkin.', that's for sure," Lexie said.

Huey let loose a barrage of barks, and turned in a circle near the back door.

"Okay, that's just freaking me out," Carla said. "You think that other one is out there?"

Cam had walked over to try and calm the dog down. "Somebody's out there," he said. "Or some*thing*. That's his intruder bark. I'd suggest no one take a stroll on the porch right at this moment."

No one laughed.

Father Mike said to Lexie, "How bad do you think they want those drugs?"

She laugh-snorted. "Well, they kidnapped me, tied me naked to a bed, were going to gang-rape me and then torture me. Or maybe that *was* the torture, to get me to tell them where the stuff was. And I'm pretty sure they were going to kill me when they were done. So, I'm guessin' they want that shit pretty bad."

Mike got the point. "Take some balls to make a run at us in this wind."

"They're coming," she said.

No sooner had she spoken than gunfire erupted from out front. The *pops* and *thunks* of rounds hitting the outside wall made everyone inside dive for cover. Then it stopped.

Troy stole a look outside, and a flash of lightning told him the story.

"I'll be damned."

Cam ran over and looked out. The gangbangers, and presumably Roland, were inside the Town Car, which was now pulling out of the parking lot of the DQ. Cam saw one of the back windows going up just as the big Lincoln accelerated down the road, headed out of town.

"They're leaving," Cam said, master of the obvious.

"Not going far," Lexie said. "No way out, remember?"

"I don't give a shit, as long as they're gone from there," Cam replied.

Joanie walked over, cradling the .22 rifle in her hands. "Then it's over?"

"Could be," Cam said. "Between our firepower and Mother Nature, maybe they called it a night."

"Just the same," Lexie said. "Let's be careful."

A horrendous screech, followed by a metallic crash outside made everyone jump. Troy looked outside again.

"Holy crap, Cam. A whole slice of your roof just flew off. It's headed down the road."

Cam took a quick look and saw a huge piece of tin roofing go skating down the road. The wind got under it and it flipped three times before wrapping itself around an oak tree.

"Not good," he said. "When you lose one..." And before he could finish the sentence, another screech and crash, and another piece of the roof sailed down the road. Blowing rain hit the bayou side of the building so hard, it sounded like a wave hit the place. Huey jumped back.

"The hits just keep on a-comin'," Troy said.

Even though the gangbangers had bugged out, the storm kept everyone tense. Cam decided it would be a good idea if they all had a hot meal. He warmed up a pot of gumbo, fixed some rice and threw some French bread into the oven. M'Lou wandered out from the back, a little bleary eyed, when she smelled the food. He tore open a box of Styrofoam bowls, and everyone ladled in the hot gumbo over rice. They hit the cooler for beers or sodas, and sat around watching the TV. Lexie, though, kept her eyes on the doors.

Outside, Hurricane Tammy raged, as the wind speed crept up to 100 mph and climbed. The rain was relentless, pounding the little building like a thundering waterfall. The sound of the storm also changed. It howled and whistled, moaned and crackled. It was like a living, breathing monster overhead, devouring everything in its path, trying desperately to get inside and swallow up everyone in there.

But the real monsters were just outside, too, with those and other thoughts in their heads. The female had inched close to the bank and pulled herself out into the raging maelstrom of Hurricane Tammy. She staggered against the wind, keeping low until she reached the little building on the side of Fort St. Jesus Bait and Tackle. She didn't know what it was used for, but it would make excellent shelter until the male arrived. Had she been observant and come by here anytime in the past, she would have noticed that the smart things cleaned their vehicles inside. It was a carwash. Not the fancy automatic kind. Just a pull-through with a high-powered hose. It was just big enough for her to crawl into, and it sheltered her from the wind and rain. She hunkered down, sent another vibration out to the male, and waited.

Raymond eased the Town Car down the residential street that ran parallel to the main road in Alcide. His lights were off. Tree and the rest of the gang, along with Roland, ensconced in the trunk again, didn't say a word. The occasional flash of lightning gave Raymond enough guidance to stay on the narrow street and not roll into someone's mailbox. All of the homes here were unoccupied, their owners holed up in Lafayette or points north, at relatives or hotels, until the storm blew through.

The street eventually connected to the main highway, which curved through town, but Raymond wasn't going that far. A block before that, the street ran behind some of the businesses that fronted the main road, including the old Dairy Queen. He pulled the Town Car into a gravel parking area behind the abandoned restaurant and shut her down.

Rain slashed across the windshield and roof, and the car shook with a gust of wind.

"Lock and load, motherfuckers," Tree said. He pulled the bolt back on the AK47. Similar metallic sounds emanated from the back seat. "This gonna be an *operation*, like them special forces do," Tree said. "Hit 'em front, back, all which-a-ways."

The three in the back nodded. T-Roy even smiled, but he winced again as a pain shot down his arm. Raymond just looked out at the storm and grimaced. He hoped Tree didn't see his expression.

The female creature rested in the car wash. She had a perfect view of the road coming into town, as well as most of the buildings, too. Fatigue overcame her and she closed her huge eyes. She'd been on the move now for days, and her strength was waning. It felt good to be on dry ground again. Well, it wasn't *dry*, but at least she didn't have to hold her breath. She was about to drift off when vibrations in the ground caught her attention. Her first thought was that the male was here. But when she opened her eyes, it wasn't the male at all.

Across the street, she could see six of the smart things moving her way. They were carrying things. They struggled against the powerful wind and rain, but the movement looked predatory as they dashed behind trees, stopped, and then ran to more cover. They were fighting the weather, hunched low. One fell down and rolled before regaining his feet. It seemed their attention wasn't on her per se, but the building to her left. As far as she could tell with her superb night vision, they hadn't seen her. But they looked determined.

What the hell were they doing, especially on a night like this? She knew the damned things were unpredictable, even if they were smart. *Crap*, she thought, *they were going to screw up the screwing she was about to get from the male.* He was getting closer now. *Real* close. Would he get spooked and hide? Or would he come on in, ready to rock and roll?

Well, he was young and a little foolish. And he'd be crazy with horniness and hunger. So chances are, he'd come in hot, the hell with the smart things. He might even eat one or two on the way in.

She kept one huge eye on the smart things, and the other on the road that led north out of town. She'd see how this would play out.

Chapter 44:
"Lights Out, For Real"

Lexie walked back into the storeroom. She saw where Cam and Troy had set up their cots, along with some battery-operated lanterns. M'Lou was out cold in one of them, the hot food having both filled her up and made her sleepy. She probably hadn't slept for days anyway.

In one corner, not far from the cots and next to some stacks of beer cases sat Roland's little chemistry project. Bags of meth, plus some coke, all destined for the big city, feeding the addictions of adults and probably some kids. Payment for it all would surely fuel the purchase of more drugs, and certainly more guns. In other words, the profits would be poured back into the business. It all disgusted her.

Lexie ran her finger over the bags, and for a moment, she felt like grabbing all of it and taking it outside to throw into the bayou. But there would be reports to fill out, and this was a pile of evidence to put Roland away with, so her better judgment kicked in.

"Asshole," she said out loud.

The other cot looked inviting. She was coming down off her latest adrenaline high, and fatigue was setting in for her, too. She had slept some in the woods last night, but it hadn't done the trick. She couldn't sleep just yet. While the others were more relaxed, she had to keep her ears up. She was the law in these parts, and she was sworn to preserve and protect.

Maybe those thugs had left. Maybe not the parish, but certainly out of town. Maybe they went to Roland's shitty trailer. That would be an excellent idea in a category three hurricane. Tammy would take the whole lot of them and the trailer and dump them all three miles away in the Atchafalaya River, and then shoot them down all the way to the Gulf.

That thought made her smile.

Then the lights went out and her smile vanished.

"What the hell?" Cam said.

With the power out now, the hum of the coolers had ceased, as well as the chatter on the TV, so the noise of the storm outside seemed louder.

"So much for the ginny," Troy said.

It had gone pitch black inside the store, but a flash of lightning or two brought some disco strobing to the darkness. Cam grabbed a flashlight off the counter and switched it on. Lexie came out from the back.

"Cam, what happened?" she said.

"Don't know. We filled the tanks yesterday. Unless a branch or something hit it and knocked something out of whack."

In the light of the flashlight, Cam saw Huey get up off the floor by the back door and run to the front. He let loose with another barrage of barks. No sooner had he done that than he ran back to the other door and did the same. Then he would glance back at the front, as if he weren't sure which one to go to.

Everyone was focused on the dog.

Then the proverbial caca hit the fan.

The front door disintegrated near the doorknob as automatic rounds from the outside tore it to shreds. In seconds, the back door did the same. The bullets that managed to pierce the doors lodged into the ancient oak floor of the bait shop, but some ricocheted and tore into Cam's inventory. The sound was ear splitting as the glass in the coolers shattered from the wayward bullets. Some of them were tracer rounds, lit up like something out of a *Star Wars* movie, hot glowing metal that could be seen dancing from floor to ceiling to wall inside the store.

Cam, Troy and Lexie dove for cover behind the counter. Mike and Joanie retreated towards the back of the store, with Huey right behind them. Carla ducked behind an ice cream cooler at the end of one of the aisles. She put her arms around her head and screamed.

The machine-gun fire stopped and both the front and the back doors were kicked in. The gangbangers spilled into the room from both entrances. All opened up with their weapons toward the front counter. Dozens of rounds of ammunition hit the wall above Cam, Troy and Lexie. Debris went flying everywhere—pieces of wood, metal fragments from the cash register, pictures on the wall, glass, plastic, paper–all filled the air and fell to the ground on top of them.

Cam grabbed Lexie by the collar and pulled her with him toward the door that led into the back kitchen area. Troy slid on his belly like an awkward snake-man and followed them through. None of them thought about returning fire. The hailstorm of bullets would have cut them to pieces.

Mike and Joanie made it into the storeroom, where they found M'Lou standing, her eyes wide and her arms wrapped around herself.

"Get behind those boxes!" Mike yelled, and pointed to a stack of beer cases in the corner. M'Lou didn't hesitate and ran for cover.

"Stay here," he said to Joanie. "Give me the rifle." He got low and made his way back into the store. The room was filled with smoke, illuminated by the flashes from the automatic weapons trained on Cam, Troy and Lexie, as well as from the lightning outside. Thunder boomed over the sound of the guns. It was surreal to Mike. He could see the backs of six shapes. They were all standing in a line like a firing squad. He raised the .22 rifle and took aim at one of the shapes in the middle of the group. He squeezed off a round and hit the guy high in the shoulder. The impact spun him around and he screamed, reaching for the wound, but he didn't go down. Mike knew the .22 didn't have a lot of stopping power, but it would get somebody's attention. Quickly, he pulled the bolt back and chambered another round, and fired at the guy next to him. It struck him in the right upper arm, and the force caused the small machine pistoled in his hand to go flying in the air.

Now Mike had everyone's full attention. The rest of the gangbangers turned as one and opened up in Mike's direction.

Cam noticed the change in sound and direction of the fire. He looked at Lexie and Troy, who had both found cover behind a table. He pumped the slide on the shotgun, stood up and eased toward the door that led out to the back of the counter.

He also got the full disco effect of gunfire and lightning flashing in the smoke. The gangbangers were now spread out to the right and left and were crouched down, as far as he could see. He figured they must be shooting at Mike. The *crack* of the single-shot .22 rifle confirmed that. The good Father was shooting back. Cam had an opening.

He stood up, aimed the shotgun to the left, toward the front door, and squeezed the trigger. A tight grouping of pellets sailed over the head of the big guy, but a few caught him in the shoulder and he went down. Cam pumped again, turned to his right, and fired. He didn't know if he hit anything, because he ducked back just in time before some well-placed rounds from an Uzi tore the door jam apart where his head had been just a moment before.

The front door was wide open, as was the back, and wind and rain poured into the store from both directions. The wet, salty air of the Gulf filled the room, as well as the fragrant smell of freshly broken trees. The wind blew the gun smoke around in whirls that circled the interior of the bait shop. Lightning flashed again, and with it he saw the gangbangers running out of both doors, crouched low, but still firing blindly in both directions.

In a moment, the only sound Cam could hear was the ferocious storm howling above them. There was another screeching metallic tearing sound. More sheets of tin were being peeled away from the roof. The entire building shook.

"Mike!" Cam yelled. "You okay?" He switched on his flashlight.

"Good!" he responded.

"Stay down. Don't know if they're coming back."

Lexie and Troy slid behind Cam, their guns at the ready. Lexie said, "You hit?"

Cam shook his head. He didn't think so, but his adrenaline was pumping so fast, he could be missing a leg and he wouldn't know it. "Come on," he said.

He stayed low and crawled out from behind the counter. Troy and Lexie were right behind him. They spread out left and right, and then carefully stood up, guns raised at both doors.

Troy went to the back. Cam and Lexie to the front. They tried to shut the doors, but with no latches left after the attack, the doors were useless. Cam pulled a newspaper vending machine in front of his door to keep it closed. Lexie helped him. Troy saw what they were doing and found a display of fishing rods and reels and pulled it in front of the back door to hold it closed. The wind was too strong, and it moved the whole thing over. He grabbed a metal stop he found on the floor and jammed it under the door.

"Carla!" he said.

"Here," she replied. She crawled down the aisle on all fours, whimpering as she went. When she got to Troy, she wrapped her arms around him and started crying. He held her tightly.

Joanie and M'Lou eased out of the back. "They gone?" she said.

Father Mike stood up, but held the rifle at the ready. "I think I got a couple of them," he said.

"Stay sharp," Lexie said. She held her pistol with two hands, pointed to the floor. Her eyes darted to the front door, and then to the back.

Cam figured her training had kicked in. Even though she wore a Saints jersey and nothing else, she still had that cop air about her. Badass. And hot. A nice combination in his book.

Above the din of the storm, more shots rang out and rounds peppered the walls. Everyone hit the floor.

"I do believe they're pissed," Troy said. He winked at Cam.

The firing stopped and all that was left was the storm.

"Shit. Mike!" Joanie said.

They all turned to her. Cam shone his flashlight that way. Joanie was on her knees and looked down at Father Mike. Blood covered his right leg.

Cam scrambled over to take a look. "Did you just get hit?"

Father Mike grimaced. He had both hands around his calf. "I guess so. Maybe. I don't remember. Might have got it when they busted in."

Cam pulled Mike's pants leg up and looked at the wound. It was bleeding a lot. "Through and through," he said. "Don't go anywhere." He kept low and ran behind the counter and down the back hall to the vet clinic. In a moment he returned with a first aid kit and some other supplies. He cleaned the wound and put a compression bandage on it. He then wrapped it tightly.

Joanie knelt there with her hands over her mouth, eyes wide.

"That's gonna hurt like a mother," said Troy.

Mike gave a brave smile. "Might have to give my next sermon sitting down."

Lexie took a deep breath and said to Cam, "We were very lucky. They brought some serious firepower in here."

Cam nodded. "Spray and pray."

"What?" Carla said. She had stopped crying.

"It's what they teach you not to do in the Army," Cam said. "When you put your weapon on full auto and just spray the enemy with fire and pray you hit something. Kind of a waste of ammunition."

Over the howling of the wind and the rain slashing the bait store, a new sound caught everyone's attention. It was a distinct *crack*. But before anyone had a chance to offer their commentary on the noise's origin, the whole east side of the bait shop collapsed in a deafening roar.

The female creature hid comfortably in the carwash and had watched as the gangbangers approached the bait shop and launched their attack. When the shooting started, she knew exactly what it was. Over her years here, she had seen and heard the smart thing's weapons. They were deadly for most creatures. She herself had never been shot, but one time, many decades ago, she had been *shot at* when some trappers had spotted her on the surface of one of the bayous. They didn't have a clean view of her entire body, just her head that had broken the surface. The bullets had plunked harmlessly in the water nearby, and she had dove into the murky depths for safety.

She didn't think the bullets could harm her. Her hide was very thick. But she wasn't taking any chances. If the smart things wanted to kill each other, more power to them. She had other things to worry about.

There was a great flash of lightning, and with it, the entire downtown of Alcide was illuminated. And there in the distance she saw him. The male. Her lover. Her husband. The father of her children. The asshole who had forced her to travel this far in her condition.

She didn't know whether to rejoice or just kill him on the spot.

Chapter 45:
"Eye of the Storm"

Tree, Roland and the gang had returned to the relative safety of the abandoned Dairy Queen. He had his leather coat off and looked at it.

"Motherfuckers ruint my coat," he said. Got fucking holes in it now." He eyed where a few of Cam's shotgun pellets had pierced the jacket high in the back left, near the shoulder. There were specks of blood there, too. He felt his back and looked at his hand. Blood.

"Fucker shot me," he pronounced.

Two of his other guys just looked at him. Fucker had shot them, too. Or, some other fucker had. They each had a .22 round inside them. One could feel the bullet embedded in some muscle in his back. The round had shattered a rib and lodged there. The other gangbanger had his .22 lodged in the meaty part of his upper right arm. It might have been broken, too. This matched the wound he had in his other arm, when the shooting had first begun in round one of their little battle.

"What now, Tree?" Raymond said. He was drenched, and wiped rain out of his eyes.

"Fuck if I know," he said. "Gotta think this through. But we goin' back, and this time we're gettin' the shit. And every last one of those motherfuckers is dead!" He pointed back across the street. "Well, look at dat."

Raymond turned, and in the flashes of lightning, he saw that a large tree had fallen over onto the east side of the bait store. The whole end of the building was destroyed, replaced by the shiny, wet leaves of an oak whose canopy now rested on the ground in front of the store. The huge trunk had acted like a blunt, dull knife and sliced the structure open, causing it to collapse.

"I think we just found us a way in," Tree said.

The male creature stood on his back legs. Or maybe they were just legs now. Unlike squirrels and bears and other animals that occasionally stood on their hind legs, the male creature's back legs were designed to mimic those of the smart things. He was bi-pedal when he wanted to be, and could walk on those indefinitely. Now he was at his full height, and surveyed the community of Alcide.

The storm was really picking up now, and he had to squint his big eyes against the blowing rain and debris. In a very human-like gesture, he even put one hand over them to protect him while he checked out the situation. The female was *here*. He could smell her and sense the powerful vibration she was putting off. But there was another smell in the air that made his stomach growl and reminded him just how hungry he was.

It was the smell of the smart things, and in particular, their blood. To get some perspective, to him it was like the smell of French fries. Or a juicy grilled filet. Or frying bacon. And you might as well throw in hot, freshly baked bread.

He didn't know anything about those foods, of course, but the effect was the same.

He was *starving.* And somebody had laid out a feast.

The darkened bait store was filled with cold, blowing rain and the smell of fresh oak sap mixed with ozone from the electrified air outside. The shiny green leaves of the huge tree's canopy shimmered in their wetness, like the skin of some huge dragon. Branches of all shapes and sizes reached out like the arms and hands of a monstrous beast. The strobing effect of the lightning added to the surreal view.

Cam and Troy had fallen backwards towards the counter. Lexie was there, too. Huey licked Cam's face.

"I'm okay, buddy," he said, and gave the dog a once over to make sure *he* was okay. Cam stood up and did a head count. Troy and Lexie were getting up off their asses as well. He couldn't see Father Mike, Sister Joanie, Carla or M'Lou. They had all been standing near the other end of the store, the one now covered in oak and fallen beams and roofing.

Lexie looked at Cam and back at the debris. They ran over and began to search for everyone. Troy was right behind them.

"Mike, Joanie!" Cam yelled.

He tripped over something and looked down. It was Carla, crawling out of the mess.

"This night's just getting better and better," she said, more angry than scared. She got out from the destruction, and turned back towards everyone. Cam shone his flashlight at her. Aside from a few scratches, she was okay.

Lexie had found Father Mike and Sister Joanie. The good sister had fallen over on Mike, who had been on his back before the roof fell in. A piece of the tin roof half covered them. Lexie pulled it off.

Mike mumbled loud enough for Lexie to hear, "Joanie, get off me. Not a good image for the church bulletin."

Joanie moved slowly. But before she got off him, she stroked his face and hair with her hand. "You okay?"

"Well, I don't think I have to read myself the Last Rites, if that's what you mean."

Joanie got up on all fours and helped Lexie pull Mike up and out of the tree's fallen canopy. Troy appeared out of the mass of green, holding M'Lou up. She looked a little dazed, but she had looked that way all night, so no one was worried. He walked her out and back around the counter.

Troy said over the din of the storm, "Hey, Cam. Hope you're square with the insurance company."

Cam ignored him and surveyed the damage. The whole back half of the store was destroyed, including the storeroom where the drugs were hidden. He pointed the flashlight that way and could see all the way out into the turbulent night.

"Fantastic," he said.

The front door had blown open again and was half off its hinges. There was no longer a back door, just a wide opening that led to the back deck and the bayou, which right now looked like the inside of a washing machine set on the crazy cycle.

"Everybody still have their guns?" he yelled.

Troy and Lexie nodded, each holding up their pistols. Cam picked up the shotgun off the floor. Mike said, "Don't know where the rifle went."

"Okay, back into the kitchen. This way," Cam ordered.

They all made their way into the small room behind the counter. No sooner had they done that, than gunfire erupted again from outside. Everyone hit the deck, waiting for the gangbangers to emerge into the store. Three came in from the back and opened up towards the counter. The kitchen offered good protection, so everyone just stayed down and out of the line of fire.

Troy aimed his pistol around the doorjamb and fired off a couple of rounds. The gangbangers dove for cover. "That'll keep 'em honest," Troy said.

Cam thought for a second that he was right. Until an explosion of automatic gunfire erupted from behind them somewhere. It was coming from the vet clinic. Someone was blowing holes through the front door. Cam and friends were about to get caught in a crossfire.

Tree was in the tree. Well, he was actually standing in what was left of Fort St. Jesus Bait and Tackle's storeroom, surrounded by what was left of the oak tree. Roland was with him. They were pushing away cases of Bud Light that had been smashed by the falling oak. The smell of hot beer filled their nostrils.

"Here, here," Roland said. He picked up a brick of cocaine, still wrapped in plastic and unharmed by the destruction. "This one, too." It was some of the crystal meth, also intact.

The racket was ear splitting, and Tree could barely hear what Roland was saying, but he could see all right. His guys were pinning down those assholes, driving them right into a little trap he had set. While they were doing that, he and Roland had found the mother lode.

"Put that shit in here," Tree ordered. He had brought a large canvas satchel that had been in the trunk, where they stored their weapons and ammo. Now it would be used to collect the dope.

Roland began to stuff the bag with as much meth and coke as he could find. Most of it was still wrapped and dry, but some had split open. He threw them in anyway.

"Hurry up, motherfucker," Tree yelled. "Storm's gettin' worse. Gotta get back to the DQ."

Roland nodded and got to work.

No sooner than Tree had said that than the storm did just the opposite. The winds died down quickly, and the rain stopped as if someone had just turned off a showerhead.

T-Roy was focused. Even though he was wounded in both arms now, he didn't give a shit. He was going to kill someone. He blew through one clip of his Uzi to take out the door that led into the vet clinic's lobby. He popped out the empty clip, and with practiced ease, slipped a new one into the evil little Israeli-made machine pistol.

He moved to the side and waited a beat, and then kicked the door in. He stuck the little gun inside and squeezed off a few rounds just for good measure. The wind behind him howled, but something just changed. The roar of the hurricane-force winds swelled and ended with a great sigh, as if Mother Nature caught her breath. The rain let up and quickly ended as well.

The audible change was so dramatic, T-Roy turned from his assault and looked out into the now-still night. Above his head and to the south he could see stars in the rinsed out sky. To the north, there was still a solid wall of dark, fast moving clouds. The wall advanced to the north. Flashes of distant lightning illuminated the area.

"What the fuck?" he said.

He suddenly remembered he was about to make his assault into the vet clinic and catch those crackers from behind. He'd make 'em hurt just like they made him hurt. The pain in his arms where he had been shot was now a dull, throbbing ache, but he fought through it. He fired off a few more rounds into the small lobby and was about to run in when he heard footsteps behind him. It would be Tree or some of the other guys, although they were all supposed to be inside getting the white boys' attention.

"I got dis," he said without turning, somewhat annoyed the others weren't sticking to the plan. He heard the footsteps again along with some heavy breathing. "I got it," he said, and turned back to make sure the others knew he had things under control.

When he did turn, he realized in one, epic moment of clarity that he really didn't have things under control at all. Not by a long shot.

"What the fuck!" he half choked out of his mouth.

Standing before him, all 20 feet of it, was something out of his worst nightmares. Or some scary-as-shit horror movie. "Monster" was the first thought that came to mind. Then the next noun his mind managed to conjure up was "Jesus." A very *proper* noun, under the circumstances. He hadn't been to church for a very long time. Maybe when he was six and his grandmother took him. He was sort of wishing he was in one right now. At this moment, as he looked into the jaws of the monster and at its razor sharp teeth and giant bug eyes, he tried to think of a Jesus prayer, but nothing came to mind. So he did the next best thing. He squeezed the trigger on his weapon. Nothing happened. He had emptied the clip. He pulled another one out of his pocket and fumbled with it. He was shaking so badly, he couldn't slip it into the weapon. It fell to the ground. His legs went rubbery. He screamed, dropped the empty Uzi and ran into the vet clinic lobby.

Cam and the others, still crouched in the kitchen, heard the storm give out. It was dramatic, even over the sound of gunfire aimed in their direction. That had stopped, too, as if all humanity called a timeout to see what was going on.

He looked at Troy. "Was the eye supposed to pass over us?"

Troy nodded. "Think so. It jiggled east a little and was kind of headed this way."

"So much for cover," Lexie said. "I was hoping it would drive them back across the street."

A weird scream caught their attention from behind. It was scary because it was so childlike. Pure terror. Primal. As they turned, they saw one of the gangbangers run into the clinic's lobby. He had his head turned behind him. There was another sound. Whip-like and somehow *liquid*. Something else had entered the clinic behind the gangbanger. He fell to the floor, onto his back and screamed even louder. That's when Troy said, "Holy shit."

The tongue-thing had grabbed the guy by the leg and pulled him back out into the night.

T-Roy, who had never been the philosophical type, pondered his immortality in the few seconds he had left to live. His whole shitty life flashed before his eyes. It was a short film, though, so not a lot to review. Raised by his grandmother. Occasional visits by his strung-out mother. Never a sign of his father. Running the streets of the Ninth Ward at the age of seven. Doing dope. A couple of hold-ups and robberies. Some time in juvey. Meeting up with Tree and running with him.

And now this.

T-Roy yelled out for Tree to save him, but heard nothing in reply. He kicked as much as he could as he was dragged through the door of the clinic and out onto the wet gravel parking lot, but he couldn't escape the tongue. He went into the thing's mouth feet first, heard the big crunch, felt the searing pain, gurgled out another scream, thought about the movie *Jurassic Park* for one fleeting nanosecond and then it was lights out.

Huey didn't bark this time. This time he howled. He had smelled the bad things really well for the last few hours and knew at least one of them was close, maybe two. Part of him wanted to run into a corner and hide, part of him wanted to protect his master, Cam. His brave dog persona won out and he charged down the hall toward the lobby of the vet clinic. He barked and snarled as he tried to run and gain traction on the old linoleum floor. He slewed left and right until he got some momentum going.

Behind him, he heard his master call his name, but he ignored it. He charged into the little lobby and headed out the front door.

Chapter 46:
"All-You-Can-Eat at the Fort"

All of Tree's guys re-loaded and let loose another volley into the counter and kitchen. They had heard T-Roy's screams and figured he had been shot. This enraged them and they turned their vengeance onto Cam and the rest.

"Everybody down the hall, stay low," Cam said as round after round chewed up the sheetrock above his head. "Into the clinic!"

"Are you fucking crazy?" Troy said. "That thing's out there."

"It's okay, it's eating that guy," Carla said. "It's occupied."

Lexie wasn't wasting time. She crawled down the hallway, leading Father Mike and Sister Joanie behind her. Carla followed. Cam and Troy raised their guns up and fired a few more rounds toward the gangbangers and followed behind Carla.

"You got a plan?" Troy yelled as he followed Cam on all fours.

"No," was all he got back in return. "Don't die."

"I like that plan," Troy said.

They all scampered into the lobby and turned left into the little receptionist's area and into the back examination room, putting as many walls as they could between them and the outside. When Troy and Cam made it into the little office, they turned toward the open door and caught a glimpse of the thing munching on what was left of T-Roy. Huge amounts of blood were dripping from its mouth, and Cam could swear the thing was smiling as if it were savoring a flavorful barbecued rib or something.

Or something.

"That it?" Cam yelled.

Troy looked at him and back at the creature. "Hmmm. Let me see. Yeah, I think so. How many weird fucking monsters we got running around, anyway? Of course that's it!"

Cam was mesmerized. He should have screamed and run for cover, but he just froze. It was like people watching an approaching tornado. They knew it was dangerous, but the sheer awesomeness of the thing seemed to override their instincts. That was what was happening to him. He pulled out his iPhone and snapped a picture. He figured the strobing lightning and darknesss probably screwed up the shot.

"What the..." was all he could say. Until the thing saw him. Its huge eyes focused on him as it swallowed the rest of the gangbanger. The creature, still on its back legs, rose up and charged for the door.

"Run!" Cam said.

With one great crash, the massive creature ran into the front of the clinic and took out the whole wall. The old wooden siding splintered and cracked and the roof slid over to the right, exposing the entire lobby to the elements.

Cam and Troy spider-walked backwards on their asses into the examination area, turned on their sides and got up, pushing Lexie and the rest of the gang before them. Carla and Joanie screamed.

There was that whip-like sound again and the tongue thing flew above Cam's head and hit a back wall with a *thud*. It retracted back the way it had come with frightening quickness. The quick flashes of distant lightning made the scene seem otherworldly.

"Shoot that fucker," Troy said.

He and Cam turned as one and emptied their weapons in the general direction of the creature. It didn't do any good. The thing was ripping its way into the clinic, tearing out walls, ceilings and anything else that was in its way, like a hungry cat after some mice trying to escape into a hidey hole.

The gangbangers who stood in the bait shot got a glimpse of the thing and stopped firing. The three of them froze in disbelief.

"What is *that?*" one of them said.

"Fuck if I know. Shoot it!"

They all let loose with another barrage. That got the creature's attention. It turned toward them and hissed. Its tongue-thing shot out of its mouth, down what was left of the hall, over the counter and attached itself to the face of the gangbanger who stood in the middle. He went airborne without a sound, head first over the counter, down the hall and into the huge mouth. In two quick bites he was gone. It all happened in less than four seconds.

The remaining two guys ran out the back of the bait shop, onto the porch that overlooked the bayou, screaming like little girls.

Tree saw them run by. That whole back side of the store had been destroyed, and he could see through the debris and the fallen tree canopy as his guys ran. Occasional flashes of lightning from the north silently lit the scene.

"Hey, fuckers. Where you goin?" he yelled.

Roland looked up from his drug recovery duties, took notice of the fleeing gang members, and resumed his work. He wondered what scared the shit out of those guys.

The female creature lay hunkered down in the carwash. She had watched with some dismay as the male entered town, ignored her, and headed over to the building for a bite to eat. Actually, she was more than a little dismayed. She was supremely pissed. For days she had been anticipating this moment, and when it finally came, the male chose food over sex. Typical.

She concentrated and sent out another low vibration, her version of a mating call. It was the strongest yet, and this close it must have made the male shake where he stood. But, no. That asshole was eating his way through the building. Might have been *eating* the building for all she knew. The storm had subsided, and the moment was right, yet he was so crazy with hunger he completely ignored her.

She thought for a moment about dragging her ass out of there, running over to him, slapping him around a bit to get his attention, and maybe raping him. But while she let this movie play through her head, something caught her attention from behind. It was two of the smart things. They came running out of the back of the structure and would pass right by the carwash. And they had guns. *This was just getting better and better,* she thought. Could she have worse luck?

Sure enough, they passed directly in front of her. In a fit of anger, she flicked her long oral arm out of her mouth, grabbed one of them, picked him up off his feet and slammed him into the ground. The smart thing lay unconscious on the side of the road, blood oozing out of its mouth. She would eat it later before she high-tailed it back into the bayou.

The second smart thing turned and watched its friend go airborne. It backed away but tripped over its own feet and dropped the weapon it was holding. Without retracting her tongue, she let go of the unconscious body of the first smart thing and grabbed the second by the legs. The angle was all wrong and she couldn't pick him up, so she dragged him her way, right towards her mouth, and bit off his two feet to keep him from running off. He howled in pain. She figured he might drag himself off, but that would be okay. The young ones would be hungry when they were born and might want something to chase and nibble on. Or maybe she would eat him, too. Whatever.

That done, she sent out another vibration.

The male was feeling pretty jacked up. He'd eaten two of the smart things in just a few minutes. *Man, that was some good eatin',* he thought. His appetite wasn't sated, not by a long shot. If anything, the wonderful flavors he was now enjoying made his stomach growl even more. *Bet ya can't eat just one!*

He turned his attention back on the group of smart things he'd cornered in the back of the building. They were holed up back there and hard to get at, so he began tearing the structure apart again. There was a veritable feast just waiting in there, and he meant to have him some more.

Cam pumped the action on the shotgun again and fired at the monster that was slowly working its way toward them. He saw the tight pattern of pellets hit the thing in its chest. Something oozed out of the gray/white skin. It was black and viscous. Probably the thing's blood. But that skin looked dense and tightly wound, and rather than blowing a hole into its body, the pellets merely embedded themselves on the surface.

Troy popped away with the pistol. Lexie was kneeling and held her gun out in a classic two-handed combat position. She aimed carefully at the monster's head and fired off one shot after another, but with no effect. The rounds just seemed to bounce off the thing's thick skull.

One thing was for certain, though. They were definitely pissing the thing off. Rather than just a malevolent blank stare, as one would expect a nightmare like this to have, it possessed an almost human expression. Its huge eyes narrowed and its mouth worked in a frown of frustration and concentration. Its face contorted, and there were almost comical grimaces as the bullets hit it. *Comical in a kind of noncomical way,* Cam thought. There was nothing funny about being eaten alive.

Closer and closer it came to them as it tore through sheetrock, doorframes and the partially collapsed roof. Cam and friends were now with their backs to the wall inside the kennel area. Cages of various sizes were stacked here and there, some small for cats, others much bigger. The force of the creature's efforts had toppled some to the floor. Once, the thing's tongue shot out and flicked a couple of the cages out of the way.

Cam was out of shells. Lexie reloaded and kept firing, as did Troy, but nothing was stopping the creature.

Suddenly, its eyes went wide and it stopped its attack. It turned its head to the right and the left as it tried to look behind it. The narrow hallway prevented that, so it backed out.

Cam could now see all the way into the lobby and out onto the parking area. It was now just a huge open space lit up by distant lightning. The creature got itself out and turned 180 degrees, still trying to look behind it.

And that was when Cam saw the most amazing thing he'd seen that night. Okay, maybe not *the* most amazing thing, but at the moment, it was pretty high up there.

Attached to the thing's tail was one badass thrashing, biting, tearing, growling yellow Lab of a dog named Huey. He had his big canines sunk into the thing's rat-like tail, near the end where it was about as thick as a bicycle tire. He was thrashing his head back and forth, snarling for all he was worth.

"Get him, Huey! Get him, boy!" Cam yelled.

The creature next tried to swat Huey off his tail, first with one clawed hand and then the other, but with no success. The thing made that weird hissing sound again. If Cam had been in a comfortable movie theater watching this, it might be somewhat comical. The monster and the dog in a dance of death. But this was real, and his good buddy was in danger of being the thing's next snack.

"Huey, get out of there! Let go!" Cam yelled again.

But it was too late. With one violent twist of its body, the creature flicked its tail left and Huey went with it, but the big dog didn't let go. The thing then flicked its tail the other way, and this time Huey went flying right out into the parking lot. Cam heard a loud yelp and then nothing.

The creature turned its attention back to Cam.

"Oh, shit," Lexie said behind him. "Here he comes again."

Carla screamed as the huge thing leaped back into the clinic. He was now on all fours and looked like a huge burrowing rat/frog/dinosaur coming right at them.

No sooner had it had gotten to within five feet of them than it stopped. Its eyes glanced off to its left and then up behind him. Was Huey coming back for more?

The creature backed out and turned its attention to the street. Cam could see that Huey was not attached to the thing's tail. Something else was distracting it.

"I gotta go get some more shells," Cam said.

Lexie took a quick check of her ammo availability. "Down to just a few more rounds myself." She was breathing heavily.

"You okay?" Cam said.

"Long day," she said and gave him a wink.

Cam smiled and took inventory of his compatriots. Troy gave him a thumbs up. Father Mike was in some pain from his leg wound, but the bleeding had stopped. Sister Joanie looked like she could use a drink. Carla was fixing her hair with her hand, but was otherwise okay. M'Lou still had that blank look on her face. He looked back toward the outside and tried to spot Huey. He whistled. "Huey, here boy!" Cam waited a beat but didn't hear the dog respond. Even though the calm eye of the storm was overhead, there was some residual wind, a mild breeze that scattered a few leaves on the gravel parking lot outside. A silent flash of lightning took a snapshot of the road beyond and the old Dairy Queen across from the clinic. There was no sign of any of the gangbangers, and the firing had stopped.

He knew for sure that two had been eaten. That left three more, four if you counted Roland, who hadn't been seen in a while.

Cam gave Lexie a head nod, and he proceeded around the corner and down what was left of the hallway, back into the bait store. Lexie followed close behind, staying low and covering Cam's advance.

He dug around the shelves under the counter and found one more box of shells. He loaded the shotgun and stuffed his pockets with a few more. He tossed Lexie the box of ammo for her pistol, and she reloaded as well.

They both began to crawl back to the others when they heard an unearthly sound from outside. It was an animal cry combined with a multi-syllabic phrase, like an unidentifiable foreign language. And it seemed to come from a very, very big mouth.

Chapter 47:
"Let's Get It On"

Troy met Cam and Lexie in what was left of the vet clinic's lobby. "What made that sound?" he said.

Carla, Father Mike, M'Lou and Sister Joanie eased up behind him.

"Y'all heard that?" Joanie said

"It's the thing," M'Lou replied. It was as if she was talking about a blue jay.

They all looked at her and then back outside.

Cam and Lexie cautiously headed out that way. They both had their weapons up, scanning left and right. Troy and the rest followed, and he covered the rear.

The lightning continued to flash in the distance, and they noticed a big patch of blood on the gravel parking lot where the creature had spilled his food–namely T-Roy, or what was left of him. The women turned their heads.

Cam whispered, "Came from over there." He pointed the shotgun barrel off to their right. He crouched around Troy's truck, moving closer to the other side of the bait store. The others followed suit.

"We probably shouldn't be out here," M'Lou said. There was a mechanical tone to her voice, devoid of any emotion. Just the facts.

Carla nodded. "Heard that, sister."

Joanie helped Mike limp along. They stopped when Cam raised his hand and they bunched up behind him, between his truck and Troy's.

"Look," he whispered.

They all eased up and looked over the hood of the pickup, toward the carwash.

Troy said, "Well, there's something you don't see every day."

The male creature was so focused on eating he had forgotten about getting laid. He had the smart things trapped and was close to grabbing a few more bites when the female let out a vibration like none he had ever felt before. It snapped him out of his desire for food and filled him with a different kind of desire.

He turned out of the building and loped over to the carwash. The female was inside it. Her eyes were wide and she was focused directly on him. She hissed at him and worked her mouth open and closed. He got the message.

He started to go around behind her when he spotted two more of the smart things. One was immobile and lay in front of the female. There was a second one that was dragging itself off into a vacant lot, whimpering and moaning. Blood trailed out of its two legs, where its feet should have been.

The male made a move toward that one, but before he could take two steps, the female made a noise with her mouth that got his attention. It had been a long time since he had heard those words.

He smartly changed his mind about eating the smart thing and moved back around the female. She had her back side up and waiting for him. It was party time. He mounted her, used his forearms to hold on tight and got down to some bayou boogie.

She screamed. He screamed. There was a lot of shaking and vibrating, a little hissing and scratching and finally he released himself into her. He let out a low, guttural cry, she yelled out a couple of "oh baby's"—at least, what passed for that in their own language, and it was all over. He pulled out of her, shuddered for a few seconds, shook his head and stood on his hind legs. He raised his head to the stars and hissed loudly. The female didn't move, but her stomach sure as hell did.

"That thing just boinked that other thing," Carla noted.

"I feel kinda dirty," Troy added. "And horny."

"Monster porn," Cam said. "Sucker's hung, too."

"This is just getting weirder and weirder," Lexie replied.

Father Mike and Sister Joanie gave each other a quick glance and smiled. "Won't see that on *Animal Planet*," Mike said.

Something moved to their left. Cam, Troy and Lexie all turned and pointed their weapons that way. It was Huey. He was limping on his left front leg, and there was a big, bloody scratch on his hip, but otherwise, he looked okay.

Cam eased over and checked the dog out. "Good boy, Huey. You okay, buddy?"

The dog whimpered and licked Cam's face.

"Uh oh," Lexie said.

Cam turned around. She was looking back over toward the part of the bait store that had been destroyed by the falling pin oak. The big black dude and Roland had emerged from the fallen canopy. Roland had a large satchel in his hand. They were talking to each other, and neither noticed the creature standing behind the carwash, or the other thing inside the carwash. But all that changed in a second, when the female raised her head and let out a wail of pain.

The male creature turned her way and looked down at her. Tree and Roland stopped dead in their tracks and saw the two monsters and stood there speechless. Their attention was also focused on the female.

Her hind end shook and undulated and she spread her back legs. Suddenly a cavity opened up, and to all of the humans in the vicinity, it looked like a pack of gray, hairless wolves emerged, with impossibly large heads and equally impossible large teeth. There were two or three at first, followed by more. They snarled and snapped at each other, some turning back toward their mother, others standing on their hind legs and looking at their father. Now they looked like very scary meerkats, the way they stood tall at attention, their heads looking from side to side in perfect unison.

"Tell me I'm not seeing this," Lexie said.

"We are totally fucked," Cam said. He pumped the shotgun.

Tree screamed and started running across the road, toward the old DQ and his car. He turned and fired his Glock at nothing in particular.

The screaming and the running and the shooting were probably the wrong things to do at that particular moment.

By then, there were about twenty of the baby monsters milling about, with more piling out of Momma Monster by the second. The ones that were already active took off after Tree with a vengeance. They were on him in seconds, knocking him down. His pistol went flying, and he rolled onto his back and tried to fight the things off. He screamed and kicked, but those noises ended rather quickly as they tore his throat out and eviscerated him. Then they got down to some serious eating.

"Motherfucker," Troy said with awe.

"Nobody move," Cam said.

"Not a problem," Lexie said.

Roland hadn't moved an inch. He held onto the satchel full of drugs and took in the whole spectacle. Thunder rumbled in, deep and menacing, and the wind picked up, this time from the west.

He was probably 20 yards away from the male creature, between it and the bayou, and started to walk toward the thing.

"Gaston! My man!" he said. He smiled up at the creature. "Where the hell you been, you big fucker?"

The male creature turned his attention away from his rambunctious children and towards Roland. He looked down at the approaching human, blinked his eyes a couple of times and walked toward him.

"Dude, is that your chick?" Roland said. He pointed to the female.

The creature reached Roland and towered over him. He cocked his head to the left, hissed, and quickly bent down, and his mouth covered Roland down to the knees. He grabbed hold, pulled him off his feet and gulped him and the satchel of drugs down in a couple of bites. He didn't need the tongue.

It was an extremely easy kill he would be wondering about for a long time.

Carla and Joanie gasped in unison as they watched the demise of Roland Avant. Cam, Troy, Lexie and Father Mike were mesmerized. M'Lou just watched dispassionately. Been there. Done that. Got the feet of Floyd to prove it.

Lexie said, "Did he just call that thing 'Gaston?'"

"He did," Cam said.

"He doesn't look French," added Troy.

"There's a joke forming here, but for the life of me, I can't think of a punch line," Father Mike said.

They were startled out of their musing by the sound of metal and wood ripping and tearing. Another sheet of the bait store's rusted tin roof went flying across the parking lot and into the road. The roar of the storm began again in earnest, as if God turned up the fan and the volume on his awesome wind machine.

The backside of the hurricane had arrived as the eye completed its pass over little Alcide, Louisiana. Now the powerful winds were coming from the opposite direction, this time from the west.

The creatures sensed it, too. The male dropped to all fours, turned and took one last look at the female and then bounded into the wind-whipped bayou. He stayed on the surface for a second, turned toward the west and went under.

The female didn't move yet. At least, not her body. With her tongue, she grabbed the still-alive-but-unconscious gangbanger, pulled him over her way and proceeded to eat him. One for the road.

Cam watched as the pack of baby monsters, now totaling over 40, turn as one and run into the adjacent parking lot. A flash of lightning revealed a footless man dragging himself toward some trees. He wasn't going to make it. The babies ripped him to pieces and enjoyed what few bites each could share with their siblings. They were done in under a minute. They turned toward their mother and watched as she dragged herself out of the carwash. For a second, Cam thought they would attack her. They had that *look* about them. Instead, they followed her movements with their heads. If they had ears, Cam figured they would be up right now. It was as if they were *listening* to something she was telling them. For kids, they were pretty focused.

The female got herself out and walked on all fours toward the water. She looked like she was hurting a bit. The vet in Cam figured giving birth to a pack of 40 wolves might do that to a woman.

The female took one last look at her offspring and walked into the bayou. She immediately went under, towards the east. The pack of young ones took off behind her. When they hit the water, it reminded Cam of footage of a herd of wildebeests crossing a river in Africa. He noticed that they scattered in all directions. Some going east, some going west. *Maybe Dad got custody of some of the kids,* he thought. They all disappeared under the water.

The wind was in full force now and heavy rain began and went horizontal.

Another part of the roof ripped up and over them. It fell on Troy's truck.

Cam yelled, "Back inside!"

Chapter 48:
"More Bait. Bigger Tackle."

The group shielded their eyes as the high-velocity rain peppered them. They staggered through the front door of what was left of Fort St. Jesus Bait and Tackle. Rain fell hard in what was once the eastern half of the bait shop. Even inside, the steady wind made the shiny wet leaves of the fallen tree shimmer as if it were alive. Tammy was back, and the whole place shook and rattled. The overpressure of a big peal of thunder felt like a fist had slammed onto the roof.

The seven of them piled into the small kitchen. It was the only part of the building not exposed to the elements. Cam found an electric lantern and switched it on. He shut the door that led into the bait shop and Lexie shut the one that led to the clinic. No one spoke, and as if on cue, they each found a place on the floor and sat down.

It was a long night. Everyone huddled next to each other as the rest of Hurricane Tammy raged outside. Over the next several hours, the wind speed diminished from over 110 mph to under 40 mph. Yet despite the earlier damage, the rest of the building held its ground. Or held on to the ground. The Dairy Queen across the road didn't fare as well. Sometime after 3 a.m., the roof collapsed and that was the end of the old DQ. The gangbangers' Town Car was destroyed when the brick wall fell on top of it. No one would be driving it back to New Orleans anyway.

They sat like that through the early hours. No one talked much, just quick snippets of dialogue followed by silence. Some muted, nervous laughter. Mostly though they just listened to the storm. Tammy shrieked and groaned and screamed with delight at her unique ability to destroy the world in large bites. After a while, it just became one big roar.

Cam sat on the floor with his back to the tiny pantry door, knees up, head down. He jerked up with a start. He must have dozed off. The absence of sound was now as deafening as the storm had been earlier. He glanced at his watch and saw that it was just after 7am. Lexie was next to him, leaning into his shoulder with her eyes closed. She looked cute in her black-and-gold Saints jersey, almost like a little girl. Almost. As totally spent as he was, he thought of a warm bed with her in it next to him. Something he had to get working on.

Troy sat across from him, head back and sound asleep. Carla lay with her head in his lap. *Familiar territory for her,* Cam thought.

Father Mike and Sister Joanie were on the other end by the stove. She was curled in the fetal position. Mike spooned her from behind. A touching image that probably wouldn't make the Vatican annual report. *Those two just had to be doing it,* he thought. *Good for them.*

M'Lou, the rocking red head, had also fallen asleep on the floor. She still had on Cam's white lab coat, except somehow in the middle of the night, it had hiked itself up over her waist. He had a full view of the splendors of M'Lou. Floyd had been partaking of that for some time. Probably the last thing he saw on Earth. *Good for him.*

Cam took a deep breath and tried to move.

Lexie moaned and slowly opened her eyes. She looked left and right. "Is it passed?" she said.

Cam stood up and opened the door that led out into the bait shop. He looked around at the store and began to check off the damage. The fallen tree had taken out most of the back half of the place. The roof was gone. Piles of fishing tackle, gear, food and bottles of soda lay everywhere. A total loss. The clinic fared better, even though it was missing the front wall by the lobby. It was monster-related damage. Probably not covered. But who could tell the difference? As far as he knew, the storm did it. So, all wind and rain-related. No flooding from the bayou. This was an important distinction for the insurance companies. Wind and rain were covered. Flooding, either by the sea or inland waterways, was a bit more problematic. Which just meant you were screwed.

One by one, the survivors from Saturday night woke up and stood. Except for Father Mike. His leg had stiffened up some from the gunshot wound and he plopped back down. Cam checked it. A little swollen, but no signs of infection. Father Mike used the counter to help himself get back up. Joanie lent him her shoulder.

They all walked through the gaping hole in the back wall that led onto the long porch that looked out onto the bayou. The sky was still overcast, but the rain had stopped. Cam's boathouse had collapsed, taking his boat with it. The bayou was strewn with shiny green leaves and branches, debris from nearby homes and businesses, and one small aluminum bass boat floating upside. Cam figured it had probably flown in during the night from points south.

No one, though, was paying too much attention to the storm damage. They all scanned the area for something else.

"You think they're gone for good?" Lexie said.

Cam looked up and down the bayou. "Gone? Maybe. But not for good, I'm sure."

Troy said, "They had enough to eat for a while. Good Lord,"

"I'm never going back up in there with you again," Carla added. "Those two big ones, and the bunch of little ones. All out there? No way in hell."

"They came here to breed," Cam said. "Like it's their spawning ground or something. But no one's ever seen them before. Maybe they don't do this that often."

Joanie snorted. "Right. He banged her, got her pregnant, and she delivered a ton of babies, all in under two minutes? That's some fertile reproductive cycle."

Cam shook his head. "I think she was already pregnant. That's why she was laid up in the carwash. Like a nest."

Carla said, "And he screwed her anyway? Horny bastard."

Cam saw that Lexie had walked to the other end of the long porch. She was talking to someone on her cell phone. After a few quick nods, she hung up and joined the others.

"Checked in with the sheriff, let him know we're all okay," she told Cam. "Told him I found M'Lou. Gonna have to make something up about the fate of our visitors and Roland, though."

"That should be some serious bullshit," he said. He put his arm around Lexie and pulled her close. "We survived, though."

"Yeah, but I'll be working on that report for some time."

Cam looked down at Huey. The scratch on his side scabbed over some. He'd have to dress it later. The dog sat on his haunches, tongue hanging down, with that stupid dog grin on his face. He looked relaxed.

"Nothin' out there, Huey?" Cam said.

The dog turned to him and wagged his tail. It thumped on the wooden porch like a drum.

"I'll take that as a 'yes,'"

Father Mike and Sister Joanie were at the other end of the porch, looking at the tree damage.

Joanie said to him, "A hurricane, monsters, drug dealers, a gunshot wound...quite a night, Reverend."

He scratched the back of his neck and massaged it some. "Yeah. Quite a night." He looked back at the others, who seemed to be discussing something about the dog. Mike turned back to Joanie. "About that..."

She put her finger to his lips. "It's okay. I enjoyed last night. At least that part."

Mike glanced nervously back at the others and lowered his voice more. "That was wrong. We shouldn't have done that. It was a sin."

"Didn't feel like a sin," she said. "And it wasn't like we...you know...went all the way. Just some lovin', touchin', squeezin'. Pretty innocent."

"Yeah, for high school," he said. "We took vows, Joanie. Went way over the line."

"Yeah, we fogged up the car last night pretty good, didn't we?" she said, and winked at him.

Mike looked back out at the bayou and sighed.

"Okay, I'm sorry. What do you want to do?" Joanie said. "Turn in our badges and get hitched?"

"No. I like being a priest."

"And I like being a nun," she replied.

He looked at her. "And I like you. Love you," Mike said. "The Christian way. And also the 'my-one-and-only way'."

Joanie stole a quick look over at the others. Satisfied no one was looking, she leaned over and gave Mike a quick kiss on the lips. "I love you, too."

Mike put his hand over his eyes, and then pinched the bridge of his nose. "Gotta go to confession," Mike said. He shook his head back and forth. "Gotta go. And you should, too."

"Wow, that should be an interesting day in the box."

"Confused," he said.

"Conflicted," she replied.

"C'mon, let's get back over there before they start talking."

Joanie laughed. "They've *been* talking, idiot."

They joined the others. M'Lou was now sitting on the porch with her face in her hands. Lexie knelt down and put an arm around her.

M'Lou sniffled. "I want to go home. I need to call my parents."

Lexie rubbed her back. "Already told the sheriff. He's letting them know."

Cam turned toward the bayou and the distant swamp. He sighed.

"What?" Troy said.

"How many of those little ones you think there were?"

Troy let his gaze settle on the destroyed boathouse. "Hell, three or four dozen, maybe?

"And momma and daddy," added Cam.

"Yeah. The whole Brady Brunch from hell. What you thinking?"

"That no one's gonna believe this shit."

"Nope."

"*Sportsman's Paradise* just got a lot more sporty," Cam said.

"I may take up golf," Troy said.

Lexie walked over. "What are you two planning over here?"

Cam and Troy turned to her. Cam said, "Swamp sure just got a lot more interesting, didn't it?"

Lexie just rubbed her face.

"So what are we gonna do?" asked Troy.

Cam smiled, looked at Lexie, and then out over the water. "Not sure," he said. "But one thing I do know. Fort St. Jesus Bait and Tackle is gonna need a lot more bait. And much bigger tackle."

Four miles away, on a bit of high ground deep in the Atchafalaya Swamp, the male creature stood on its hind legs, hugging the trunk of a big tupelo tree. He slowly tapped his big head against the solid wood. His huge eyes rolled back and forth into their sockets. He made a *churring* sound that pretty much ran off every animal within a mile due to its weird *otherworldliness*.

He groaned and thought, *I am seriously fucked up.*

It wasn't the shotgun wound in his chest, a little gift he got in last night's fun and games. That really didn't hurt that much. In fact, he could barely feel it or anything else at the moment.

He was wasted.

He had swallowed Roland last night, and in the process, had gotten a chaser of meth, cocaine and a little weed mixed in. The drugs Roland had in the satchel.

But damn if he didn't feel *awesome*.

He had gotten laid last night, had some seriously fantastic food, and was now officially a bachelor again. Free to do whatever the hell he wanted. He had been hallucinating most of the night and morning. Sex dreams about the female. The young ones eating the smart things and bringing him some to enjoy. Weird stuff.

A little while ago, he had mistaken the tree for the female and dry-humped it for an hour. That didn't turn out so well. When he realized what he was doing, he had laughed hysterically for another hour. That must have been the weed. He puked his guts out a few minutes later. Some weird shit came out.

Now, it was time to sleep this one off. He lay down on his side and then rolled onto his back. His huge legs and arms splayed out. He looked up into the overcast sky and took a deep breath. Before he drifted off for some much-needed sleep, he recounted the last few days and what he had learned.

First, being a husband and father was a bitch. The sex was good, but all that running around hungry and pissed off was ridiculous. And those little ones were mean as hell. Lesson: stay away from the female. Forever.

Second, those smart things were crazy. Unpredictable, too. One minute they're running from you. The next, they're talking to you, like that last one he ate. It wasn't afraid of him at all. The whole scene had totally fucked him up. The buzz had been cool, but it kind of freaked him out some. Lesson: eat hogs and deer instead.

Satisfied that he had his world in order, the male creature closed his eyes and began to slip away into a deep, dream-filled sleep. But just before he went completely out, he had one last thought that made him smile. He now knew his name.

"Gaston."

Chapter 49:
"Two Weeks Later"

The first cool front of the season had passed over South Louisiana, bringing with it a crispness to the air and a blueness to the sky that signaled beginnings and endings. Fishing was still good. Hunting would soon kick in, with deer season still over a month away. Gator season had ended. Some said one of the best in years. Hurricane season was ending, too. One of the best or worst, depending on your perspective.

Hurricane Tammy had knocked a lot of trees down, and there was some street flooding in New Orleans, but the new levees had held, so no Katrina Part Deux.

Same for Baton Rouge. Trees down, power out for a week or so.

All told, only 12 dead. Not bad. Unless you were one of the 12.

And as for Alcide, things were getting back in order. Power was restored in three days. The water receded back into the Basin, and all roads leading into the town were now open.

Four miles outside of town, behind a rambling one-story home along the bayou, the smell of gumbo filled the cool October air. Out on the back lawn, just behind an old wooden patio deck, two old men sat in rickety wooden chairs near a gas burner. The low jet roar of a propane-fueled blue flame heated a bubbling pot.

"Damn, Boudreaux. Dis might be your best gumbo yet." Tommy Thibodeaux forked another bite of gumbo into his mouth. He was eating out of a Styrofoam bowl. He reached for a Bud longneck that sat on the ground next to him and took a pull. A light breeze caught the wisps of thinning gray hair on the top of his head, lifted them, and then set them back into place.

"Did sumpin' diff'rent dis time," Sonny Boudreaux replied. He sat back in the ancient Adirondack chair and rested his bowl on top of his substantial paunch. A small piece of French bread rested in the bowl on top of the gumbo. He reached in and snatched it into his mouth.

Thibodeaux took another bite. He savored this one as if it were a fine wine. He closed his eyes and smacked his lips a bit. "Yeah, you did. Same spice. But there's a kinda sweetness to it, too. Musky and sweet, kinda combined. Shit, I don't know. It good, though."

"Hell, yeah, it good. Sausage, chicken in dere, alright," Boudreaux said. "But sumpin' new, too."

"What? Gator? Turtle?" Thibodeaux said. "Nutria?"

"Ain't got no nutria in dere, man," Boudreaux replied, somewhat indignantly. "Better. C'mere." He put his bowl on the arm of the Adirondack and eased himself out of the low chair with some grunting and wheezing thrown in. He walked toward the small pier he had on the bayou.

Thibodeaux got up and followed him. But he kept his bowl for the trip.

Boudreaux led him down the walkway onto the small floating pier. A big aluminum tub lay on it, covered by a blue plastic tarp. He flipped the tarp off.

Thibodeaux's jaw dropped and his eyes went wide. "What da fuck is *dat*?"

"Hell if I know. Shot it and its brother this morning."

Thibodeaux squatted down for a closer look. He squinted his eyes and 75 years of crows' feet splayed out across the sides of his leathered face. "Looks like a dog fucked a frog."

"Yeah, and then *dat* went and fucked a gator."

"Sumbitch," Thibodeaux said, and whistled. "It in season?"

"Hell if I know. It is now, dat fo' sure."

"Whatch you gonna do wit it?"

Boudreaux laughed, which turned into a cough. "Do wit it? Shit, man. You *eatin'* it."

Thibodeaux looked up at his friend. "Dat what you got in here?" He nodded toward his gumbo.

"Hell yeah," Boudreaux said. "It good, yeah."

Thibodeaux looked at the thing, and then at his bowl of gumbo. He took another bite. "Damn, dat good."

"I could make some sausage wit dat, too," Boudreaux said. "Might try to fry some, too. Tro' on some corn meal."

Thibodeaux thought this over some. "Jambalaya?"

Boudreaux nodded his head. "With the chicken or instead of?"

Thibodeaux shrugged. "Try it without. Dis shit good."

And so, just like their Cajun ancestors before them, Boudreaux and Thibodeaux had stayed true to their ancient culinary heritage. Whatever the swamp offered up, you thanked the good Lord and dropped it into the pot. Even if you didn't know what the hell it was. You lived by the Cajun kitchen code of old:

"If it moves, eat it."

Author's Note

A couple of quick things. First, thank you for reading my book. I had a lot of fun hanging out with these characters. I hope you enjoyed it, too. Next, there's no such place as Alcide, Louisiana, so don't go looking for it. You'll just get lost back in the swamps and that may not work out so well for you. However, the *area* where I set Alcide does exist. There really is a little town called Butte La Rose down the road from I-10. Ask the nice ladies at the Visitor's Center at exit number 121 how to find it. You'll see a lot of my inspiration for the book there, too. When you're in Butte La Rose, be sure to stop at Doucet's Grocery for a cold drink. Henderson, Bayou Chene, Breaux Bridge, St. Martinville and Lafayette are all there, too. As is the Atchafalaya River. It's beautiful country full of some wonderful people. And, of course, the food is incredible. And please don't feed the gators. They've got plenty enough to eat without you being some of it. Some thanks also go out to a few people. Rosalind Tuminello, for her additional insight into all things Looziana. Jim and Audrey Shanks, our Cabo buddies, for all the encouragement and needed laughs. Chad Smith (no relation to Lexie), for helping me work through the story. Candy Peterson, for her creative support and cover inspiration; and Chad Vander Lugt for that awesome cover design. And, of course, my Official First Reader and Critic—my wonderful wife, Debra.

Look for my next book in 2013:
"The Haunting of Bayou Potomac"

A Cajun president, his crazy friends, one voodoo priest-ess, a looming military confrontation with China, and the ghosts of dead presidents popping in to offer advice, drink his beer, and ogle the First Lady. Can the country survive the weekend?

About the Author

Louis Tridico grew up in Louisiana's bayou and plantation country, listening to the swamp stories his father and uncles told. Some were even true. After graduating from LSU, he began his career in advertising, PR and political consulting. He also served a while as media spokesman for the East Baton Rouge Parish Sheriff's Department. He currently lives in Texas as a Louisiana expatriate with his wife, two kids, two dogs and one box turtle.

They make regular pilgrimages back to the swamps.

Visit him at his author website: www.LouisTridico.com

Made in the USA
Lexington, KY
20 January 2013